Infectious

L. Chambers Wright

Published by:
Machen Society Press
11876 Stanley Valley Road
Gate City, Virginia 24251
Email: Publisher@machensocietypress.com
Printed in the United States of America.
Book Cover Design: Laura Wright

ISBN-13: 978-1-967310-06-7

Chapter 1

"Congratulations, Ms. Smallwood. You're the owner of this unique property." The portly realtor vigorously shook her hand and broke her from her thoughts. His forced smile suited his exaggerated handshake, but neither convinced her. The dark rings around his eyes made his round face even paler. His appearance grew worse every time they met.

She barely managed a smile of her own, despite genuine elation. She was a home *owner.* Not a renter, not a lessee, but an owner. She dreamed of homeownership all her life but never believed it would happen. It was an unattainable dream that remained high above, like dreams of success in any other realm.

Elysium belonged to her. She had admired the estate for as far back as her memory traveled. It was neglected. Time had widened the cracks in the concrete, and ivy vines almost overwhelmed it, but it was magical.

Taylor's beady eyes anxiously darted around the structure's exterior. She watched him from the corner of her eye. The curious habit was both amusing and unnerving in Elysium's sunlight. *What are you looking for, John?* He didn't look at his cell phone, or his watch, but he looked for something. She almost asked but decided against it.

He assembled the documents and stacked them on the glass top of the antique iron table. His gray tweed jacket strained in protest as he locked them in his briefcase. He suddenly erupted in a fit of coughing. Seconds passed, but it didn't stop. She sprinted into the kitchen for a bottle of water from the fridge. Taylor's white face had turned purple by the time she returned.

He fumbled off the lid and drained the drink. He managed a meager smile as his unusually pale pallor reemerged. He thanked her for her hospitality, and with another excited handshake, congratulated her again on her purchase. He mumbled something about allergies and left without another glance. He either hadn't made a sale in a long time or was just elated to sell Elysium. Maybe it was both.

She ran her hand across the nearest concrete column as he drove away. It was one of a dozen magnificent Corinthian columns twenty feet high and eight feet around. Its age was obvious. The ancient, grainy concrete was sharp where the outer plaster had fallen away. She needed to inspect the entire property and create a list of what needed repair. She wanted to preserve all she could.

Something about the estate gnawed at her since she assumed ownership. She thought she heard things in there. She thought she saw someone out on the grounds. She needed to verify no squatters lived on the property. The last thing she wanted was a struggle with an intruder. The house had been vacant for a long time, and it was possible vagrants had taken up occupancy. After all, she'd been tempted to be an unlawful occupant of Elysium, herself, a time or two.

In thirty years, she hadn't been lucky enough to go to college, have a family, or locate employment that paid remotely viable wages. It all changed in one morning—along with everything else remotely familiar. Essentially, her entire identity changed forever.

She still didn't understand how it happened to someone who'd never known fortune. Life betrayed her. It made her assume things would always be harsh and treacherous, only to erode what meager security she managed to find in that. Millions of people played the lottery and never won. Many played for years or even lifetimes, without any benefit whatsoever. Why her? It was a cosmic puzzle, and the pieces may or may not ever properly fit together.

Despite the flaws, Elysium belonged to her, and it was gorgeous. Uncle Ian warned her about the hazards of impetuous real estate purchases. She could hear him say, "A home is the largest investment in a person's life. It requires months of research and preparation."

He would be so disappointed in her. She'd plunged into ownership without time for either prerequisite, but none of that mattered because it was *Elysium.* That made a world of difference to her. Who was she to doubt good luck? No. She'd had nothing but good luck since she won. She was exactly where she was supposed to be.

Chapter 2

He wouldn't be sick if he hadn't visited Elysium. He knew it in his gut. That's when the weird shit started. Everything there that could possibly go wrong went wrong. He'd jumped at the opportunity to represent Elysium after losing eight high-end properties to the new realtor. *Thank you, Tara Blair, and your miniskirts.* He should've let her have this one, too.

Harold was a successful broker, and a good boss, but when his wandering eye drove yet another secretary away, Blair assumed the open position, as well as that of the "new realtor." His women got the best properties when first under his thumb. That was, until they realized he would not actually leave his wife, and his marriage was not actually on the rocks.

At least this was over, and he sold the damned thing. It was a small consolation for another bout with the flu. He hoped. If he could get Elysium sold, maybe the Blythe family would ask him to list one of their more valuable properties. It would at least compensate for this eyesore.

He just didn't feel optimistic. It was wrong. It was all wrong. The sale was shady as hell, in nearly every way, and he hated to even be involved. The house was so damned weird, and the sellers were even weirder. He could overlook the impulsive purchaser. She had new money, and new money was dumb money. Naturally, she'd want the biggest estate in the area, because most people, who'd never known money or a large house, associated size with wealth. He wished her the best but was glad to be rid of it.

The price was yet another strange element in that morbid equation. The house wasn't listed long, so there was no reason for seller's desperation. Most sellers go a year or two without a successful sale. Not a month or so. That meant there was something wrong with it. Something *really* wrong. *But it isn't my problem any longer.*

So long as he didn't have to return, he was a happy camper. It was a House of Horror. He wasn't sure why he felt that way but why didn't matter. He just did. Concerns for motive or price weren't part of his contract. His commission worried him far less than his health. Or his sanity. Not that contracts or formalities had helped him.

He breached many of his own professional rules to take on Elysium. In retrospect, he'd been much like Elysium's purchaser, which was probably why he pitied her. He didn't thoroughly inspect the premises before he agreed to represent it. He should've stayed away. *I should've given it to Blair.*

The sellers were so dismissive, it just didn't seem necessary to perform the customary staging. They had no interest in the house or the price, which should've sent up a dozen red flags. The whole damned thing needed sweeping, scrubbing, and a possible overhaul. The former owners couldn't be bothered. He'd only physically ventured onto the property with the new owner. She was the only person to show any interest.

That was when he first caught this bug. When he first started encountering the same woman in those dreams. Those damned bizarre flashes had kept him awake for two nights. No, he would not deter any brave soul who wanted to buy it, if it meant he never had to go back. He kept thinking of the line from Dante's *Inferno*, *"Abandon all hope, ye who enter here."*

He swerved around a creeping gold Lincoln before he pulled into his drive. The long, straight stretch of road in front of his house had a 55-mph speed limit, but far too many drivers went around at 35 mph. He was already far later and more irritable than he'd hoped due to those slow-assed idiots.

The girl stood in the same garage corner she'd used for the past several days. He ran over her the day before, but it didn't do any good. It was purely accidental because Toby, the amazing hyperactive golden retriever, darted in front of his car.

He swerved to avoid the dog, but hit the girl—the spirit, or whatever it was. He assumed she would be enraged, but it didn't change anything. He got out to check on her and laughed to himself. He'd checked on the body of a ghost when there was no body to examine. It disappeared as soon as his car went in her direction.

4

It didn't matter. Whatever it was, he suspected it was already pissed. At least Jess hadn't noticed the threatening presence skulk around the corners and shadows of their home. It didn't seem quite as serious so long as it didn't bother Jess or Michael. Toby liked to bark at it, but it didn't acknowledge him, either. Regardless of who or what it was, it came from Elysium. God, he was fucking peachy until he visited that house.

He sneezed again as he raised out of the car. *Damned cold.* Not only did some *thing* follow him, the house gave him the flu. It must've been the low-hanging trees and damp grounds. It was chilly on Elysium's grounds, even in the heavy heat of summer. The house didn't have cold spots... the entire property was a cold spot.

He'd been in real estate long enough to know some properties were just bad. History didn't make much difference. No amount of history ever fixed them. Some places were just cursed, regardless of whether a structure stood atop it or not. There was no better word for them. It wasn't good for professional reputation if it got out, but once you handled enough properties, you knew.

He was too chilled and fatigued to normally move. His hands trembled with each shudder. She now stood in the shrubbery next to the front porch. "Leave me alone... I sold the house." He whispered as he passed.

She didn't acknowledge he spoke, as was customary. He was certain the Elysium bug would pass since he wasn't connected with the property any longer. He hoped she would leave with it. His heart did reach out to her if she couldn't find peace. That probably wasn't her fault, but he couldn't help. He wasn't a medium. He didn't predict futures or psychically solve crimes. He was just a mild-mannered realtor.

She was shoulder-height when he passed. He was six feet two inches tall. Her head was always down, and that dark hair hung in matted tendrils across her shoulders. He couldn't understand why she hung her head. She seemed like such a threatening figure yet stood as if her world was destroyed. She never looked up, even when the car hit her.

He glanced back when he reached the front door. The same pattern had repeated for days. She was as substantial as a corporeal person but vanished when he turned his back or looked away. Maybe he should tell Jess. She probably wouldn't believe him, but he couldn't keep silent if it continued.

The hardwood flooring made his tender feet ache with the slightest of steps. He changed into his Dio tee shirt, now faded almost white, and a pair of flannel pants. He wasn't going anywhere until his body made a dramatic recovery. The mere act of walking had drained him of the residual energy left in his body. He just wanted to lie down.

Chapter 3

Melanie still didn't have any desire to return inside, despite the work that awaited her. She just wanted to exist in that moment, while she had it. It was like a dream she never wanted to end.

Tree branches rustled overhead. The high grasses in the unkempt yard whispered with the breeze. A beautiful symphony of nature surrounded her and in this new world where everything was fresh and clean. Birds sang amid magnolia and willow trees in the front glade beside the paved drive. The organic concerto was eons away from the constant traffic at the apartment. The apartment's entrance was like every other place she'd lived: decrepit, neglected, and caked with a thick layer of filth.

So much for Alicia Davenport. That wound would be tender for some time. Alicia had been the sister she always wanted through the years, and she abhorred Elysium. Alicia knew she'd loved that house, but still insisted her instincts said the house was *wrong*. The idea that a structure was "right" or "wrong" was just foolish. A house was an elaborate box for human storage. A shelter that securely held personal items. It was a *thing*; therefore, it wasn't possible to be good or evil.

She sat on the first concrete step and reclined against the nearest pillar. Virginia creeper crawled across much of the home's exterior. Several breeds of wildflowers had overtaken the front garden. The concrete angel presiding over the old fountain had developed green moss on the north and east sides. She wasn't ready to destroy the grounds. Nature had become the gardener, and her graceful work was far more stunning than anything a host of landscapers would produce.

She closed her eyes. Generations of children had played across the grounds. She could vividly imagine their laughter in her mind. There would've been beautiful ladies and dashing gentlemen in that bygone era. She imagined fathers walking with children and mothers wearing contented smiles from rocking chairs in the shade.

Her mind drifted to the questions that plagued her. That was something she'd only dreamed of: a father. Even Elysium's old-world opulence couldn't abolish thoughts of him. What happened?

Perhaps even more puzzling was the question of what happened to her. She'd survived two decades without him. It was a little late to develop that obsession. She'd never regretted his loss, never really even mourned it. Uncle Ian assumed the paternal role when her father stepped out, or whatever happened to him. She didn't yearn for a father figure because she had one. She had far more pressing worries to focus on by the time she reached adulthood.

What would his face look like? The only feature she couldn't really recall was his face. She was so certain he would return when that wave of luck came. She imagined he would arrive like a sleazy attorney at the scene of an accident. He would want money, bless his avaricious heart. He would be the saintly father that never truly left in heart, just in body. He would want something for the seed which helped create her... but he never came, and that silence was far bleaker than her negative character assumptions.

Her wayward imagination had taken advantage of the influx of unexpected free time. People didn't just *disappear.* They weren't swallowed into the ground. Something had to happen. She sighed as she toyed with a tall cluster of wild rye that had crept up through the iron railing. She had no business thinking about him. Why did it matter? Why couldn't she dismiss him as she always had?

She opened her eyes as a cardinal flew by. Her thoughts returned to the private investigator's final report. *"I'm sorry, but there's just no trace of him. We've searched for a month. We can continue, but there's no reason. I think we should abandon the effort. We can always resume if you discover anything, but his Social Security number hasn't been run at any time in recent history. There's no court documents, tax documents, public records... It could take a decade, or more, to find him, if we ever find what happened at all."*

She wondered if he would have liked Elysium. If he would've helped her restore it. *Stop it.* She shook her head to ward off those thoughts. She would drive herself mad. She had a house to focus on

8

and could immerse herself in restoration. Eventually, the questions would subside, and she would forget about her father.

She stood to turn but paused. Something moved in the house—sounded like it was right across the porch in the parlor. She strained to hear more, but the brief rustle was gone. It was probably from those thick velvet draperies. Elysium had tall plantation windows throughout and all of them still had their opulent curtains. The exquisite original windows were carefully maintained through the years. It might've been decades since sunlight was allowed inside the house. The change in temperature might create a lot of noise.

She turned off the central air and opened the windows on both floors when Taylor prepared the final documentation. Enough natural light poured into the house to forgo artificial light. If there was one thing she couldn't stand, it was dark and dreary houses. She'd lived in enough of them. Elysium's antique draperies made the interior look like a gloomy castle. The sizable rooms could do nicely with some simple fabric panels that accentuated the abundant natural light.

Strange noises and dark houses were traits only Alicia appreciated. She was the ghost hunter. Uncle Ian always said structures adapted to people, just as people needed time to adjust to an unfamiliar environment. Spooky noises in a new house were usually signs of repetitive weight shifts across the floors or the home's overall skeleton adjusting to temperature and pressure changes. She didn't really know just how long Elysium stood abandoned. Cars on the property were a rarity, even when she passed in childhood.

She kicked off her white canvas shoes and slipped out of her socks. The aged concrete was grainy on the soles of her feet. That gorgeous overgrown yard was now her gorgeous overgrown yard, weeds, and all. She descended the concrete steps into the soft and cool grass with her arms raised. She felt the mild gusts of the soft and fragrant air with outstretched hands. The sweet aroma of honeysuckle wafted across the yard.

A few minutes later, she folded her socks and stuffed them in her sneakers as she carried the shoes back up the steps. It was too bright and sunny not to take advantage of all that light inside. Her fingers trailed the patina along the wrought iron rail.

She reentered the home and felt a twinge of intimidation in her stomach. What would she really do with so much space? Her stomach knotted with thoughts of the labor needed to maintain it. She would live alone in a house with twenty rooms, if not more. There could be rooms Taylor hadn't known about. He wasn't the most knowledgeable individual on the house. Every question was met with, "Would you like to ask the owners?"

No, of course not. She didn't trust people with money. She chuckled to herself. She certainly couldn't say that anymore. She was one of them. It had been months since the win, and she still couldn't wrap her brain around that alien notion.

Even the ordeal with getting everything settled, taxes and delinquent accounts, fees, and days of tedious paperwork with a half-interested accountant, hadn't made it any more real. The grueling sessions of numbers and monotony made her brain feel like jelly.

She didn't accomplish anything aside from work when she lived at the apartment, even after the win. She continued life as normally as possible to avoid attention. It would've been ridiculous to buy big ticket items knowing they'd just have to be moved... if they weren't stolen first. There were many community members with habits to support at the Happy Hell.

She memorized the soft thud of her bare feet against the wooden floors as she ambled through the main hall. The new kitchen appliances were installed two days earlier. The new appliances were the only modern amenities included with the sale, all else was "as-is."

It was just as well. She wouldn't have thought of buying super-sized professional appliances, but the kitchen required them. A regular electric range would've left glaring gaps in the counter. The wall on the left side of the room was constructed for two ovens. The refrigerator nook would have swallowed a standard-sized appliance.

She grabbed a hot soapy rag from the sink and a clean dish towel from the box. The fridge was empty aside from a few cans of soda and bottles of water. She wiped around the few meager items and covered the rest of the appliance. When she finished the other appliances, she moved on to dust out the cabinets. She would order pizza today and get groceries tomorrow.

Groceries. An entire life of struggle, eliminated by one tiny piece of paper—she stopped for a moment—she had the distinct feeling that someone was there. Someone was in the house. She stepped to the back door, but it was locked. The hall and dining room were empty.

After a few more minutes of silence, she returned to work. She peeled back the flaps of the next box and caught a glimpse of her arms in the bright sunlight. The bright red burns had almost disappeared, and there weren't new ones to replace them. Ink stains, blisters, and second-degree burns were perks for employees at Hayden Graphics. People could look at you and know where you worked. The scar tissue from those earlier burns likewise showed signs of healing.

She came to the last box from the apartment kitchen and paused. Several other boxes were stacked below, but there was little initiative to continue. She'd taken such pride in her things before. None of it meant anything now. Most of the items she considered extravagant splurges now looked cheap in Elysium's imposing kitchen. Maybe she just needed to take those boxes to the Salvation Army. It was a new life. She was starting over in every other way, why not that, too?

Her eyes returned to the view through the windows over the sink. She needed curtains, something to frame the picturesque gardens. Natural beauty surrounded her now and she had no idea of how to appreciate it. It felt like she'd spent all her life in the dregs of the dark, nasty pit at Hayden. In fact, the apartment didn't look much different from work.

She paused for a drink. She assumed it was a stereotype, but silent houses really were lonely. She'd never had a place of any real size, or one that had any real silence, to know. The big buildings she was familiar with were constantly filled with tens of families and all the noises they made. Families and kids screaming; people coming and going; now, she didn't even have that.

She reached into the box and laid the breakables on the counter as quickly as she pulled them out of the newspaper. She had to do something, even if she gave the stuff away. She wasn't accustomed to inactivity. She'd had relied on the mad rush of working life to alleviate negative thoughts and feelings for years.

She would be getting ready for second shift now if she hadn't won. The Friedman couple would be screaming at each other in the opposing apartment. The prostitutes down the hall would be welcoming customers and their beds would be banging against the walls within minutes. It was a bizarre symphony of poverty; the drums of communicable disease beating in rhythm with the screeching octaves of rage.

Alicia was alone there now. *Well, that's not my fault.* Fault or not, she felt guilty. *Alicia was just pissed she didn't buy that damned ticket.* She was going to but backed out at the counter. She just followed their normal routine. That wasn't a crime, was it? It was their weekly entertainment. If Alicia had listened to her instincts, she would've had the money. She'd even offered her half, but she refused. That was fine. She'd never had enough of anything. Ever. Never again.

Blame wasn't an adequate distraction. She couldn't pretend Alicia was jealous or petty, it wasn't in her nature. They'd both said things in the heat of anger, and they'd both made completely outlandish accusations. It hadn't benefited either of them. She needed to call her. She probably wouldn't have much to say, but she would call and invite her over.

Another noise in the home broke her concentration. It almost sounded like a solitary footstep upstairs, but it just happened once. It was probably a draft. At the worst, it would be vermin, and that was nothing new. Every home she'd ever lived in had vermin. It wasn't all bad; after all, the company of vermin was far more pleasant than the company of most of her former neighbors.

Chapter 4

Taylor gently lowered his aching body onto the queen-sized mattress. *A nice, long nap should fix the aches.* He shoved Jess's numerous floral pillows and the coverlet off the bed. He didn't want her to catch the flu and, no doubt, he would contaminate the frilly bedclothes. Unfortunately, it wasn't better in bed. Sleep was a cruel and fickle fiend that teased him with peace. Instead of repose, he found brutally vivid dreams. In those lucid scenes he rode a black horse within a group of horsemen.

"We'll burn it all." A stranger commanded from the front of the group.

"Hey!" He shouted, but not a single rider acknowledged him. "Hey, get me off this thing." He couldn't move his body... couldn't make himself talk. The horse wouldn't recognize his commands because his body wouldn't make them. He willed himself to grab the nearly petrified saddle horn and, through some miracle, wasn't thrown from the bouncing equine.

He hated horses. He hadn't ridden one since childhood. He fell from a thoroughbred and broke his arm when he was seven. He hadn't liked them since. *No, you didn't get back on the horse when you fell off. You went in to have the bones reset, followed by several months of pain and physical therapy.*

The group's pace finally slowed and the form he inhabited moved with them. "Lookie here, boys...." The rider spoke with menacing excitement. "Here comes a rat."

The evening sped by in an instant as soon as those words were uttered. Flashes whirled before him too quickly to process. He dismounted the horse, just like the rest of them, as if he'd ridden for years. They gathered next to a small building in the darkness. He stood behind the group of men.

The torch light fluctuated but did little to illuminate the wooded area. The only thing he discerned, with any certainty, was the thick forest around them. The strange new body wasn't shaky or unstable. He felt taller as he looked down at his unadorned black boots. He looked around to his fellow riders and noticed he was a couple of inches taller than the rest of them. That couldn't be right. He was only 5'10" tall. That was merely average by Appalachian standards.

Another jump in time happened before he could focus on the group's target. It was just enough time to see their leader run a cruel blade across a man's throat. The victim ran around the small structure as he bled, the men in his ranks laughed. The poor man put his hand to his throat, but blood spurted through his fingers. John protested from inside the host body, but his mouth wouldn't form the words. He tried to run to help the injured man, but his feet wouldn't move.

He jumped when another rider yelled in the distance. A small explosion thundered, and a tall plume of fire rose towards the sky. What had they done? *Damn it, it's too dark.* He just stood there. His body's inactivity made him an accomplice. Involuntary or not, he was there, and he didn't help.

The bleeding man circled the structure although his pace slowed with each pass. John couldn't stop his physical body as it approached the bleeding man. It grabbed him, "Where the hell you think you're going?" The body forced him to look into the man's vacant and utterly despondent eyes. His strange body muttered, "You're already dead... You're just too stupid to realize it." He didn't want to say that... didn't want to be so cruel. His heart shrank within him.

He released the dying man, but the bleeding body continued the same path. Why wouldn't he stop? He studied the thick line of blood that developed in the man's tracks. The line grew brighter and more prominent with each pass. Every beat of his heart sent another wave of gore out of his throat. He felt this strange body want to kill him, partly out of anger, but mostly out of fear. He wanted to kill him and get it over with. It was unnatural. He shouldn't be alive, shouldn't be walking, but he continued around the structure.

The new body stepped back as the dead man circled back around. Gore continued to flow from the gash. Blood had soaked his clothing several passes before, and it now coated the ground.

"Finish it, Wilson." The leader jabbed him with the handle of the long bowie knife. "Finish it now."

"With pleasure." He protested within. He pushed the obstinate body to heed to his desire, but it was a vain effort. The host body reached for the weapon, and he felt its belligerent relief. He didn't want to. He didn't want to touch him again. He still chilled from the first time. The body held out the knife as the dying man approached. He couldn't do it. It wasn't in him. He couldn't take another life.

He clenched his eyes and tried to force the body to run. He wouldn't kill another man. A limb groaned overhead, so loud it drowned out the men's voices. He reopened his eyes, but now he had a slit throat. He couldn't stop moving. His body was determined to continue around the structure. Mad laughter chorused through the trees as the torches cast strange shadows everywhere.

Wake up. He tried to force his body awake. *It must be a dream. It must.* He applied pressure to the wound at his throat, but blood pumped out through his fingers. The wicked stinging sensation in his throat made his eyes water. His flesh was on fire. Just as with the previous form, this body wouldn't stop moving. He looked around the rim of the trees that surrounded them. Where was she? She should be here somewhere. For some reason, he knew she should be.

He made two more circles around the structure as smoke filled the air. He couldn't see. It was everywhere. His lungs burned as badly as his throat. He finally jerked hard enough to move his body. He sat up on the bed. He could smell smoke. The room even looked smoky. He sold the goddamned house. It wasn't his problem any longer. She was still here, though. She was still here.

Chapter 5

She organized kitchen cabinets and arranged furniture until her muscles ached. She dropped onto the shabby green armchair and caught her breath. Her favorite chair didn't fit in any room, and she wasn't sure if she cared. The home's historic grandeur made it appear even more worn. Maybe she should've left it at the apartment, but she couldn't part with it. It was all she had from her grandmother.

She needed help—a bitter realization after years of ill-will towards the previous owners, but Elysium was no vacation home. Maybe the Blythe family really had been unable to maintain the property. She had the means to bring in a maid or housekeeper. It was a viable option, but she couldn't bring in help just yet. She had to try as hard as possible to be independent. She'd always enjoyed independence. If you couldn't clean your home, unassisted, without a medical reason, what could you do? She had to at least try.

Something still felt out of kilter. The gnawing feeling had lingered for days. It was easy to dismiss it as residual damage from her argument with Alicia, but it wasn't that. She sensed it even before. The urgent suspicion was immediate and foreboding. She checked and rechecked the apartment and hadn't forgotten anything. She'd just spoken with her mother an hour earlier and she was fine. Aside from developing Taylor's sinus infection, or whatever it was, life was fine.

She gently rubbed her bloated stomach. She'd gorged for weeks. She needed to stop. There was just so much food, more than she'd ever dreamed of, and it tasted so good. Rent and bills usually took everything every month. It was impossible to save enough to move elsewhere or change jobs. She was never concerned about weight, but if she kept eating, she would be.

Her mind drifted through the entire gamut of things that may have slipped her mind. There wasn't much to forget. She didn't have a boyfriend, didn't have kids. Her ailing mother was seldom able to leave her house. That was the extent of her immediate family she might have an instinctive connection with. She hadn't spoken with distant relatives or cousins in years.

She probably just needed a good night's sleep. Exhaustion played tricks on the mind and emotions. Life had been hectic enough since the win, moving made it worse. It was an exciting new world.

There was much potential for the house after the renovation. She never had a decent place to welcome guests before. She'd always wanted a presentable home with an intact ceiling. A good place where vermin didn't openly roam the halls. Perhaps she might even open a bed-and-breakfast.

Tenants at the Happy Hell watched everything. Your water was usually tapped into your neighbor's. You coordinated your telephone use due to the noise from other apartments. The landlords had no desire to interfere in their tenants' lives. In all actuality, they didn't want to interfere with those Section 8 vouchers. She pulled her head from that place. She didn't even need to think about it anymore. It wasn't her problem any longer.

She was secure just by owning a house like Elysium. She could conduct home tours and, if worse ever came to worse, host weddings, receptions, and anything else. There were probably enough curious people locally to support her as well as those who came in for the NASCAR races or tourists traveling through the area.

At the Happy Hell Apartment Complex, neighbors developed a keen interest in her after the initial announcement. Luckily, she convinced them it wasn't her. Thank God no one watched the news, it was always "a friend of mine heard...." It was dodgy for weeks.

When they noticed her moving boxes, she fobbed off curiosity by saying she had to move in with her sick mother. She covered her steps; even told the landlord her ailing mother needed her. She stood and stretched her sore arms out. A shower would ease those exhausted muscles and get her ready for bed.

She had stumbled into a bittersweet place in life. She really didn't want all she had; it was too much, and she had no one to share it with. Her mother was comfortable. She'd ensured Janet would never have to worry about anything again. Still, there was so much left.

She tried to give Alicia half, but she wouldn't take it. If she could've trusted her neighbors to do something beyond overdosing, she would've eagerly given them all a small fortune. Every person she knew there except for Alicia, was lazy and wasteful.

The fighting couple down the hall was on disability but weren't remotely disabled or elderly. The lady of the house was her age. The couple violently fought on a daily basis. He was healthy enough to do frequent engine work on his car, and she cleaned house for the brothel women down the hall. Most of their money went to illegal prescription drugs, or meth, maybe both.

The prostitutes weren't any better. They didn't have children but received rental assistance and any extra funds kept up their own habits. The worst factor was, out of all that everyone regularly received, no one had anything for it.

She wished her mother were healthy. Janet smoked her lungs into oblivion after her husband left. *Gone. Vanished. Disappeared.* It didn't matter how you labeled it. She said it was just a nasty habit, but there was more to it than that.

Coffee and nicotine ushered through years of single parenthood. She felt partly responsible for her mother's illness. She knew how difficult it was to survive on a single income by experience, she still marveled that her own mother did it *and* provided for a child.

Bastard of a father. If only he'd supported them. If only he lent a sliver of help during her childhood. That could've saved them from years of expired food bank food, years of used clothing... it wasn't any use. She stopped herself... again.

She couldn't rant as she had for months. The dependable loathing had worn paper thin, just as her anger towards Alicia. She couldn't harbor such hate. Maybe he couldn't help what happened. He could've just as easily been hit by a car and left for dead or robbed and killed. His body might be buried anywhere or may still lie atop the place he died.

She'd always held her father responsible for their poverty, but that was convenient, wasn't it? He'd been an easy scapegoat. It wasn't so easy to utilize those comfortable assumptions now that time had passed. He was a missing person. The investigator even provided copies of the paperwork from decades earlier which reported him missing.

The investigators verified his side of the family hadn't heard from him since he disappeared. That obliterated one of her most logical theories. She'd considered there was a vast conspiracy among his family to keep her and Janet from him. The investigators eliminated that suspicion in one fell visit.

The investigator summed it up quickly, and sharply. His family didn't like him to begin with. His disappearance was just another black sheep eliminated. She already knew they felt Janet was beneath him, and her offspring was just as subhuman. She was surprised his family cared so little about him. He disappeared from the face of the Earth, as far as they knew. He just walked to the store and was gone forever.

At least her mother wasn't so alone now. The retirement community had friendly residents and activities, even for the ill. The single-level homes were equipped to alert medical staff with the touch of a button. Janet's emphysema hadn't flared once since moving from the last slum. She could provide her with the finest care, now. The doctors spoke as if her condition was rapidly worsening, but maybe she could slow it, even if it was just for a little while.

She lugged the weighty overnight bag into the bathroom. It was her first piece of leather luggage. She got it second-hand and was fairly sure it came out of the 1970s, but it belonged to her. She flipped the shower to hot as she undressed. The house's pipes were remarkably quiet. There weren't any harsh clangs or groans within the walls. She couldn't even hear water leaks or drips. It was a bizarre tradition that always followed her before. Every house had something wrong with the pipes.

She gasped for breath as she stepped under the spray. *God, that's hot. It's really, really hot.* She eased under the shower while the steaming water pummeled the tight muscles of her back and shoulders. Showering was heavenly when you didn't have neighbors who stole the hot water. She washed away that former life and all the muck that went with it.

A face came to mind when she closed her eyes. She knew him. He was—she opened her eyes as lather drained into them. She cursed as she rinsed them in a frantic attempt to quench the burning. She didn't know him, but she did. He had shoulder-length dark hair and bright blue eyes. She shook her head and tried to push the invasive image away. She must be more exhausted than she thought. He was probably an actor in some forgettable movie.

She toweled off and dressed while the image lingered in her mind. At least something positive had overtaken those hopeless thoughts of her father. If that was common, she would be showering often at Elysium. She pulled her toothbrush from the crumpled aluminum foil.

Maybe the stranger was her father. She wouldn't know. She couldn't recall his face. She remembered his hugs, his voice, and his stories, but not his face. Time was cruel as to leave so much, but the most human element was gone. *Well, he's gorgeous, regardless of who he is.*

No, that can't be right. She brushed her teeth. He couldn't be her father. Her father was several years older than Janet. He wouldn't have looked that young even when she was a baby.

She finished her nightly routine and strolled into the bedroom. She spread the old, familiar sheets on the bed. She needed new linens as well as furnishings, but at least most of Elysium's bedrooms came with their own furniture. The old cotton sheets looked even more worn in contrast to the rich wood and the intricate detail of the headboard.

She fluffed her favorite pillow and laid back for a moment. The idea of sleeping at Elysium remained surreal. At any minute, she would wake up at the apartment. The smell of musty age and cheap lavender air freshener would assault her senses. The lingering sounds of people in the hall would emanate through the decrepit front door. It didn't happen.

Two ivory hurricane nightlight lamps sat on either side of the bed. Both sizable pieces needed dusting, the brass embellishments needed polishing, as did most of the abandoned wares. Most of Elysium's antiques were quite valuable.

Several Hummel figurines gathered dust on the mantel in the parlor. Two Tiffany Venetian lamps stood on either side of a massive oak desk in the library. Several Wedgwood china pieces were scattered in the hutch as if they were cheap stoneware. Other pieces, with other expensive-sounding names, were strewn elsewhere through the house, all left like trash.

She stood back up and assembled the last of the bedding. She hit her knuckle on the headboard, rubbed it for a moment, and again noticed the home's silence. She expected the house would be peaceful, but not dead quiet. Her bedroom had never been quiet at any point in her life. She'd always lived with fighting neighbors, blaring electronics, or heavy traffic, sometimes all combined.

She extinguished the lamps and slipped into bed. Her eyes wouldn't close. She waited for the soft embrace of slumber to pull her into rest. Everything was ready for sleep... except her brain. Her thoughts raced. Her consciousness refused to soften in the new atmosphere. She strode to the balcony's French double-doors and pulled them open. The soft night air should help her sleep. She momentarily watched the gentle mist waft around below.

It was fortunate the veranda overlooked the backyard. The first thing vandals aimed for were the largest windows, and if this side of the property faced the street, they would've been destroyed. All of Elysium's windows would've been broken decades earlier, regardless, were they in any other neighborhood.

She inhaled the cool night air. Normally, she could never do that before bed and wouldn't have wanted to. There was always something horrible in the air, smells of traffic and dirty pavement, maybe a subtle whiff of sewer overflow.

She noticed a trace of something else in the air. A hint of smoke drifted in the breeze, just beneath the fragrances of trees and flora. She stepped to the balcony's edge to get a better view of the area.

No one burned rubbish or grilled at night. Elysium bordered the prestigious Dogwood subdivision, a gated community where all houses looked alike. She hadn't decided if the fencing was meant to keep people out or in. In Dogwood, they paid others to do their grilling over the weekend, not in the middle of the night. She wasn't even certain they allowed outdoor grilling. The gardeners probably even took the trimmings from the lawn elsewhere for disposal.

Rich people didn't burn trash. The very act had to go against the homeowner's association. All ritzy places had the same rules, and all homes had to conform. Every basketball goal had to be centered over the garage door, if allowed. Every blade of grass had to be precisely 2 inches in height. Every car needed proper shelter, and every person had a proper place.

She sniffed the air again. It wasn't charcoal or food smoke. It wasn't smoke from burning trash, either. It was wood smoke with a trace of something rotten. She lived in a crappy house on Sycamore Street years earlier that used a woodstove. The familiar smell pungently lingered, noticeable even in trace amounts, but it didn't have that acrid note. She left the doors open and returned to bed. It wasn't anything she hadn't lived with before; at least the sweet scent camouflaged the smoky tinge.

She lay on the bed and closed her tired eyes. It seemed like only a few minutes passed before she shivered, despite the covers. The temperature didn't just drop, it plummeted. Maybe it wasn't a good idea to leave those doors open. The night's bizarre frigidity saturated the bedroom with what felt like a thick arctic fog. She shut the terrace doors, threw the lock, and returned to bed.

She adjusted herself in an honest-to-God bed, not the warped cot. The California king pillow-top mattress had posture support. It was a challenge because her posture had never been supported, as far as she could recall. The cot was only a "cot" in the loosest definition of the word. Springs protruded from the thin mattress's sides and the edges were so old they'd bowed. It was more like a big bag of old cotton and some saggy, rusting springs.

She meant to burn it earlier but forgot amid the rush of unpacking. Her first order of intentional destruction at Elysium remained the incineration of the God-awful cot. There would never be another. Luckily, her old sheets were for a king-sized bed, the only sheets in good condition at the consignment store. She'd just tucked the extra fabric in around the cot. Now, they fit her bed.

Her mind returned to the mysterious man she envisioned while in the shower. His face remained so clear, even though it had only been a split-second flash. He had clear, fair skin with the softest lips. She shook her head to calm her racing mind. *Enough of that.*

He was nothing more than a figment of her imagination. He was no memory because she wouldn't forget someone like that. She would feel a familial connection had he been her father. She didn't have features similar to the man she witnessed, and she'd heard she resembled her father all her life.

Choruses of cicadas and forest noises grew louder. Her heavy eyes were gritty as she struggled to get them back open. She could've sworn she closed the veranda doors, but maybe she hadn't.

She sat up, but she wasn't in her bed or even in the house. She was lying on the ground. The soft radiance of several fires shone through the clustered trees ahead. She stood as quietly as possible in a strange outfit. Her bare feet slightly sank into the ground as the cool moss rose between her toes.

An ethereal white gown draped down past her feet. She had to lift the front hem to walk. A small train of white fabric extended behind her, but it didn't look like a bridal dress, just an elaborate nightgown. The thin straps loosely draped across her shoulders. A corset style waist fitted her form but didn't constrict her breathing. A near-by growl emanated from the brush when she passed. She crept faster towards the amber glow ahead, away from the animal.

Moonlight fell through the random jumbles of branches overhead. Cool night air chilled her skin. Gooseflesh prickled across her bare shoulders and crossed arms. Her skin felt foreign beneath her touch, unnaturally smooth and cold. A thin string of pearls weighed lightly on her throat. There was a scuffle ahead. Men's angry voices erupted from the direction of the lights. She peeked around a large tree trunk to see a group of men on horses circle a wagon.

It wasn't a covered wagon like from western movies. This was a well-constructed vehicle unlike any she had seen in known memory, but it still looked familiar. The side of the wagon had numerous small doors with shiny silver latches. The black iron roof appeared to have some kind of embellishment around its base.

She studied the details as the torches surrounded it. There wasn't a section without a door of some kind. A tall, thin door on the side had small steps extending downward. Some primitive instinct pushed her to run through the door. The feeling promised safety, it implied answers to every question lay just inside.

"Damn you! Not here..." the thin door crashed opened and a man with a familiar voice shouted from inside. It shouldn't be familiar, and she shouldn't love the sound as she did. She couldn't even see him for the horsemen. Every man on horseback covered his lower face with a black bandanna and wore a tall, wide-brimmed black hat. Their eyes glimmered evil in the fickle torchlight. She knelt closer to the tree in front of her.

A twig snapped beneath her feet. Her body went rigid in the abrupt silence. Her extremities trembled. She didn't want to look back up. *No, please no, they've seen me...*

She prayed they hadn't paid attention, but her heart sank within her. They saw her. She somehow knew they would see her no matter how silent she was, or how quietly she approached.

A towering rider trotted towards her, but she didn't have an opportunity to see him, either. His pale face was shadowy above the black bandanna. His hat was pulled low on his forehead. He glared at her for a moment. His eyes were as sinister as the darkness surrounding them. He tossed something at her, but it landed in the darkness.

She was stunned by a loud whirring noise as a raging fire encompassed her. There was no time for flight. The raging wall separated them, but it would consume her. She already knew. The chest-high flames suddenly shot far overhead. The voracious inferno rose so high above it seemed it would ignite the sky.

She cried as the circle closed in. The scalding air blistered her skin before the fire even touched her. She was suffocating. The fire stole all precious oxygen from within the circle. Her flesh burned as the insatiable heat stole the last breathable air. She smothered in the soot-filled smoke. Her heart pounded so hard her chest hurt. She couldn't breathe. *Can't breathe... Can't breathe... I'm dying....*

She bolted upright and gasped for air with such force her lungs wheezed. Her pulse slowed, but her chest still ached. The long, white curtains billowed in the smoke-laden breeze at the veranda door. Her eyes burned and watered as if the air was still filled with smoke. Her skin was unusually warm, but there was no fire or smoke. It was all a dream.

She rolled her shoulders to relax the tight knot of muscles in her neck. She could only guess what might've brought on such violent, lucid dreams. She couldn't recall ever suffering that vivid horror. She massaged a stubborn mass of tense muscles on her left shoulder. *God, help me. No more pizza before bed.*

She laid back and tried to relax in the rush of night air. The cool zephyr felt amazing after the nightmare of fire and suffocation.

The sheer curtains on the other side of her room swelled with each gust. *At least it might remove some of the dust.*

She thought she locked the veranda doors before going to sleep. Or was that a dream? You locked everything with hinges at the Happiness Apartment Complex; otherwise something would be stolen within hours, if you, yourself, weren't stolen within hours. She wouldn't forget that in a day. She should probably close them before she nodded off.

She groggily stumbled across the room and peered down into the yard as she closed the doors. She paused. *That's strange.* It was familiar. That yard, from that angle, was familiar. It shouldn't be, but it was. She had seen that before, but it made no sense. She'd never been to Elysium. She'd never been past the iron gates that blocked the long gravel drive. Nothing here should be recognizable. The previous owners never even allowed historical photographers inside.

Shit. She just needed to return to bed. She sounded like Alicia. She was not a reincarnated former resident; she did not visit in a past life and had no desire to entertain her spiritual self. The sleepy coincidence would be cured via a good night's sleep.

Her spirit had already improved, despite the lingering symptoms of a sinus infection. The physical move, in combination with her congestion, was too much. She was already psychologically exhausted from months of dodging people. In addition to everything, she worked normally to avoid unnecessary attention, while she packed her apartment. It wasn't a stretch of imagination that the home's unique character would have an impact.

She needed preoccupation. Something to take her mind from questions that hadn't relented in weeks. Maybe her mom was right. Maybe she needed a boyfriend. They were the best preoccupation, and the most practical answer for loneliness. It was one thing to say, however, and quite another to accomplish.

She returned to her pillow with a mind full of vain wishes. The thick draperies of the massive four-post canopy bed matched those on the windows. She'd tied the bed curtains back against their respective posts. Her eyes roamed the dimly lit room in search of something to focus on.

Her fickle train of thought jumped to the previous owners. Why did they abandon the house? Maybe, since they were wealthy, and had always been wealthy, they felt the house was beneath them. It still didn't make any sense. Why not just give it to distant relatives, or turn it into a museum? It was a family estate.

She didn't know much about the Blythes, but there were a number of them still in the area. The current mayor, several city council members, and various other political figures posted signs every election season that bore the Blythe name.

Another troubling factor was the absolute disregard for the remaining valuables. *Hummel figurines and Wedgwood china?* Those weren't exactly second-hand goods. *Tiffany glass?* They weren't cheap antiquities you could find at a yard sale. Even those with wealth didn't usually treat them like dime-store merchandise.

Suspicion crept deep into her mind as she lay in the dark. *There is something wrong with the place.* Maybe it wasn't just a discarded eyesore. Maybe something terrible prevented the previous owners from returning. There was also the fact that the house wasn't cleaned. Sellers usually tidied up their products before they went on the market. Some of the upper rooms had so much dust on the floors they left footprints when they walked through.

She started fifty thousand dollars below asking price to see if they were open to negotiation, but there was no negotiation. She'd wanted to barter and bargain on her first house, but the offer was accepted that day. Taylor didn't know why they were so eager and, apparently, didn't care. The fast transaction hadn't bothered her when it happened. It never crossed her mind during the rush to get away from the apartment. It did now.

Taylor acted like he'd never been there before when she first visited. He didn't seem to care what the price was. She should've started a hundred thousand below to see if that might bring some reaction. He wasn't concerned about his commission in the least. He was preoccupied, even on the first visit. Thoughts of his beady eyes darting here and there didn't bring any comfort. He was looking for something.

Uncle Ian warned her about impetuous purchases. He was her surrogate father after her real father disappeared. The retired city building inspector had no family of his own. Ian's wife died in childbirth, and he never remarried. He stepped in as a surrogate father.

He warned her repeatedly, and the first opportunity she had to use his advice, she ignored it. He administered his knowledge over the years, and she thought she'd paid careful attention. She listened to those random facts and figures, followed every procedure and every precaution, except the primary one: she purchased impulsively and not intelligently.

She sighed and rolled on her side. *Well, it didn't do any good now.* She had to force those nagging doubts as far back into the recesses of her mind as possible. The pessimistic residue of her former life had initiated its demeaning urge. Her decisions were flawed. She wasn't capable of good choices because she was flawed. She couldn't trust herself.

Negative thoughts had berated her for years and those insecurities just gained a new arena for worry. No matter what those suspicions stated, life was not the same and never would be. Things weren't like that any longer. Wasn't the win enough? It wasn't something bad. It was a miracle, and miracles did not need elaboration. They weren't supposed to be logical. That's why they were miracles.

Her eyes grew heavier as she watched the shadows from the branches outside moving on the wall. The tallest elm had the longest shadow that nearly touched the ceiling. She'd already forgotten why she woke up. Something disturbing forced her awake. She couldn't remember much aside from fire—so much fire—and it burned like nothing she'd ever experienced. The image of the man she'd seen in the shower came again. She smiled as she drifted off into blackness.

Chapter 6

The biological week of doom approached faster than she hoped. Her body would change, as it did every month, into a foreign host that brought only pain and misery. Alicia Davenport stretched her arms high above, until they almost touched the ceiling. No amount of exercise loosened her cramping abdomen or her tightening back.

Every month her body rebelled against all that was natural for seven days. It brought near-crippling cramps and migraines. She tightened the straps of her bra to stabilize her tender, swollen breasts. She gently pulled the tee shirt down over the tightened apparatus.

One day, it will be different. She had to maintain hope things wouldn't always be as they were. She wouldn't always be stuck in Happy Hell. One day she would afford medicine to thwart the monthly avenger. She must've accidentally unleashed some evil karma, at some point, for life to be this way.

She slipped out of her dingy denim work pants and pulled on a pair of blue cotton shorts. A whisper rose behind her from somewhere. She turned, but the room was empty. It wasn't the wind, or the tattered blanket over the window would move. The windows were little more than slivers of glass, cracked and worn from the elements. One day, a final gust of wind would shatter them.

She waited for an indication of what caused the sound, but the apartment remained silent. She needed a shower. She was covered in a film of dirt and sweat. Of course, that was no use. No matter what hour it was, as soon as she turned the hot water on, the assholes next door would turn their faucet on.

The whisper was probably a draft from the ever-crumbling ceiling or the ancient air ducts. She went to the mirror and brushed her hair out. *Damned landlord, it wasn't as if he ever fixed anything.*

The entire floor was crumbling in, and nothing was ever done. She'd complained a thousand times, but they always put her on hold, or said they'd get to it the next week. After a few months, they stopped taking her calls altogether.

The brush was half-way through the eleventh stroke when it made a loud snap. Several of the brush's teeth cracked off deep into her auburn hair. She dug them out as she grumbled. *There's nothing worse than a damned dollar brush that breaks the week after you bought it. Damn Hayden Graphics for being so cheap.* She abruptly stopped when she glanced in the chipped oval mirror. A girl in a dingy white dress stood in the corner behind her.

She whispered, "Who are you?" She looked back to the corner, but there wasn't anyone there. She returned to the mirror and saw the room was now empty in the reflection.

Okay. She took a deep breath and lowered the brush. Spectral presences appeared for two reasons. The first was communication. The second was mindless repetition of past events. If it were a mere repetition, the entity would be commonplace. She'd been in the same apartment for years. The building was paranormally active, but none of the activity inhabited her apartment, or this floor.

She toyed with the blue brush's remaining bristles. There was something familiar about the phantom. It was the figure of a woman with dark hair, who kept her head down. Her clothing and hair were filthy. The posture implied shame, but the strong negativity said otherwise. Shame, like rage, was an incredibly destructive passion to carry in the next world. Those destructive potentials compounded if the person died while suffering.

She'd witnessed activity before, but never so pronounced in recent memory. Why was the spirit filthy? Did it feel unclean? When it came to the mysteries of the mind, there could be a host of reasons for filth in the ethereal realm. It might be a physical event, or an emotional betrayal, or a bitter regret might manifest if she died with something on her conscience.

32

She'd heard many stories about the apartment building over the years. Other residents frequently discussed the building's quirks and habits going back decades. Lost loves, wasted lives, yearning, hunger, misery, there were tens of stories with a variety of conclusions. Activity of all kinds had been reported as far back as the building had been operational.

The abortion butcher, "The Mad Doctor," ran his operation out of an apartment on the bottom floor through 1991. Most of his patients required major reconstruction surgery after his work... and that was just those who survived.

For years, authorities couldn't figure out why perforated organs and internal infections were so common in the region. Finally, one brave woman revealed the true cause. They eventually linked the doctor to 40 female corpses found around the region. His license to practice medicine was revoked two decades before due to drug abuse.

Instinctively, she knew none of that applied to the figure. This was not something connected with the apartment building, or the residents. The spirit was familiar, but it was not from here. That troubled her.

A faint memory drifted from the back of her mind. *Elysium... Yes, I know her.* Twenty years earlier, she'd witnessed the same form in Elysium's gardens. She walked by the old estate every day on the way to elementary school. She walked alone that crisp autumn morning because her sister had strep throat. The strange woman then walked through the overgrown grounds behind the house. She'd studied the stranger through the break in the iron fence. She'd never seen life at Elysium, let alone a woman.

She first saw her at nine years old. The memory returned as vividly as if it happened yesterday, not twenty-one years earlier. It was before she knew anything about Elysium's infamy. It was just a lonely old house and the woman who resided there was just as lonely.

She told her schoolmates about the strange woman. The other kids eagerly recounted tales of horror and tragedy in Elysium's history. They warned her to never approach or communicate with her. They told her she would end up like the "Pennsylvania Five."

Pennsylvania Five. That was a jolt from the past. She hadn't heard that term since. She never thought of investigating what it meant. She still didn't know who they were, or how they related to Elysium.

She sat on the folding chair at the milk crate vanity. No matter what happened between them, she had to help Melanie. She had no idea what she'd gotten herself into. She couldn't shake the insidious misgiving that things were going to get much worse for both of them.

Melanie just refused to listen to reason when it came to Elysium. Why? It was completely unlike her. She was not normally irrational or impulsive. She didn't make purchases without considering them—unless it was Elysium. It was a buyer's market. There were hundreds of beautiful estates to choose from. Many of them were just as historic as Elysium. Every home was huge, surrounded by gardens and woods.

Melanie fixation went to the point of obsession. She ran to that place as soon as she could afford it. The calm and certain skeptic grew just as stubbornly unwilling to see fact as any delusional zealot... but none of that mattered. She couldn't remain angry. Maybe it wasn't just her choice. Melanie didn't believe in things like that, but belief didn't impact their existence.

Maybe something influenced her friend's level-headed nature. Melanie had discussed her affinity for the home since they'd been friends, so that wasn't new. Maybe she had an innate connection. Maybe the purchase was intuitive, but she had no idea what that place was. She wouldn't listen.

She lay across the tiny bed. She pulled the shabby, patched quilt up to ward off a shiver. She knew Elysium. Melanie clung to her skepticism, not surprising because most hardened skeptics shared the trait of oppositional logic. Any "explanation," no matter how ludicrous, no matter how impossibly far-fetched, was always more believable than the obvious. They prided themselves on science and reason, so long as it coincided with their opinion.

Of course, even if she remembered the woman earlier, she could never bring herself to tell Melanie. She would've laughed at her. Pride was not worth a human life, and especially not her only family. She should call her before something happens.

Melanie became her surrogate family through the years. Her own family refused to recognize her. Now, her last remaining relative abided with an adversary she had no hope of conquering alone. Melanie believed it was just some neglected structure that needed attention, but the genteel overgrowth and graceful disrepair was a mask.

Life slowly disintegrated after Kevin left. It seemed impossible that five years had passed. Any hope of moving to a better place was the first to disappear. The hope of a better job through her father's connections was the next wish to fade into oblivion. Her unforgiving parents had no pity, even when the object of their contempt had vanished, and she begged to come home. Her sister refused to speak to her because they threatened her with financial abandonment, too.

She couldn't get a job anywhere else in the city, region, or state. Hayden was some kind of curse for employment. Life was shit, but she had Melanie. Skeptic though she was, she was an honest and reliable friend.

Melanie didn't have anything growing up, which equaled no regrets. It was an unspoken blessing that no one dared to mention at other status levels in life. Poverty allowed certain freedoms, in comparison to the life she'd lived with her parents. There wasn't anyone to impress or snub because everyone was in the same desperate situation.

Her apartment grew oddly silent. The atmosphere was dark and heavy. Where were the neighbors? The prostitutes' customers should be coming and going, no pun intended. They should slam doors and yell in the hall. She didn't like thinking of Elysium. She was so afraid of it all those years ago, and it still scared the hell out of her.

There had to be a connection between Melanie and Elysium. Some unknown psychic attachment beyond a whim or urge. Melanie feared frivolously spending her newly acquired money too much to spend several hundred thousand on an impulse.

Melanie had never known "status," not in the traditional sense. The purchase had nothing to do with regard for other people's attentions or status advancement. Of all the beautiful homes in the area, she chose an aging structure that likely needed more work than it was worth.

She, on the other hand, would keep going as usual, and hope someday God would smile on her and a better employer would respond. She turned to her side in the despicably tiny bed as another round of cramping began. Melanie probably had no use for her cot any longer.

Poor Melanie.

She had to help her. There was no way she could take on Elysium alone. No one could, but especially not a skeptic who didn't have the first clue about paranormal things. Elysium would eat her alive.

Chapter 7

She ate a sensible breakfast for the first time in weeks, partly out of compulsion, and partly because it was all she had left. She ate a slice of dry, whole-wheat toast, a hard-boiled egg, and the remaining cup of milk. It only reaffirmed her suspicion that health food was a form of sadism only practiced by those who were a glutton for punishment. The food was neither flavorful nor filling. She finished the last of her coffee before she dressed to go to the grocery store. It was time to stock the house.

She hated shopping on an empty stomach, or even a half-empty stomach. She grabbed a sausage biscuit from the drive-thru and ate it in the car. She watched traffic on the main road as she dined. The world was weird. Most people enjoyed thoughts of not having to go to work. Most dreamed of the day when they could do as they pleased, when they pleased, and forget responsibility. She did the same thing for most of her life.

"Carefree living," as was glamorized, wasn't care-free at all. It was difficult to adapt to life without routine, particularly when drudgery was all you knew. The convention and predictability of life, what she'd grown accustomed to, was gone. She wasn't as ready as she'd believed for the subsequent isolation.

She crumpled the wrapper into the bag. She returned into traffic as soon as the flow allowed. The store was relatively deserted. She grabbed what was needed faster than anticipated. She crammed everything into the hatch and backseat. The 1980 Pinto gave all it had to transport her and her wares back to Elysium. The pitiful thing moaned and coughed as she came to a stop in front of the front door.

She transferred tens of shopping bags to the kitchen. The sunny day was already intense, humidity radiated, and it wasn't even lunchtime. She really couldn't complain about discomfort. Sunlight cascaded through the windows and brought the place to life.

L. Chambers Wright

She purchased several bottles of wine for the barren wine cellar. It would probably never be entirely filled, unless she hosted many more events than planned, or she opened a bed-and-breakfast. She occasionally drank wine, but she preferred mixed drinks and hard liquor.

She worried she wouldn't have enough room for the goods until she had everything in the cabinets. She stocked the shelves nearly as quickly as she'd unpacked the foodstuffs. She thought she'd purchased plenty, but it was barely enough to fill a few shelves. She still had room for much more.

She eyed the Wedgwood in the hutch. Cobwebs and a layer of dust blanketed the plates, but they were fine, no fractures or cracks. The previous owners were a puzzle. They couldn't be bothered to take antiques, but they certainly stripped the wine cellar. Who cared about Tiffany lamps or Hummel figures?

She grabbed a can of soda and dropped into a chair at the table. It was barely ten, but she was exhausted. There was so much to do, but any initiative had vanished. Maybe she needed a boss. Self-discipline was an alien concept when someone else was always there to motivate you.

She studied the overgrown backyard beyond the French glass double-doors. Birds flittered from limb to limb as they serenaded one another. Butterflies flittered from daisies to dandelions. Bumblebees and honeybees shared their colorful and fragrant workspaces in patterns that resembled shifts at work.

She just needed a temporary diversion. A walk should help her tense muscles relax as well as provide exercise and clean air. There was no better time to explore the acreage. It would only get hotter as the day went on. The house came with thirty acres of forested farmland, around half a mile. It was a lengthy journey on foot. She wouldn't explore all of it today, but a stroll might boost her energy.

She slipped into her old jeans. They were covered with ink and grease stains that never washed out. She stepped into her well-worn, steel-toed boots that still carried golden residue from the gilding machines.

She grabbed a bottle of water from the fridge as she went out the back door. She and Alicia often hiked on local trails. Not only were hiking trails free, but standard work footwear also made excellent hiking shoes.

Uncle Ian would've loved the gardens, had he lived. Bittersweet thoughts of him plagued her as much as thoughts of her father. He died the year before, and the only biological family left was her mother.

Ian would've been disappointed with her impulsiveness. No amount of nostalgia would change that. She went against the most important real estate rule to obtain Elysium. *"A home is the biggest investment any individual will ever make and should be treated with necessary respect."* Well, there was no need to dwell on that. She'd made her purchase.

Sunlight streamed through the branches above to create random lacy patterns of light across the ground. Massive oak and beech trees grew across the wide back yard. A clear stream trickled through the forest. Its constant flow created a miniature in-ground canyon. She stepped across the divide, between two tall willows.

She looked upstream to find a series of willow trees following the waterway as far back as she could see. Many of the trees' graceful tendril branches snaked down into the water where they flowed with the current. Black ash and tall elm trees grew in haphazard clusters.

It should all be new and beautiful, yet it wasn't as new as it should be. She sensed there was some intuitive pattern to complete, but she had no idea of what it was. Logically, it was preposterous. Elysium wasn't *familiar* in any way. It was novel and wondrous, a grand mystery to keep her spellbound for years. There should be no sensation of déjà vu.

She glanced back towards the house after she reached the next clearing. Even the rear of the home was stunning. She thought back to the sweet doll house they lived in when she was small. The tiny yard was manicured with pansies and azaleas around the front porch. A clean sidewalk framed the front of the property.

That rare elation had been dismally short-lived. When she walked out to explore the backyard, she found it was like any other slum. Rusted pipes jutted out of an equally rusted roof. The white siding had blackened with age... a stark contrast with the seemingly new siding in front. Dying grass grew in sparse patches atop dry red clay earth and the tall, wobbly fence was filthy. The house wore a disappointing mask.

She began to wonder if Elysium wore a mask, too. Elysium's grounds were strange and mysterious within the forest. The unkempt trees had thick, ancient trunks. Their gnarled roots jutted above the soil. Dark branches poked heavenward and gave the infiltrating sunlight odd shadows. The forest felt old and secretive, as if many important things had happened there, but humans weren't supposed to remember.

She had intended to landscape the courtyard grounds, but after seeing nature, she couldn't destroy it. The transition from an overgrown yard into a majestic forest added to the home's mystique. She passed eastward through a dense group of trees and paused at the next elm.

A strange barren patch of ground lay directly ahead. The circular spot was around fifteen feet across and completely bald. It wasn't just bare soil... the ground was white. There had to be salt or sand, some kind of contamination in the earth, but Uncle Ian showed her ground that was contaminated by both. This looked nothing like it.

She uprooted a handful of weeds that bordered the circle. The bordering soil was normal. The dark earth was rich with organic matter, which was nourishing for greenery. There was no hint of discoloration. The soil didn't even harbor traces of white just an inch outside.

Forest soil was nature's best, where clay earth mixed with years of organic waste. The natural mix produced soil that nearly all vegetation thrived upon. There shouldn't be such a straight edge if it were a natural formation. The polluted soil should taper to some degree, even if slight.

She reached out to feel the texture of the powder but hesitated. It could be meth lab residue. They were common in the region, and she didn't know anything about the process, or the resulting waste. Drug busts involving portable meth labs were frequently on the news. It was yet another chore to bring the place up to speed. She needed to summon the authorities to ensure it wasn't anything so toxic. For now, she would continue her relaxing walk.

She circled the barren ring and continued northward. Another thick glade lay ahead, behind the next line of trees. Trees camouflaged several caves on the right. Their entrances went back into a sharp-sided mound of dirt and rock, almost as tall as the trees. No trees grew on the mound, but the sides were covered in thick moss and grass grew on the flat top. It resembled a small butte.

The presence of caves also meant she needed to contact an extermination service to verify the caves were free of animal life. *Better safe than bitten.* Caves often harbored snakes and bats if left alone. People didn't die from snakebites, but a bite could disfigure limbs or require extended hospitalization. Bats didn't attack out of hostility, but people were bitten by accident, and their bites required rabies treatment.

She wished her mom could see the caves and explore the land with her. *"Tell me the story again, daddy..."* she told her father when she was a child. It was a strange recollection to surface. His old yarn was nearly forgotten. Now she only recalled something about a beautiful princess, a traveling magician, and a band of cruel highwaymen.

His family probably had pictures of him, but that did no good. They wouldn't speak with her, even after she won the money. His family only visited once when she was a baby. The only pictures

Janet had of her father were destroyed when their basement apartment flooded.

She rounded another group of trees and walked into the next open dell. The world abruptly silenced. Animal sounds and insect calls vanished. Nature's resonance fled as a whirring wall of flames developed twenty feet away.

She couldn't move, but part of her didn't want to. It was a mesmerizing display. She had watched that somewhere before. She blinked several times, but the blaze remained. The flames subtly drifted towards her. She spun, desperate to find some kind of exit or a clearance that allowed escape. It was too late. She was surrounded.

The wall of fire drew closer. The tongues leapt up four feet, just high enough that she couldn't jump over. The circle continued to enclose as it grew taller. The heat was unbearable, but the ground didn't burn. When the burning circle came within three feet of engulfing her, it vanished. She dropped to her knees and gasped for air. *Cool, clean air.* She was nearly immolated, but the dried tips of the wild wheat surrounding her remained unscathed.

She fell to her side and waited for her lungs to clear. Her heart wouldn't stop racing. *That wall...* That circle was familiar. Dear God, she'd seen that somewhere before. She just couldn't remember where.

She stood back up once her breathing leveled out. She examined her arms and clothing for damage. She now had black scorch marks and several singed holes on the back of her pants, behind the knees. Two blisters on her left hand were already the size of dimes. The hem of her shirt had burned.

Okay, pause, breathe slowly, it's over. There was no reason to panic. There was a perfectly rational explanation for the fire. She'd probably just stumbled onto a natural gas leak. A natural gas bubble could've seeped through the surface and ignited.

The long, humid week had offered only scant breezes with none of the typical summer precipitation. The last storm was brief and without measurable precipitation. It could've been ignited by

42

anything, daytime lightening, even a static charge from her clothes. She was incredibly lucky that it burned out before it reached her.

Her normally iron-clad logic suffered a few dents. Even though she knew there was a rational cause, she also had rational questions. Why was the grass untouched, even where the fire originated? The parched weeds should've at least been singed. The flames also formed in the shape of a ring. A bubble of gas wouldn't. It would've been an immediate flash. A continual leak would continue to burn where it seeped through, if it didn't blow up altogether.

Likewise, it couldn't have been a hallucination. Blisters didn't appear, nor did fire damage clothing, from a figment of imagination. She shook her head. Both theories had flaws, but they were the most logical. Maybe both happened at the same time. She could've disturbed an underground methane pocket. That would explain the fire and the damage. Maybe she crossed an unstable patch of ground and a trace of gas somehow ignited.

Logical explanations were as fantastically coincidental as the paranormal. She shuttered to consider the paranormal. *No, not that.* Even the idea of methane was flawed. The authorities would've been involved years ago if something as toxic and volatile as methane seeped through the ground. If it were real, the grass would have been scorched just as her fabric had been.

Alicia knew everything about the unnatural, or *unexplained*, but she was reluctant to ask. She had some reasonable opinions, but she was biased when it came to Elysium. She would automatically believe it was *ghosts*. It was the terrible curse of the mummy. It was the curse of Dracula. It was the monkey's paw or whatever the current trend was.

Of course, sarcasm didn't help when you had the problem, and skepticism wasn't reassuring. She shouldn't have mocked Alicia's beliefs. That was bad karma and would come back to bite her. That may very well be what it was. All those years of laughing at her friend might be coming home. The concept of the paranormal didn't seem so far-fetched when you were alone in Elysium.

She needed to pull herself together. *Paranormal, my ass.* She'd completely overlooked the other possibilities. She could be experiencing chemical imbalances, a sinus infection, allergies, or a host of other health problems. Physical ailments combined with the drastic and rapid life changes could do anything.

Logic's discrepancies came with everything she considered plausible. If there was that amount of natural fuel, the Blythes would've installed a natural gas well, and made a small fortune running natural gas into the subdivision. There had to be an astounding supply below for it to seep through the ground. Elysium used natural gas for the appliances, but it didn't come from here, it was from "Buck and Sons' Gas." They would've at least hooked their own house up to it.

Hell, maybe it is Alicia's ghosts. She wasn't prepared any more for home ownership than a brush with the unknown. She only knew there was something strange at Elysium. Her dream home didn't seem so dreamlike now.

She walked to a nearby stump to rest. She slowly drank the water as the natural sounds returned. She rolled the cool liquid over her tongue and savored the feeling. The fire, or whatever it was, left her parched. Maybe she needed a break from the house and the money. The two combined to open a world of shit she'd never dealt with before.

The cell phone in her pocket played, "Ring of Fire," and she jumped. She'd loved the Johnny Cash song for years, but it held an eerie implication at Elysium. For a split second, she looked for the flames. She quickly scanned the area as she pulled the phone out. It was... Alicia?

"Hi, um, Mel, I wanted to talk to you."

"Hi, Alli." The argument seemed to be a hundred years in the past. She felt like she'd been isolated for months from the outside world. The quiet fears vanished as they made small talk. The greatest way to relieve a grudge was to release it. "So, you want to come over and see the place?"

"Well, no... not yet I mean. I have to go to work in a minute." Alli stumbled through her speech and tried to cover her awkward loss of words. "I... I needed to ask you a question."

"Okay...say, aren't you supposed to be at work already?"

"Yeah," she lightly chuckled. "Overslept.... I'm getting ready to go in. It's not like Fillmore will do anything, but bitch, anyways."

"True. I thought I'd gotten my shifts confused. I'm out-of-the-loop. What'd you need?"

"You might think this is silly, but I had to ask if you have you seen anything... unusual."

"Unusual? Like what?" The conversation became familiar, but she wasn't as confident in skepticism this time. She stared at the blisters. If something *unknown* could cause that circle of fire, then anything was possible. The universe was limitless, and she was marooned in uncharted territory.

"Well, anything. Strange noises or... even odd circles?" The mention broke her focus. How did Alicia know? She wasn't there, but she knew something.

"I...." She slowly responded. She wanted to blurt everything out. *Yes, I have seen odd circles. I just witnessed one hell of an odd circle minutes ago.* "Actually, I think so. Why?" She was an inadvertent hypocrite, but a hypocrite, nonetheless. She'd always been so certain it was nothing. Haunted houses promoted tourism. People enjoyed the adrenalin rush from a safe scare, no harm done. It wasn't like it was anything *serious*.

Alicia had every right to gloat, and she couldn't cheat her friend out of the opportunity. All those years she aggravated her for believing in the supernatural had come full circle. Now she was in the middle of something bizarre.

She had no one else to confide in. No one from work called or cared. She didn't dare worry her mother. Janet needed rest and relaxation. Her health had just started to improve. Any stress might reverse it.

"I was curious." Alicia held back but had to know something. It was a tremendous coincidence that she called as soon as the fire was gone.

"Come on, Alli. What is it?"

"Don't worry about it right now. Just let me know if you need to talk about... anything." She quickly changed the subject and forfeited the opportunity to revel. "How's the house?"

She reflected on her own behavior while they talked. Maybe it really had seemed like she wallowed in her fortune earlier. She was never known for patience... or choosing her words carefully. Alicia, however, was the opposite.

She had wanted to talk about the win as much as possible. She never meant anything malicious. It was just the newness of good luck. Something *good* had happened to *her.* It proved good things do happen. There wasn't a universal caste system, and even the poorest people could escape the voracious arms of poverty. It verified a few hundred thousand dollars wasn't a prerequisite to financial gain.

They talked aimlessly of work and the latest gossip. The environment lightened even more when Alicia agreed to visit after work. They spoke a moment longer before she had to leave. Melanie returned the cell to her pocket as she walked back towards the house.

A straight cut through the open field would be faster than returning through the forest. She'd already wasted more time than she wanted outside. Her burned skin throbbed in waves of pain. The blisters stung in random intervals as if she moved her hand in and out of fire. She needed lots of aloe and ice.

The trail ended in the cluster trees at the caves. A faint male voice resonated within the caverns as she passed by. *"Do what you need to doctor."* A menacing male voice whispered, *"You know what you're doing."*

The voice was almost too distant to fully understand. She was so attuned to the whispers that she stumbled over a protruding tree root. An auditory hallucination this far from the leak was impossible. The gas would've cleared her lungs much earlier. Even if her equilibrium was shot from the flu, she wouldn't experience hallucinations. *God, it's just a sinus infection, not LSD.*

A black feeling came over her. Her stomach knotted in trepidation. Instinctively, she knew she was not supposed to hear what was said in those caves. She wasn't supposed to hear it, and she shouldn't even be in the forest. She quickened her pace.

The sound of horses galloped nearby, from out of oblivion. The phantom riders drew so close she heard the strain of saddle leather and the jingle of the reigns. *What the hell?* There weren't any horses in the community, or the region. Those sounds shouldn't be there. It wasn't the turn of the Twentieth Century, but the Twenty-First. She felt misplaced and disoriented.

She heard a child laugh nearby... or was it a group of children? It had to come from the subdivision next door. She darted through outstretched limbs and dodged saplings until she was out of the forest's density.

The branches overhead thinned and allowed more light in as she neared the house. Leaves shivered behind her from movement. She didn't look back and her sprint slowed into a rapid walk. She didn't want to see whatever was back there.

The air changed as she emerged from the woods. She shook the daze off as her sinuses cleared. The rattling congestion in her lungs was gone. She stood on the lanai to catch her breath. She hadn't noticed earlier, but the hair on the back of her neck stood on end. A slight breeze whispered through the forest.

A tickle arose in the back of her throat that became a violent cough, like Taylor's cough. Her chest constricted and her breath left her body in one harsh outburst. Something came out. She looked down on the ground to see a sprinkle of bright red blood. She'd coughed up blood? *Well, that figured.* It was irrefutable proof that she'd caught Taylor's sinus infection. *Allergies, my ass.*

She'd done that the previous year. The doctor charged her nearly six hundred dollars to let her know her sinuses were infected. Congestion made her cough so hard she tore the membranes of her throat. This was nothing like that. She wasn't nearly as sick as she was then. As quickly as the episode erupted, it ended. Her breathing was normal. The sounds and disorientation disappeared. All that remained was the sensation of being watched.

She looked back into the forest from the safety of the back porch. It felt like someone was watching her. She knew there wasn't anyone out there. She'd just come from that very spot. She listened, but the woods were again, like they were before the fiery circle.

Who was in the woods? She knelt and peered beneath the low branches. There was no sign of human shoe or animal paw. She felt them, though, those eyes seemed to watch from all directions.

She went in the kitchen and locked the door behind her. She shouldn't have invited Alicia over. She shouldn't have anyone over until a professional inspected the entire estate. It might not be safe. She couldn't have guests if events like that were common. *"Houses weren't haunted."* She heard herself say the year before. *"It's bullshit to get viewers to watch and readers to buy books. People are haunted."*

She paced the tile floor in the kitchen as she rubbed aloe on her burns. She couldn't very well resell the house. That fiery circle in the back field alone would kill someone if they had a heart ailment.

Her problems went beyond fears for the next possible owner. Something deep in her body had latched on to Elysium and, like it or not, it wouldn't let go. There was something there and she had to be a part of it. There was no leaving or running away. For some reason, she had to fix something. There was no alternative.

Chapter 8

She nearly burned her lasagna in the new stove. Her old oven's customary ninety-minute baking time was just forty-five minutes in a normal appliance. She'd forgotten to subtract the old cooking time. The apartment oven was at least forty years old and required at least double the package baking time for everything. It had been two years since she last ate lasagna. She'd almost forgotten its richness in scent as well as taste.

Alicia's Ford Escort crawled up the drive around ten o'clock. It was a later supper than usual, but they would likely be up to the wee hours. She arrived at the front door as the first knock resounded. She waited a moment and opened the door. Alicia smiled, "Nice digs."

"Thanks. It needs some work. I have dust bunnies large enough to retire."

They walked into the kitchen and sat at the rectangular table. It was another antique the previous owners left. The massive oak piece was a dark shade she'd never seen before, a mix of dark pecan and mahogany. She draped a sheet over it to use as a temporary tablecloth. She needed to inspect the underside with a flashlight to see if there was any information on who made it or where it came from. That would help her figure out how to clean and maintain it.

She poured two tall glasses of Chianti as they caught up on what she missed at work. Alicia scrubbed up in the bathroom off the main hall as she put a final sprinkle of Parmesan on the baked casserole.

"I'm sorry I jumped on you before," Alicia pulled the salad bowl from the fridge. "I was afraid you didn't know what you were getting into."

"You've never liked Elysium." She sat at the table with the hand-washed Wedgwood and her regular silverware. "Why?" She almost snickered at the austere contrast of substandard steel utensils atop fine china.

"You'd think I was ridiculous... I just have my reasons."

"This isn't something new... and you've never told me why. When we became friends, if I mentioned this place, you didn't like it."

"It's just a feeling. That's all it comes down to."

"Can't you tell me more? I am curious." Alicia toyed with her napkin, clearly uncomfortable with the questions.

"It is a piece of history." Melanie broke the awkward silence as she sat the main dish on the table. She always tried to defend the home before, but now she wasn't certain of what she defended. After the ring of fire, she didn't know if any defense was necessary.

Alicia sipped the wine. "You've never believed in the paranormal. I thought you wouldn't want to hear about it."

"Oh, yeah." She wouldn't defend her former attitude. In retrospect, she had been an overtly aggressive skeptic. She cut into the pasta casserole with the spatula and let her friend take her time. She wiggled the first piece out, but it fell apart anyway. She distributed the garlic bread in silence.

Alicia finally began, "When I was little, I saw things here... I passed it every day on the way to elementary school."

"What kind of things? You went to school near here?"

"Just things that should not have been... shadows, voices, whatever. I attended the old elementary school down the road. I think it's a community center of some kind for Dogwood now."

"Can you describe your encounter?" She gently encouraged the conversation onward.

Alicia eyed her suspiciously. She ultimately sighed, "Okay, you'll probably see it, anyway. I'd say you've already seen a little. I heard children playing once, out by the fence. I heard a woman crying before. The first time, a woman stood in the yard with her head down. I felt sorry for her. I told the kids at school. They didn't want me to talk to her. You heard all kinds of noises, but no one lived here."

She struggled to find the right response. She took a bite of salad to try and think of something. She had to tell Alicia it was happening. She had to tell someone. She couldn't find the words. She needed to get it out in the open and couldn't. She was half-way through her salad when Alicia triumphantly voiced, "I'm not alone, am I?"

"No, you aren't alone." At least she didn't have to start the conversation. She wasn't sure of how to begin. Even if she reduced the events to black-and-white science and logic, it was fantastic. The odds of being at just the right spot to be engulfed in a natural gas explosion, that miraculously didn't kill her or even singe the foliage, were microscopic, if not altogether impossible.

"You saw the ring?"

"Well, yes."

"How many times?"

"A few, I think."

"A few, already? Jeez, it must really like you."

"Oh, stop it." She rolled her eyes. She'd missed her friend. She didn't want to hear about anything strange having some kind of conscious affinity or personal attachment. The joviality diminished and the room went silent.

Alicia took another sip, "I worry about you, Mel. I don't say it out of jealousy or pettiness. This is a big place and it's a... questionable place, to say the least."

"Questionable? So, what? My house has a reputation? Do I need to defend its honor?"

"Yes, it has a reputation, and no, you don't have to defend it," she laughed. "You just seem to be the only person unaware of the reputation."

"Prove it," she retorted. "Who are all these informed people?"

"Neighbors, residents, potential buyers who wouldn't come near this place...?"

"I just beat them to it?"

"You were ripe for the realtor's picking." She said between mouthfuls.

"Ah, but a ripe apple or peach?"

"Why be typical? A lovely pomegranate."

"Why not a passion fruit?"

"I've seen your realtor. You really want passion in the same discussion as John Taylor?" They heartily ate with no further discussion of the house.

She felt foolish. Was the world really attuned to some history she knew nothing of? Yes, it was entirely possible. Most of the people she grew up around knew nothing of local history, or lifestyles of the local rich and famous, or infamous. More facts supported Alicia's claims than her own.

The house had been for sale, on and off, through other realty companies for a while. John said she was the first client to view it with him. Who knew? It could've just been a shoddy housing market. Maybe she was jumping to conclusions from exhaustion. It had been a long exhaustive day.

They wandered into the living room after they cleaned the kitchen. She left the windows open all evening to clear the air. Her eyes left the television screen to watch the sheers billow in the breeze. Each curtain gently danced over one of the two massive leather couches. The luxurious furniture was draped with white cotton sheets and abandoned by the late owners. They lay opposite one another with an enormous coffee table between them.

Alicia's understandable reluctance couldn't have come at a more inopportune time. She needed comforting words from someone who wouldn't think she was delusional. Alicia was the only person in that position. She was the only individual whom she could tell anything without that same unfair sarcasm or skepticism.

She ventured again after another bottle of wine, "Will you tell me more about the house?" She added, "I'll tell you some of the things that have happened, since I moved in, I mean."

"Okay. We lived in Dogwood... when I was in elementary school. My sister lives somewhere over there with her husband, now."

"You never told me you grew up so close."

"Well, it was a long time ago. A long time before we were friends. I used to walk by here on the way to school."

"The Tipton-Haynes Elementary school. Didn't it close?"

"Yeah. I was in the last fifth grade before it closed."

"What happened?"

"I went to the sixth grade?" She paused and laughed. "I'm kidding. Not enough kids attended to keep it open. They consolidated it with Lincoln Elementary a few miles away. Anyways, all the kids knew this place was haunted, but kids often do. Here was this massive house, but no one lived here. No one stayed. There would be a car in the drive for a few hours and then they would leave."

She sipped her wine. "We assumed, but adults knew. We were taught to ignore it. I guess they figured any questions would disappear if they ignored them."

"They never do."

"Ain't that the truth?"

"But what happened? Why was it haunted?" Melanie rolled on her side.

"Legend has it there was something wrong because of what happened with Sherman."

"Sherman? The tank guy?"

"No. You know, the Civil War Sherman?"

"Here? In Bristol? My God, did he get lost? What sorry map led him here?"

"He refused to ask for directions."

"So, what was he doing here?"

"It wasn't established... but like I said, all I know is from rumors and most details are sketchy. The story goes that there was an attack on the house. The only survivor was a slave girl."

"What did she say?"

"We have very few plantation houses in this area, as you know. Most families were far too poor. The families who had them were divided on which side they chose. Most residents were simply indifferent."

"I know that feeling."

"Don't we all? Simple survival was an accomplishment into itself. The family that lived here leaned towards the Confederacy."

Mel grabbed a pillow and propped it behind her back. Alicia continued, "No one knows why the group chose Elysium. It was suspected that the family living here was the richest 'Rebs' in the area, and they were killed for it. The men attended a political meeting in town. Back then, they ran late into the night. That's when a band of soldiers showed up. They were called mercenaries, but that's just a label, and according to the legend they were in uniform."

"Did they attack the women?"

"They did more than that. The slave girl said the women, free and slave, were repeatedly raped and beaten. The soldiers referred to even them as 'the enemy.' While a group was busy with attacking the women, the rest raided the home and left with everything. They even took food from the pantry and the chickens."

"Geez..."

"Yeah, it was horrific, even for such a time as the Civil War. Everyone was murdered. The slaves, the women, any children they saw, the slave girl was lucky enough to hide in near-by caves when things became violent. She was never the same after that."

"How did they kill? Didn't neighbors hear gunshots?"

"No guns were used. The closest neighbors were still miles away. Most victims were stabbed. A few were beaten, but all bodies, dead or semi-deceased, were stacked outside on an old piano and set on fire. The poor girl remembered hearing screams from the fire from when some of the victims woke up."

"Good Lord. Why did they do it?"

"To make a point. And of course there is greed... not that they would be greedy."

"Those sainted men? Never! They just needed to unwind." She followed the sarcasm.

"And the rape?"

"What rape? Just ask the media. Only a few select cases are actually 'rape' per se. The rest are just evil female predators looking to harass poor, defenseless rich men."

"Of course. Welcome to war."

"That story makes it seem as if the actual ring of fire is just a minor element, but that's the only thing I've seen since moving in."

"Maybe they burned the bodies in a circle? Maybe they poured something flammable around the piano to start the blaze?"

"Maybe." It didn't feel right. Even with that story's merits, it felt false. "It doesn't feel like it, though."

"Excuse me? So now, you're *feeling* things?" Alicia grinned. "*You are feeling things?* Since when?"

"Well, yea. Since the move." She sheepishly replied. It was karma. She just had to deal with it. She'd given Alicia a hard time for her beliefs. She had the right to gloat.

"What do your feelings state?" Alicia smirked.

"It tells me that was a really long story, and I almost fell asleep." She gravely answered and barely caught the pillow Alicia threw. "I'm kidding, kidding. I just don't feel like that's what's going on."

"I bet I know of someone who could find out."

"Who?"

"You remember Kevin?" He was the reason her parents disowned her and, even when he left, refused to welcome her back. *He really was a bastard.* He dropped her like she was nothing and she still respected him. It was infuriating but also astounding. She was an amazing person. She would never have been so forgiving with Aiden. She never wanted to be, but that's how she was. "Yes... unfortunately."

"He knows a local paranormal group, the Secret Society. One of his relatives needed them to investigate their house. I could give them a call."

"That would be great... I think. Do you believe it's that serious?"

"What could it hurt? Besides, there's always a chance that they won't find anything and you're just crazy."

The darkness of the midnight hour came and left. "You want to stay here tonight?" Melanie sat up and peered out the window. "I don't know if it's safe to drive after a bottle."

"A bottle?" Alicia laughed, "I think we passed that at dinner. Try three or four... or ten, but who's counting?" She sat up, "Why I can drive anywhere—" She stood, staggered two feet, and fell.

She laughed as she struggled to get back up. "That's why they call me Grace!" When she caught her breath, she relented, "Well, maybe I'll stay. You can't shake your groove thang in a hospital. They frown upon that."

"I didn't know you had a groove thang." Melanie laughed and laid back down. She could barely move. "But thank you. I won't have to get out at the crack of dawn to identify any bodies."

"Does that happen often?"

"Not really, but that's a good thing. I'm not a morning person. I can't tell you how many I've misidentified."

The conversation went in aimless circles and touched on everything as they relaxed on the couches. It was a relief to talk about all things aside from Elysium. She'd only been in the home a few days but felt like she'd been alone for a year.

She assumed Elysium had a past. It was ancient for houses in the region. She also anticipated a little negative history. That came with age. She hadn't expected such brutality. Maybe it was haunted, or *active*, or whatever the proper term was.

The ring of fire went beyond standard lore, even considering a war raged around the estate. Many houses stood today that were engulfed by war, epidemics, and all other tragedies. It didn't mean they were *haunted* or harbored forces that could harm you. Why did Elysium?

Chapter 9

They were still in the living room when she woke. Alicia was fast asleep on the other couch. She hadn't moved from her earlier position, either. Melanie stood, too quickly, she sat back down, blood rushed through her body and her eardrums thumped.

Now ... a little slower. She gradually rose and waited for some semblance of stability to return. The television said it was four in the morning. She turned it off.

She waited a moment, still slightly disoriented. She needed to go to bed. She would have a terrible hangover when morning came, without the aches and pains of sleeping on a couch.

She tossed a throw quilt across her slumbering friend as well as she could before she closed the windows. She cautiously entered the hall and ascended the steps. *Thank God, the rail is sturdy.*

A wave of nausea struck deep within her stomach when she crested the top of the steps. She needed air. She couldn't go all the way back to the front door. She wouldn't make it back up. Her instable legs barely made it up the steps to start with. The closest exit was her bedroom balcony.

She would've anticipated such a punch from liquor, but not wine. She used the wall for support as she stumbled down the hall. She peered into the bedroom with a start. Flashes of light played off the objects outside her windows. The bright light made her head hurt. She blinked repeatedly to see if it would stop.

It almost looked like lightening, but the clouds were far in the distance. The pattern of illumination and stark darkness repeated until she felt blinded by the intensity, as if the moon had turned into a molten strobe light against a darkness that absorbed light.

She arrived at the veranda doors and pushed them open. The familiar sound of horses galloping approached below, from the left of the house. She turned to retreat back into the bedroom—her alcohol-affected legs didn't move fast enough— she fell, her chin hit the concrete floor. She crawled behind the massive concrete flowerpot in the veranda's left corner and peered down through the railing's scrollwork.

A cluster of phantom horsemen slowed their pace as they crept by directly below. They were solid for a few seconds—then transparent. The riders wore black hats with black bandanas covering the bottom half of their faces. "Get his horse," one man whispered loudly. She looked off into the distance to see a tiny flame lazily approach.

After more unintelligible whispering, the men divided up into two groups as they advanced towards the light. The noise faded along with the fire in the distance. She leaned against the huge vase to pull herself up. She would never overindulge again. Her legs ached from the awkward hiding position. Her head swam. She looked below, but the riders hadn't even left hoof prints behind.

The headache worsened and she raised her hand to her temple. Another loud sound came that she never wanted to hear. A roaring fire raged somewhere near. The roar was so loud she had to cover her ears. The stifling air carried an unbearable stench of death and ash, but there was no visible fire.

She was light-headed. She'd heard it before. She knew what it was. God, her ears hurt. She rubbed them as she covered them with her hands to try and ease the pressure. Something leaked out of her ears. She pulled her hands away and squinted. There was blood on her hands. The familiar fiery ring appeared below and ascended towards her.

She couldn't move. Her legs wouldn't move.

It floated higher, now even with the tall treetops.

The bright ring of white fire came at her, and she couldn't force her body to react. It was in front of her. She fell to her knees and covered her face. The flames would engulf her. She shut her eyes and trembled. She didn't want to die.

One second...

Two seconds...

Three seconds... She opened her eyes. The ring was gone. She stood back up. She couldn't pull her eyes from the ground below. It might be waiting. She leaned over the rail to look over everything.

A tree branch groaned somewhere deep in the forest. It was followed by the sound of a rope strain with a heavy weight. She looked through the trees, but none of the limbs shuddered or moved. She slowly came back inside. Any sudden movement might bring it back.

"Mel...." a faint whisper came behind her. Alicia stood poker straight. Her eyes were wide, and her face was filled with shock. Any residual giddiness from the alcohol dissipated. "This is what you've been seeing?"

"Yes." Finally, a witness. There was no reason to deny or dismiss any longer. It was more of a relief than she anticipated because she didn't have to explain it. Someone else witnessed it and maybe she knew the right words. She knew about that stuff. It also meant it wasn't natural. People couldn't share dreams and, as far as she knew, hallucinations fell into that spectrum.

"Are you sure you want to stay here?" Alicia put a hand on her shoulder. "You don't have to do this."

"I have to be here, Alicia. I can't explain it." Alicia would probably disagree now that she'd seen the activity herself. She could hear it already. *Why the hell did you buy this house? What were you thinking? How stupid could you be for buying Elysium without knowing about it?*

The silence was broken only by her softly stating, "Then, you need help."

"You aren't going to fuss?" She thought aloud before she considered the repercussions of her words. She felt her ears, now dry, her hands were now clean.

Alicia only repeated, "You need help."

"Thank you," she embraced her friend. Her heart smiled. Any residual negativity between them vanished. She had a friend again.

"But what is it?" She looked back out to the balcony. "Alli, you know about this stuff. What is that? That damned ring was there again."

"Ring? I didn't see a ring. I saw lights... and the horsemen, but I didn't see a ring. I don't know. Maybe it's haunted... or maybe the past repeats itself here. That's why we need people who know."

"What's the guy's name from the group?"

"I think it was Ash... Ashton Lane. I haven't spoken with them, myself. They were starting out back then, but I think they've helped a number of people."

"We need to talk to him." It was a step in the right direction. Maybe they could even find some bizarre organic reason for it all. *That's some damned gas leak.* The once-plausible explanation no longer seemed rational. Maybe it was some kind of weird psychic residue from the attack, but that made no sense. The men in the group weren't in uniform. Civil War soldiers were called "the blue and the gray" because of the uniforms. This group didn't even carry a flag, and both sides had their own respective flags in that war.

She crawled into the right side of the bed. Alicia followed on the left. They briefly discussed the events before sleep came again. She drifted in and out, her mind returned to the same answerless questions. How did Alicia see the men and not the ring? She believed far more strongly in everything. Melanie tossed again before settling on her left side. She wasn't sure what she believed now. It seemed like anything supernatural would be far more eager to show itself to Alicia.

The curtains moved in the slight breeze. A whisper of fabric laden with secrets and answers she couldn't hear yet. Those windows only opened when she was nearly asleep. The sheers ebbed and flowed like a white tide; softly moving as the breeze came.

It still seemed improbable that the ring was supernatural. It physically injured her, so it couldn't be anything paranormal. Who heard of physical injuries from a *haunting*? Sure, there might be some self-induced afflictions, but not from a spirit.

Alicia sniffled and sneezed as she dozed. She heard her friend's hand hit the table and grab a handful of tissues from the box by the bed. She soon settled back into position. She eventually stopped moving and her breathing became regular. It was that damned bug. What the hell did Taylor bring to the house? It was bad enough that something was amiss at Elysium without that stupid cold.

She drifted into a deep and troubling darkness that offered no escape. Ashton might help, but he might not. He may not have any idea of what is happening at Elysium. He may dismiss them both as delusional. There might not be any information available to even point them in the right direction to find answers. It may simply be hopeless.

The images from the veranda repeated every time she closed her eyes. The men whispered, *"Get his horse...."* She felt malevolence just from that phrase. They weren't soldiers, but they planned something wicked.

She saw the ring of the sun, the moon, a ring of gold, a circle-shaped pond, flowers growing in rings, and the concrete columns along the entrance. Circles and rings were everywhere at Elysium, and she'd never paid attention.

Chapter 10

Sleep came in random intervals but didn't provide rest. If only the second night were as peaceful as the first. The bright morning magnified her hangover. She laid still a moment for her head to clear and that first wave of nausea to subside. She struggled with the wine's aftereffects as she rose.

She washed and dressed in the bathroom. The step-down marble tub had two seats opposite the faucet. The double shower had a massive flat chrome shower head. She was a universe away from the worn iron bathtubs and antiquated toilets she'd grown accustomed to. Most of her shower heads were so cheap they flew off after 100 uses. She nearly obtained a concussion when the last one broke, mid-shower.

She felt awkward and conspicuous as she stood there. She might own Elysium, but she didn't belong. She didn't know if that would ever change. She felt called to solve some mystery that lingered on the grounds, but she would never fit the house. She wasn't the mistress of a fine manor, any more than she was an astronaut. She was a custodian. A steward.

The balcony doors were now closed. Alicia must've closed them... if they were open to begin with. It was difficult to distinguish between what happened and what she dreamed.

She squinted as she inched down the hall. The previous night was surreal, full of strange visions. She thought Alicia said something about the Civil War, some kind of attack. She remembered hearing people were killed, but not much else. Why did she take the bottle into the living room? Why did she return for another? They could've moderated their alcohol much better if she had just left it in the kitchen.

She clutched the rail as she descended the steps. She'd always loved dreams of a bright, happy home. Elysium's numerous original windows seemed like a unique benefit, but right now, she longed for a dark and dreary castle.

She needed caffeine to settle her stomach and soothe her headache. The sunlight in the kitchen was blinding as it shone through the glass doors. She got the grounds in the coffeepot filter after two failed attempts. She cleaned up the spilled grounds as she waited for the brew to perk.

She poured a bit of the early brew when it was its strongest. She sipped the espresso-like liquid. Her body jolted awake. She was now somewhat ready to face the day. She reached to get Alicia a cup and caught a glimpse of her arms. She hadn't seen the flesh of her arms without mark or blister in years. They were gone. The pink bubbles had almost faded into normal skin.

She was so used to blisters from the damned laminator, the hot glue machine, and various cuts from the binder. Books were great to read, but a hell of a lot of blood, sweat and tears went into their production. Hayden Graphics didn't handle paperbacks. Oh, no. They produced hardcover books that required nearly all work to be done with dangerous equipment.

"Hi," a soft, raspy voice called behind her.

"Have a cup, the elixir of life." She poured Alicia a cappuccino mug full of strong black coffee. She didn't look well. Her puffy face emphasized the dark circles under her gray eyes. Her dull blond hair was tangled from sleep. "Are you okay?"

"We... we just had to over-do-it, huh?" Alicia nearly dropped the heavy cup.

"Well, if you're going to the trouble of doing it, that's the only way to go." She finished her own cup and poured another.

"Ugh. I never want another night like that. By the way, about the curtains, what is it with them? Don't you close your doors?"

"My drapes don't like to be oppressed."

"They burned their sashes, huh?"

"Yep, free and flapping in the wind."

"Seriously, what if someone tried to break in?"

"Alli, I don't know what to tell you. I do lock them... they just don't stay locked. I would worry about burglars, but considering what happens in my backyard after dark, I don't think that's a problem." They slowly migrated to the stools at the bar. She scooted the coffee pot within reach.

"The men?"

"Do you remember much?" She leaned forward on her elbows. Try as she might, she couldn't put the previous night's events in any logical order.

Alicia nodded, "I had the worst dream. Angry men... a group of angry horsemen were in front of me, like a lynch mob or something." She shook her head. "It's all so hazy." She sneezed and sniffed again.

"Did you see them standing around anything?"

"Sort of. Maybe it was a wagon?"

"I wondered if the wagon was part of their group."

"I don't know. It might be." She grabbed a tissue and wiped her nose. "My sinuses are killing me."

"Were you in the forest in your dream?" She scooted the stool closer to the counter. "I had that cold yesterday. I think it's some sort of bug, give it a day or two. It's awful, but at least it passes quickly."

"Yeah. I was hiding in the brush. I wore a white dress or gown. It was pretty, but I don't know why I wore it."

"Hm.... Just like my dream." They finished their coffee in uneasy silence. "Welcome to the club, Alli. I think it's exclusive."

"Ya think?" She laughed, "I need to get in touch with Ashton."

"Yes. They're probably used to both natural and unnatural weird stuff."

"I think they specialize in 'weird stuff' so yes, even if it isn't supernatural, they should have answers. Care if I use your phone? I was supposed to come in for a day shift today."

"What? You risked Fillmore's wrath?"

"I know. I'm such a disappointing employee."

L. Chambers Wright

"And look at what he's given us, Alli!" She summoned all the melodrama she could muster. "Honestly! All that paid vacation time and look at those benefits! We only have a $10,000 deductible on hospital stays. How can you beat that?"

"I'm such an ingrate!" She did her best crying impression.

"Phone is on the buffet," she nodded with her chin. Fillmore would just utilize it as more ammo against those present. Everyone was expendable at Hayden. It was common knowledge. For every person hired, five potential applicants remained on file. The two of them had somehow managed to last longer than the majority of those around them. Their history and production records afforded them a few missed days here and there.

Alicia called in to work, and luckily, missed Fillmore. She spent an hour attempting to reach Kevin. Melanie never understood why she kept in contact with him, but it was a benefit if he could help.

She never wanted to see Aiden after he left. He had the unmitigated gall to contact her after the win and tried to weasel his way back in her life. She told him to kiss her ass. He proved his feelings long ago, and she had no fond memories of his lies. They weren't true then and wouldn't be now. It was all a lie, and always a lie. Every time they woke, every time they fell asleep in one another's arms.

The worst thing was he made her the other woman. He said he was divorced, and she accepted his story. It took a year to discover he was married and had no intention of leaving his wife. Oh, they separated on and off, but never actually stopped their relationship. They even continued date nights every month. She'd felt so dirty for so long. She would've dropped him instantly, had she known he was married. It took nearly a year to forgive herself, and to stop feeling so stupid.

Apparently, staying in touch didn't help Alicia, either. She gave up and telephoned information to find Ashton's number. He wasn't listed. She took it a step further and asked the operator about the group, but they weren't listed, either. It was hard to be patient even when things moved as quickly as possible.

She tugged the cardboard crate of paperwork from the bank out from beneath the counter as Alicia worked her way through local areas with the operator.

There was too much information in the world. It was the first time in her life she needed a calculator to figure out what she had. How the hell did people crunch numbers for a living? She couldn't balance her checkbook without mathematical sedation. For one brief second, the numbers resembled Greek characters a little too closely for comfort. The bank representatives gave her pamphlets on investing and interest rates and CDs and every other maniacal financial term imaginable. *Stocks and bonds and bears, oh, my!*

Waterboarding seemed mundane in comparison to the excruciating migraines brought on by numbers. It had to be torture somewhere in the world. It took concentration and discipline to deduct and calculate for five minutes. She pushed herself until she couldn't do it any longer. Her head throbbed and her temples ached as she returned the materials to the box. Addition and subtraction did not mix with hangovers.

Alicia struggled with the search in three of the closest cities. It didn't look hopeful. She repeated the name several times, as well as the organization's name. The operator finally found a general number for the group.

She sighed as she sat the receiver down, "I got a number, but I don't know if it's current or working." She poured a glass of iced tea and returned to the telephone. The search lasted nearly two hours, but they finally got Ashton's information from someone named Janelle. Janelle provided the group's primary number.

Alicia took a deep breath and called Ashton. She watched her friend slowly pace from one side of the kitchen to the other. She should be calling, but it was so damned embarrassing. She could barely discuss it with Alicia, let alone a complete stranger. She still felt foolish for bothering her friend.

Alicia triumphantly grinned and gave a thumbs up when he answered. She eventually explained to the man that they were at Elysium. The caller became excited. Alicia developed a pattern of, "Excuse me?" and "Yes, the Elysium in Bristol."

She pulled a box of Lucky Charms from the cabinet as her friend continued. The hard marshmallows jingled against the ceramic bowl. Her stomach calmed and her headache subsided. Alicia returned the phone to its cradle and giggled, "I'll be damned."

"Is it that bad?"

"He's coming over to talk to us. He said he'd probably need to conduct two or three meetings. He wants to interview us both."

"Now? I thought they needed time to prepare... wow, an interview. I feel famous."

"He said he's already prepared and it's his week off. He's been collecting information on this house for years."

"Will he bring Mr. De Mille? I'm ready for my close-up," she grinned. "That is convenient. I'm glad *I* thought of it."

"Yea, right," she rolled her eyes. "Anyways, you might just have answers today, Mel."

Breakfast concluded on a hopeful note, and she sat the bowl in the dishwasher. It was a glorious day outside, but she didn't feel like walking. "It's amazing out there." She sighed.

"Yes, it is." Alicia's agreement surprised her.

"Thank you for helping," she patted her friend's arm. "I'm in a new world here."

"Yes, you are... but you'll get used to it."

She'd be smoking if she smoked. It was a recent temptation considering her home's behavior. *Behavior.* That was good. Her home was an unruly relative. She needed an intervention before it got out of hand. It was more difficult to sit and do nothing than it was to encounter something. At least time passed with some swiftness when the thing out there unleashed. It didn't just crawl by like it did now.

She mopped the kitchen while Alicia dusted the study. Activity was the only way to pass the sluggish time. After she mopped, she grabbed the Windex to start on the windows. She strolled to the front door to see if any cars had come up the road.

What was taking him so long? It felt like hours had passed. She sprayed the first parlor window she came to. She was impatient, but patience had never been a virtue for her, just a pain in the ass.

She peered out the window when she came to the second pane. *I'll be damned.* There he was again. She didn't know him, or what he did, but his attachment to Elysium must've rivaled her own. She'd driven by several times before she purchased the place, and he always watched the house. She named him "Creepy" after the fourth or fifth time.

He wore generic business suits and alternated his jacket based on the day's temperature. He would be a "Man in Black" if she were into conspiracies. Sadly, he seldom wore black suits, so that designation was unwarranted. He did look like a leering government official.

He watched the house for hours. If a car turned down the street, he always turned and walked, as if he were going somewhere. Once the prospective witness passed, he returned to the same spot. He stood by the tall hedges in front of the white Federal house at Dogwood's entrance.

It would be a waste of time to involve the authorities. He never actually came towards her home. He just stood there. It wasn't as if she didn't understand that attraction. His interests had nothing to do with her. It was all Elysium. She would've stared at the house for hours, herself. She returned to the kitchen, "My house has a stalker."

"What?"

"Some guy stands across the street and stares at my house."

"Alli. I don't like that."

"Oh, don't worry. He did that before I even toured it with Taylor. I drove by several times before I contacted the realtor, and he watched it the same, then."

"Have you tried talking to him?"

"No, not yet. I thought he'd stopped since I moved in. I hadn't noticed him for the past few days. I guess not."

"Maybe there is someone else, somewhere, who wanted to buy it."

"Maybe. If it continues, I'll talk to him."

A knock finally resounded, and she dashed to the front door. She knew it was Ashton when she opened the door. He held a thick black briefcase that was filled to capacity. "Hey, I'm Ashton."

"Hi, I'm Melanie." She eagerly shook his hand.

"Thanks for calling. I can't wait to talk with you."

"Come in. I'll introduce you to Alicia. She's the one you spoke with."

She introduced Ashton and Alicia in the kitchen and the room went silent. She smiled to herself and slowly backed away, without drawing attention. The two seemed oblivious to her presence. Maybe Kevin's memory had met its match. It was about time. Alicia deserved someone better.

"Ashton?" Melanie tried to politely break their stare after several minutes. "The house?"

He blushed, "Sorry." He sat the briefcase on the table. "Our group is simply called the 'Secret Society.' We primarily work with the paranormal but offer resources for anyone with questions about things like cryptids or UAPs. I've collected information on Elysium for years. It's a pastime, although you can't imagine how difficult this stuff is to come by. It's an honor to be here. Thank you again for inviting me. This is a hot topic in the paranormal world."

"This place? I didn't think anyone knew anything about it." Melanie sighed. *It figured.* Everyone knew more about her home than she did. Maybe it served her right. She'd jumped without considering where she might land. "How is it so popular and I've never heard the lore behind it?"

He grinned, "Well... that's the difference in the 'normal' world. It's hard to locate information on most historic landmarks if you try to find anything 'paranormal.' The only exception is if the establishment wants to use the paranormal as a promotional angle. Sadly, not many do."

"Why is Elysium popular?" They gathered at the table as he unpacked several folders.

"Mostly, because of its known history. It's been 'forbidden fruit' for decades. The owners never allowed others on the premises, for any reason, for as long as anyone can recall. They wouldn't even allow representatives from the local historical societies to visit."

He rummaged through his case and picked out handfuls of papers in random sections. "The only reason I have my collection is from estate or yard sales. Sometimes you find miscellaneous items from people who visited decades ago. There are also renegade photographers that risked trespassing charges to snap a few pictures over the fence. They're taken without permission so, you can imagine, they are nearly impossible to view at all. There's also a few on record at the courthouse."

"Is it the legend about Sherman's raid? Is that why?" Alicia took the chair across from him.

"No. That's an urban legend. The only documents I found on an attack described the culprits as highwaymen or bushwhackers. There are no facts supporting a Union or Confederate attack, and no evidence of such a notorious figure in our area. Plus, the Civil War hadn't started when the attack happened. Lincoln was just campaigning at that time, so it would've most likely been late 1859 or early 1860.

"Elysium was several miles from its neighbors back then. There was also a tuberculosis epidemic at the turn of the Twentieth Century. Elysium was a quarantine hospital for this region. To be honest, Elysium may be active, or not, it just has an extremely high probability due to history. That's the primary reason investigators are so attracted."

She sat back. "Is there anything that *hasn't* occurred in my home? I'm the last one to know about everything."

"Don't be alarmed," he stacked his paperwork. "I have tons of information. Most of the past has no influence at all on the present. It's just history... nothing more. I doubt even the previous owners knew much of it... and it was their own ancestors."

"But sometimes the past influences the present." Everything that happened presently at Elysium was due to events in the past. She felt as much in her doubtful gut.

He nodded, "Yes. Sometimes, it doesn't want to remain in its rightful place. Tell me what you've seen." He flipped a yellow legal pad open and grabbed a pen.

Now that a professional was visiting and she had the opportunity for answers, her mind went blank. "I'm... I'm not really sure how to start."

"Then, let me help." He seemed to expect her loss for words. "Have you liked the house for a long, or was it just an interest once you could buy it?"

"I've loved this place all my life."

"Do you have any psychic abilities?"

"Not even close. I can't tell much about the present, let alone the future."

"That isn't necessarily what 'psychic' means. Psychic abilities often have little to do with the future. Otherwise, everyone with psychic abilities would be wealthy. Unlike the romanticized demonstrations on television, a psychic ability is often just a specific knowledge or awareness that shouldn't be there. Some people read personalities. Some guess cards. A few read expressions, and others almost seem to read minds. Some psychics can look at a crime scene and tell police what happened. Do you just feel or see things you can't explain?"

"Only since moving here... I can't remember ever doing that before."

"Okay. What do those instincts think it is?"

"Instincts?" She didn't want to go on instincts or answer from feelings. She sat back, "I don't know. I'm not an expert. *You're* supposed to tell *me* these things. I didn't believe in any of this until I came here... It wasn't supposed to be like this."

Her disappointment faded when she realized how curt her tone had become. "I'm sorry. Elysium was just supposed to be an old house, empty and abandoned. It wasn't supposed to be *haunted*. It wasn't supposed to cause this...." She held out her blistered hand. Alicia gawked at her injuries but remained silent.

"That's not how it works, Melanie." He ignored her initial aggravation with the patience of an experienced listener. "I apologize, but I can't wave a magic wand and make answers appear. I believe in the paranormal, but I'm a skeptic, too. I must be. I need to know everything before reaching a conclusion. The more you let me know, the better for all involved."

"I don't want anything to be wrong with my home."

"Maybe there isn't, not the way you assume. Maybe it's just the past repeating itself."

"How does the past repeat in a *thing*? It isn't a person, it isn't living...."

"It's just residue. A random array of pictures and sounds that repeat over time. Maybe the burns just came from being in the middle of it when it was at its strongest. We need to approach it with as much objectivity as possible."

"There's so much to consider. How can we narrow anything down to a single event or individual? Who knows how many people have died here? Why is it angry? Why did it hurt me? I didn't do anything."

"It may not be about death... or even anger. Have a little faith. We'll find out everything about this house. It just takes time and patience. It seems you are running low on both, and you need to relax. First, tell me in detail how you were blistered."

She recounted the previous day as quickly as she could, the sounds and the disorientation. He listened intently and didn't speak for a moment. "Okay. Now, I need to establish some things."

"Sure."

"I need to consult with the group to offer anything aside from personal theory. I can give you a guesstimate right now as to what I believe, but it doesn't mean it's the definitive answer. Our policy is to keep the property owner as informed as possible, even in the earliest stages."

"Go on." She sat up.

"Hauntings most often common symptoms. These can be cold spots, noises, flashes of light, shadows, or other minor disturbances. They can be frightening but are generally harmless. Your ordeal seems a little more... interactive. Elysium is beyond a normal activity range. At this point, based upon your account, it sounds like you have a poltergeist or an entity. "

"What's the difference?"

"Poltergeists are playful, known for impish pranks. They like to aggravate and annoy, rarely do they ever cause any real fear, and even if they do, it's playful. They hide your keys, move small objects, and some people have had furniture rearranged. We call living people who do the same thing pranksters or jokers."

"And entities?"

"There are many definitions, but we reserve this title for an extremely specific group. Entities are the 'badasses' to put it simply." He flipped through his papers. "You can also call them 'demons.' Initially, most present themselves as poltergeists, but their behavior progressively worsens. It isn't uncommon for entities to attack people."

"How do you get rid of them?"

"Poltergeists? There are several methods for dealing with them, and we'll need to tailor it to your situation. If it's an entity, well, I'm afraid entities require much, much more work. Their wrath is far worse than any other spirit. They like spiritually weak people. Our Western society doesn't really prepare people, spiritually, for such encounters. It's easy for them to take over. The weak are like fish in a barrel when it comes to entities."

"Can you tell us more about the Civil War attack, Ashton?" Alicia finally chimed in. "I told Mel about the stories I'd heard. She said she didn't feel it matched the impressions she had. Do you know more about that particular time?"

"Yes, there are many stories although I'm fairly sure they're just stories. Melanie, do you see anything that would confirm or conflict with the story of Sherman, for example?"

"I see a group of bandits... highwaymen... whatever they're called. I saw them first in my dreams. Alicia had the same dream last night. It's always from the perspective of someone in a long white dress or gown. It's nighttime. I was outside in a forest of trees, to the left of the backyard, hiding in the bushes. The bandits aren't in uniform, but they wear black hats and black bandannas."

"It sounds like an organized mob, but I don't think stories involving the military apply. Also, I don't know of any pre-Civil War groups like that. What happens when you see them?"

"The horsemen crowd around something. They move towards an object that looks like a wagon, but it isn't a normal wagon... it's a big wooden box with doors everywhere. The men are so angry. One looked at me and he had the blackest and cruelest eyes. He enjoyed what they were doing."

"Good. Tell me more." He continued writing as she spoke.

"They appear faded, almost black-and-white. They are in period clothing, but I'm not sure what era. They're wearing plain pants and white, long-sleeved shirts."

"Wouldn't it be the group from the burning?" Alicia tilted her head.

"The only document I found on that attack was from an undated piece of newspaper. The group that annihilated

Rotherwood, the estate here before Elysium, couldn't be identified. Local people recalled a band of unknown travelers on the far side of the estate, but after they attacked, they just disappeared. They were never seen off this estate."

"Is that concrete?"

"Not at all, and it doesn't mean that the story couldn't have changed a week or a month later, either." He shrugged, "However, as usual, history has been rewritten a number of times to suit the writer. We won't know the full truth until we find more information... if we ever do."

Alicia leaned slightly towards him, "What is confirmed?"

"It is known, for whatever reason, Lincoln heard of the ordeal and was horrified. This was his first election. Maybe that's why so many assumed it was related to the war. War hadn't been declared, and wouldn't for years, but early rumors mention Union involvement.

"Eventually, legend states he toured the destruction and commissioned an architect to reconstruct a home for the family. A slave girl, named Esther, escaped into the caves on the night of the attack. She carried the Rotherwood family's infant daughter and the youngest son. She also managed to save numerous slave children. I think she saved 15 children in total. She was granted her freedom but chose to remain with her family."

He handed her a stack of papers. "Keep this for your records. It's some general documentation on the types of entities and spirits that are common in our investigations."

"Thank you," she nodded. "Do you know more about back then?"

"That's all from that far back. Most of the construction workers were volunteers who wanted to help the family. Lincoln briefly inspected the work afterward. I don't know if it was intentional or not, but no wartime fighting took place anywhere near the property."

She finished looking over the documents and handed them to Alicia. "The group's leader noticed me... in the dream, I mean. Just as I looked into his eyes, a ring of fire circled and engulfed me. Every time I've encountered it. The flames are in a perfect circle. It narrows until it feels like you will be burned alive, and then it vanishes... every time."

"Hmm... I've heard reports of the ring, but always from afar. I don't think there is an account where the person is inside or even near the ring." Ashton further noted. His blue eyes sparkled as he flipped through the papers. He tossed a picture on the table and continued digging. "Does this look familiar?"

The faded black-and-white picture was of a beautiful girl in a long white dress. She had fair skin with light eyes. Her dark hair was fashioned in a loose bun on the crown of her head with ringlets cascading down over her shoulders. "I can't tell. It was dark and I couldn't see the dress's details. The necklace looks familiar."

"Well, the necklace was commonplace, so that doesn't tell us much." He smiled, "That is one of the few photographs of Isabelle Blythe. You purchased the house from her relatives. Hunter Rotherwood, the infant son, grew up here. He eventually became Old Man Rotherwood. He held on to Elysium until he turned 30. He always said the house was the last of his original family. He moved on after he turned 35. The Blythe family bought the home sometime in the 1890s."

It still didn't bring a sense of finality. "I don't feel like she's a key figure. She was a rich kid, what did she know of hardship?"

"Are you psychic?" He looked inquisitively at her. "Is that a true sense, or just an assumptive one?"

"I said before, no. I don't think I'm psychic. I don't know why I feel things."

"Maybe you're open to the house. See where it takes you. There might be answers that way."

"Are there attacks on this property that aren't connected to a war or epidemic?"

"None that I've found, so far." He stopped flipping and thought. "There could be, again, time and patience."

"What about a psychic?" Alicia broke from her fascination with the documents. "Couldn't a psychic help?"

Ashton gave her a grimace at the question, "You can try. I'm not sure what your feelings are. I tend to shy away from them, especially this early." He folded his hands on the table. "We've worked with them before. None offered information that could be substantiated. That is the most essential element for a scientific process. Any information supporting their claims always fell victim to a fire, or had been destroyed in another way, according to them all. If you make claims in a paranormal investigation, you need at least one source proving it. Otherwise, why bother? We can all guess without paying others to guess."

He sheepishly grinned. Dimples formed on either side of his mouth. "Sorry, I'm biased. We put forth good effort on several, but it was no use. Maybe you will have better luck. A lot of people achieve the results they are looking for with them."

"I wouldn't be interested if you wouldn't recommend them. I have trouble accepting that stuff... even after what I've been through."

"The first order of business is to return with some equipment. Can I officially report that this house is under investigation?" He paused a moment and sneezed again.

"Bless you." Alicia smiled.

"Yes, do." She nodded. "Will a group come with you?"

"Probably, but a little later on. I hope to do a full individual preliminary investigation before group involvement. This place sounds extremely active, but the original owners never released information, and there aren't any other witnesses we can contact. I'll do further research to see if any descendants are alive. I'd also like to narrow the geography down before the group arrives. Our typical investigation goes from a few hours to overnight. We need to know precisely which areas are active. Otherwise, we have a massive house, and over 30 acres to investigate. That's a lot of space to cover."

He picked up the white ballpoint pen and started writing again. "The last formal report of paranormal activity here was by a driver on the street, I think in the 1970s. Even with that, we have nothing more than speculation and hearsay until now. I'd like to have more."

He flipped through the nearest file. "Our group has believers, but also skeptics. It maintains a healthy balance. I think our believers would go anywhere on suspicion, but our skeptics want something tangible."

"What will you do?" She walked to the cabinet to fix drinks. She pulled out three glasses and filled them with ice.

"Mostly photograph. I may take some E.V.P. recordings."

"Which are?" She poured the lemony tea over the cubes.

"It's an acronym for 'electronic voice phenomena.' Voices, noises, things caught in an audio recording that shouldn't be there. Sounds on frequencies our ears can't hear." He brushed a strand of unruly dark hair behind his ear. His fingers were long and pale.

"Are those reliable?" Alicia leaned slightly towards him.

"There are some who refute the validity, but I can't. I mean, honestly, how do you get random television wavelengths, or obscure radio frequencies to provide relevant answers? It's a little too convenient to dismiss it all as electronic backwash. Also, manmade noise would be consistent, perpetual, and predictable, in some way. EVPs aren't."

"Do we need to leave?"

"No. Although, if you would, turn off any televisions and radios, unplug them if it isn't too inconvenient. It's just a precaution to ensure no electrical interference. We utilize EMF detectors for electromagnetic fields. We like to keep our work environment as clean as possible."

"What about phones?"

"Just turn them off when we're investigating the house. Disconnect any landline phones. We need to visit when you don't have company. Family members may offer moral support, but we can't work with another group hovering over us. So, given all that, when would you like to begin?"

They arranged a time for his initial inspection. He gathered his papers and left the photograph for her to examine. He left a few copied documents on the history of Elysium for her to examine. Maybe something would make sense of what she had seen. Alicia escorted him to his car.

She wished she could say the visit clarified the situation, but she felt worse. The truth could just as easily be lost. Who could say what happened, without documentation? Even if they found more, could it be trusted? Newspaper publishers could have been bribed, or threatened, to omit or alter facts. Most simple textbooks today were full of bias and prejudice, authored with deliberate misinterpretation and manipulation, and that was without any pressures or temptations of wealth.

She looked over the papers again. The definition of "entities" came from the *Paradox Dictionary of Paranormal Terms.*

"An entity is a powerful malevolent spirit, or demon, who attempts to contact, harm, or possess. It is recommended to only approach with relevant spiritual leadership. Any professional consultation should be done with a fully trained demonologist."

Well, shit. That made matters worse. What if Elysium harbored an entity? They had to locate the specialist, bring him or her here, and who knew how long that would take? She rested her head on her folded arms on the table. She couldn't think of that so early in. It was too much.

The front door closed, and she heard a giggle. Alicia must've made a good impression on Ash, or the other way around. "This is going to be so exciting!" Alicia exclaimed as she entered the kitchen.

Her bubbly demeanor was a welcome change from the previous gloom. Alicia was supposed to be perky and optimistic. Everything was bleak if even her spirit was diminished. They spent the hour flipping through the various documents. Resolution was a fickle friend that wouldn't answer when called. They eventually wandered into the living room to watch television. Alicia continued to smile, her eyes bright and happy.

She couldn't take more than an hour of the mind-numbing tedium of daytime programming. Alicia's expression remained dreamy and distant. She wouldn't disturb the love-induced bliss. It never lasted long enough in any regard.

She strode to the kitchen to find something to do. She didn't have anyone to enjoy dreamy thoughts of, but her house needed an overhaul. The cream-colored porcelain tile flooring had remnants of a sealant, but the aged grout was caked with dirt. It wouldn't come up with simple mopping. That was a job she would procrastinate while she could.

She retrieved the Windex and paper towels and returned to finish the parlor. She could see it now, once everyone had a good laugh at her expense. *Sure, let's have a cotillion. We'll start the festivities with smoked salmon and caviar. Appetizers will be followed with demonic summoning and group incineration. Toast marshmallows at your own risk.*

She scrubbed the final set of windows in the room. The glass now gleamed like a diamond. It was so beautiful once you removed the thick coating of grime. Elysium's interior windows were far dirtier than the exterior. She paid attention to the corners where gunk hid from the cloth.

She started to do the same with the living room but stopped on her way back to the kitchen. She could look through the papers a little more. The cleaning could wait. It wouldn't clean itself without her. She stared at the girl's photograph that lay atop the papers. Isabelle was beautiful. She was envious of the Victorian beauty.

She probably had a string of handsome, wealthy suitors and privilege of every kind. The photograph seemed to come alive beneath her gaze. The girl twirled her necklace, happy and carefree. She looked so familiar in that light, but she couldn't be familiar. Isabelle quickly returned to her original pose and the photograph was again lifeless.

Nothing was as it should be. A house was a structure, something static and lifeless that provided shelter. Elysium wasn't. It wasn't enjoyable. It was anything but constant.

Alicia emerged. "Care if I take a shower?"

"Out of Ashton Land?" She winked.

"For just a bit." She giggled as she walked towards the foyer. Melanie leaned back in the chair and listened to the steps fade up the stairs.

"What do you know, Isabelle?" She whispered to the photograph. "What can you tell me?" She flipped through the papers, but it was hopeless. There was no way to know the home's history when documentation was so sparse and irregular. There were decades between several of Ashton's articles.

Her concentration was broken by the sound of tiny feet running overhead. She slowly stood and backed away from the table. Alicia's steps didn't sound like that. She looked around the kitchen and living room, but there wasn't anything there. She listened a moment longer and heard a strange *thonk* in the parlor, followed by another. Something approached.

A large white rubber ball bounced into the kitchen, and she heard the faint laughter of a child. She reached out and picked up the large toy but dropped it as soon as she did. It was slimy and frigid. She wiped her hands on her jeans but only smeared the substance across the fabric. She still felt it between her fingers.

"Hello?" She ran to the sink and washed her hands before Alicia needed the water. She wet a paper towel and tried to clean the oily residue from her pants. "Is anyone there?"

She started back through the home. Did a child sneak through the door when Ashton left? She avoided the disgusting ball as she walked into the corridor. The tiny steps still darted about upstairs. She crept up the stairway as quickly as she could.

The shower ran in the master bedroom down the hall. A muffled giggle came from the tiny room across from the steps. The strange little space had no identity, not even Taylor knew what it was. She neared the closed door and heard little feet repeatedly jump on the floor inside.

"Isabelle, Isabelle, where did you go?" A little girl's voice sang. *"Are you hanging in the trees like you were before?"* The rhythmic movement was isolated to one spot. She put an ear to the door and listened to the sound of someone jumping rope. *"Who did you tell your daddy you would marry? It better be the one who's big and scary."*

The jumping continued as she reached for the brass knob. Maybe the child wouldn't notice her. She peeked inside so as not to scare the little girl, but it was too late for silence. The child already stopped and suspiciously eyed the adult intruder.

"Hi?" She whispered. "Who are you?"

The room had changed. Tiny Victorian flowers lined delicate pale blue wallpaper. Toys were scattered around the room. A white ball, exactly like the one in the kitchen, sat in the corner. There was a jump rope with wooden handles, a beautifully adorned rocking horse next to the window, and two porcelain dolls on the pillow of a tiny childbed. It was a nursery.

"You shouldn't be here." The little girl pouted. Her cascading sandy blond ringlets moved with her movement. Her frilly white dress had countless layers of lace. "This isn't your home." She had the tiniest black shoes.

"I just bought it." She carefully disagreed. "I live here now."

83

"You'll get infected if you stay." The little girl pleaded with her eyes. "You should leave."

"I can't just yet, sweetie. I need to know what happened."

"The men started it." She spoke with all the indignation her innocent mind could gather. "It's their fault."

"Which ones? The attackers?" Was that the pre-Civil War massacre, after all? It had to be.

The little curls shook with her affirmative nod, "Yes, they attacked... and they killed."

"How do I stop it?"

"You can't. You should just leave."

"Where should I go?" She blinked back the emotion she felt as she watched the child. Someone so young and precious had died there, in the house she wanted. She had to know something.

"Far away."

"What will I be infected with?"

The little girl's big brown eyes widened. Her face grew pale until she was sheet white. She opened her mouth wide and breathed in a heavy erratic pattern. She almost panted and then she choked.

Melanie ran to her and slapped the middle of her back. The baby girl couldn't breathe. She tried to listen to her chest, but it was too noisy. God, she couldn't be a spirit, she was flesh and blood, and she was warm. She was alive and tried to breathe. She wasn't transparent or a vapor, she was as solid as Alicia was.

"Breathe, honey! Breathe!" The little girl didn't hear. *What did they say about CPR? What did they say? Shit!* The little girl managed a deep gasp that erupted into a powerful scream. The piercing shriek was so sharp Melanie quickly covered her ears; the horrible, raspy cry made her skin crawl.

"Please, stop." She cried. The scream abruptly disappeared. The sweet dress fell to the floor. Melanie dug through the layers of fabric to locate some reason as to why she vanished. She was just standing there. She was solid... how could a spirit do that?

She darted to the door to see if the girl might've run into the hall. She expected to see her run away, but the hall was empty and silent. She turned back and stared at the mysterious room. Everything had returned to the way it was. The clothing and toys had disappeared along with the child. All that remained was the skeleton of the old bed and two decrepit dolls in the corner.

So the small platform was an ancient child's bed. There was no way to tell now. It was covered in a tattered, dingy fabric that barely covered the metal spring frame. The dolls' delicate dresses were wrinkled and worn. The floor remained as dusty as it was when she purchased the place. The only signs of movement in the room were her own footprints and the marks from her knees.

Her stomach dropped. *Not in here, too.* There was already so much going on outside. Now there was a little girl inside? What had she suffered to make her scream like that? Her queasy stomach worsened, and her head pounded. Maybe she needed a hotel room. Were bizarre things going to appear everywhere? She just had to have this place. She *had* to have Elysium.

She waited a few minutes for something else to happen, but all remained still. The white ball in the kitchen was gone by the time she returned. She took two Tylenol and started another pot of coffee. She flipped through Ash's papers while she waited on it to brew.

Something happened in the 1940s. Elysium held lavish annual social gatherings until then. The practice became a figment of memory. A copy of a faded newspaper fragment from the 1880s also spoke of some tragedy that occurred at Elysium, but it was equally vague and ambiguous.

She knew the house was used as a hospital. It was a scene of war-era atrocities. The lovely home was tainted by something dark and unknown, with no certain origin. The little girl upstairs was proof enough that things weren't right, inside, or out. There was copy of a tiny newspaper clipping from *The Knoxville Herald* for September 12, 1918:

"A girl died yesterday in the Clark area of Knoxville. It is feared she suffered the same form of tuberculosis that started the White Death Epidemic of 1912-1916. The epidemic caused mass panic when it first began. In total, over 1,000 people died throughout Southwest Virginia and Northeast Tennessee...."

The epidemic article stirred a strange trepidation. Instincts told her the epidemic was related to the situation but didn't provide clarity. It presented another round of questions. A hospital couldn't cause terror or rage. They cared for people. They might've been primitive, but they only had so much to work with. The patients would have known no one could work miracles.

Alicia returned with a towel wrapped around her wet hair. She poured a cup of coffee.

"Alicia?" She looked up from the notes. "Could you stay here a while, at Elysium? You can pick out a bedroom. I don't really care to be here alone, until this blows over, anyway."

Alicia smiled. "And leave my happy home? But I've grown so accustomed to the unique sights and smells of the Happy Hell."

"Well, so long as it isn't an Unhappy Hell."

She rolled her eyes. "I'd be glad to be out of there. I'll need to go home to get my things."

"Did you hear all that upstairs?"

"Hear what? I enjoyed that shower. You have a hell of a tub here."

"I know, I love it.... I heard something upstairs."

"Uh-oh. What happened?"

"There is a little room up there. I guess it was a nursery. I saw a little girl in there...."

"Do you want to go with me?" She sat down in the next chair.

"I don't think so. I'm a little sick to my stomach."

"You sure? Need me to pick up some medicine or anything?"

"Nah. I think I'll be fine."

"Does Trigger still run?" She smiled. "Why on Earth do you have your Pinto parked out front?"

"Hey, it's a good car."

"You need a better one."

"I'll get one... eventually."

"You should tomorrow, at least for our sakes. I'm sure Janet wants you to get a better car, too. Trigger may still run, but he deserves retirement. You never know when he'll die, and you don't want to be stranded." Alicia finished her coffee, "I need to get dressed and I'll be off."

Part of her wanted desperately to leave with her friend. She wanted to be as far from the house as possible. She wanted two tickets to a Hawaiian beach for an endless series of massages and cocktails, in either order.

Her mind drifted to postcard scenes of warm, soft sand and delicious tropical drinks. That was what she would look forward to. If she had to drag Alicia with her, they would go to Hawaii when this was over. She could repay her whenever; however... it didn't matter, and she didn't care.

She was marooned right now. No matter how far she traveled, the house would be waiting on her. Running would not fix it or even alleviate the situation. She just had to live with it. She bought it. It was her mess, and her responsibility to fix it.

She waved from the porch when Alicia pulled out of the drive. The street was barren of life, not even Creepy stood in his usual spot. He must have a day job after all.

She missed working. She sat in the nearest wicker rocking chair and watched the yard. She never had to worry about this bullshit when she worked. There was always nice, normal conflict with coworkers, or Fillmore.

Time passed quickly and no unusual problems ever surfaced... but she didn't work anymore. She couldn't go back to Hayden, even if she wanted. She turned in a resignation and, at

Hayden, which was one of several ways to ensure you were never hired again.

Isabelle's picture drifted through her mind, like the soft breezes through the lilac. The exact area from her photograph was now occupied by the strange white circle out back. The spot wasn't white or barren at that point in time. There wasn't even an indication of a bald patch. The grass was lush and full all around her. The trees and the foliage breaks looked relatively the same as they do now.

Isabelle looked like she was hiding a wonderful secret. That's one of the striking qualities of the picture: a pretty girl with secrets. They were both girls with secrets. Sadly, her secrets were only a haunted house and a faceless father. Isabelle's was likely a dashing suitor and an exciting, whirlwind romance.

She stood and took a deep breath of the clean air. She needed to get busy. Maybe nothing would happen so long as she kept busy. She grabbed supplies from the pantry and returned to the foyer. She turned on Apocalyptica loud enough to drown out any abnormal sounds that might emerge. She wiped the balustrade down with her mind focused on the photograph.

Something emerged from the recesses of her brain. She was related to the glamorous girl of yesteryear... somehow. Of course, that had to be a mistake. Her impoverished ancestors had struggled to survive as far back as anyone cared to recall. She wouldn't be connected to someone wealthy—unless perhaps a great-grandmother was jealous. Isabelle might've stolen the suitor of someone she was related to.

As much as she'd tried to avoid such thoughts, she couldn't help wondering how talking to her father might help. Any potential connection would have to come through his side of the family. Her mother knew nothing of Elysium. When she was a little girl, they marveled at it every time they passed. She finished dusting the stairway and started wiping down the hall between the foyer and the kitchen.

She didn't want to return to that vain circle of thought. She didn't know her father and never would. She had one parent and one sperm donor, by will or not.

No, she couldn't think of him that way. She remembered his holding her hand. In her heart, she knew he'd never been just a "sperm donor." Just thinking it made her feel guilty. His huge hands had been rough and worn from work in a lumber mill. She remembered sitting on his lap. She even remembered his voice, but not his face.

She exchanged the cleaning cloth for a broom and swept the walls down. It seemed safe to assume Elysium's activities started with either the Civil War attack, or something from the epidemic. The little girl said it was from "the attack," but those gut feelings didn't emerge when they discussed it. It didn't make the atrocities less severe, but something powerful happened during the epidemic.

She couldn't sell the house. The idea turned her stomach as she dusted the threshold. That was a last resort. She couldn't let it go, even if it were poisoned. It wasn't fair to relinquish the only good thing that came into her life in a long time.

She also couldn't live with herself if she knew something horrible happened because she'd sold it to the wrong family. The estate wasn't a replica of the ideal she held, but it was close, and if they solved the puzzles, there was a good chance it would be ideal.

Chapter 11

Taylor's body did not echo the bright sentiments of the new day. Harsh sunlight glared through the slits in the blind and spread across the hardwood floor in elongated lines. He squinted at its unbearable presence. The light hurt even with the blinds drawn.

Fourteen hours of sleep didn't improve his fatigue or aching body. Jess's cold medicine didn't help. He needed to go to the emergency clinic. Again. For the third time this year. It was cheaper than the emergency room, and faster than waiting on his physician to work him in, but it was an inconvenience, nonetheless.

It was probably another bout with the flu. It just developed a little faster than the two previous instances. Dr. Jacobs probably expected his return any day. It felt like he'd visited the clinic every few months, as it was. He just didn't want to miss work if it could be helped. Hopefully, it wasn't too late. Now that Elysium was gone, he was ready to get back out there and sell. Mentally, he was ready. Physically, it was going to take some time.

He staggered to the bathroom, washed his face, and dressed. He was ready to return to bed by the time he slipped into his shoes. He slowly made his way out to the car, determined to put one foot in front of the other. He passed the girl. She was near the shrubs again, but he was too sick to speak. It was her fault, but no amount of blame improved his health. He needed medical attention.

Hours seemed to pass as he maneuvered in and out of wearisome traffic. He donned sunglasses to divert the sun's intensity. *God, it's so damned bright.* The clinic's parking lot wasn't crowded when he pulled up to the front. Maybe it wouldn't take long, and he could return to his warm bed. He parked the car crooked but didn't care. They should be happy he made it without an ambulance.

Judging by the reception area, the other patients were already in with the doctor. Occasionally, the door opened, and a man

90

or woman exited. The white and pale charcoal blue that decorated the office seemed starker. The lines were sharper. The colors contrasted more.

An old woman emerged from the back, with piercing blue eyes and a sour face. A man approached her from behind the large potted tree. He hadn't noticed him earlier. He walked to her side. The elderly woman glared at him when she turned away from the desk. Her bobbed white hair was so stiff it didn't move.

He recognized the man who hovered behind her. It was the same man who often stood across from Elysium. He just stared at the estate. He started to say something but didn't have the energy. The old woman reached him and hissed, "Elysium."

His heart jumped within him. The man-who-stared briskly apologized and ushered her towards the exit. He struggled to follow. He needed to understand what she meant. By the time his exhausted body reached the door, their Cadillac had pulled out onto the highway.

He was taken back before he returned to his chair. He'd been sixty pounds overweight on his last visit but somehow lost twenty. The nurse's congratulatory praise didn't help his spirits. "Dr. Jacobs encouraged you to go on a diet when you were last here. I'm delighted to see the change." He would've been happy under normal circumstances, but the unexpected change seemed sinister. It was an ominous gift from Elysium that was bound to have a price.

Dr. Jacobs rushed in as quickly as usual, "Mr. Taylor, this is getting to be a habit." He smiled as he sat at the computer and began typing.

"Sorry, doc."

"Is it the same thing?"

"I believe so. I don't know why I keep getting this. Do you think it's H1N1? Covid? West Nile? It keeps coming back."

"Absolutely not. You've been checked several times already for all of them, every visit. Your sample likewise today was negative. It's good, old-fashioned influenza. If your symptoms are the same, I don't think extra testing is in order. You aren't really running a high fever. I'll have the nurse give you a vaccination and maybe we can avoid this for the rest of the year. How long have you had it this time?"

"It just started getting bad yesterday. I feel horrible."

"I'll give you some medicine to curb the symptoms. That should shorten your recovery time."

Thank God, the visit went quickly. He would've hugged the doctor if he had the energy to move. He could now return to his bed for more rest. His body felt like it would collapse at any moment. The work to place one foot in front of the other was a formidable task that required all the determination he could gather. He had to take small steps.

He vividly recalled both instances of illness, but neither seemed quite like this. The symptoms were the same, but he felt different, somehow. He would stay in bed a few days and see if that helped.

Chapter 12

She inspected the foyer a moment longer. She returned to the kitchen once she was satisfied. She sat on the bar stool for a moment and studied the backyard outside the window. It was so beautiful.

Butterflies fluttered through the air. Wildflowers swayed in the breeze. She imagined Isabelle strolling through the yard in that gorgeous flowing gown. It didn't feel like anything was amiss before the Blythe family came. Isabelle would have played beneath those trees. She would've lived contentedly without a care in the world.

An abrupt tug of instinct came to mind. It was just an assumption, wasn't it? Isabelle was no more content, regardless of what her parents had, than she was. Something about those initial romantic notions suddenly became false. She looked at her picture through a haze of bias, not reality.

She stepped over and retrieved the image. In reality, the picture said otherwise, didn't it? She'd been too prejudiced to notice. She brought it into the sunlight at the door. The photograph was different in direct light. Her smile wasn't happy, it was feigned. Her eyes didn't shine with joy, they were misty and melancholy. There was something somber in her eyes. That was what lay beneath the façade.

A photocopy of a newspaper article from 1912 was taped to the back of the paper. The headline read, "Sign of the Times." She read:

> "Tuberculosis has spread to all corners of our region. Residents of Northeast Tennessee and Southwest Virginia have witnessed the horrors of a plague only matched by that of the European Black Death. This type of tuberculosis is fast and merciless.

"The virulent disease has caused more horror than any other previous. It spreads between humans and animals. Quarantine hospitals have been set up in homes and churches through the area. The number of available physicians decreases daily. Several towns have lost the only doctor for tens or hundreds of miles. The rapid decline of public officials has also caused crime to skyrocket. Many local men, who remain unnamed, have started a group to preserve law and order.

"The Black Riders of the White Death will maintain peace and justice as we wait for this heinous pestilence to end. Several residents believe this to be the end times, but regardless, we are a civilized area. We should all behave in a manner befitting civility...."

The tuberculosis epidemic started the same year the Titanic sank. Her heart raced at the group's mention, *the Black Riders*. Her semi-queasy stomach grew fully nauseous. Instincts screamed they had a key part in Elysium's past.

The angry group from her dream drifted into her mind but they didn't protect anyone. Why didn't Ashton mention them? Maybe he hadn't made any connection, or maybe there was no connection. The Riders probably had badges or something formal.

The group she'd witnessed creeping through the forest had to be from the first attack, like the little girl said. The name from the article simply struck a chord because the article suggested it, and those men happened to wear some black. The riders from the epidemic likely hid their faces for the same reason police officers hide their identifying information today.

The article continued to discuss the bizarre lethality of the epidemic. She knew nothing of medicine, but tuberculosis was something humanity suffered for eons. It was far from fast. It could be active today, go into remission tomorrow, and stay hidden fifty years, or more. The article made it sound like the doctors died faster than their patients. The original physicians had contracted consumption and died by 1913. That was only the beginning of the epidemic's reign. No younger physicians dared enter the area.

She scanned through the documentation, but still didn't find any mention of marauding bandits. There weren't any further references to crime of any magnitude. Gangs of brutal horsemen couldn't have been *that* common.

It must be yet another facet of Elysium lost to time. There was no logic in sifting through the past when no more newspaper coverage existed. Either the newspapers didn't print regularly, or often, or someone at Elysium had meticulously intercepted any mention of the place.

Chapter 13

John woke in a cold sweat. The recliner was soaked. The drive home from the doctor's office was awful, but healing was worse. It didn't seem possible to feel worse than he did earlier, but here he was. God, those dreams didn't relent now. They kept on and on, the same scenario over and over. He needed to go to the bathroom, but his body wouldn't move. "Hi, honey," Jess spoke as she came through the door. "Are you okay?"

He forced his body to answer, "No."

She came around to his chair and gasped, "My God, John. You need to go to the hospital."

"I need... bathroom."

She helped him into the bathroom. He was mortified that his wife had to help him take a piss, but he didn't have the energy to protest. She left to dial the paramedics while he fixed his pants. He felt dizzy. The room violently spun around him. He felt his body hit the floor and heard the bathroom door open. There was only darkness after.

He only saw flashes of life for the next few minutes. Jess cried as two paramedics worked on him. He was in the back of the ambulance. He was then in an emergency room, but the staff wasn't frantic. He saw blackness that brought peace, no dreams, and no visions. If he was going through this, due to Elysium, what did he do to the girl who bought it? He had to warn her.

Chapter 14

She reached across the papers on the table to answer the phone. Alicia grumbled she had to pull a shift or lose her job. She wouldn't be back until around midnight. It didn't surprise her because Fillmore was waiting. God forbid that he was inconvenienced or had to wait.

Poor Alicia. He was probably still pissed she quit and wanted to take it out on Alicia. It's not like there weren't people standing in line for any job there. There was no reason to take it personally.

The silence magnified as she looked around the kitchen, *alone again at Elysium.* She needed to get her mind off her questions. She pulled out the vacuum and cleaning supplies. She walked up the now shiny staircase to the second floor.

She passed the closed door of the playroom. She would clean and restore it with a new daybed and Victorian toys. The ripped and jagged wallpaper were remnants of the delicate floral. She would work on that next.

The bedroom opposite the playroom was in dire need of cleaning, as was most of the upper floor. She wiped walls down and scrubbed windows.

She didn't turn her attention to the closet until the room was finished. She stripped the bed of dusty linens and vacuumed everything. She would overhaul all the closets. They were dated and most of the shelf supports looked fragile.

She tugged on the closet's glass knob, but it wouldn't budge. The door was probably swollen from the humidity. Taylor could barely open the bedroom door when she first toured the place. She yanked on the stubborn door and finally felt it jerk. She brutalized the handle for another 60 seconds and hit the stubborn entry with the palm of her hand. It was time to arm herself against the forces of nature. She pulled a long-handled screwdriver from the cleaning caddy and used it like a crowbar.

The door's frame splintered beneath the force of the tool. She would have to replace the frame, but it was her frame to do with as she pleased. She worked the screwdriver harder and finally pried the door loose. She stopped when she peered into the opening. It wasn't a closet—it was a bedroom off a bedroom.

The space was large enough to be a second room. She felt around the entryway for a light switch. She managed to get a splinter from the crack in the frame. She entered the new room as she shook her injured hand. *Impressive.*

So, that made 21 rooms at Elysium. How many other spaces were carefully hidden? An elaborate scroll top desk sat next to the far wall. The wall across from her was filled with empty shelves.

She cleaned the new room just as she had the previous two bedrooms. She chuckled when she found another small door hidden at the back of this room. It was a maze. She'd always wanted a house with secret passages and mysterious halls. The fondness grew from a childhood of ancient detective books.

The tiny door was built into the wall, around five feet high and three feet wide. She paused a moment. She had to approach with caution. The musty smell had been strong in the house when she first entered. It would probably be overwhelming in an enclosed place.

She would let the new room air out before venturing into yet another. She propped opened the newly discovered office door and opened the bedroom windows as wide as possible. The windows at Elysium were double hung to allow optimal air circulation.

She inspected the new piece of furniture. The walnut desk was beautiful, even though the scroll needed repair. Another beautiful antiquity snubbed by the contemporary Blythe family.

When the new office aired out, she pushed on the small door. The little entry door was wedged into place. She gingerly pried it from its frame and winced with each crack of protest. It would be more practical to repair the tiny door than to construct a new wall entirely. She needed minimal damage if she was going to keep the place as original as possible.

She finally loosened the entryway. She stood back as she held it open with her foot. She hadn't inflicted a great deal of mutilation on the piece, but it was close. Cracks had spider-webbed across the left side of the bothersome frame.

Clouds of dust eventually settled in the flashlight's beam, but instead of another room, this opening went to a narrow set of steps. This couldn't be part of the attic. She already checked that, and there was only one door in and out. The attic's entrance was down the hall from the master bedroom. The attic itself was a small, unfinished space. The bare walls held several antique tools, and a few old coats hung from rusty nails. The rest of the space was primarily exposed beams and insulation.

She angled the beam of light up the steps to the secret room. She shouldn't have bought the house. It was foolish. She didn't even know how many rooms it contained.

Of course, it didn't do any good to complain. It was her instinctive choice. There was no other place for her. She could've bought something modern, with all the latest conveniences and amenities, but it never crossed her mind. It was all Elysium, and always Elysium.

She knelt as she entered the doorway. The space didn't harbor any traces of animal inhabitants or nests. She didn't see any bats hanging from the ceiling up the steps.

She ducked under the low threshold and stood back up. The ceiling on the other side had a clearance a little over six feet. It was around half a foot above her head when she stood, and she was five feet-seven.

She ascended the narrow stairs, up to a small room, barely 10-by-12-feet. A small bay window lay in front of her. She assumed all the third story dormer windows were purely aesthetic. She neared the foggy pane and wiped the grime away with her hand. The window looked out across the back acreage, but the angle slanted towards the white bald spot.

A worn wooden bench sat beneath the window. She threw the latch and pressed against the pane, but the window held fast. The single-layer glass felt so fragile it would crack beneath her fingers. She couldn't let that happen. It wouldn't be the same if she had to install new windows in the dormers. Older homes had character left from a time when owners wanted unique and personal architectural value. They didn't create lavish cookie-cutter boxes, just like the house next door. They built masterpieces.

She turned to go down the steps but stopped so hard her shoes almost squeaked on the dusty floor. Countless papers were attached to the back wall, from floor to the ceiling. The mismatched collage contained index cards, notebook pages, and handwritten notes. It was homemade, patchwork wallpaper. Every piece of paper had a drawing or printed notes. Various small newspaper clippings were tacked around the wall's midsection.

She picked up a small canvas from the floor, one of several leaning against the wall. They were drawn with pencil or paint, arranged in haphazard groupings. Some circles were created with white, others with yellow, and one with blue flames. The airtight room must've preserved them. She had to bring Ashton up when he returned.

The artist hadn't created plain circles. Each was an elaborate circle of fire. One newspaper clipping discussed a wreck in front of the estate. In 1965, a man claimed a circle of flames came from nowhere and he swerved to avoid it. The skeptical reporting implied the driver was intoxicated and dismissed his words as nonsense.

One clipping caught her eye, nearly transparent with age. The faded gray ink reported that Edgar Blythe was attacked in the caves behind the house. He was sent to a hospital in Kentucky to recuperate and would be there indefinitely. *Edgar was attacked?* Maybe that was what she'd witnessed. It had to be the men from her dream. They attacked Edgar while he drove his wagon.

She gawked at the room a while longer. Morbid curiosity overshadowed her shock. Who did this? Why? Someone was smitten by that circle of flames, and their obsession was far stronger than her own. Elysium had never been leased or rented, so it had to be a Blythe.

The family became incredibly private around World War II. The newspaper clipping was from 1965. It wasn't just seclusion or eccentricity—something made them go into hiding. They were hiding from something that terrified them. None of the newspaper articles said anything about it, other than the family was no longer holding public celebrations due to rationing in the war.

She returned the picture to its place. She felt a degree of morbid comfort that she wasn't the only one so curious, but it wasn't right to disturb it. Someone invested years to create the layered wall. She pitied them. She prayed she'd never be in the same predicament. Consumed by an impossible puzzle, reduced her to scribbling circles in a little, forgotten room, completely hidden from the world.

The room's original curator surveilled the circle for some reason. *Isabelle...* The word whispered through her mind. Isabelle must've sat in here. The bench was an antique. It was worn and plain. It could've easily come from her time. She might've lived decades after the photograph was taken.

She returned to the kitchen. She was determined to find answers. She was not going to end up in the Puzzle Room. That was a good name for the newly discovered space. That was not her fate, even if it had happened before. She wouldn't allow it. She couldn't.

Ash was generous to share his stockpile of information, but she needed facts of her own. The first logical step in any home investigation was the courthouse. It had to be the same for paranormal research.

Ash was a member of a paranormal group, but there was a chance he'd overlooked something. The group probably had many locations to research. If they were so thorough with every property, they probably already amassed a warehouse of information on

106

previous investigations. Elysium was her own. Her home and her responsibility. The fact she'd witnessed so much firsthand also meant she might have a better perception.

She quickly showered and dressed. She grabbed a yellow legal pad and her purse as she walked out to the car. Wagner Street was empty. The oppressive humidity had likely driven everyone inside. The distant mountains were blanketed in a white haze.

She drove down streets devoid of people into the equally inactive city. A few regulars were brave enough to window-shop or walk to various classes on State Street. The shops on the left were in Virginia, while the shops on the right were in Tennessee due to the street's placement. She admired the Cameo Theater as she drove through downtown Bristol.

She made the customary pilgrimage for those in Washington County who wanted information on decades past. Abingdon was a small, artsy town that prided itself on its history and its hotel, the Martha Washington Inn. The oldest of the county records were held in the basement of the courthouse.

Deeds were the best place to start. Those would at least provide specific names and dates from the property's history. She could use those to filter through vital records and wills. She needed to start from the very beginning. She had the rest of the day free, and it was hours before the courthouse closed.

Chapter 15

She walked into the courthouse behind a chattering mob. They had to be relatives. All were dressed and talked much the same way. Just as with all accents in the world, Appalachian accents varied not only by community, but often by household. Some were pronounced and lazy while others were rapid and barely discernible. Some families used strong phonetics almost as proper as British English. Others had a rapid Gaelic tongue.

Court was in session and people moved back and forth to their respective rooms. She looked ahead and saw the hem of a dingy white dress around the corner to the right. Whoever it was remained completely still as she approached. She rounded the corner, but no one was there. The hall ahead was silent and empty. A brown plaque above noted that the records were straight ahead.

She found her way down to the archives in the basement. The overfilled room smelled of aging paper and dusty binding. The fluorescent bulbs overhead provided adequate lighting, but one bulb needed to be changed. It flickered and flashed as she sat her things down. She grabbed the massive deed index from the circa 1950 green industrial shelf and searched for her home's address. She should've done this to begin with, before she even purchased the place.

She paid little attention to names as she traveled through time. She wasn't concerned with the Blythe family at this point. She wanted early history. After she trudged through three equally sizable books, she finally found the answer. The earliest deed was 1796. The property was a land grant given to Ivan Rotherwood in exchange for military service.

When Ivan died in 1840, his son, Jeremiah, inherited the property. The legendary attack happened while he was the owner.

She grabbed several ancient newspaper books and flipped through the dates. Many years were missing, but she was in the right era.

She nearly laughed aloud when she found a formal mention of the horrendous attack, dated: June 2, 1860. Finally, she found something substantial. The report attributed the atrocity to a band of bushwhackers that were heading west.

Sixteen bodies were recovered from the fire in front of the Rotherwood Plantation house. The account listed the Rotherwood slaves' deaths separately, but the overall mortality count was 257. The attack occurred at night when most inhabitants were asleep. The family pets were killed first so they couldn't alert residents. Jeremiah Rotherwood was in Bristol for the week on business.

She cringed at the article's content. Even the cautious Victorian verbiage couldn't fully mask the brutality. The estate was annihilated. Crops were uprooted. The home was just as brutalized as the victims and set afire as well.

The grand piano really was pulled outside and set on fire, as she'd heard. Bodies of the household victims, human and animal, were thrown into the fire. Those clearing the destruction found three dog and five cat carcasses, alongside the charred human remains.

Anna, a fourteen-year-old slave, had single-handedly taken Hunter, 10-year-old son, and Maria, 2-year-old daughter, to Jeremiah. Thanks to her forbearance and tact, a dozen children survived by hiding in the Rotherwood caves.

The next relevant article came a year later. Jeremiah Rotherwood's health had declined after the tragedy. He authored a public letter of appreciation to the community's prayers and kindness. The Rotherwood family dropped out of the spotlight until ten years later when Elysium's final courtyard was complete. Jeremiah was grateful for the beautiful home, but bedridden by that time. He died right after.

In 1895, Hunter Rotherwood sold Elysium to Horace Blythe. The story depicted it as the end of an age for the estate. There weren't any notations as to what happened to Hunter after the sale. He seemed to disappear from Virginia altogether.

The ring of fire had to originate with the piano. It was the most logical origin. The paper said the fire was hard and fast, fueled by kerosene.

She jotted notes on the precious few details available on the estate's reconstruction. The nation was rocked by a massacre that brought unimaginable cruelty to the blossoming America. Lincoln did sponsor the reconstruction, because the established portion of the nation hadn't witnessed such carnage before.

She made copies of the articles and slipped them in the bottom of the pad. While there was mention that newly elected President Lincoln commissioned reconstruction, nothing mentioned his return to visit. The new home was built, not to squelch rumors or gossip of Union involvement, but out of sympathy for a distraught community.

Elysium physically belonged to the Rotherwood family, but reconstruction was meant to restore the community. Many notable weddings and celebrations from all over the region were held on Elysium's grounds, not just the Rotherwood celebrations.

The Blythe family was the polar opposite of the Rotherwoods. They prospered through flourishing railroad and mining industries. Their familial numbers multiplied as quickly as their net worth. Horace continued to invest in local development. It seemed their success couldn't be stopped. She pulled their documents. A haunting that came from the attack would be there when the Blythe family purchased it.

The family didn't seem to be affected by negativity, paranormal or otherwise. Horace died from a stroke at the rich age of 90 in 1900. His advanced age alone implied he enjoyed a comfortable life. Edgar, his only son, became the owner, and the father of twelve children, himself.

The Blythe family's first daughter, named Isabelle, was born in 1897. The next child was named Andrew. She tried to cross-reference the records with no luck. Andrew became the owner after Edgar died... or left. There was no record of what happened to him after he went to Kentucky.

She returned the volume to the shelf. A clerk came in the door beside her, "Just thought I'd check on you. Have you found everything you need?" He was young to be behind the desk in a courthouse, just a few years older than she. He had a clean-shaven, baby face and sandy blond hair, accentuated by a white dress shirt and gray slacks.

"I'm okay. Thank you, though."

"I'm Dawson Kelly, a clerk's assistant. Is there anything I can help you with? We try to give visitors a tour when they come to the records department, but it's been hectic. I'm just now able to leave my desk." She couldn't suppress a smile as the incredibly cute assistant explained himself.

"I'm Melanie Smallwood. I'm looking for information on the old Elysium property in Bristol."

"I heard someone bought it."

"Yes. I didn't know much about it. I was curious." She didn't want to say too much. If Keller knew any substantial information, he might go silent rather than offend the owner. It seemed best to say as little as possible. She could avoid lies and still maintain a degree of anonymity.

He walked to the far wall, "As a matter of fact, we have a photo album from the estate. It was donated decades ago."

He climbed a rolling ladder and tugged a massive book hidden back on a high shelf. "These are much more sensitive than our standard documentation. Do you care to wear gloves?"

"Not at all," she smiled.

He opened a filing cabinet and pulled two pairs of purple nitrile gloves from inside. He handed her a pair, "Everyone who views the albums must wear gloves. It's amazing how quickly skin oils can damage old photographs." He waited until she gave the last glove a final tug, "What kind of information are you looking for? Are you with a paranormal group?"

"No... I'm not with a group. I recently heard the estate had a long and fascinating history. I've lived here all my life and seem to be out-of-the-loop. I had some free time today and thought I would check it out."

"A lot of groups come here for that."

"Yes, I've heard there was a big interest in Elysium, but I can't figure out why. It's fascinating."

"My grandmother attended the final cotillion at Elysium."

"I heard the family hosted gatherings. What made them stop?"

"Well, nothing... that was ever explained. Gran went every year, as did most of the people in the area. She believed it was the disappearance and the suicide... well, that and the ghosts." Dawson invited her to join him at the nearest research table.

"Disappearance? Suicide? Ghosts?" The back of her neck prickled. *Finally.* It wasn't exactly first-hand information, but it was close enough. It might provide something a little more concrete than what she had.

"It was kept quiet, but Gran was there. A young mother and her daughter went outside to explore the gardens, but they never came back. At that time, the home's backyard was an elaborate courtyard." He leaned back when he finished.

She immediately recalled the little girl on the second floor. "Did they ever find them?"

"The mother was found hanging in a tree, but the baby vanished."

"Why wasn't there more attention for that?"

"The Blythe family maintained close relationships with the Mayor and Governor... for a reason. Elysium was kept out of the papers. To thwart civilian investigation, or future casualties, they stopped all social events."

"Are there historic references to a ring of some kind?"

He grinned. "You've heard about the infamous ring? Gran talked about it. That's part of the haunting, I guess. It was popular for a little while but lost its luster when it seemed to disappear."

"What was it?" He seemed to suspect something, but she quickly smoothed it over. "Were there any theories?"

"There was never an answer. Most locals dismissed it as spirits from the Civil War attack. Rumor had it a group of Union soldiers became frenzied for some reason. When they burned the people and the property, they poured kerosene in a ring around everything they burned. Gran said the land was bad long before because the Cherokee wouldn't use it before the settlers came."

Well, hell. Instead of narrowing possibilities down, they'd compounded. Dawson pulled out another book of newspaper clippings from a lower shelf, "These are some articles from the 1940s. All we have on record for the last cotillion is here." He looked at his watch. "I need to get back to my desk. If you have any questions, my office is at the top of the stairs, the second door on your right."

"Okay, thanks." She smiled. He ascended the steps. Wow, she needed to come to the courthouse more often. A life of crime didn't seem so bad if all the staff were handsome.

Her smile faded when she looked at the book. She had the proverbial thorn in her side. It wouldn't be particularly attractive to own a *haunted* house.

She couldn't very well say she was the new owner of the infamous estate. He'd probably assume she was a weirdo for buying it. Now, she also wondered why she bought such a place. Maybe she was a weirdo. *Oh, well.* So much for handsome clerks or a social life. It just wasn't the time.

She gently opened the aged leather cover. The spine creaked as she nudged it flat. Elysium was a picture of elegance, just as she'd imagined. Manicured yards were separated into distinct areas by elaborate hedges and lavish flower gardens. One photograph showed an intricate hedge maze from one of the second-story windows. That was now a formless wall of green in the far-left corner of the backyard. It had long since lost any shape. Now, it just looked like an impenetrable wall of weeds and brush.

There were several unnamed photographs of Isabelle in lavish party gowns. She was pictured with several different men, all of them dashing and impeccably dressed. They must've been suitors. She finally fit that carefree image she first had of a rich and privileged girl.

The next page had the photograph of a stern, older man on Elysium's front porch. He wore a black tuxedo and top hat with neatly groomed gray hair. His gray moustache's pointed ends nearly touched his goatee. That must've been Edgar. His expression was deathly serious, well-fitting the piercing stare of icy blue eyes.

She stopped at a photograph of a familiar man. She'd seen him before, although she didn't know where or when. She stared at the photograph until she thought her eyes would cross. She flipped the picture to see, "Heath Buckner." *Heath?* She shouldn't know him, but she did, and she didn't like the feelings the photo stirred.

She didn't know anyone surnamed Buckner. It wasn't common in the area. He had striking dark eyes and medium length dark hair that just brushed the shoulders of his suit. He had a perfect, yet wicked smile that could be interpreted as flirtatious... or dangerous.

The next page held a photograph of Heath and Isabelle together, but something was wrong. Isabelle was haunted, miserable under a phony smile. For some reason, the more photographs she saw of Isabelle, the more familiar she became. By the time she reached the volume's latter pictures, the girl's face was pallid, her eyes had lost their sparkle. The people in the album should have no significance to the present, but they did. She felt that much.

She used her phone to collect images of the photographs. It seemed fitting and appropriate to keep them at her home. She'd wanted a wall in the study or living room that featured historic photographs of Elysium. Images of the previous owners would be perfect. If only the photographs were dated. She could narrow down the dates. She returned to the earlier photographs in the album.

Isabelle was sparkling and vivacious in those early pictures. Something crushed that contentment, and she became haunted. She looked over at the gray metal utilitarian clock on the wall. The courthouse closed at four and she had around fifteen minutes to finish. Time had flown by while she examined the album and the deeds.

She ascended the steps and Dawson stepped out of his office. "Are you leaving?"

"Yes, I am. Thanks for your help."

"Did you find everything okay?"

"As much as possible for now, but I'll probably come back."

"Do you know the person who brought the place?"

"Sort of." Better to say nothing, than to lie. "I'm not at liberty to say right now, they just purchased it. Maybe I'll see you again when I come back."

"Probably." He sheepishly grinned. "I always feel like I'm behind here. Would you like my number in case you have any questions?"

"Sure."

They spoke a moment longer before she returned to her car. It was obvious he was very curious, if not a little suspicious, but she couldn't tell him the truth. Not just now. She wanted to get to know him before she said anything... if they talked further. It was easy to presume now that the mad rush of work didn't overshadow life.

Life was so mechanical before. Her entire existence revolved around that struggle, and she didn't even realize it. You went to work, did your job, came home, slept, and the next day you did it again. It was a reliable pattern. It was exhausting and predictable. Now, it wasn't her life anymore. It felt like her entire identity had been altered, and she didn't even know it was happening until it had.

Elysium was a big pill for anyone to swallow with any grace. She'd learned an impressive amount on her first visit. She could at least have hope of some sort of answer. It didn't matter what the future held because she could go home and rest for a moment. Maybe it wasn't as impossible as she feared. Maybe it was all leading her in a direction that would become singular. She just had to have patience.

Trigger coughed several times before his alternator turned over. *The poor thing.* It didn't sound good. She let the car idle a moment just to make sure it would run. Alicia was right. She couldn't depend on the old Pinto much longer. Several new warning lights indicated problems, and those were just the warning lights that functioned.

She should just get it over with. She needed a car and there was no promise that Trigger would restart tomorrow. She didn't really have a promise it would even make it back to the house. She hated looking at cars. They were gorgeous and sexy, but the process to acquire one was as appealing as a root canal. She slowed as she approached a car lot.

She pulled into Humphrey Bob's Auto Mall, which promised the largest selection of certified, used vehicles in the region. Regardless of where she went, she would be treated the same. She already knew it. A high-end dealer wouldn't look on her with any more favor than a typical dealer would. They would assume she didn't have anything and, when they found out she did, they would try to sell her the lot. She was in love with several before she stepped out of the Pinto.

The new Mustangs were amazing, but the insurance would probably cost as much as the car. There was a Dodge truck, gloss black and beautiful, at the end of the line of used vehicles. She peered around the lot. She was a distance from the office and there weren't any salespeople out. They wouldn't be in a hurry to greet someone driving a Pinto.

She strolled past the sportier cars: Corvette, BMWs, and she nearly fell over a new Camaro. Man's greatest contribution to humanity was the machine. She could get them. She could get any car in that lot, and as many as she liked, but that foreign security still felt false. Everything still felt too good to be true.

She couldn't shake the feeling there was something sinister at work because good things didn't happen to her. They never happened to her. The fact that luck waited 30 years to even approach her sent up a dozen warning lights, red flags, and a klaxon siren that was nearly deafening.

She made her way into the used car section and saw the car she needed. A shiny black Jeep reflected the approaching evening behind her. That was it. A nice, practical vehicle that had was small enough to easily drive but had room for supplies.

She took a deep breath and trudged into the dealership. The interior was incredibly shiny despite the dimming light outside. The industrial tile floor shone as brilliantly as the chrome on the newest Corvette. The staff stood in clusters of two and three and chatted. One lazily ambled over to her, "Can I help you?"

"I would like to buy the black Jeep Grand Cherokee."

"Will you be trading in?" He glanced out at the Pinto. His expression was unimpressed.

"No, I would like to buy it, outright. I want to keep the old car."

"Do you have a down payment of some kind?" He was less than enthusiastic.

She didn't really have time for the chase. She was already tired, and something told her she needed to get home as quickly as possible. "I will pay for it with a check."

He laughed, "Ma'am? You have that amount of money in your account?"

She ignored his obnoxious disbelief. Rather than acknowledge his tone, she haggled the asking price down two thousand dollars. She followed him into his office and several other salespeople followed, apparently curious at a cash payment. She filled out paperwork as looks of curiosity were exchanged between those the little room, "Can I have your bank information?"

She handed him a check without flinching. He seemed to be waiting on a punch line for a moment. She ignored his lingering disbelief and continued filling out forms. He took the check elsewhere.

She wasn't surprised. It was so damned typical, but the sooner this was over, the sooner she could leave. Ten minutes later, the salesman nearly ran back into the office. "Ms. Smallwood, I had no idea it was you. Please meet our manager, David Frey."

A short, round manager came in to shake her hand. "Are you certain I can't interest you in a finer automobile, Ms. Smallwood?" He smiled widely and she thought of a hammerhead shark. He looked just like a hammerhead.

"No, thank you. I'm looking for something practical right now, and I'm in a bit of a hurry."

Salespeople abruptly clustered around her. She tolerated their questions and attention but was ready to leave. The dealer finally handed her the keys thirty minutes later. They granted her escape, but only after taking free coffee, a tee shirt, and a hat.

She arranged to have the Pinto delivered the next day and left the keys with the salesman. She grabbed her purse and paperwork before she climbed into the new car. She pulled out of the lot and stopped at the next block. It felt like she couldn't drive.

She had easy acceleration and gentle braking. She wasn't accustomed to mechanical efficiency. The car was used, but it had the new car smell, and she relished the scent. She hadn't smelled a new car since Uncle Ian purchased his Lincoln when she was little. She hadn't driven a remotely recent car since Aiden left. In the Pinto, you nearly had to stand on the gas and brake pedals.

She pulled into the drive at Elysium. She stood on the porch and just gawked at everything. Whose life was this? Whose car was that? It couldn't belong to her. She was still the underpaid drone at Hayden.

Chapter 16

She unlocked the door and stepped inside. She still reeled from the swift and merciless realization. Life was no longer her own, and no longer familiar. There was no security in having nothing, but now she had everything, and didn't feel any security. She wasn't the bitter worker with no hope of life otherwise—to pretend otherwise was false.

She was none other than one of the very people she hated. *Had hated...* or thought she hated. The words slithered forth from the depths of her mind like a repressed memory. She had *money.* She had enough for everything she ever wanted, but now her life belonged to Elysium.

She walked down the silent hall into the kitchen. She laid her purse and the tablet on the table with the rest of the information. The red answering machine light flashed from the dark granite counter. She hit the button and waited for the mechanical voice to recite the day and time of the call. She poured a glass of tea as she waited.

Alicia hyperventilated, "Mel, please pick up... Please... If you aren't home, call me as soon as you get back. Ash is gone. I tried to call him when I was on break, just to see if he'd figured anything out. Someone named Matthew answered. Ash had two appointments he never arrived at. I'm at work. I can't do anything. Ash's car was outside his house, his cell phone was there... but he wasn't. Matthew Peterson... He's President of the Society. He checked Ash's house and found his keys and wallet, everything, but Ash was gone... Please call..."

What the hell? She picked up her telephone and dialed Alicia. Fillmore could go do whatever with himself. She prayed Alicia's pay-by-minute phone still had a few minutes left.

Alicia's voice cracked as she nearly yelled, "Thank God! Did you get my message?" She heard machinery clanging in the background.

"Yes, just now. What happened? Have they heard anything?"

"No, no one knows anything. They can't do anything until 24 hours have passed. We aren't sure what to do."

"What can I do?"

"Call Matt. He needs to talk to you."

"Me? Why?"

"About Elysium."

"What?" That was ridiculous. "They think I had something to do with it?"

"No, no." She huffed. "It's the house. Look, just call and talk to him. That way, this will all be cleared up."

"Okay. I'll call... but I don't understand how that will help." She would offer what she could, but she didn't have special knowledge. Elysium wouldn't have anything to do with the disappearance. Alicia saw him drive away, and his car was at his house.

She sighed and tried to clear her head. Maybe she was being defensive. It was ridiculous to even think they would accuse her of anything. She was paranoid. He probably just wanted to see if Ash mentioned going somewhere else. That was it. She took a drink and dialed the number. Someone picked up on the first ring. "Hello?"

"Hello? This is Melanie Smallwood. I'm calling—"

"You're from Elysium!" He sounded almost triumphant. She couldn't tell if he was angry or worried. "I've been waiting for you to call."

"Okay. I would've called earlier, but I'm just getting home. Can I help in the search or whatever you plan?"

"No, no...." he trailed off for a moment. "It's not that. We can't organize anything like for 24 hours. I need your help in another way."

"Um... Sure. What do you mean, exactly?"

"Can you meet me at Starbucks on Exit 7?"

"Now?"

"In ten minutes? Please... It would help me a lot."

"Okay. Sure. Whatever I can do."

Dread bloomed in her stomach after she hung up. She could see it now. They would blame her. She knew they would. How on earth was Elysium connected with Ash's disappearance? He didn't disappear on the grounds. Everyone acknowledges his things were at his house, not at Elysium. She had a sinking feeling that she should've stayed at the courthouse.

Doubts about the estate plagued her as she went back out the door. What good was having a thing of beauty if it was nothing but trouble? There hadn't been anything but problems since day one. She grudgingly returned to the car and pulled back onto the road. God, she was sick of driving.

Creepy again stood by the side of the road and she had no time to talk with him. Would she ever get to just sit down? Every mile felt like she'd traveled twice that over. She drove down the ramp onto the Interstate and tried not to think of the situation. If he'd just wanted to know Ash's plans, he would've asked over the phone. He didn't do that. He wanted to meet her. He wanted to see her reaction for some reason, in person.

She shouldn't have even called the group. She should've known something would happen. Would they really blame her house or would suspicion fall on her, personally? A paranormal investigator undertook risks from the start. How could they know if it was Elysium or if it was another case?

She was in no mood for an irrational argument. Elysium wasn't responsible for a disappearance... at least not at that kind of distance. It might scare the hell out of you, might even give you a blister or two, but a disappearance miles away? *Couldn't happen.*

She flipped through the stations in an attempt to prevent the driving lull. She would be fine if she got some coffee in her. At the moment, she was exhausted from the previous night's lack of sleep.

The day had been long and wearisome. She rolled her shoulders and moved her back to ease the tension.

She needed to be optimistic. Her lingering pessimism wasn't even swayed by her newly found luck. It should be gone. She had a car, and everything on it worked. The poor Pinto lost most of its standard factory functions years earlier. Trigger slowed down if you turned the volume up. She could hit fast forward on the tape deck and the bass would nearly break the windshields. She hit eject on the tape player to work the headlights. It didn't happen in this car.

Poor Ash. She worried as much for him as for the oncoming confrontation. She feared for him, even though she didn't feel the house was a factor. *Bless his heart.* He just wanted to help. She tried to repress those negative thoughts, but they emerged.

She didn't want to acknowledge her biggest fear but ultimately had no choice. What if Elysium did cause it? Something awful could've happened. The ring of fire could've consumed him. It was on the road beyond Elysium's boundaries, in the 1960s. What if it could travel?

It was blood on her hands, if that were true. She couldn't live with herself knowing a place, she had no business buying to begin with, had caused it. No, she couldn't think that. She couldn't think of her home as a living thing. It wasn't *alive.* She had to focus on the fact that he didn't disappear while there. Alicia said his stuff was at home. Elysium couldn't be at fault.

Why couldn't logic, and not unexplainable insanity, rule the moment? It was supposed to be easy, after she came into money. It was supposed to be a typical life. She had a home, some security, and she could enjoy things she couldn't before. It didn't feel like that would ever apply. She might've gained in one of life's skirmishes, but she could still lose the war.

She approached the Exit 7 signs and turned down the exit ramp. A solid black rocketing rig whipped by so close the car jerked. She stopped at the intersection and waited for the light to turn as traffic backed up behind her. She eventually emerged through the crowded intersections at the series of red lights. She crossed the road to Starbucks.

The air in the coffee shop was laden with smells of coffee beans, cinnamon, and baked apples, but food didn't appeal to her. She ordered the largest black coffee she could. She needed it. She didn't want food until this was straightened out. Maybe then, she could relax enough to avoid an upset stomach. They would talk, get details sorted, and it would be cleared up. She hoped it was as easy as it seemed.

"Melanie?" Someone called from the rear of the room. He stood by a table in the back. Papers were scattered across the top. She hoped he didn't notice her initial stare. *Well, it was a good day as far as men went.*

She admonished herself. It was ridiculous. She shouldn't be contemplating anything as frivolous as romance. The stab of guilt overshadowed her worry. Attraction to the opposite sex was the least of her concerns with everything that was going on. She still admired him, even as she berated herself. He was tall and lanky with slightly muscular arms. The dark hint of a tattoo on his left shoulder peeked from beneath the sleeve of his tee shirt.

It figured. She gave a slight smile as she approached him. She was out of those worn work clothes, she had decent cosmetics, and could even style her hair beyond a ponytail, but it did no good. Now, she could enjoy all the lonely nights she had inside a mammoth haunted house. It was chained to her ankle, along with the suspicion that it might also make people disappear. *What timing.*

"I'm Matt," he reached his hand.

"Hi." He had a strong, firm grasp.

They sat down across from one another. "So, what can I help you with?" Curiosity raced along with her pulse. She just wanted to get it over and go home. She had to be realistic. He wouldn't be any more interested in her than Dawson at the courthouse. She was a bound woman, and there was a good chance the other end of the chain connected her to a monster.

His blue eyes were filled with worry. "Well, it's a long story." He began. "I'm sure Ash told you... Elysium has some history with people disappearing."

"Yes, he mentioned the disappearance." *So much for polite conversation.* Wow. He went right for the jugular. She'd at least hoped for some small talk.

"That's what I wanted to talk to you about. Do you know what this means?"

"Look, Matt," she disagreed as amicably as possible. "I don't see the significance. Ash visited the house, but he returned to his own home before he disappeared. Alicia told me that much."

"She also mentioned Elysium was your dream home. I know you had great hopes for the house. I don't want you to think we're singling you out for no legitimate reason. I suspect the house may've had something to do with it."

"Okay... so, what can I do?" She didn't mind if they wanted to examine her house. She just wanted to understand *why* they felt it had anything to do with Ash's disappearance. It had been sixty years since anyone disappeared from the property, and that was probably due to another person, not a ghost. Above all, it happened on the grounds.

"Tell me everything that has happened since moving in." He sipped his coffee. "Any event, no matter how slightly abnormal or simple, if there was a piece of paper that seemed out-of-place, I want to know."

"I can't say anything important happened that might relate to Ash. He just visited the one time, earlier today." The meeting took on a sinister feeling. What if they believed she was responsible? She couldn't speak freely knowing anything she said might be manipulated against her.

It was possible. Would she actually get in legal trouble? It might be best to downplay the paranormal for now. She could always elaborate further later. "Really, it's mostly just dreams. Nothing I can

124

confidently label paranormal, though. I've been very tired with all the moving and adjusting."

"You know, exhaustion can only be attributed to so much. I think there's more than that."

"Do you?"

"Yes. I think you are uncomfortable with it all. Perhaps even so much to lie."

Whoa. Her heartbeat began to pulse faster. "Lie? Why would I lie? If I believed Elysium had caused Ash to disappear, I wouldn't hold anything back."

"I'm not saying you would intentionally hide it... but downplaying the paranormal is easier than discussing it."

"That's ridiculous." She looked down. How the hell did he know what to say? She prayed he really couldn't read her thoughts.

"So let's discuss the ridiculous." He began. "First, you contacted Ash. You wanted the group to help. Why? Because of bad dreams?"

"Some of them are very vivid and disturbing... very unusual. It's not like I'm used to this."

"Yes, they were. Some of the 'dreams' happened during the day, didn't they?"

"Daydreams and hallucinations are common. People who are fatigued or tired often report hallucinations. Not to mention, I had a cold for a few days."

"So everyone who gets tired or has the sniffles is supposed to see things?"

"Don't they?" She suspected she was supposed to admit something, but there was nothing related to Ash. Maybe he thought she was to blame. His actions and language spoke volumes about his intent. It was a little much to believe a house could do that, even if it had a history. How many paranormal investigators disappeared due to property? It was unheard of.

What's the worst thing that could happen? The ring of fire came through her mind, but she'd been there, done that, and she didn't go anywhere. The little girl? She sat down and had a conversation with her, and still didn't disappear.

He eventually replied. "Occasionally... but none of them are scared enough to contact a paranormal group."

"Look, if I knew anything that might help you find Ash, I'd tell you." The conversation pointless and she was so tired. Even the coffee lacked the punch she thought it would have. A house couldn't abduct people who were miles away. She couldn't believe she had that thought. It sounded even crazier in her head.

Whatever was at Elysium played with people, it toyed with them. She would readily acknowledge that it could hurt people, but the idea of its causing people to vanish was ludicrous.

If, by some miracle, the house did it, where was he supposed to go? Was he sucked into the woodwork? Maybe he suspected Ash was in the little room on the third floor, but she hadn't told him about that, and she wouldn't. She wasn't saying any more than she had to. Ash was not at her house and hadn't been since he left. "Why are you so eager to link my home with this?"

"It could be a valid link."

"Look, I didn't kidnap him. I find it difficult to accept my house is a factor because he arrived at his home. The supposed disappearance at Elysium was probably a vengeful father or neighbor. Doesn't that make more sense?" His eyes weren't worried any longer. They challenged her.

"I wondered if you would take this personally." He sat back. His azure eyes glittered with intensity. For some strange reason, she wasn't sure she liked him at all. She missed talking to Ash. Ash didn't act like that over the house.

She sighed. "How could I not? You're badgering me." She looked back to her coffee cup to avoid a prolonged stare. He had wonderful eyes but look at how he behaved. It was just as she assumed. She was the freak with the supernatural ball-and-chain of a house.

"I apologize if you think I'm badgering, I'm not. My questions have nothing to do with you, personally. You don't have to believe what I do. You may never believe the paranormal, or supernatural, has that kind of capacity. I do. I hope you understand that."

"Fine." She looked back at him. His smug expression had dissipated and left fatigue in its stead. He almost looked as tired as she felt.

She nearly jumped when he laid his hand on her own. It was unexpected. His fingertips sent a jolt through her body. He didn't seem to share the feeling, "It's just a house that shouldn't be that important to you, right now, but it is. Doesn't that make you curious? Ash told me the other day that you just moved in. How long have you been there? A week?"

"A few days."

He took a drink of coffee and continued, "Yet you become angry over my suspicions about the house. Why are *you* so sensitive? You know the paranormal is what we do. If you don't believe, that's all the more reason to simply answer my questions."

"I have my reasons." She didn't want to tell him about anything. She didn't want to say that Elysium was the epitome of success... until she actually attained it. Now, everything she believed in that former life was becoming increasingly false. The purchase of Elysium, the dream of her life, might be the biggest mistake she's ever made.

He withdrew his hand and sighed. "There are hundreds, if not thousands, of beautiful houses in the area. Plenty of new ones every day. Why did you choose Elysium?"

"It's history. It has character. It has—"

"Something no other house has?"

"Precisely."

"You had an ideal that all would be beautiful and graceful at Elysium."

"Doesn't everyone with a new house?" She already recognized and accepted she was not in a mature frame of mind when she bought the home. He had no right to use that against her. "What does it matter what I thought? What does that have to do with Ash?"

He was silent for a moment and looked down at his cup. He toyed with the lid. "Not many people feel that kind of connection with a house, but you did, Melanie. Like it or not, it ties in with what happened to Ash. Why did you feel that?"

"I just told you—"

He interrupted, "There's something else, something you aren't even aware of." She casually glanced at the clock on the wall. She was tired of trying to create logic from little more than moonshine, but she couldn't just walk out. She didn't want a legal battle. What he made a scene about her and Alicia being the last people to see him? If Ash turned up dead, that could very well be the case.

After a few moments of silence, she conceded. "I respect your position. I just don't understand what you're saying. I mean, yes or no, do you believe that I'm responsible for Ash's disappearance."

"No, not you personally. I—"

"Then, you should understand how infuriating this is. How could my *house* have anything to do with a person's disappearance when they were miles away?" She controlled the conversation, now.

"But look at its history." He weakly defended.

"There's one alleged disappearance, that we know of, and that was on the grounds, was it not?"

"Yes."

"In the entire history of the home, just one, and that's probably some freak incident that was enacted by a human being, perpetrated by enemies who were very much alive, couldn't it? A scorned lover? A husband who wanted to be free of his wife and child? There are a hundred possibilities just with that one case, and that was about sixty years ago."

"Yes."

"Okay, now this is most important, wasn't Ash's vehicle in *his* drive?" She kept the questions coming as rapidly as possible. He seemed uncomfortable with being on the receiving side of an interrogation.

"Yes, it was."

"Okay. He was at home, not on my property, as with the original disappearance. Now, wouldn't you have issues trying to connect Ash's disappearance to my house?"

He didn't seem to know how to answer. "Okay. I'm sorry if I was harsh."

An unexpected wave of sympathy and guilt came. He was just looking for his friend, but she couldn't let him push it off on her. She had to fight it. Why should she feel sorry for him? A minute ago, he interrogated her as if she had kidnapped Ash herself. "It's okay."

He pulled his notes out of the folder beside his coffee cup, "I'm just trying to find Ash. We know what kind of reputation Elysium has, even if there isn't formal information on the subject. Janelle, she keeps everyone in the group up to date on developments, was particularly upset because she knew Ash would be calling a meeting immediately. It was Elysium. He's been interested in that for as long as any of us have known him."

She arrived at a familiar stretch of road in life. Everyone knew more about her home. She felt like an even bigger ass every time she heard about the home's history. *So much for a dream home.* The world probably laughed at her.

"How could you know?" She sat back on the hard chair and just looked at him. "How could anyone know what reputation my house has when I didn't? No one investigated there. There aren't stories beyond rumors. Why is it so bad?"

She didn't try to hide her frustration. "I didn't suspect anything before I purchased it. My closest uncle was a building inspector. It was just a beautiful house that needed some TLC, not some evil place. Why am I the last to know?"

He leaned closer and looked her squarely in the eye. "Have you developed abnormal instinctive feelings since you moved in? About people or events, things you should know nothing about?"

"Yes." There was no reason to hold back. They couldn't build a legal case against her with the paranormal, and it felt good to involve an unrelated party. She felt the weight lift from her shoulders.

Alicia couldn't be there, and she didn't want to burden her. As an employee at Hayden, her friend endured stress enough. Matt didn't know either of them. He probably wondered why the hell she bought Elysium, but it wasn't like he would be making social calls if he suspected her home caused disappearances. She leaned back against the wall behind her and relaxed her shoulders. "I haven't seen peace since moving in."

"You know what I think?"

In a bizarre twist on her first impression, he was friendly and open. He didn't play detective or force his opinions on her. He was normal and she liked him that way. "What?"

"I think you were duped. Don't berate yourself for it."

"Should I move out?" Why bother avoiding the question? It was the proverbial bruise no makeup would hide. It was the white elephant she pretended she couldn't see. It was her worst fear, and she didn't know why. She just couldn't leave.

Selling seemed as horrible as living with whatever was there. There was something about the place she couldn't let go of. Admittedly, the price was of little worry, but something instinctive held her there.

"I don't think so." She nearly fainted with relief when he answered. "That's a last resort. We only encourage that if we feel someone is in immediate danger, or if there is nothing further to do, and the property owner is suffering. I think there's a pattern repeating... something that might end if the right actions are taken. I know that's what Ash would want us to look at."

"Such as?"

"That's where you come in." He flipped through his paper until he found a clean sheet. "That's why I need to hear everything. What repeats? What connects everything that has happened to you since you moved?" He grabbed his empty cup. "I'll give you a moment to think of everything. I'm going to get a refill."

How could she tell him everything? She wasn't sure of some things... didn't know how to describe some things... and the rest was so jumbled she didn't know if she could keep it straight. Maybe it was a blessing in disguise. She didn't have to hold back with him. She could tell him everything that she couldn't tell Alicia.

"Okay." He sat down. "Now, what is the first object or event you see repeating."

"The ring of fire?"

"Okay. That's a good start. The ring has been reported for years. You aren't the first to see it, and if we can't stop it, you won't be the last."

"What happens if we can't stop it?"

"It'll continue."

"And?"

"Probably more disappearances and more things you can't explain. But 'what if' scenarios aren't important. You can say 'what if' in any situation until you're insane. What if the stock market crashes? What if you lose your job? What's important is stopping it. In truth, most paranormal presences are not something people should worry about. Most are completely benign and want nothing to do with the living, if they're even aware of the living. Elysium is unknown and that worries me. We don't know what we're dealing with. It may be benign... or not."

"Where are people supposed to go when they disappear?" She thought aloud. "Dead? Stuck in some kind of time warp? A dimension of some kind?"

"I wish I knew. We might be able to find Ash."

"Do you really think he's somewhere on the property?"

"I don't know. I honestly don't. I do encourage you, though, to do whatever possible to uncover more about the house. What else happened?"

"Vivid, reoccurring dreams...." It probably wouldn't make sense, but if he wanted information, he could have it. Maybe he could sort it through if she blurted out things as they came. They would just have to figure out a logical order if one existed. "A band of men encircling a wagon, not a covered wagon, but a boxy wagon. It has many little doors and nooks on the outside."

"Sounds like a peddler's wagon."

"Peddler?"

"You know, traveling salesmen. They kept their wares organized and arranged on carriages like that. They could stop in a village or town and just open the display doors instead of packing and unpacking an entire wagon. I think some models even had a compartment in the center for the salesman to rest or sleep."

"That sounds like it."

"What are they doing in the dream? Are they protective or confrontational?"

"They're incredibly angry. I never see the man in the wagon."

"How do you know it's a man?" He returned to his notes.

"He yells at them... tells the group to stop."

"Good. What then?"

"I'm always in unfamiliar clothes. It looks like a nightgown, but is elaborate, like a wedding gown."

"Okay."

"I'm wearing a string of pearls."

"And?"

"I creep closer to the conflict, but step on a twig. The men hear me. They approached me on horseback. There's one, I assume he is the leader, who comes forward like he knows me."

"Do you remember any clothing details?"

"Just period clothing. The men seem to have on white shirts with dark pants."

"Seem?"

"It's night. The only light is from torches. They all have on black jackets, hats, and bandanas over their lower faces."

His eyes widened. His mouth developed a crooked, sneaky smile. "I'll be damned. I should have known."

"Known what?"

"I always suspected something. I guess this proves it."

"What are you talking about?"

He grinned, "None of us had given it much thought. I doubt if Ash thought much about it. During the tuberculosis epidemic, officials were the first to die, the police, and physicians. They presided over funerals, and policemen often doubled as substitute doctors. The disease was fatally contagious. With no medication or hygiene regulation, officials were the first to die. Since the region was labeled a 'plague area,' no new professionals would venture in. The odds dictated you wouldn't survive."

"I read about that."

"So then came the Black Riders, the Black Riders of the White Death."

"I've seen them mentioned in articles. Where did they get the 'White Death' anyway?"

"Tuberculosis is an ancient disease. Mummies exhumed in Egypt have had traces of the disease, and its damage, still evident in their corpses. Tuberculosis is the White Death. Bubonic plague is the Black Death."

"Why is it white?"

"One of the most obvious symptoms is the victim's pallor. They grew paler as the disease progressed. The Black Plague wasn't just a name, either. Victims of the Black Death had large sores in their skin that turned black while they were alive. It often encompassed entire limbs. Today, it's called necrosis."

He remained oblivious to her revulsion, "Anyway, the riders were the only lawmen. Before they organized, crime skyrocketed. Thieves made a healthy living from stealing, despite the worry of contagion. Family homes were robbed before the next of kin even arrived. The community who buried the dead today would find the graves robbed tomorrow. Some believed it was the end of the world and strived to keep things under control. Even more lost control. Alcoholism, violence, prostitution... vice-related crime rates skyrocketed. People believed they were going to die, so why not?"

"Sounds horrible."

"The Riders seemed to be the great white knights. Crime rates plummeted, and people felt safe again."

"Who were they?"

"No one ever established who they were. People suspected neighbors or relatives, but that's all. The riders maintained secrecy to protect their families. That was an era of feuding, or at least that was what everyone assumed. A grudge might be ten or twenty years old, but people got killed."

"Were the riders a lynch mob?"

"They weren't supposed to be like that, but there were probably bad ones, somewhere. It's only probable with any group. We've seen accounts where the riders were noble, even selfless, in protecting the infected, but it was not a small organization. Each community had a branch. What else do you see?"

"I always wake when they see me. There's also a little girl in the house... she isn't related to that dream. This is something I saw while cleaning."

"Did she look like this?" He pulled an old photograph from a folder and handed it to her.

She gasped and smiled. It was the sweet girl as a toddler. "That's her as a toddler. She was in her playroom in the house. She was about 4 or 5 when I saw her."

"Her playroom? It's been believed all these years that she was just a visitor. Wait—older? That's impossible. She disappeared the year this photograph was taken."

"I just know what I saw. She played in the old nursery."

"Very peculiar."

The nursery girl wasn't a baby. There was a few years lapse somewhere. "Maybe she was kidnapped as an infant, and was returned to the estate a few years later?"

"I guess that's possible."

"Maybe it's completely unrelated. I don't know... I went to the courthouse."

He shook his head. "I don't think what we need is at the courthouse. We need something personal, something from inside the Blythe family. There has to be something. Have you ever found any kind of personal documents in the house, maybe something in the attic or basement?"

Her mind flashed to the little room on the third floor. *Consumed like me.* Then again, maybe she should forget it. She spoke before she caught herself, "There's a strange little room, something I just found. I had no idea it was there."

"Where?"

"The house is supposed to be two floors and a fully finished basement. There's only a small storage area on the third floor for an attic. I hadn't found anything abnormal about the house before. I found several hidden rooms today while cleaning."

"Tell me about them. I mean, a nook or a crawlspace doesn't necessarily mean anything. Lots of times people used every square inch of their home."

"There's a regular bedroom across from the nursery I mentioned, but there's a room connected to it. You can only reach it through a paneled door. It still had an old scroll top desk. I think it was a private study. Anyway, there's another even smaller door off of that study. It didn't have a knob or anything. You have to push the wall. You kneel through and there's a stairway to a tiny room on the third floor."

His eyebrows furrowed as she continued, "Someone hung drawings of the ring all over the back wall in that little third-floor space. They made notes, left a few newspaper clippings, but I didn't stop to read them all. It was creepy."

"Do you think it was just a storage space, or something else?"

"I don't know. I was too unsettled. I just expected dust and debris. It looked like any other empty storage area until I turned to go down the steps."

"The papers were on the rear wall?"

"Yes."

"So the person hanging them didn't want anyone to see them?"

"I don't think so."

"If they hadn't been concerned with secrecy, they would have hung them over all the room."

"What does that prove?"

"That he or she lived with others who might be upset by such materials. They didn't want anyone to know who might worry... Or ask questions."

"Who do you think it was?"

"I think it was one of the Blythe men. If it were a female figure, you would've found that room off the kitchen or basement, a place more suited for a woman's routine in a typical day back then, not off a personal study."

"Edgar?"

"Maybe... or Andrew."

They ran through possibilities, but none seemed probable. They ruled out the old Cherokee legend. She had to consider her instincts were off. She was too involved. She wasn't debating the estate from afar like everyone else. She owned it.

The conversation lightened as they drifted away from talk of Elysium. At least the meeting had taken on some semblance of normality. She still couldn't quite wrap her mind around the idea that Elysium took Ash, but Matt seemed convinced.

Maybe he grasped at straws. She would do the same had Alicia vanished. Apparently, he was pleased to learn what he had. She would tell everything once she found him to be trustworthy.

Chapter 17

Alicia stumbled out of her old Escort and up the steps to Elysium's front door. She survived another shift and, if only for a brief time, it was over. She was tempted to stop at the apartment and fall over in her tiny bed, but she told Melanie she'd be back.

Fillmore was so incensed by her "erratic" behavior during the previous days that he'd given her a double job in the pit. She ran the glue machine and stacked books for inspection. Her back hurt. Her legs hurt. Everything hurt.

Melanie answered the door, blurry eyed, in the preliminary stages of sleep delirium. It had been a long day for them both. Mel was sympathetic but exhausted as well. Neither of them expected apologies. They both knew how it was. Working for Fillmore was little more than paid slavery: no breaks, no talking, and no distractions. All attention had to be paid to whatever machine you were assigned to operate. Of course, that was with reason.

Hayden Printing was a dirty, dangerous pit where fatality lurked around every corner. Amid industrial cutters, binding machines, and stacked skids of books, accident or injury promised permanent disability.

At Hayden, there was no hope of working your way up for any standard employee. Management and office workers, just like the majority of plants in the area, were from elsewhere. It ensured the commoners were kept in their place.

Mel quickly summarized the day's events between yawns as they walked to their respective rooms. There was still no sign of Ash. Melanie insisted she take the bedroom beside the master for the time being. She took a quick shower to rinse Hayden's residue away.

She returned to the bedroom after she dried her hair. It looked like a different place. She stopped looking for her tee shirt when Melanie grew unusually quiet.

Mel mumbled, "You're so pale. Are you okay?"

"Yes," she tried to smile. "I just feel awful."

"Get a good night's sleep... you'll feel better. It's been a long day. That bug just lasts a couple of days." Melanie bid her goodnight.

She heard her friend switch her light off in her bedroom and crawl into bed. The darkness magnified the sounds of the house. She fitfully tossed, but she was too tired to sleep, and she couldn't stop worrying over Ash.

Why bother? It wouldn't do any good because Elysium won. She wouldn't tell Melanie, but she knew Elysium caused his disappearance. Ash wouldn't do that. She sensed he wasn't the type to intentionally cause fear or worry. Something happened to him.

Melanie wouldn't admit it, but Elysium was eating her up, too. Maybe she just couldn't see it. She wasn't anything like she'd been at the apartment, but then that's when life was simple. The one thing she currently had, that her parents never had, and Melanie recently lost, was simplicity. Poverty made life simple. Period.

Despite the hardships faced at the Happiness, the people in that area, not necessarily their floor neighbors, but the others, were incredibly human. They were kind, helpful, and honest. There was no competition because there was nothing to compete over. It was a struggle to survive, and many struggled together. Progress stopped there decades earlier, but people reflected that halt in wonderfully human ways.

Both of them moved into the Happiness with their boyfriends a year or so after high school. She couldn't believe that much time had passed. The stay was supposed to be temporary, just until they could afford houses. Those sweet ideals of marriage and family had betrayed them.

She savored the feel of a real mattress. *God, a real bed feels so good.* Time had flown by at the Happy Hell. Through the passage of time, both men passed out of their lives, and they passed from the janitorial staff into the pit at Hayden.

It was a sad promotion, but it was a sad place to work, and it was even sadder considering few other jobs in the area paid as much without a degree. She shook her head. None of that mattered now.

She was in the world here, and all of that was outside, in that world. She closed her eyes and drifted. It felt like she was floating on the clouds. Her body relaxed and she finally slept.

She woke to a soft singsong voice that emanated from the hall. She picked up her watch from the stand and pressed the backlight button. It was three o'clock, exceedingly early for children to be playing. She was surprisingly energized for a few hours of sleep.

Well, there's no sense in tossing and turning. It must be the little girl Melanie spoke of. She would check it out for herself. Melanie was probably nearly dead, if not completely comatose, from exhaustion.

She opened her door and listened to the house. Through Melanie's open bedroom door, she watched the veranda curtains flutter for a moment. *Open again.* The doors and windows didn't behave at Elysium. She wouldn't tell Melanie, but something was in the house, as well as outside. It wasn't just the courtyard.

She followed the voice. It had to be the child Melanie encountered. She didn't mind children, in flesh or spirit. She loved kids. She heard the little girl's words, *"Isabelle... Isabelle... Where did you go?"* She heard something creak like a rocking chair in the little room. The child continued, *"Are you hanging in the trees like you were before...?"*

She let her finish, *"Who did you tell your daddy that you would marry?"* The child finished the line with all the gruff emphasis her dainty voice would allow. *"It better be the one who's big and scary."*

She opened the door. "Hi." She had to smile. *God, she's precious.* Her golden curls hung down around her shoulders. Her big blue eyes were so clear. "Who are you? You aren't the lady I talked to before."

"No, that was Melanie. I'm her friend, Alicia."

"She was nice. I like to talk... I don't have anyone to talk to."

"Are you here alone?"

"No, but I don't have no one to talk to."

"Who else is here?"

"Isabelle is." She looked away and continued rocking.

"Isabelle is in the house?"

"She doesn't like the house... seldom comes inside. I think something happened here, don't you? I have to go out to see anyone."

"Who else is here?"

"Monsters." She crept over and sat on the tiny bed, but she didn't seem to fear whatever monsters she spoke of. Alicia slipped in the room. The child didn't seem concerned of her approach. She continued, "There are monsters out there."

"What kind of monsters?"

"I don't know. They're sick."

"What is your name?"

"Dahlia."

"How did you get here?"

"Mamma brought me here to a party. I'm still trying to find her. She let Isabelle hold me and I haven't seen her since."

"Hold you? Are you as old as Isabelle?"

"No," she giggled. "That's silly. Isabelle is ancient. I don't know everything about life here. Only what she tells me. She took me to her real home, and I lived there for a long time. I got sick, though. I was so sick... I slept for a long time. I woke up. I could return here, to the real Elysium. I wasn't sick anymore."

If Isabelle didn't live in the real Elysium, then where did she live? Maybe Ash would be there. She cautiously pried. "Have you seen any strangers there?"

"No, it's right through the cave. Do you want me to show you?"

"Sure. Can I come back?"

"As long as you don't get sick. They're sick over there. If you get sick, you'll be like me. I'm stuck at Elysium, for some reason."

"What do you know about Isabelle?"

"She has two sides. There's a good Isabelle and a bad one, but I don't get to see the good one much."

"Okay. So, why is she bad?"

"Something happened to her. That's all I know. She never had anyone to tell before, but she tells everyone now. She said the deed had to be done."

"What deed?"

"She never said.... Anyway, let's go."

She followed the little girl out of the room. The child's legs moved, but her feet never touched the steps as they descended. Her bubbling chatter was almost too fast to understand. "I don't ever get to show anyone where I play. This is exciting!" Her curls bounced as she skipped ahead. "Just follow me."

She followed her out the back door and across the yard. Her eyes darted from one tree to the next. Was Isabelle out there, waiting on both of them? How could she defend Dahlia against Isabelle? How could she defend herself? Or was Dahlia stronger? The little girl ran into the center cave. She called, "Dahlia! Be careful. You don't know what's in there."

She followed the sweet voice as it laughed ahead, "Sure, I do. I've been here lots, all the time, in fact."

The cave changed as she went deeper. The dark became dense. The blackness had a weight to it. The deep tunnel started cold and dark but became humid as they drifted into the subterranean murk. The sickly atmosphere became muggy, the humidity felt slimy. She wiped at her skin trying to clear the sticky matter away, but it clung.

"Dahlia!" The little girl was far ahead by the time they reached the opening. "Please slow down. I can't follow as quickly."

"Come on, slowpoke." The little girl called from beyond.

She stepped through the entrance and shielded her eyes. It was too bright, but the sun shouldn't be shining. She hadn't been in the cave that long. It had just been five or ten minutes since she got out of bed. She started to run towards the house but caught herself. It didn't feel right.

Her eyes finally adjusted to the light in an almost sepia-toned world. The monochrome landscape was a mixture of light and dark brownish gray. The sky was white and gray. The grass was black and gray. She blinked several times, but it wouldn't clear, it couldn't be her vision. "Where am I?" She called to Dahlia.

The child stopped long enough to say, "We're here. This is where she lives.... Come on."

She crept behind the child in the bizarre realm. She didn't want to go near the house because there was something terrible there. She felt it from hundreds of yards away. This was not the Elysium she should be in. There was something terrible all around. The grass didn't look right. A slimy film coated every blade. Barren patches of gray earth were littered with puddles of the slick substance. She rubbed her fingers together and wrinkled her nose. The humidity maintained an almost petroleum-based feel, but it had to be an aquatic substance because it naturally misted in the air, like water.

She walked under another cluster of thick overhanging trees and emerged in another meadow. She stopped when she heard movement nearby. A herd of dead sheep lay in the field to her right. Their coats were streaked with black and gray stains. Huge open boils and sores were clustered around their throats. Their stomachs were distended as if they were ready to pop. She put a hand over her mouth as each one stood up and began to graze. Their bleating was horse and raspy. Two of the animals had deformed spines and walked with pronounced limps.

She inched back from the field and hit her back on a fencepost. The barbed wire ripped her shirt. There was another meadow behind her. Two horses with white eyes watched her as pale green foam dripped from their mouths. Their breathing was labored and ragged, just like the sheep.

One of the dead steeds reached its nose towards her as it neared. She bit her lip to avoid mouthing the scream building in her throat. She couldn't make any unusual noise that might make them panic.

It would be a domino effect. One scream might make the animals panic. That would draw attention from whatever was in the house. She didn't want to touch them, but they neared as if they expected it. She stroked the dry parts of their muzzle and patted their heads just behind the eyes.

She assumed their skin would be frigid, but they weren't cold. Their coats felt the same it did on living horses. They eventually returned to graze, as if their wounds had no effect. Panic grew in her stomach.

She should be waking but she wasn't. She shouldn't be here. She shouldn't have followed Dahlia. She whimpered as she looked around. What was this? Was this another dimension... or was it hell? It had to be hell. It was Elysium's hell, and she was stranded in it.

A flock of chickens lazily passed like they were perfectly normal. Most of the fowl missed half their plumage. Their bare skin was littered with the same sores as the other animals. Their clucking sounded more like crowing. How did such life exist? The animals should be dead. The plants should be dead. What sustained them?

Dahlia had already reached the porch of the house. She conversed with the people who inhabited the line of rocking chairs by the door. If the animals were this gruesome, what would the people look like? She watched that little hand rise up and beckon her closer, but she couldn't go. How long would it be before someone noticed her, before they came to get her? Would it be Isabelle?

A heavy footprint thudded behind her. She turned to see an enormous black bull with the same white eyes the horses had. He aggressively lowered his head and stomped his mighty right hoof. Each strike rumbled through the nearby ground. The spiked points of his long, black horns were turned ahead to impale whatever got in his way. He had the same sores around his neck and couldn't move normally.

She had two equally dismal options, as he snorted and glared at her. She could face him or go to the house and see what the plague had done. She didn't want to move. Swift death from a demonic bull was far less frightening than the malevolent world she was in.

He slowly moved towards her. She closed her eyes and just braced for the impact. With his bulk, he would be a brick wall once he built up momentum. She felt his steps near, but he didn't run or gallop. He walked slightly faster towards her and lowered his head.

He was going to kill her. He leaned his head farther to hit her with a spike. She wouldn't run or struggle. She didn't want to be in this world. Maybe death here meant life back in the real world. She felt the sharp impact of the point and the force of the horn. It was like getting hit with a steep pipe. She flew backwards and hit her head on the wooden post. Not even pain could keep her tethered. It faded into nothing, just as the world went black.

Chapter 18

The bed was warm and soft, but sleep was intermittent. She needed a shift at work so she would be exhausted again. Sometimes, she missed being too tired to think. She was accustomed to hard labor. Her body needed it.

She briefly dreamed of a strange place where there was no color. The little girl from the playroom ran towards Elysium, but she hesitated. That wasn't her house. The grass and sky were faded gray, dead animals littered the ground and there wasn't another person anywhere. The animals didn't sound right.

The veranda doors were open by the time she looked their way. She walked to them and peered down into the backyard. It was still difficult to accept rings of fire and ghostly riders inhabited such a peaceful place. She would never believe it if she hadn't experienced it. Thunderheads rolled over the azure mountains in the distance. Bright lavender lightening flashed across the edges of the indolent, silver-lined clouds.

Why wasn't it easier to solve the mysteries that surrounded the place? Ash was the primary concern, even more so than answers. If anyone deserved Elysium's wrath, it was her alone. He'd done nothing aside from try to help. That implied he was willing to help whatever force was here. He had to be somewhere in the world out there. A gust of wind came through the trees below and she expected the sounds of ghostly riders, but the yard remained silent. She closed the doors and locked them.

She didn't rest. She woke several times with a splitting headache. Her eyes were swollen and gritty. She barely recalled what she dreamed. Even the time with Matthew seemed surreal. Things were changing at Elysium, and she prayed it was working in their favor.

Chapter 19

John shivered in the cold hospital air. He fought to pull the sterile covers tighter against his body, but it didn't help. He was so damned tired. All he'd done was doze, but when sleep came, it was filled with macabre visions. He wished he'd never accepted Elysium. His own greed caused his trouble. His gut told him not to take the property and he ignored it.

The group within that reoccurring scene was from the Civil War attack. There couldn't be any other explanation. He'd always assumed it was a myth, but apparently something happened. *Those poor people.* What kind of monsters could do that?

That girl wanted to tell her story. He knew it. What they did to her... and to that poor man. He dreamed he was a part of it and woke nauseous every time. He watched himself take part in the vilest acts imaginable as if they were nothing.

His arm itched beneath the white bandage. A strange burn formed on his arm after he passed out. The staff didn't believe the injury was serious, but they were curious. So was he.

The doctor attributed it to something that happened after he fainted. Jess suggested his arm hit the radiator and the doctor concurred. It would help if he could recall what made him faint in the first place, or why the burn was the perfect shape of a human hand. He remembered chaotic flashes but only recalled going to the bathroom and waking in the hospital.

He couldn't argue. Distinguishing between those visions and reality was a Herculean task that sapped most of his strength. The doctor's tests proved it wasn't the flu, but every negative result only brought further examination and the promise of more testing. He just wanted to go home, he was tired of being poked and prodded.

The round clock on the wall read eight o'clock. Since he'd stabilized, they assumed he was fine for the time being. Sick as a dog, but well cared for in. Michael had to see the doctor this morning and Jess probably wouldn't be back until lunchtime. The poor kid wasn't feeling well. He prayed it wasn't the same illness he had. It was bad enough for an adult to deal with it. He didn't want to even think this could be passed onto his son.

He stretched his tender arms up as high as he could. His shoulder sockets felt like he'd tried to push a bulldozer. He glanced over to the other side of the private room. The nurse had shut the door when he came in earlier. He'd wondered why his room was so quiet.

A black shadow grew in the corner. He blinked a few times, the vision morphed into a familiar figure as he watched. She stood motionless in the corner, just as clear here as she had been at home. "Who are you?" He whispered.

She didn't acknowledge his voice here anymore than she did at home. Maybe she couldn't communicate. A drop of the gunk from her dress splattered on the floor beneath her. It was such a shame. She hung her head because of what they did. It was hard to hate her after seeing what he had, after watching what they did.

There was a flash of light, and she was instantly by his bed. Her dress smudged filth onto his sheets, even though her head remained down. He saw her face. He saw her white-blue eyes, but she kept them on the floor. If only he could get through to her. What did she need to hear? A strand of her hair brushed against his arm and left a wet, frigid residue. "What can I do?" He was too tired to deal with it all, enough spooks and ghouls, he just wanted to sleep.

"Suffer..." she whispered and grabbed his hand. It was the first time she'd interacted with him. His flesh ignited beneath her touch. He moaned and tried to pull away, but she was too strong. Her grip was like molten iron that held fast against mere flesh.

He had to tell someone. He grabbed the white patient telephone from its clip on the sheet with his free hand. She backhanded it away with her free hand. The device ripped the sheet as it flew back behind the bed and burst against the metal bed supports. He struggled a moment and managed to twist his free arm around her. He opened the nightstand and grabbed the cell phone from bedside stand. Smoke filled the room from some unknown source.

He dialed Jess's number, but she didn't answer. She must be in the doctor's office. He couldn't call the hospital. He would have to go through the main switchboard and there was no time.

He dialed Smallwood's number. He should warn her. He might not survive, but he might save someone. He hurriedly scrolled through the previous call and hit her number. He coughed as it started to ring. By the time she picked up, he could barely breathe, "Get out of the house...It's cursed..."

"Ash?" The voice was distant and far off. "Ash? Is that you?"

"She's there, she's here." He swallowed the next urge to cough. "It's here." He couldn't breathe, couldn't speak. He couldn't move.

He dropped the cell phone and looked up. She now looked at him. She stared at him with those dead eyes and, instead of seeing his own reflection, he watched the group attack. He watched them do everything in the reflection of her eyes.

He couldn't fight her. He dropped back on the bed. He couldn't breathe. His chest was on fire. He couldn't see the door any longer. The thick white smoke enveloped everything, but her. It was too late. It was too late.

Chapter 20

Melanie needed to occupy her mind until someone told her what they would do about Ash's disappearance. She would go mad if she dwelled on possibility. She decided to work on the third-floor nook. It would make a wonderful reading room, and she could turn the little hidden study into a storage area for her paperbacks. She could purchase a pad for the bench and a chaise lounge to relax.

She rolled her shoulders and stretched her back as she rose from the bed. She had the strangest sensation that someone was near. "Hello?" She called, but there was no answer. Alicia was probably already up. She washed her face and dressed, but the feeling of a presence didn't diminish. She started the morning coffee as usual, with her guard raised. Something wasn't right.

She heard a sigh and a whisper, but there wasn't any way to decipher what was said or where it came from. The kitchen and hall were both empty. She returned her attention to the percolating coffeepot. A shade at the backdoor caught her eye through the reflection in the glass. A woman stood outside the back door. Alicia must've gone for a walk. She turned, "Hi! Are you explor—" she stopped. There wasn't anyone there.

She returned to the glass cabinet reflection, but the woman wasn't there, either. She knew what she saw. There was clearly a woman at the back door. If it wasn't Alicia, who was it? She thought a moment, but it couldn't have been Alicia. She didn't own clothes like that, not even work clothes. Now that she thought of it, where was Alicia? The phone rang as soon as she began up the steps to check on her. She picked it up, "Hello?"

A deep, gurgling voice rasped, "Get out of the house.... It's cursed...."

"Ash?" She raised her voice to the faint sound. "Ash? Is that you?"

"She's there, she's here." The voice cracked. "It's here."

151

"What are you talking about? Where are you? Please tell me." She pleaded, but the line went dead after another disgusting choke.

Poor Ash. She immediately dialed Matt to notify him of the call. She breathed a sigh of relief when he said he would immediately be over. She didn't say it, but Ash's time might be running out.

She tried to calm her trembling body as she drank the steaming java. Why was *her* house the bizarre one? She didn't want to think of that voice, the horrible voice that couldn't breathe, but it's exactly what stayed on her mind.

Alicia. *Damn it.* She forgot to look in on her. She must still be asleep, but she would check on her. She wanted to make sure that flu, or whatever it was, hadn't turned into something serious. Alicia was normally a morning person even when she worked.

She started down the hall. Now, how could she tell her about the call? Alicia was absolutely smitten with Ash. She was devastated on the phone when he went missing. She just couldn't tell her the details of the call, not yet. She would say the connection was unreliable. She would get Matt alone and tell him the truth.

Of course, she didn't *have* to wake her. She just wanted to make sure she was okay, so she could just let her sleep through it. She didn't look good the night before, even considering work at Hayden. She was far too pale, and her eyes had been swollen. She knocked on the door and waited a moment, but there was no answer. She cracked the door and whispered, "Alli? You up?"

There was still silence. She knocked louder on the door and spoke with a nasally voice, "Housekeeping..."

Alicia should've had a sarcastic response, but there was only silence. She tried to see through the dark room, but all the curtains were closed. She went to the window and drew back the heavy draperies to illuminate the room. "Hey... you okay?"

A cloud of fear draped across her heart as it pulsed faster. Alicia wasn't a heavy sleeper. She couldn't sleep if a mosquito buzzed around her. The bed was empty.

"Alicia?" She whispered. *Not another one, not again.* She ran to the bed and yanked the sheets and coverlet back. "No..." she whimpered. Her friend was not there. She looked around the bed and in the en suite bathroom. Her purse was on the dresser, her shoes behind the door, just as she left them the previous night.

She ran into the master bedroom. She checked on the veranda and in the bathroom. She scoured the top floor as quickly as she could, even throwing open the door to the third-floor nook. The house must've taken her, too. She couldn't stop herself from shouting, *"You bitch, what did you do to her?"* That thing did something, she knew it. It wasn't happy with doing whatever it did to Ash, it had to have Alicia, too.

She half-ran and half-slid back down the steps. There was no time for caution. She needed to find Alicia. *Oh, God, poor Ash, poor Alicia,* now they were both gone. She skated by the front door just as someone knocked. She should've worn shoes, her cotton socks had no traction, and she slid three feet before coming to a stop.

"Melanie?" Matt called through the door.

"Matt!" She threw the door open. "Oh, thank God Matt. Alicia is gone."

"What? Your friend?"

"Yes, she was staying with me. She went to bed after work last night and this morning, she's... gone."

"Would she have gone to the store?"

"She left her purse and shoes." She looked out on the front drive. Alicia's Escort sat in the same spot. "Her car hasn't been moved, either."

"Oh, God." Matt sighed. "Not again."

She gave him a whirlwind tour of the house, through the upstairs and downstairs. There wasn't any trace of anyone. They walked out through the double doors in the kitchen. "Damn... you can feel it out here."

"Feel what?"

"Unrest. Panic... Everything. It's so thick you could cut it. Amazing."

"We don't have time to feel or be amazed, Matt." She urged. "We just have to go."

"Easy, Melanie. That might be your problem."

"My problem? I don't think now is the appropriate time for that."

"Whoa." He put both hands on her shoulders and held her. "Close your eyes and take a deep breath."

"We have people to find." She tried to squirm away, but his grasp remained firm.

"It's the best time. Stand... and close your eyes." She followed his lead. Maybe he would get back to searching faster if she got it over with. Her pulse slowed and everything went quiet around her. "Are you relaxed?"

"Yes, yes, as much as possible."

"Now, concentrate. Think of Alicia. Where do you feel like going? Remember *you* are the one with the connection with this place. You may be capable of many things here that weren't possible before. Just try."

"Feel..." she stopped. He was right. Instincts pulled her onward. She whispered, "...follow me."

She followed the innate tug across the backyard and towards the bald circle. She came to the white circle, walked around it, and crept towards the caves. She started to go in the central opening and felt him lay his hand on her shoulder again. "Wait. Are you sure that's safe?"

"No, but it's leading me."

"Let me go first." He pulled a keychain flashlight from his back pocket. He shone it into the caves.

"Where do you think it goes?"

"There's only one way to find out." He entered the dark space of the largest cave. "I don't see anything, no bats, no snakes..." He

154

was so far in she couldn't see him. The light from the flashlight grew dim. "Wow, this is huge. Did the realtor say much about it?"

"Not a word. I don't think he even knew it was out here."

"Well, I can't tell you where it goes. It's too big" He called back. "I think I see a... a... wait a minute." His movements echoed wherever he was in that darkness. She heard footsteps return. The flashlight gleamed as he neared. "Look at what I found."

He held out his hand, he was holding something. She took a tiny pair of shoes from him. They were dainty little shoes with faded pastel blue bows on the heels. "Do you think these belonged to the little girl?"

"Yes."

"Do you want to walk behind me? We'll see what else we can find in here."

She followed him into the depths of the cave. It felt murky and an occasional sound of water dripping echoed through the cavern. There was the strangest smell coming from somewhere. "How far did you get?"

"Just ahead. There are some other things I didn't have time to look at."

She tightened her grip on the shoes, so precious and small. They looked too small to fit a human. Did they really belong to the same little girl? What happened to her? She couldn't remember her shoes in the nursery or even if she had any. "I wonder if she died in here."

"I don't know. It would be impossible to find out after all this time, unless you actually found a body. Here they were," he stopped. He shone the beam down towards the ground. There were two clear imprints where the shoes had been. A faded piece of lace lay beyond spot. "That must've come from her dress." She walked on past the sad memorial. "I wish I'd known her name."

The air in the cave abruptly changed as they stood. It became unbearably humid. "Matt, what's happening?" The change grew intense even though they remained stationary.

"I don't know. We should leave."

"What about Alicia? Ash?"

"We'll cover the ground outside." She followed his quickened pace and curt tone even though it made no sense. Why did he want to leave when they hadn't explored, but a small part of the cave?

It was only moments before she understood why he'd changed his mind. Something was behind them. She quieted her internal voice long enough to realize something followed them. "Matt, what is that?"

He broke into a jog "Walk faster... quickly as possible."

She tried to see what was back there in between strides, but there was nothing in that blackness. She could only feel something sinister approach. Matt wrapped his arm around her waist to ensure she kept up. The humid pressure continued to build in the air around them. "Why hasn't that feeling gone? It didn't feel like this earlier." She panted.

"We'll talk when we're out." They were up to a run, but the thing back there remained close.

It was coming faster.

She heard a familiar whirring roar.

Where had she heard it?

Where had she heard that noise—the ring. "Oh, God, Matt. It's the ring...."

They sprinted out of the cave's mouth and crossed the yard before they looked back. There was nothing. She bent over and put her hands on her knees, her sides were aflame. "God, that about killed me, you know how long it's been since I've moved like that?"

"I don't think either one of us was ready." He fell across the ground on his back. "That was not wise. Okay, we stay away from the cave unless we have a group."

"Why did it get so humid?"

"It's difficult to say, but I didn't like it. It was unnatural. You should have the air tested or the cave sealed. Bacteria of all kinds can harbor in humidity like that, but I guess when you consider everything here, what lurks in there won't go under a microscope."

"Will we find them?" She sat cross-legged on the grass beside him.

"Be positive." The cluster of tall trees overhead shaded them from the sun's rays. "Stay positive."

"I can't. I'm exhausted, I've been panicking since yesterday, there aren't any answers, there's nowhere to turn... shall I continue?"

"Here," he patted the ground beside him. "Kick back and relax, just for a minute. Take a deep breath and count to 8. If we panic, we'll overlook everything, and miss the obvious. We'll pick it back up in a minute or two. We'll look for another thirty minutes by ourselves, and if we haven't found anything, we'll call the rest of the group."

"I don't think I can rest." She forced herself to be still. Matt took charge of the situation for the moment, which was fine. She was clueless. She delegated her issues to a responsible person and admitted her own weakness. She couldn't deal with it on her own. She couldn't bear the thought that two of the sweetest people were just gone. "I'm so glad you came to help."

"Me, too." She heard a smile in his voice. "We'll find them both—I know it, alive and well."

A blue butterfly fluttered through the overgrown grass. It wasn't likely anything would manifest with someone else there. Whatever it was seemed to avoid situations where people were together.

The little girl waited until Alicia was in the shower. The ring of fire didn't reveal itself to Alicia on the balcony. Like this morning when... when... she needed to tell him about the girl. "Oh, my God. I can't believe I forgot it."

"What?" He leaned on an elbow beside her.

"This morning... I thought Alicia was asleep and came down to make coffee. I saw a girl in the reflection off the glass in my kitchen cabinets. She was standing at the back door."

"Was it Alicia?"

"I thought it was at first glance, but she was faded, like she stepped out of an old black-and-white photograph. I turned and she was gone."

"How strange. Was it Isabelle?"

"No. This girl was a mess. In all the pictures I've seen, Isabelle is very distinctive and very beautiful."

"I don't know." He looked off from her. "Ash mentioned there might be an entity here. Maybe it's taken her shape?"

"What do you mean, 'taken her shape'?"

"Some powerful entities take the shape of people. It isn't actually the spirit of that person; it's like a mask." He rolled on his side and propped his head up with his arm. His head was above her, looking down on her as she lay on her back.

"What causes entities?"

His eyes shone in the sunlight. He watched the cave for a moment, "Anything powerful or horrible can bring about an entity. Experts debate whether a situation actually creates an entity, or if it just invokes one. Suicides and brutal murders are nearly guaranteed to draw something because the victim often clings to something or someone from their life, but any traumatic circumstance is fuel enough. From documented cases, entities prefer extreme stuff: brutal murders, torture, utter desperation, any atmosphere of complete rage or sorrow."

"Misery loves company?"

"Sort of." He then looked down at her. She smiled back up at him. He was comfortable to be close to. It didn't feel like he regarded her as strange, despite the chaos that surrounded her. His skin looked so soft, and he was so close.

She should look back out into the yard. She didn't need anything to interfere with the situation. She couldn't get involved, anyways, until things cleared up. She should let the situation go and look for a distraction. She couldn't.

He leaned over her and kissed her. She didn't pull away as his kiss became deeper. She didn't want to, regardless of what the wisest course of action was. She felt every muscle in her body let go, her back fully relaxed, her mind cleared. She hadn't been so comfortable since moving in the house. He pulled back with a somber smile. "Time is wasting."

"I know."

He stood and held out his hand to help her up. They already covered the property near the cave. It was time to search elsewhere. "By the way," Matt stopped. "What's that white spot in the yard?" He pointed towards the bald area.

"I don't know. I was afraid to touch it."

"Well, couldn't be too bad."

"What if it's contaminants from cooking meth, or something dangerous?"

"In this backyard?" It seemed far-fetched when he said it. Who would be making anything in Elysium's backyard? It was bad enough to see those things sober. Who knew what you would see under the influence? They headed back towards the clearing.

The entire estate was enclosed in a mammoth 12 feet high fence. The black wrought iron had numerous spots of green patina from age but hadn't lost its solidity. Columns of solid beige brick were placed every 12 feet along the iron. Even if a cooker could scale the fence, there would be a shitload of bizarre stuff on the other side. "So what do you think it is?"

He ran his hand over the surface. "It feels like sand, but it's too fine..." He licked his finger, touched it, and then tasted the residue on his fingers. "It's... salt?"

"Salt? *Salt?* Like table salt?"

"Why would someone put salt here?" He scratched his head and stood back up. She knelt down and tasted the substance for herself. He was right, it was plain salt. Traces of bitter iodine were still detectable.

Elysium's oddities were perpetual and continued to show themselves after all this time. She heard a soft noise somewhere beneath the surface. There was the sound of a faint whimper below. She held her breath for a moment. "What the hell was that?"

Matt dropped to his knees and dug with both hands. She quickly followed and helped him unearth whatever was down there. Something was down there. She touched a hand beneath the soil. She screamed and drew back.

Someone was down there. *Oh, god it's a corpse.* Matt continued throwing the salt outward as he dug. Her stomach knotted when she got a clear glimpse of the flesh beneath. She knew that hand. "Alicia," she wept. "Oh, God, no."

She pushed the sediment away from her friend's body as Matt dug deeper. She lay a just few inches below the surface. If Alicia was dead, she would burn the house to the ground and sow salt across every acre. Nothing would ever live there again.

She brushed more of the corrosive substance away from her friend's skin. Alicia was warm. *Thank God she isn't cold.* She felt for a pulse as he continued to dig around her body. She had a pulse. Matt got her torso uncovered as she brushed the sand away from Alicia's hair and face.

"Alicia, Alicia... please talk to me." She quickly wiped the sand from her eyes and mouth.

"Mel?" She whispered. Melanie locked her arms around her friend's body and dug her heels into the ground. She needed to be in the grass. She pulled Alicia outside the circle. "Alli, Alli, please talk to me," she whispered. Matt laid Alicia's legs in the grass. She quickly smiled at him and returned to her friend.

Matt sat beside them. "How is she?" He felt her pulse and checked her forehead for a temperature. "She's alive. I bet Ash is, too."

"I don't know." She whispered. "Why won't she wake up?" She continued brushing the salt particulates from her face. Alicia's expression finally changed, she blinked, "Melanie?"

"Alicia. I'm here." She scrunched her face. Her skin was pink from the grit of the sediment. She reached up and wiped her eyes. "Where am I?"

"You're in the backyard. How did you get in the ground?"

"In the ground?" She managed a chuckle. "I wasn't in the ground... I think I fell."

"Where did you go?"

Alicia sat up and shook her head to get the salt out of her hair. "I woke up early this morning... it was dark out. I heard someone in the little room down the hall. It was a little girl. I thought she might know where Ash was. I followed her...followed her into the cave. I couldn't see... forgot a flashlight. I... I...." She tried to sit up. "It kept getting humid. I couldn't breathe."

"*Where* did you go?" She brushed some of the sediment from her friend's shoulders and hair.

"I don't know. The cave ended and it looked like I was back here. It was daylight. I thought I'd just made a circle inside the cave, but everything was gray. The animals... oh, God, the animals...."

"Animals?"

"The animals, goats, cows, sheep... they were diseased. They had such sores... I couldn't stand to look at them. Everything seemed so angry."

"Angry?" That must've been one hell of a dream. She had the strangest sense that the world she described was familiar, but there were no gray worlds, and no farm animals for miles.

"How did you get back?" Maybe Alicia would make more sense if she changed the subject.

"I was so sick. My chest hurt... my neck hurt... felt like I was burning up with fever. I must've passed out. I woke up when you called me."

Matt put a hand gently on her shoulder, "Did you see Ash?"

They stood on either side of her. They escorted her back to the house, "No. I hoped I would, but I didn't."

Melanie's stomach loudly growled as they entered the house. The other two grinned at her, "I'm famished."

"Me, too." Alicia weakly agreed.

"Who's hungry?" She washed her hands at the sink.

"I need a shower. How did I get covered in sand, or is this salt?"

"Salt." Matt sat at the table and looked through the paperwork. "You should. The salt will dry out your skin. You're lucky it hasn't fallen in your eyes yet."

Alicia rolled her shoulders as she walked out of the kitchen. Melanie cracked half a dozen eggs into a bowl and mixed in cream. Everything that could be backwards in life was backwards. She shared breakfast with someone she'd met the previous day, to discuss a curse that may be on her house. That didn't even include the fact that she'd just dug her friend out of the ground.

She felt so damned foolish, even if it did no good. Perhaps she was too hard on herself. If it hadn't been her, some other unsuspecting soul would've purchased the house. They would've dealt with the same problems, as well. Even if she'd inspected the house from attic to basement, as Uncle Ian stressed, she wouldn't have considered the paranormal as a potential issue.

"She doesn't believe it, you know." Matt finally spoke from the table. "Doesn't believe she was in the ground."

"I know... I don't know what to do."

"Maybe we shouldn't say anything—" A knock resounded from the front door. She scooted the skillet off the range. "Coming," she shouted towards the door.

She opened the wide front door and paused. She looked left and then right. There wasn't anyone in the yard. There wasn't anyone within the vicinity; even Creepy wasn't in his usual position across the street.

"Okay, I get it." She told the empty porch. "I know you're here." She had a haunted house as well as haunted land. She was woman enough to know when something was out of her hands.

"Melanie?" She jumped at the sudden voice from nowhere. Matt stood at the end of the hall behind her.

"God, you scared me." She leaned against the door frame until her pounding heart slowed.

"What happened?"

She sighed and shut the door, "Oh, the usual. You know, unseen knocks, disembodied voices, just the same ol' same old."

"Business as usual?" He smiled.

"Unfortunately." They returned to the kitchen. "Do you want coffee, soda, tea, or orange juice? Take your pick." She nodded towards the large Kelvinator. He got the juice out while she pulled the buttered toast from the oven.

It was the strangest social situation she could've imagined, but it felt so natural. She watched him from the corner of her eye as she sat everything on the counter. It shouldn't be so relaxed. She should feel awkward or something. It had been years since she'd had a male companion for breakfast. Had she had any at all since Aiden? No faces came to mind.

They carried their breakfast plates to the table, "Thanks again for coming over. That call was unsettling... then, all that with Alicia...."

"I'd say so." He sat down across from her, "Are you positive it was Ash?"

"Well, considering all things, I don't know many others who sound like they have a throat full of sand. Oh, by the way, watch what you say about that with Alicia, at least right now. She doesn't know about the call. It'll scare her."

"That bothers me." He said between bites. "Ash has a clear telephone voice, consistent, I mean. He's one of the few people I know that sounds in life as he does on the telephone. Even when he's sick, you can tell it's him."

"Then, maybe it wasn't Ash. Sorry, if you think I called you for nothing."

"It's okay. What did your phone display?"

"It was a 'not provided." She grabbed her phone from the counter. "No one has called since so it should just take a moment to find it." She scrolled to the number and read it aloud, but apparently, it meant nothing.

"That's not his number."

He smiled, but the rest of the meal was in silence. She was so certain it was Ash on the other end. How could it not be? "That number sounds familiar, though." She thought aloud. She knew that number, she'd recently called it. "What a morning." She felt his stare. "I didn't disturb you or make you miss work did I?"

"Yes, I just got fired and my family disowned me over it." His deadly serious expression faded into a wide grin.

"You know what I mean," she rolled her eyes. "I'm serious."

"It's okay." He laughed as he stabbed the last bit of omelet with his fork. "I work the graveyard shift, so I was just getting in from work when you called. My family couldn't care less about what I do. It's not like I'm married or have a family or anything."

"Okay. Good. Just wanted to make sure everything was cool." She put her fork down on her empty plate. She stood to take it to the dishwasher.

"It's cool," he walked up beside her, as close to her as he was outside. She looked up to see a mischievous look in his eye. She quickly looked away and walked over to the appliance. *Not that look*, she thought. You didn't forget it once you knew what it meant, but at least it was a far more positive problem. The distraction was brief, but it was a wonderful coping mechanism.

She fixed Alicia a plate and covered it with plastic cling wrap. She sat it in the refrigerator. She would be hungry when she finished showering. She arranged the dirty dishes in the dishwasher as Matt came around her. He set his plate in the rack, "So... what about you?"

"What about me?"

"You know. Where's your family?"

164

"Well, I only have my mom. I'm not married, but I guess you sort of figured that out. My house has far more dead occupants than living."

"You know, we're a dying breed." The impish glimmer returned to his eyes.

"The living? Oh, that's a terrible pun." She giggled even if it was a bad pun. She wasn't expecting humor. The greatest element of any relationship between the sexes had to be humor. The combination of fun and affection was a luxury for people who didn't have it.

She rarely let her mind wander there after Aiden. The consistent lack of time and energy after work left virtually nothing for herself, let alone someone else. Aiden had been her best friend when things were good. She told him things she wouldn't dream of telling anyone else, even Alicia. When things went to hell, she lost several relationships at once. That was in the past, though, and Matt wasn't Aiden.

She closed the dishwasher as he continued, "No, we single people. Every day we lose more of our kind to matrimony. It's an epidemic." He retained his sober expression. She laughed loudly at the feigned severity.

"Come on," she started into the hall. "I'll show you the little room while you're here. We found Alicia... now we just need to locate Ash." She grabbed a flashlight from the hall closet.

"Really, it's a problem." He followed. "If it isn't matrimony, its gender mutiny, and then they change their orientation altogether, and without warning."

"What are you talking about?"

"I'm making a joke. I'm just trying not to think about what's going on." He grew quiet as they climbed the steps. "Do you think there's a time frame on our discovery?"

"Like a stopwatch?"

"Yea."

"Yes, it feels that way. I just can't figure out why."

"Maybe that answer will come when we figure everything out."

The shower ran down the hall. She opened the bedroom door and the approached the newly found study. She retraced her steps the day before, again opening windows. Maybe he could make sense of it. She shone the light at the little panel and pushed it open. The now overcast day decreased the light in the tiny stairwell. She shone the flashlight behind her so he could see the steps. "Wow. What purpose did these rooms serve?"

"The realtor didn't mention it. I don't think he knew about it."

"Something bad happened here, too." He looked around the stairwell. "No offense, don't mean to insult you."

"Uh-huh, I bet." It was her turn to smirk as they entered the room.

"Hey, I heard that."

"You were supposed to."

She stepped aside so he could explore. "Someone didn't want anyone else knowing about this place."

"Did you see out the window?"

"No, why?" He walked over and peered down into the yard.

"Look at the ground." It was heartening to confide in someone, but strange not to confide in Alicia. She hadn't even mentioned the room to her best friend.

It just seemed Alicia already had too much to worry about. She was sick the night before and God only knew what happened during the night. She needed to get better and rest up before she became further vested in the situation.

He walked to the wall and looked through the paperwork. "Amazing. Do you think someone made this part of the house before or after the circle?" He didn't seem to expect any genuine answer.

"I don't know. I just found it yesterday." She shrugged and leaned against the opposite wall.

He returned to the window. "They wanted to watch that exact spot. Why just that place... what did they expect to see?"

"Maybe people commonly wound up beneath that salt? Maybe whoever it was could see it from here? Maybe the salt created some kind of doorway?" She sat on the bench by the window.

He walked over to the paper-covered wall. "This is a lot, but it can't be all. The person, or persons, who did this should have a goldmine of research, documents, articles, everything. I wish we could find where it was." He felt of the room's ledges, panels, and finally studied the floor. "This was no simple hobby. Someone in an obsessive state of that magnitude wouldn't just leave papers on the wall. They would have a trove of documentation and probably wouldn't want anyone to find it."

He gently scuffed his shoes on the floor to see if he could force any of the aged boards aside. He stopped at set of loose boards in the corner to the left of the window and kneeled down. He gently wiggled the boards to loosen them. The central board popped up when he applied pressure to the end nearest the wall. "Ah, what do we have here?"

He knelt down by the opening. "One board down, let's see if the other two move as easily. There's something down there." He shone the flashlight down as he felt the remaining boards. None of them budged when he pushed them. He returned his attention to the cache of materials below. She already saw numerous papers and books shoved inside.

He leaned down to the gap and quickly came back up coughing. "Dust cloud." He wheezed. She fanned the air trying to disperse the thick cloud that had puffed up from the new opening. He opened the window for fresh air.

"What is down here?" She got down in the opening when the dust cleared and peered down. "Hey, how'd you do open that window? I couldn't get it to budge yesterday." She tried to lift it with everything she had, and it didn't even scoot an inch. Maybe she just pissed the place off.

"It needed a man's touch." He smiled with a suggestive tone. She quickly half-smiled and returned to the materials. Flirting encouraged similar comments and who knew what trouble that might lead to? Maybe even the enjoyable kind. She cleared her throat and snapped back to the present. She had no business thinking of that. She turned all focus to the discovery.

The nook below wasn't particularly large, but it was wide and flat, almost as if it had been created specifically for books and papers. She reached into the darkness and pulled out a thick, hardcover book. Several other volumes sat below the first. She stacked book after dusty book on the wooden floor.

"Now, why didn't I think of that?" It only made sense. If the room was hidden, and the previous occupant's hobby was hidden, logic suggested anything that the remainder of the room's original contents would likewise be hidden.

She fished out countless aged papers and newspaper clippings scattered below. She had to nearly crawl into the space as she emptied the documents. Her face was an inch above the floor. Her shoulder down within the opening.

After the last piece was apprehended, she sat up and stared at the mismatched mound. "Now, what is all this?"

"You can open a museum if we can't figure it out." He sat by her. "Surprised?"

"Completely. What was this?"

"It appears we're not the first to take notes."

She looked through the closest stack. "*The Complete Works of William Shakespeare*. Why is this here?"

"Hey, being a lunatic is no excuse for neglecting the classics." He smiled, "at least we know they respected literature."

She flipped the cover open. "Printed in Chicago, in 1888. How did it get here...? *Why* is it here?"

"Well, you know, they did sell books back then." He smirked.

"Oh, very funny. *Why* is it *here*? There's an empty library downstairs. They left several few books. Why didn't they put this there?" She flipped the book open. A picture of Isabelle marked the most famous romance. "*Romeo and Juliet.* What does this have to do with Isabelle? It's very romantic." She had to smile. The person who owned the book had marked several stanzas, all of them Romeo's words:

> When the devout religion of mine eye
> Maintains such falsehood, then turn tears to fires;
> And these, who often drown'd could never die,
> Transparent heretics, be burnt for liars!
> One fairer than my love! the all-seeing sun
> Ne'er saw her match since first the world begun.

She flipped the page to read another portion:

> But, soft! what light through yonder window breaks?
> It is the east, and Juliet is the sun.
> Arise, fair sun, and kill the envious moon,
> Who is already sick and pale with grief,
> That thou her maid art far more fair than she:
> Be not her maid, since she is envious;
> Her vestal livery is but sick and green...

She continued to read, where marked. Now some of Juliet's immortal lines were highlighted:

How camest thou hither, tell me, and wherefore?
The orchard walls are high and hard to climb,
And the place death, considering who thou art,
If any of my kinsmen find thee here.
O, bid me leap, rather than marry Paris,
From off the battlements of yonder tower;
Or walk in thievish ways; or bid me lurk
Where serpents are; chain me with roaring bears;
Or shut me nightly in a charnel-house,
O'er-cover'd quite with dead men's rattling bones,
With reeky shanks and yellow chapless skulls;
Or bid me go into a new-made grave
And hide me with a dead man in his shroud;

The person who outlined the portions of text had gone throughout the play. She stopped at Romeo's immortal words, **"Thus with a kiss I die."**

She would have to read them more thoroughly. The words haunted her, even as she sat the book down. *Thus with a kiss I die.* It had meaning. She felt it related to the events happening now. "Thus with a kiss I die," she whispered aloud.

"Fan of Shakespeare?" He smiled beside her.

"Certain lines in the play are marked. There's something about that line... it's most important. I just can't figure out why."

She pulled out logbooks filled with dates and other mundane information. "These are records for something."

"It looks like supply or inventory records." He looked over her shoulder. "See the date, goods, and delivery person?"

"Why keep records?"

"I guess when you maintained large stores of supplies, you needed everything documented. You couldn't exactly run to the store and pick up some Hamburger Helper back then."

"Do you think these records have something to do with what's going on here?"

"Apparently, although I can't imagine why. They wouldn't need this if the activity stems from the Civil War attack. It's dated 1909-1914. Was this Isabelle's room?"

His question set off an alarm in her mind. It was Isabelle's room? "Was this what happened to her?" The image made her feel constricted and claustrophobic. Why did that resonate? She felt she was trapped in the room, herself. Isabelle must've been here against her will.

"What do you mean?"

"I've seen a number of pictures where she is happy and vibrant, just what you'd think a wealthy girl was, but a picture or two show her different. She is sad and so lost. I wonder what pushed her over the edge. Did they lock her in here or something?"

"Maybe. Here's a name, Felix McLain was the peddler."

As soon as he spoke the name, her stomach knotted. *Felix.* She knew that name. She gasped. She shouldn't, but she knew it. It was familiar, it was so familiar. "How often did he visit?"

"Looks like once a month. The purchases in here are around a month apart."

They scoured the clippings after they stacked books. Several articles discussed the mother's suicide and child's disappearance. The last grand cotillion held at Elysium. "Wait, these are from the 1940s. Was Isabelle in here collecting things?"

"Maybe. Maybe whatever is here draws someone in and makes them obsessed?" She paused to consider her words. If that were the process, how far had she gone herself? It might be an eternal mystery that cursed people to search for an impossible truth.

Several tattered articles clung to the books' dusty edges. "What's this?" She picked the volume up and flipped it open. She

171

gently pulled the pieces out and studied them. The first newspaper piece came from *The Bristol Courier.* The article was from 1915, but the month and day were lost:

> "Isabelle Blythe, daughter of Edgar Blythe, died two days ago. The seventeen-year-old young lady was formally educated and engaged to Heath Buckner. We are all devastated to learn of this tragedy. We will provide further details as soon as they are given."

"Heath!" She yelped. "That's him. That's the man that was in the photo album at the courthouse."

"What killed her?" Matt reflected as he picked up another volume. "I don't guess she had anything to do with this room, after all. She was dead."

"It doesn't say what happened to her."

He pulled two more clippings out, "Here's an obituary, and a small memorial, but no details. Oddly brief for a rich man's daughter, don't you think?"

"Maybe it was the epidemic? Why?" She was just as curious. Isabelle had been young and vivacious. She didn't look ill in any of the pictures. Tuberculosis wasn't instant. It was an extended sickness where the victim suffered for a long time.

"It just doesn't sit right with me."

She didn't admit it, but her instincts questioned everything. It aggravated her. She probably simply contracted the illness and died.

Matt continued, "And, if she died in 1915, who was in here, collecting all this?"

"She should've had a memorial... of some kind." She tried to organize the various clippings into the books. They were too fragile to be left out in the open.

"I don't want to get focused on that just yet. Maybe she really suffered from the epidemic, and they couldn't hold memorials for fear of contagion? Epidemics routinely hit typhoid, tuberculosis, and pneumonia. There weren't any antibiotics then. Most people believed the dead were contagious."

An epidemic was the most logical possibility, but it didn't feel right. Why did those instincts rage so hard against what was probable? Isabelle shouldn't matter. It shouldn't matter how she died. She wasn't even alive when the massacre happened. Heath wasn't. Edgar wasn't.

"I don't feel it, but you're probably right." She sighed and returned to the bench's hard surface.

"Well, what do you feel?"

"I can't give you anything concrete... I don't understand what's going on. Elysium has altered my intuition. I don't trust it. I feel some things so strong now, and they aren't logical at all. I've never encountered anything beyond logic... Now, nothing seems to fit the word 'reasonable.'"

"Maybe it shouldn't. Maybe you should listen to your internal voice."

"It would be so much easier if we knew more about these people."

"Maybe the courthouse could provide more information. I could've been wrong. Did you check the records for the Blythe family?"

"Well, no, nothing aside from Horace, Edgar's father. I didn't really go into the Blythe family. I didn't think that would turn up anything. I was looking for something from before they lived here."

"Can I bring the group to look for Ash, Melanie? Today?"

"Sure." She already missed having him to herself, and he didn't belong to her to miss. She was selfish. Her mind needed to be on rescuing a friend, not entertaining sentiment.

He stood, "It would mean a lot to all of us. We're making progress, but we need help. The group is accustomed to looking for subtleties. It's what we do. I know you may still have difficulty accepting a connection between Elysium and Ash, and you could be right."

He helped her stand. "It would be better to start a search, and fail, than to do nothing. Maybe he's asleep, like Alicia was, and we need to dig deeper. Maybe he's somewhere else."

"It's fine, really. Please call them."

They divided the trove to carry downstairs, both lugged armfuls of paperwork. They missed one book and, as they both reached for it, they stopped when their hands touched. She was caught less than an inch from him. He sat the books down and quickly reached his arms around her. He furiously kissed her. She couldn't stop a whimper of delight from escaping her lips.

She needed to protest, needed to demand he stop. She should pull away. They had so much to do, and they were wasting time, but just for a moment, she was free and let him do as he wished. She didn't want him to stop. His hands traveled from her back to her shoulders. His mouth kissed her chin, her neck. She backed away, "We need to continue searching."

She let it go further than anticipated. She carried the stack of books as quietly as he did. Every place that he touched burned for more. It was ridiculous. She couldn't allow herself to become so involved, not while so much was going on. She acted like a schoolgirl.

They sat the newly found treasure on the kitchen table. Her phone rang. "I'll just be a minute."

He pulled out his cell phone and walked into the backyard, "I'll call the Janelle to see how many she can gather."

She answered her phone as a telemarketer began a rehearsed speech on why she needed replacement windows. She grew tired of the forceful lecture and hung up. Matt's face was the color of bleached cotton when she stepped outside. His blue eyes wild, filled with fear and elation, "I saw it." He whispered. "The ring...."

"Are you okay?"

"I'm wonderful." He grinned, seemingly lost in a daze. "I'm ecstatic. I've always believed in the paranormal from instinct, but this proves it. I actually witnessed an aggressive supernatural phenomenon. Not just the standard figures, hazes, or orbs, but a total, active, physical manifestation. It's... it's beautiful...." he trailed off in bewilderment.

"I can't share that sentiment. Where do we go first?"

"Probably back to the circle. We dug quite a bit out getting Alicia out of that pit. We could look a little further. Maybe we can find a clue about Ash, or maybe there's something under the salt that might give us some information."

She led him onward. "I thought I was just exhausted when I first saw the ring."

"It's astounding. You know, that's not typical of a spirit or entity." He marveled. "I don't understand it. The spirit, or presence, is clearly trying to communicate."

"I don't have a preference, call it what you like. It's all new to me. But what really is typical behavior with something like that?"

"Occasionally, a living person will feel a connection with a presence. They might see one another, briefly talk, or even physically interact. They may even recognize each another as they are. Then, some forces simply repeat the past. They go through decades or centuries, just doing what they did in life, with no sign they know hundreds of years have passed. They're oblivious."

"Not the most exciting of eternities."

"Then, there are these." He lifted his hand and made a gesture towards the bald spot. "It's aggressive, assertive... maybe even wrathful. It doesn't interact; it demands attention."

"This is supposed to be comforting?"

"Sorry," he awkwardly grinned. "I got carried away." He came back to her side. "What's here is making a statement. It will have your attention, regardless. Janelle and the rest will be here shortly, so take heart, we won't leave you hanging."

"What could something like that have to say after all this time? Why linger over a place?"

"I think it's pissed."

175

"Oh, thank you, thank you, Sylvia Brown. I can now sleep better at night."

"Don't be so sensitive. I've seen accounts where home occupants had a demon and were bitten and scratched daily."

"Wouldn't you be sensitive? What if that starts happening? It's already burned me."

"No, I wouldn't. Not just yet. Look, it only happens in the back yard, doesn't it?"

"As far as I know."

"So, aside from the child, there's little activity in the house?"

"No, nothing pronounced aside from her."

"Then maybe the demon can't, or won't, enter the house, for some reason. A child's spirit is often just searching for love. They don't really have a reason for negativity. I've yet to hear of a situation where any kind of wrath or rage carried over into the spiritual realm by a child. It's always about love and tenderness. They didn't live to see a special event or couldn't find a parent. It's most often innocent things."

She didn't want to acknowledge her suspicion that things would get worse before they got better. Matt coughed and cleared his throat. After a sneeze, he seemed to be better. She sighed, "What if it gets worse before it gets better?"

"Are you getting a legitimate sense or is it just panic?"

"I wish I knew." She shook her head. "I wish I knew everything already."

"It'll be okay."

"I wish I could believe that, too."

"We'll find answers."

She reached out and put a hand on his shoulder. "We're on a schedule. Something is becoming more active and more assertive and it's getting stronger. I feel it."

"I see."

"I have no proof and no idea why I feel like I do."

"Maybe it's because no one has lived here in decades? Who knows how long it's been since a visitor has come here? Maybe it was asleep and woke up?" They walked together towards the circle. "Come on. Don't think about a schedule just yet."

Easier said than done. There was a rhythm to the events at Elysium. She felt the passage of time on a deep and instinctive level. Every second brought them closer to something. She tried to force the thoughts away because there were positive things happening.

She knew the circle wasn't contaminated with toxic waste, so that was one less worry. Of course, even summoning the authorities wasn't simple. There was no promise they wouldn't become the next victims.

Cynicism wasn't the constant friend it once was. Now, it was tired and clingy. The more she tried to free herself of its influence, the stronger it gripped. She didn't want to be the girl in the tenement any longer. Elysium belonged to her, not the Happy Hell.

She didn't have a massive mortgage. She owned something. She may never live there in peace, but she owned it... *Christ, so much for counting blessings.* Sure, she had the house of her dreams, not to mention pissed off demon, a child ghost, and one hell of a bonfire in the courtyard. Life was alien and unknown. She now followed feelings because she couldn't depend on logic. Logic didn't exist here. "One thing bothers me...."

Matt grabbed a nearby stick and scraped the soil outside the ring. "What?"

"If it all stems from that night, from the massacre, why isn't there more relevant activity? Different stuff, I mean, why just the ring? Why does the only spirit here resemble a person? Shouldn't there be different people reliving different events?"

"Maybe, or maybe not."

"I've considered talking to a psychic."

"We don't really condone the use of psychics, especially this early, as I'm sure Ash already said."

"He did."

"But, we have a few on record. Do you want to consult one?"

"Do you think it would help?"

"Honestly? I wouldn't pin my hopes on it, but other people have had some luck with them. Maybe this would be an exception." He studied a handful of the white dirt. He coughed a moment before continued the inspection, the crystalline grains fell between his fingers "Now, it's my turn for question."

"What?"

He stood beside her. "Who would put salt in this circle? Why? Someone sowed salt in this circle. Why here?" He rubbed his temple with his hand. "Sand? Sure, kids played in sand. Compost? Another likely element in a yard, but... salt?"

"It makes no sense."

"Wait," he had a flash of something. His eyes shone, "It could make perfect sense." He shook his head, "Why didn't I think of it earlier?"

"Excuse me?"

"It's supposed to be a method of protection. It's salt, any salt, it was used decades ago. Old timers believed you could get rid of witches, ghosts, demons, and the like, with salt. If you didn't want them in your house, you sowed salt around the exterior."

"Maybe, but this isn't around the property or the house. Do you think this might've been where they cured meat?"

"A slaughter area wouldn't be a perfect circle. Besides, meats were cured in some kind of structure, not the ground. If it were from back when they cured meat, it wouldn't be on the ground after decades of the elements. Elysium had electricity by the 1910s, so everything was modern, until the fifties or so. They was no need to slaughter after that. Salt from the fifties shouldn't even be here. It should've dissolved long ago. Someone did this much more recently. Maybe they were trying to contain something within this spot?" He walked the width of the circle, "I wonder why this spot is so huge? I bet you could fit a car in this."

"Probably."

"Someone watched this spot. Someone studied what went on here." He looked up to the window of the little room and back. A tree branch groaned overhead, as if a heavy weight was suddenly suspended from a rope. Matt didn't seem to hear. She looked up to the branches but couldn't see anything.

"Hello?" A strange female voice called from the side of the house.

"It's Janelle," Matt started towards the house. "The group has arrived." She followed as he spoke, "We'll probably set up first at the circle."

"Can you give me a minute, Matt? I need to check on Alicia." *Damn it.* She had no business being in Matt's arms or being distracted. She needed to be fully alert and aware. God, why hadn't she thought of her sooner? What if she was gone again? Worry crept across Matt's face, "Yes. I'll go with you. You care if Janelle comes?"

"Of course not."

Janelle Brown was shorter by a few inches. She had a portly figure, and her gorgeous auburn hair was loosely pulled back. "Malcolm and Ginger can't make it. I contacted everyone, but we'll have to see who shows up. Everyone had to work." She grinned, "Short notice."

"If you don't care, Janelle, we have to check on someone. Would you like to join? Maybe you can get a feel for the property."

"Sure." Janelle was one of the few people she'd met in life that seemed genuinely perky, like Alicia. It wasn't an overbearing I'm-on-speed joviality. It was warm and strangely infectious.

The three climbed to the second floor and quickly walked down the hall. She just knew Alicia was gone, that thing—or whatever it was, had come for her. The shower was silent and the door to the master bedroom was open. No sign of her in there. *Not again.*

She cracked her bedroom door, "Alli?"

"Mel?" A sleepy voice came from the vicinity of the bed. The curtains were drawn, and the lights were out. She flipped the switch.

179

"Ah, you'll make my head explode." She left Janelle and Matt at the door and went inside. Alicia had a pillow over her head.

"They're going to conduct some investigative work outside. Are you okay?"

"I'm fine. I don't think I had a wink of sleep last night. It hit me when I got out of the shower... or I would've come down. It's so strange."

"What happened last night?"

"I heard something in that little room down the hall."

"The old nursery?"

She leaned up on her elbow. "Yes, the one with the old dolls. But the room looked new. There was a little girl there."

"Girl?"

"Yes, a beautiful blond girl. She said her name was Dahlia, she knew Isabelle."

"Would you care if Matt and Janelle stepped in to listen? They're from the group." Maybe they could filter everything. They knew what questions to ask and what to look for.

"Nah, bring them in. Might help."

The three made brief introductions and returned attention to Alicia. Janelle sat on the bed beside Melanie. Alicia continued, "The little girl is Dahlia, like I told Melanie."

"What happened to her?" All Melanie could think about was those darling shoes in the cave. They were so small. She was just a little girl. How could Isabelle hurt her?

"Isabelle took her for a walk, and she doesn't know what happened after. She went to the other place and got sick. She said she slept for a long time, but when she woke, she could come and go."

"Isabelle?" *Back to the Blythe family... again.* As time passed, it seemed increasingly like the original attack had nothing to do with the activities at Elysium. How could such a vicious and brutal episode have no influence on a place? What could've possibly happened in Isabelle's time to remotely compete with that atrocity?

"I don't know how they're connected. Dahlia didn't know much. She misses her mommy."

"Bless her heart." Janelle looked down at the floor. "I can't imagine that. She still doesn't know her mommy died that night."

"She said there were two sides to Isabelle, and the bad side was strongest. Someone did something horrible to her."

"No mention of marauders, or anything related to the Civil War attack?"

"None."

"No mention of how to appease her or put her to rest, either?" Matt spoke up.

"No. Just that a deed had to be done."

"Deed?"

She shook her head. "Don't know."

"What happened then?"

"Dahlia wanted me to follow her, to see something... I don't remember."

"Where did she take you?"

"We went in the cave. I don't know where we went after. I thought we'd just turned around, but it was daylight there. Everything was so faded. The grass was gray. The sky was the same way. There were animals behind fences, but they weren't animals. They were hideous..."

Her eyes widened as she spoke. "Oh, God. I remember.... They had oozing sores.... It was disgusting, their calls were awful. The grass looked diseased. People sat on the porch at that Elysium, but I could see they were deformed. I didn't get close. I started feeling horrible, everything hurt. I turned around as a bull was walking towards me. It was black with black horns. I thought it might bypass me, but it hit me with those horns. I flew back."

"What then?" Melanie scooted closer.

"The next thing I knew, I was laying on the ground outside and you were wiping salt off my face."

The three listeners relaxed and looked at one another. "It makes no sense," Matt nearly whispered.

"I know. You all go on." Alicia rolled on her side. "I'll be down in a little while. I need to rest."

Melanie turned the lights out as they left the room. "I don't like this," she confided in the two. "I can't tell if she still has that bug. You think I need to stay with her?"

"Melanie?" Janelle gently patted her shoulder. "She'll be fine, just let her rest. We don't know what happened last night and it's better if she sleeps. Her body is depleted. Many mediums come out of a simple trance in sheer exhaustion. She physically traveled someplace. We don't know what she saw, or where she was led. If she recalls more, we'll hear about it, just let it come naturally."

"You think Ash is there?"

"Maybe. We can try the cave or the pit where you found her. I'm inclined to further explore the pit. We'll have to get proper equipment to investigate the cave, so we'll save it for later. Besides, there's a good chance it won't go anywhere without a guide like Alicia had."

"Guide?"

"Yes, Dahlia was a guide who came from that side, dimension, the 'other side,' if you will—they open doors for the living. It sounded like Alicia was led by a helpful guide, but a malevolent one might've entrapped her. That might've been why she ended up where you found her. I think the bull was a helpful presence to get her out of there. Dahlia probably didn't understand what danger she put Alicia in. At least, I hope."

They returned outside to the salt circle. A man approached from the side of the house in loose khaki shorts and a suede blue shirt. "That's Devon." Janelle whispered. She made quick introductions as Matt accompanied him to retrieve the equipment.

"Devon's tech, he manages the audio/video set-up." The men stacked equipment cases beside the circle and, two trips later, they started to connect the electronics.

"I've never been around anything like this." Melanie toyed with a thread that hung from the waist of her jeans. "I don't know what to expect."

"Expect nothing," Janelle waved her hand. "Nothing at all. Sometimes there are answers, sometimes not. Don't expect to be dazzled because it doesn't work that way."

"But there is so much equipment."

"It doesn't promise, Melanie." Janelle shook her head. "There are no promises in the paranormal, well actually, there are no promises in any field of science, but you'll never hear that anywhere else." She winked. "There aren't even promises in what is considered 'natural' science. Clouds don't always guarantee rain or snow, sometimes they blow over. Meteorologists can be right, and they can be equally wrong. Anyone can get a lottery ticket, but it doesn't mean you'll win. Equipment improves the odds but doesn't guarantee."

"I wish this were over and we knew something."

"It will be, soon enough. We need to be thorough, if we're to help, and that takes time."

"The supernatural... I never expected to be anywhere near something 'supernatural.' Isn't it funny?"

"It happens far more often than you think." She grinned, "And always to skeptics."

Matt and Devon quickly arranged the wiring. Cameras were aimed at the circle. A microphone was hung from an overhead branch. Devon used a digital camera to photograph the yard.

The equipment couldn't have been cheap. Several laptops were arranged on the white plastic table. There were sensors, recording devices, and a host of odds-and-ends rigged up together. There had to be tens of thousands of dollars in equipment. Matt darted to the car and brought back some other archaic devices. He grinned as he walked by.

"That is an EMF detector, short for electromagnetic field detector. Don't mind the men. They go all silent when we start checking a site out."

"That's okay. I don't mind."

"Unlike us, they can only do one thing at a time. That's why they can't talk and watch movies or sports."

"It's limiting." She chimed in.

"We should pity them."

"We should see what they're into."

They both headed towards the station. It was a beautiful day for investigating. The sun rained golden light down on the forest as the noisy animals carried on with their tasks.

She still couldn't fully accept a paranormal investigation group was at her home. *Good Lord, how things change.* They would probably be offended if they knew what she thought of the paranormal before. She was genuinely surprised Ash didn't show up wearing beads or crystals. He didn't chant over chicken bones or sing to Mother Earth. They were so blessedly normal.

She couldn't recall experiencing such a powerful epiphany as her brain continued to shed the tethers of that former life. No one there had assumed anything about her, at least not that she knew of. She was the one who had stereotyped and presumed.

She'd done that all her life, a habit she hadn't even realized. As far as she could recall, no one had assumed anything about her, based on her background or status. She regarded others as being snobbish or arrogant when she was the one who was haughty. At least they had the gumption to pursue their beliefs, and that was more than she could say for herself. She hadn't believed anything.

The study stretched through lunchtime. Janelle remained by the circle with a sketch pad and charcoal pencil. Melanie brought sandwiches and sodas out to everyone. She sat by Janelle's side as they ate. "Are you an artist?"

"Sort of. I do what is called 'automatic writing.' It's a fancy way of saying my hands draw what they receive instead of what I see."

"Have they gotten anything?"

"Not yet. I stay prepared in case they do."

Matt and Devon dug further through the salt-laden circle. The solid layer of salt had lost its pristine appearance as traces of gray-black earth became heavier.

After a brief verbal exchange, Matt continued to dig, but Devon climbed out to examine the surrounding area with a complex metal detector. The device had a small display near the handle. Matt sat the shovel down for a moment. He strode the circle with the EMF detector. Every so often the alert would beep, and Janelle would whisper, "He found something."

Devon returned to the circle and the device loudly resonated. "There's something metal down there."

She and Janelle returned towards the circle. "It's huge." Matt yelled. "Look at this!"

Devon swirled the sensor across the deepening salt pit and walked away. The sound silenced. He returned and it grew loud. He walked for ten feet and the sound didn't waiver. "Wow. Is there a car down there?"

No one spoke as he marched across the same tract of land several times. Matt looked at her, his eyes were wild, "Melanie? Can we exhume what's here?"

"If you don't, I will." She was as enthralled as the rest. What could be down there? They returned to their seats and watched the guys discuss what to do next.

"Don't worry. We'll return the ground as it was." A gentle hand rested on her arm.

"I'm not worried about that, Janelle." She laughed. "I don't think anyone will be seeing it any time soon." Janelle's expression changed. Her brows furrowed. She concentrated on something in the distance. Her eyes were distant, and her voice sounded dreamy. Melanie walked towards the men as they discussed what to do. It seemed every option needed her agreement, anyway.

A frantic rush of scribbling on paper came from behind her. She started to return to her new friend, but Matt grabbed her hand and held on to it, "Wait, Melanie."

"What is it?"

"Janelle's concentrating. Stand with me until she's finished."
Janelle wrote like a madwoman as they watched. She flipped an
enormous page and continued.

"What's she getting?"

"We'll have to wait and see."

After about five minutes, she stopped. Her expression was
drained and tired. She shook her writing hand like it hurt. Matt
patted her shoulder, "Thanks. That's a really delicate process, and if
it's disturbed, there's no promise it will return."

She returned to Janelle. "Did you get anything?"

"I think so. That's awful. It never gets easier."

"What's it like?"

"Honestly? It's an adrenalin rush. Your body freezes up and
words just come."

"Did she show us something?" She wondered aloud.

Janelle nodded and pointed to numerous repeating phrases,
"They attacked... The men attacked me... They're all infected... I will
not be infected."

"It looks like residue from both the epidemic and the Civil
War attack." Devon and Matt examined the pages. The general
conclusion supported the theory that residual energies were left
from both eras in Elysium's history. *Well, at least the possibilities
had narrowed down to two events.*

"Can I ask you something?" Janelle squarely looked at her
after the men returned to the circle.

"What is it?"

"Is something unusual bothering you? I mean beyond this?"

"Nothing. I mean, outside of this, I guess I'm just a little tired.
This has been an exciting day."

"Are you sure it isn't more? You know I'm an unrelated third
party."

"I don't want to burden you." Janelle seemed to read her mind. Why did she relate so easily to Matt? She believed she couldn't burden a stranger.

"We'll be watching the two stooges dig up whatever is in there for a while. Burden me."

She sighed, "Actually, I don't know how to describe it." She spoke softly, so as not to disturb the peace around them. She toyed with the bark of the old, knotty oak they sat on. It had fallen ages earlier, but the thick trunk was sturdy beneath them.

"When did it start?"

"Just after I bought the house."

"What started it?"

"Alicia didn't want me to get the house. I thought she was just jealous or angry. She started to buy that ticket but backed out at the last moment. I bought it and won. After that, something changed, and I still haven't figured it out. It became pronounced when I moved in here. Something just feels amiss. For a long time, it was like I'd forgotten something, but I know it isn't that."

"Could it be depression or anxiety? You know the purchase of a home is major event in life. It's a major change, albeit a good one." Janelle probed.

"No, nothing like that." There was no known cause for it, no reason for it to be there. The feeling just lingered. "I'm not particularly sad about anything, I mean life here is nothing like I expected, but I'm used to disappointment."

She was grateful Janelle didn't pry. "Maybe it's a culmination of things." She talked on. "I grew up poor, really poor, and suddenly have the means for everything. I don't know how to process that. I keep wondering when it's going to end because good stuff doesn't happen to me."

"But, winning was good, wasn't it?"

"Well, yeah," she smiled. "It was incredibly good. I've had so much time on my hands that I didn't have before. I even tried to find my father, believe it or not. He disappeared when I was 8."

"How did it go?"

"It didn't. There was no trace of him anywhere."

"You know he didn't leave by choice."

"What?"

"Your father didn't voluntarily leave. It's just a feeling. Sometimes I get feelings. Please continue."

"This has affected me, too. All of this. I mean... me... paranormal stuff? I laughed at this stuff before. Now, I'm... I'm in the middle of it. Sometimes I wonder if I've carried that missing feeling all my life and now I just have time to recognize it. I don't know."

"You might learn a lot from this whole experience."

"I guess."

"You know, you don't stay the same in life. Things are supposed to change, just as people are. That's just part of it."

"I know."

"And Matt?"

"Matt?"

"I can tell you like one another. How is that going?"

"What?" She didn't know how to respond. "Matt? I don't know. We just met yesterday. Really, I don't think anything is going on."

She felt a strange sense of relief and fear as Janelle looked back at the men. She hoped it wasn't that obvious. She wasn't an expert in social situations. They remained quiet for a few minutes and a new discovery emerged. The guys cleared the soil from something huge. The hole was massive. There was a strange flat slab of metal about three feet down. Devon felt of it, "Is this iron? Why won't it move?"

"Iron would have rusted after this long, especially in salt." Matt disagreed. The debate barely lasted a minute before they returned to their previous tasks. Matt pulled out a brush and began dusting sediment and salt from the crevices. There was some sort of metal embellishment around the base.

"It might be a nickel alloy," The caked salt fell away with the brushing. "I can't figure out why it isn't rusted or corroded."

Devon remained at the side and pushed the shovel at an angle into the dirt. "The slab is attached to something."

They uncovered six inches more of whatever lay down there. "Well, well, well," Matt began feeling below the metal. "What have we here?"

Devon's sharp, black eyes didn't move from the discovery. Matt felt around beneath the metal top. "It's attached to something wooden. I think it's a small building or structure."

Melanie watched the guys and felt a sudden twinge of recollection. She gasped when she noticed the scrollwork. Janelle studied her. "You okay?" Matt looked up for a moment when she spoke.

"That... those decorations." She couldn't find the words. It was useless to explain. The knotted scrollwork lined the bottom lip of the iron slab. "There's something about those decorations." She whispered to Janelle after the guys returned to digging. "I shouldn't be feeling this, shouldn't be recognizing it. I am... Am I crazy?"

"Whoa, honey." Janelle firmly held her shoulder. "It's okay." She turned her attention to the watchful eyes. The digging stopped as they tried to understand her frantic whispers. "We're fine. Carry on." She grinned.

"Melanie," she spoke firmly when the guys went back to work. "Tell me everything."

"It's the scrollwork. There's something familiar about it. It terrifies me."

"Because you recognize it?"

"But I'm not *supposed* to recognize it." She wanted to flee the courtyard and the grounds, forever. The house was cursed. It was rotten to the core. It wasn't a beautiful piece of history any more than she was meant to have it.

Janelle remained quiet for a minute. "You need a strong drink." She flatly said. "Where's your booze?"

"Third cabinet to the left of the refrigerator."

"Any preference?"

"Something so strong it walks."

Janelle left her to gather her composure. A few moments later, Melanie worried she shouldn't have gone alone. What if she vanished? Would other people be like Ash and just fall from the face of the earth? Matt and Devon continued to dig, but it didn't seem like there was any point. She couldn't tell them that. She couldn't rob them of what they obviously found comfort in.

Janelle returned with a lowball glass filled with whiskey and ice. "I don't think you need to worry about being tipsy. I'd say your body would like it." She laughed, "To be honest, with the stress you're exhibiting, I don't think a fifth could get your drunk."

She drank half the glass in one swig. Janelle waited for her to calm, "You have a connection to the house, don't you?" She looked back at the guys and seemed to take much thought in her words, "You feel a strong relation, with this place, and can't explain it?"

"What do I do?"

"Let it be." She soothed. "Just feel it and go with it. That might be the key to solving what is happening."

"But everyone knows why the house is the way it is. Everyone knows what happened during the Civil War. Everyone knows about the epidemics and tragedies here."

"People don't *know* everything," she shook her head. "I think Elysium has many secrets that no one knows."

"You don't think it is connected with the events I mentioned?"

"I didn't say that. In fact, the house is most likely due to those reasons, but every story has two sides. Let's just leave it at that."

The men started throwing dirt into another pile as they exhumed the object below. "Good God, what did they bury here? The smokehouse?" Matt looked up and smiled at her.

She returned the smile but didn't feel it. He returned to digging. His muscles flexed beneath his shirt. There was something wrong with the object that had been hidden from the world.

"He likes you, Melanie." Janelle whispered as she lightly nudged Melanie's arm.

"He is cute," she smiled back. "I'm just not feeling flirtatious."

"That's just fine. You're going through a lot. He knows that. He's very patient."

"I hope so. If anyone needed patience, it's me."

Chapter 21

Alicia smashed the cigarette filter into the ashtray and returned it to the nightstand. Melanie had no idea what she'd gotten herself into, even now. She wouldn't judge her, because she hadn't anticipated the situation, either. They were as naïve as the Pennsylvania Five had been.

The laws of science had no proper application here. She'd never read or heard of a supernatural episode where people vanished as Ash had. Her head hurt. There were too many questions. She lingered in the bedroom a while longer and marveled at those dreams. They were so vivid. So real. There was so much to do, and she lacked initiative to do anything.

Melanie had been lucky to win the lottery, but unlucky to go on instinct instead of forethought. She knew her friend wanted the property but had no idea the transaction would happen so quickly. Usually, a home purchase took months, if not a quarter or half a year. Not this time.

She had it in a week. And now, they were powerless to circumvent what had started. Whatever bewitched Melanie still held her with macabre fascination and now, it counted down. She'd been by Elysium often early in life and had an idea of what the home was capable of. There was just no way to know the full extent of it.

If she could do things over, she would've prevented that purchase at any cost. She'd been so afraid. Her heart dropped when Melanie won, not because she didn't win the money, but because she knew the first place she would go. *Of all the people to win a fortune, why Melanie?* Melanie deserved good luck, there was no doubt, but she also knew her first major purchase would be Elysium.

She strode into the master bedroom and peered down at the courtyard. The group had concentrated their efforts on the pit.

Whatever they were unearthing was huge. She needed to help. It might help them learn something that could point the way to Ash.

Her heart tugged as she watched them toil. They worked so hard and there was no way to know if it would pay off or just be wasted effort. *Of all the people to disappear, why him?* She longed to hear his voice again. It was soothing when everything else was in utter chaos. Meeting him was like meeting an old friend, and the unexpected kiss on the front porch took her breath. Then, he was gone.

Her mind repeated flashes from the nightmare. Who were the people on that porch? It was so hard to remember. Maybe they were those who'd gotten trapped there before. The bull had to represent something, but was that something harmful... or helpful? That was a disturbing thought. That Elysium wasn't of this world.

She moved her arms in a circular motion. She rolled her shoulders and tried to soothe her tender muscles. It was a new day. She should just be glad she wasn't at the Happy Hell. It was her day off and she should be ready to face anything. She was ready to go back to bed. She eyed the tempting softness a moment before she pushed herself forward. No, she had to get out there and help.

The coffee in the kitchen was still warm. She poured a cup and sat at the table. She hadn't eaten since the previous day, but her appetite vanished along with Ash. That flu really did a number on her body, and any semblance of an appetite had long since gone elsewhere. Melanie was sweet to fix her a plate. She reheated it but couldn't manage anything more than a few bites. She scraped off her uneaten food into the trash and put the dirty tableware in the dishwasher.

She couldn't be too critical of Melanie. Elysium was a beautiful place. The garden outside would've suited any historic estate in the English countryside. The wildflowers blended in with the few residual perennials that clung to life. The forests were ancient. The tree trunks gnarled and massive.

Melanie was the sister she wished she had. It didn't seem possible that only a few months earlier, they were certain no luck would find them. They were going to grow old and go to the nursing home together. As senility approached, they would forget one another and become new friends.

If she hadn't moved in with Kevin, she would never have experienced the dregs of poverty. She shook her head, there was no reason to think of that, not now. She couldn't count the times she questioned life, but to no avail.

Her father could've easily gotten them both white collar jobs with any company in the region. He played golf with most of the owners and management. He refused. He always refused. Being disowned was difficult. She was utterly alone. Not even her biological sister spoke to her, but if there had been no Kevin, she wouldn't have had the friendship she did with Melanie.

She helped more than anyone after he left. She survived the real world without hardship. She was innately realistic and down-to-earth. It was ironic that she loved Elysium as she did. Maybe it wasn't the most haunted place in the world, but it was enough to devour anyone.

She was obligated to see Melanie through a world she'd never experienced. Melanie's basic realism was a handicap now. The upbringing that centered solely on life from paycheck to paycheck, barely keeping the mounting bills paid, did not apply to life now. That limited experienced greatly neglected social complexities and had no regard for anything remotely supernatural.

Elysium was a breathtaking, but wicked Grecian beauty. It was designed by the best architect in America, and built from the finest materials, but the glamour and regality was surface matter. It was rotten beneath that handsome façade. Who knew when they would be free of it if they would ever be free? Considering its reputation, they might not live long enough to be free of it.

Chapter 22

The initial excitement faded into a chorus of labored huffs and shovels that nearly dragged from exertion. "You know, Melanie," Matt came over and sat beside her. "We may need a day or two to unearth this."

"What? Already losing steam?" She chided. "How did the pioneers dig the railroad tracks across America? How did they dig the coal mines and till the farmlands? They didn't give up, and now, you're expecting me to believe you're tired?"

"Yes, the pioneers accomplished marvelous feats... and they're all dead. Of course, to be totally honest, they didn't dig the railroads or create coal mines." He smirked.

"Well, aren't you a fount of knowledge?" She nudged his arm. "That's fine. Will you be here tomorrow?"

"We might just wait until later this afternoon, if we can." Janelle answered as she gathered her pad and charcoal pencils. "There would have been more of us today, but it was short notice. We'll be able to finish up faster with the rest of our group. Plus, those who worked the graveyard shift will have a chance to sleep," she cast a stern eye at Matt. "Collapsing from exhaustion does nothing for the team."

"How many of you are there?" She asked Janelle. Matt and Devon packed up equipment and threw a thick waterproof tarp across the excavated area.

"Seven when we're together."

"Does everyone have a purpose?"

"Yep. We all do different things."

The group exchanged farewells with the newest owner of Elysium and exited the grounds in the same direction from which they arrived. Matt lingered behind with her, he sneezed again, "You know, I'm still sneezing, but I feel much better. What was that bug? I'm an EMT, and that wasn't anything like the common cold or flu."

"I don't know, but Alicia and I both had it."

He took a long drink from his soda. "As the property owner, what do you think of what we're doing?"

"I'm still trying to process everything." She couldn't imagine a positive and polite response because there was no black-and-white. There was no simplicity to any part of Elysium. There was no stable answer when everything was unsure. Life had changed and she hadn't even considered what a drastic shift it would be. She wasn't the poor girl at the apartment, wasn't penniless with nothing to offer. There were no seemingly endless shifts at Hayden, or battles with ever-entitled neighbors.

What was left? She had no identity at all. The one faucet of life she'd been so sure of was poverty. She always struggled with the difficulties of survival. Now, even that was gone. The difficulties she faced now would've been unimaginable then. She leaned back on the fallen log. "I can't imagine why they would bury something so large and not just burn it or tear it down."

"It's probably an old utilitarian building of some kind." He finished his drink. "They had a variety of small buildings back then. Outhouses, sheds, smokehouses, it could be anything. Many estates had separate buildings for weaving, schoolhouses that doubled as churches, and laundry sheds. Some even had small buildings dedicated to specific tasks like making lye soap or candles."

"But why bury it?"

"The walls appear to be wooden... they might've been infested with termites. Some buildings will collapse if they're eaten enough. Termites start from the bottom, from the foundation. Several homes in the French Quarter of New Orleans suffer from termite infestation that started in the foundation. It may be a half-intact building or just a pile of rubble. It's just as likely to be a building that caved in due to age."

He adjusted his sweat-soaked shirt. The damp, clinging fabric outlined the muscles in his arms and back. She hoped he didn't notice her eyes tracing his shape. "Wouldn't they have eaten the remaining wood?"

"It depends. They might've used insecticide or something. You can imagine insecticide was lethal to humans back then. Many companies commonly used arsenic or cyanide."

"It's odd burial, anyway."

"Elysium is odd," he chuckled. "But, in a good sense. Despite the activity, I can see why you bought it."

"I'm glad someone does. After I bought it, and learned everything about it, I assumed most people would dismiss me as weird. It's difficult to live in a place that no one understands, including yourself. The rest of the world purchases real estate on a daily basis, but sometimes it feels like you need justification. It isn't fair. I mean, I didn't want the house for egotistical purposes. I've never had anything to show off, and don't plan on starting. I just felt like I was meant to be here."

"You assume too much about other people. I don't know anyone who believes you are anything aside from perfectly normal. We'll find out why you have that connection. It just takes time."

"Do you want to sleep in a spare room?" She wanted him to stay as badly as she'd wanted Alicia to stay. Thoughts of his absence invoked an emptiness that defied reason and irritated her sense of independence. She wasn't clingy and didn't need to be looked after. She had lived alone since Aiden left, with no regrets. Since coming to Elysium, she didn't want to be alone.

"Thanks, but I need to get home, shower and change. I have to contact Ash's mom, too. She'll probably want to file a report. We'll continue looking here, but in case he is out there, they should be looking for him."

"Where do you work?"

"Washington County Life Saving Crew."

"You've been here all day and haven't slept any." She spoke before she meant to, but he had to be exhausted.

He didn't seem to draw any insinuation from her concern. "I'll be fine," he smiled and looked at her. "Stop that. I can sleep this afternoon and be up and rested this evening."

"If you're sure... it makes me feel bad to think you'll be dead tired at work."

"Don't. I can do my job backwards and forwards. I've been there six years."

She walked with him around the house. When they reached the front yard, he said, "Call me if you see any further activity."

She probably read too much into it and assumed he had feelings for her, which he didn't. Maybe his earlier affection was sleep delirium.

She smirked to herself. There was an odd sense of humor to life. He probably wouldn't remember any of the day's events after sleep. "I will. Do I need to do anything? Will you guys need some snacks or something?" She returned with distance that equaled his.

"No, you don't have to, unless you want to. We love to be spoiled, but don't feel obligated. You get some rest, too."

They paused a moment at the front of the house. He seemed to be waiting for something. *Yes? Can I help you?* She turned to go back inside, but he didn't move. What a bizarre paranormal investigation. She played along with him, "So, this is—"

He leaned down and kissed her mid-sentence. She started to pull away but couldn't. She returned his sudden affection and wrapped her arms around him. He straightened back up and drew her closer. The surprising ferocity of his kiss stole her breath.

Fireworks exploded everywhere in her body and worries of Elysium poured from her like water. *I'm in love,* her inner voice shouted with glee. *Yes, yes, yes I love it.* She admonished herself for the ridiculousness of it all. She was no giddy schoolgirl, and right now, she was too vulnerable for a relationship. No amount of reason swayed her heart.

He withdrew first, "Was that an adequate good-bye kiss?"

"I don't know," she couldn't force away a smile. "Further analysis is necessary."

He laughed as he started towards his Jeep. "I think we're making progress. You take care of yourself."

"Sure, you, too. Let me know if you hear anything about Ash."

"I will." He walked down the sidewalk towards his car. She still felt elated and... absolutely giddy. God, she wasn't giddy, that was in the same field as perky. She wasn't perky, either.

She didn't know if she should hang her head in shame for letting herself get carried away or skip through the house. If men ever recognized the absolute power of a single kiss, the world would be thrown in turmoil. The human kiss was an irresistible influence she seldom understood. It certainly made her utterly malleable and ripe for sculpting.

"Geez... Get a room." Alicia giggled behind her.

"Hey! Are you feeling better?"

"Sure. I'm fine." Alicia grinned, "Wow, he's a cutie. What was that all about?"

"Um... Paranormal therapy?"

"It's about time," she playfully frowned as she walked closer. "I didn't think I was ever getting your lazy ass out of the house. Don't you have a life? Do I have to worry about who can occupy you?" Her blue eyes went to the Jeep. "And where did that car come from, young lady?" She grinned.

"You like it? I just got it."

Alicia looked at her again, then the car, and back to her. She broke out in a hard fit of laughter. She couldn't talk. She leaned back against a column and slid down it until she was on the ground. She calmed down after a few minutes, "Mel? You won the friggin' lottery. You could get a Lexus or Range Rover, or both, and you bought a Jeep?"

"It's practical."

Her laughter subsided and she resumed her standing position. "I know, I'm sorry, it's nice."

"We'll see. Maybe later."

"I know already... you don't want to waste it." Alicia put her arm around her as they walked to the kitchen. "So, what's the diagnosis? Did they tell you anything?"

"They uncovered something in the woods."

"Like what?"

"Matt thinks it's an old building."

"Wow. A buried building? You'll have to show that to me."

"I will."

Alicia pointed at the pile of books and papers on the table when they arrived in the kitchen. "Mel, it's called a bookcase."

"I would have never guessed." She continued with her strongest hillbilly accent, "I ain't got no use for them thar bookcases. Organ-u-zation is fur city folk... I reckon...."

"What is this stuff?"

"There's a weird closet hidden on the third floor, I found it yesterday while you were at work. I'll have to let you see that, too. This stuff was under the floorboards."

"Amazing. It's like treasure. What's it for?"

"We're trying to figure that out."

No matter how they manipulated history, it didn't make sense. There was no reason for a circle of fire, other than the Civil War attack. It was also the likeliest origin for the smoky smell. So, why did so much revolve around Isabelle? Her time was half a century *after* the attack. Why not a victim from the bushwhackers' fires?

They examined the documents for signatures, initials, anything to identify the collector. Whoever curated the documents didn't include their own information. The newspaper clippings weren't all antiquated. Several were from around World War II. The death of the mother and the child's subsequent disappearance happened on July 5, 1945, decades after Isabelle, and nearly a century after the Civil War attack.

She pushed the books from the legal pad and documented known names and events. Felix repeatedly came to mind, although she could see no reason for the return. There were no pictures of him, no information on his family or where he came from. He was a faceless name, with no connection to Elysium, aside from a few deliveries. Her gut knotted up every time she read about him. Did he murder the little girl on the second floor? Murder Isabelle?

She assumed they would abandon the evening's search as the sky darkened outside. Clouds rolled in from the west as they had the night before. There would be no further excavation if it stormed. They ate a quick sandwich and potato salad just before they meandered to the living room. The evening proceeded without event. No one called to report Ash's status, but no local news mentioned a disappearance.

Alicia attempted to call Ash, again, but still couldn't reach anything aside from voice mail. Matt was probably asleep since he had to go into work. No other group members left their contact information. It was going to be a long night. Janelle called several hours later to formally postpone the dig, and report that Ash wasn't missing any longer, but no one had news on him.

She was somewhat relieved. Everything was pushed to the next day. It provided a little extra time to process everything. There was nothing on television aside from dim-witted celebrity babble, where the unbelievably wealthy spurted unbelievable stupidity on things they were unbelievably ignorant of.

"Are you into this?" Alicia dropped the remote. "My IQ is plummeting as we watch."

"It's illegal to shoot them, so please, turn it off."

"You mean celebrity hunting season has ended?"

"Yes... I'm heartbroken."

"We have some piss-poor hunters—they multiply every year."

"You know, celebrity overpopulation is a looming concern for authorities." The banter eventually faded into mumbling. They made their sleepy ways up the stairs to their respective bedrooms. Tomorrow would be a busy day, the forecast predicted clear skies and summer humidity. The next dig might last all day.

She needed a shower after the long day of panic and confusion. She grabbed a clean change of clothes and adjusted the knobs in the shower. She stood in the spray and rolled her shoulders. She closed her eyes as the hot water flowed over her face. The dark-haired man came to mind once again. Who was he? It was possible the man was Heath, but that didn't feel likely.

She dried off and looked in the mirror. Maybe she would join a gym. She'd always wanted a toned rear-end. Her weight was average, like Alicia, but she wanted something more. Thankfully, the eating increase of the past two months hadn't made much of a visible difference. Now that she had the means, she didn't know where to start.

She turned out the lights and lay in bed. Elysium's silence became pronounced as she struggled to connect two eras of history. She slipped over to the window and cracked it so she could listen to the sounds of the night. She returned to the bed and drifted off into sleep.

She opened her eyes to light, the gray light of an overcast dusk or dawn. The moon was high above, but its pale light was muted by the smoke and fire surrounding her.

"Ha–girl." Someone grabbed her left arm and twisted it behind her back, pain shot through her shoulder and back.

A faceless man held her arm. She couldn't scream or speak—couldn't writhe free of his merciless grasp. He had no mouth, but he yelled, "See what happens when you go against me? Look at your pretty boy... he's dead. You did that to him. You should've listened to your daddy and left him alone."

She tried to use her weight as leverage against his strength, but he dragged her by her tender arm. Her shoulder socket felt like it was on fire. He ranted, "If you speak a word of this, I'll kill you and tell the world you're a whore I caught in bed with him."

She was so cold and damp, despite the humid evening. She felt like she would suffocate from the smoke wafting over the yard. He yanked her arm and threw her to the ground, but she didn't hit soil. She hit the hardwood flooring of the first-floor hall. She sat up and rubbed her forehead, but she already knew there would be a knot. Light emanated from the keyhole on the closed door beside her. She grimaced as she rose to peep through the keyhole into the dim parlor. Her parlor. The dark room inside was only lit by the fireplace.

Two men talked in hushed voices. She only saw their torsos in facing wing-back chairs. They sat across from one another; both in dark suits with ties; both held snifters of brandy and cigars.

Their clothes were strangely familiar as they murmured and muffled their laughter. She couldn't discern any features aside from their shoulders. They congratulated one another, for something. Something deep inside her trembled. She knew whatever happened in there was sinister.

She woke to a thudding noise. Something rhythmically banged against the house. She timed five seconds between each rap. It wasn't a crashing sound, or anything indicative of damage, but something large swung against the siding. The thud had a muted sound, as if at thick layer of rubber prevented the full force of impact.

She crept down the stairs in the dark house, her guard as high as it could be forced. The sound grew louder in the bottom-floor hall, and still louder in the kitchen. She peered out the window above the sink, but all was calm outside, not even a breeze swayed the branches.

It was probably a raccoon or animal caught in the brush. The wind from the storm might've tangled a broken limb in the limbs overhead. Or it could've been a phantom mob from a century ago. You didn't know with Elysium.

She couldn't understand why the noise invoked such fear. There wasn't any real activity around the house aside from Dahlia. She wasn't frightening. It seemed like the vicinity of the home was safe from whatever lay out there in the forest. It was apparent that was where the really bad stuff happened. Maybe that's where the original Rotherwood house was.

She grabbed the flashlight from the cabinet as she crept out the backdoor. She shone the beam through the darkness, but there was no nearby movement. She followed the rhythm around the left side of the house. She walked beneath the densely overhanging branches and stood by the library window.

The pounding was loudest here, but nothing moved. She shone the light in every direction, on the ground, and in the trees. She had to be nearly under it but still couldn't pinpoint the location. She stopped for a moment to just listen. Suddenly, the top of her head itched, a likely sign of a wood tick from the trees overhead.

She reached up to scratch it when something brushed her hand. She waited a moment longer to see if she could grab the branch. She would pull it down and finally get some sleep. A hard object hit the crown of her head, but it wasn't a branch. The next blow knocked her over. She sat on the ground and rubbed another developing knot, a match to the sore bump on her forehead.

She shone the flashlight up and gawked. It wasn't a branch that hit her. A pair of filthy shoes swung in unison above. *Oh, God, not shoes.* That meant someone else was here that shouldn't be. The once-black shoes were feminine, but ancient. Another phantom of Elysium's colorful past also haunted the grounds, next to the home and not in the courtyard. *So much for safety in the house.* Her stomach dropped along with her heart.

She scooted back to the next tree and leaned on the trunk to stand. She paused a moment to take a deep breath, to calm her trembling. She gathered the courage to move the light up a second time. She saw shoes, then the white legs and then the hem of a dingy white dress. Was it the girl in the picture? *Isabelle?* She knew how Isabelle died.

Isabelle fell from the branches overhead, but it didn't fall to the ground. The ghostly body stood strong and rigid, so close their bodies nearly touched. Those dead eyes were open, they were black with rage.

A gray hand grabbed the top of her left arm with mottled and sickly flesh. The skin was cold and damp, but the grip felt like steel. She couldn't breathe, she heard the sound of a distant scream, and she was instantly taken elsewhere.

She was in a beautiful glade with the most handsome man she'd ever witnessed. Being near him was enough to take her breath. It was *him.* It was the man from the shower. He was *real.* He stood there with his arms around her. His hair was cut shoulder-length and his dark eyes shone in the pale moonlight.

He said, "It's just us. No chaperone?" The body she inhabited nodded, and the beautiful man kissed her. They hid for some reason, but she didn't care. The man didn't look anything like Heath in the pictures, but primitive photography wasn't known for accuracy. They broke their embrace to look for others for few moments and agreed to meet in the cave. She heard his voice in her mind: *"Thus with a kiss I die."*

She returned to see his body on the ground, crumpled, and broken on the stark earth. She bent over, praying he'd merely fainted. She knelt beside him and reached her hand to his throat to check for a pulse. His head snapped around just before her fingers touched him, his bloody smile was full of wrath, "Welcome home," he growled. His throat was slit open from one side to the other, and with each cruel gurgle of laughter, a gush of blood spouted from the wound.

She gasped and sat up. She was in bed. Morning light poured through the windows in a golden torrent. Birds sang outside in the trees. She tried to shake the lingering fear in her mind, her body shivered from memory of that dream. Was that Heath? What happened to him?

Alicia poked her head in, "Room service?"

She slipped out from the covers and stood as her friend entered the room. Alicia looked far better than she had the previous day. Melanie struggled and tried to straighten her sleep-mussed clothes as her friend sat on the opposite side of the bed. "What a night."

"I know," Melanie yanked a stubborn thread from her boy shorts. "I haven't made coffee or anything."

"I already put some on." Alicia sat back on the bed. "Say, where's your beloved cot? I haven't seen it anywhere at Elysium. Leave it at the Happiness?"

Melanie grabbed a pair of socks from the highboy. "It's in the shed outside. I had planned on a cremation service, but all this happened. Arrangements will be completed when we figure out what's going on. There will be no cots at Elysium. Ever."

"I want to attend. You know, it is heavenly here in so many ways." Alicia smiled. "As long as you don't sleep. Or go in the backyard. Or follow any sweet, yet dead children."

"Dreams?" Melanie wiggled into her jeans.

"Yea. Bad ones. Horrible ones. Hair-curling ones."

"Hair-curling?" She grinned.

"Yes. Richard Simmons was my stylist."

"Now, was that really so bad?"

"Well, no, but I had his hair and shorts. Do you know how long it's been since I've exercised?"

"Ah. Were you sweating to the oldies?"

"Oh, yea."

Melanie went into the bathroom, "So, what'd you dream?" She asked before she brushed her teeth.

"It was strange," Alicia spoke from the other room. "It was the same dream I had earlier. I don't normally have reoccurring dreams. I was in a glade of trees. There was a group of men on horses in front of me."

Melanie returned to the bedroom after she finished. She sat down beside her friend. "Were you hiding from the group?"

Alicia looked at her strangely, "Yea. Why?"

"Been there, done that, and have the commemorative shirt. Actually, I have that dream often. You get used to it."

Alicia sprung up with a gasp. "What happened to your arm?" She looked down at her arm and held her breath. She was so caught up in waking that she hadn't even noticed. No wonder her arm had a familiar ache. Something had left a vicious burn near her left elbow. At least, it resembled a burn blister, but it was purple.

"What did you do?" Alicia examined it. "It's swollen like a blister but discolored like a bruise. Did you do something yesterday?"

"She did it," she sighed. Alicia sat beside her. She felt the insanity of Elysium leap to another, even more illogical level. "She grabbed my arm."

"Who did it?"

"Isabelle." Alicia looked at her for a minute, probably waiting for a punch line, but there wasn't one. There wasn't a joke to go with it.

"You're serious, aren't you?"

"Yes."

"Isabelle?" Alicia looked off into the distance and toyed with the ruffle on the coverlet. "Isn't it bizarre? The Melanie I lived beside wouldn't so much as think anything paranormal or supernatural."

"I know."

"You aggravated the hell out of me for watching 'Haunted History'."

"I know.'"

"And when I watched any paranormal programs, you wouldn't let me live it down."

"I know... I know."

"So, I have one thing to say to you about that."

"That is?"

"Ha-ha, told ya so, told ya so." She burst out in laughter. "I'm sorry. I know it's inappropriate. I've had the urge to say that for days."

"Yes. I deserve it."

"Now, look at us, not only are we both believers... we like investigators."

"Does that make us ghost groupies? You know, despite how we feel, we don't really know that they like us in return, in that way. We're just dabbling."

"In the paranormal or the guys?"

"Okay, fine, smarty pants. We're expanding our horizons."

"Something's bound to go bump in the night."

"We can hope." The laughter subsided and her sides hurt. It took the edge off of affection's humiliation. The giddiness, the giggling, it was all residual from youth, but it was amazing to feel young.

After a few years at Hayden, she questioned if she'd ever known youth. She was nothing more than a tired machine, continually bound to repetition and misery. Thoughts of love, the warm rush of hope, it was the quickening her exhausted soul needed.

"Okay, tell me about yesterday. Summarize what happened." Alicia sat up and crossed her legs.

"I told them everything. It started with strange dreams of the angry mob and the fire, and the ring of flames that encircles around you. I've seen things, heard things, things are just much different."

"I think I'm entitled to repeat, 'Told you, didn't I'?"

She looked at the mark on her arm, at what should be a severe injury. It didn't bother her so long as nothing touched it. It stung like a blister if fabric brushed against it. She needed to find the spandex bandage she used for when she worked on that damned laminator. It was probably in the boxes of miscellaneous items that couldn't be easily organized. They were all thrown in the parlor closet.

They made their way to the radiant kitchen to find morning sun had illuminated every inch of space. She opened the parlor curtains before she dug through the closet. Three boxes later, she found what she searched for. She coated her injury with antibiotic ointment and gently stretched the fabric over the wound.

She pulled the heavy chair out and sat beside Alicia at the kitchen table. They each picked up another volume found on the third floor. They had to do something, even if it was just scouring the contents for anything pertinent.

Alicia flipped through to the clean pages of the legal pad. "We should document our own experiences. You write down what you've seen, what you've experienced, and I'll do the same, everything, from dreams to encounters, anything at all. Maybe a written account will give us a visual aid where we can locate repetitions. Maybe there's a common factor we're overlooking."

She documented the haphazard stream of details as they flashed through her mind, but her concentration remained on the dream. Who was that in the glade? Heath and Isabelle couldn't be secretly together *and* pictured together. Why bother with secrecy if it's unnecessary? Perhaps she'd been betrothed to someone else.

In a few of those photographs, she appeared genuinely happy, but something happened later. She blurted out, "Heath and Isabelle were together." It had to be, probably one of those romantic unions that a parent or family objected to.

"What?" Alicia looked at her.

"That's got to be it. I saw them together in the glade last night in a dream. I wonder if Dahlia was the baby that disappeared at the cotillion? Or could she be her child? What if Isabelle got pregnant outside of marriage, and they did something to them? The couple was looking for spies. They didn't want to be seen together."

"Okay," Alicia jotted down notes on the emerging theory. "That's good, but why Heath? Did you find anything on a romantic connection outside of the photographs?"

She sifted through the materials. "There are pictures of them, together, at the courthouse. I made copies, they're around here, somewhere."

"I tend to doubt that, though," Alicia tapped the pen against the pad. She looked off as she concentrated. "We have to remember life during that period. It's possible but doesn't happen that often. People weren't remotely as sexually active during those eras as they are today. Back then, STDs and out-of-wedlock pregnancies, were terminal afflictions that ruined your life, if they didn't get you killed."

"That's true."

"Grandmother told me about a family in the county, in the 1930s. Their daughter became pregnant out of wedlock, and the father wouldn't marry her. They enlisted the help of a Bristol doctor and murdered her by poisoning."

"They killed her for *that*?

"Yep. And that wasn't uncommon." Alicia pulled the nearest stack of documents and searched through them. "We'll figure something out.... Say, should you call Matt?"

"Oh! I'm glad you said that." She grabbed the cordless phone from the charger. "I'll do that before he goes to sleep."

A sleepy voice answered, "Hello?"

"Matt? It's Melanie."

"Hey. How are you?"

"I'm okay. Were you asleep?"

"Well, sort of."

"I'm sorry to disturb you."

"No problem. It's fine."

"I just wanted to see if you had heard anything more Ash."

"No one called you last night?"

"Janelle did for a moment, but she didn't know any details when I spoke to her."

"Ash's mom said he came by yesterday morning, and he was fine."

"Where is he? Alicia's tried to reach him."

"His mom said that he was having his house fumigated, the day before yesterday. Today he's at a paranormal meeting. He told her he wasn't taking his cell."

"Do you believe it?"

"No, not really, but I know she wouldn't lie about seeing him. I don't buy that he has just been out and about. That sounds like a cover."

"That is strange."

"I can't figure it out. It's nothing like Ash."

"Well, you go get some sleep. Will the group dig this evening?"

"Yea, we'll be there about four."

They exchanged goodbyes and she hung up. "Ash is okay, but he's avoiding everyone." She shrugged at Alicia's questioning look. "I don't know what happened. Matt seems to think he's on to something."

"Well, that's weird. He was missing. His car was left, his wallet, his cell phone, everything lay in his house, his closest friends had no idea, and he's suddenly found? Like nothing ever happened?"

"Apparently."

"I wonder what is going on?"

"I wish I knew. At least it wasn't like with you yesterday—" She blurted and stopped herself. She hoped Alicia didn't hear. Janelle said it might be better if she didn't remember. She might not want to recall that other world. She quickly started on another topic.

She picked through the fridge. "I need to go to the grocery store, again. I forgot breakfast stuff. You want some cold cereal?" Maybe she didn't notice. Her mind might not be ready to see it. She didn't want to do something that would hurt her. She regretted even saying it.

"Is there really any other kind?" She sighed with short-lived relief. "And precisely what do you mean 'like with you yesterday'?" *Too late.* She heard.

She tried to delicately approach the topic, "Well... yesterday morning. We tried to tell you what happened."

"I remember...." Alicia's eyes became distant. She used her spoon to push her cereal into the milk. "I remember you wiped salt from my face."

They returned to the books after breakfast. "I'm supposed to work the night shift now. Fillmore called early this morning to bring the glad tidings. He was damn near giddy. They abruptly switched my schedule, so now I'm off Mondays and Thursdays."

"Typical. You should quit."

"Not all of us won the lottery, Mel." She chuckled, "not all of us can be so lucky."

Melanie flipped another book open. "You know, why don't you move in here?"

"I couldn't impose."

"Oh, I know," Melanie dramatically shook her head. "I just don't know where I could put you. I don't have, but two, three floors, and where would I put my things? I have so much to organize, you know."

"Really, Melanie," Alicia shook her head. "Don't make fun. I still live there."

"I'm not making fun, and you know it. Why don't you stay here?"

"That's generous, but what if we got on each other's nerves?"

"This isn't a tiny apartment, Alli. We won't exactly be stepping on one another's feet. There's plenty of room for us to live comfortably without crowding. When everything is clean, you can use the front part of the upper story, and I'll use the back. There are also bedrooms down here behind the stairs. It will be like having an entire apartment building to ourselves."

Alicia seemed to choose her words carefully, "Mel... That is generous—but too generous. I can't tell you how much I appreciate it. But I could never let you support me. I don't even get support from my parents. It's not your place."

"Whoa, who said anything about 'supporting,' you? Oh, no, you lazy sack, you're going to work...." She laughed. "Seriously, all I'm doing is providing a roof. I know you'd do the same for me. If you like, we can split the utilities, or taxes, or whatever. You know, you can go back and finish your studies to be an attorney. Hell, I may even go to college."

"Are you sure?"

"Positive. If it makes you feel better, you can always pay me back whenever you get it, if you want. I'm not worried about it and, if I have it, I'm spending it. So, get your things from the Happiness and just tell everyone you're moving in with your parents."

"Do you know something?"

"What?"

"I never really said it before, but you were so generous when you asked me to take half the money. I've never thanked you and I should have, then. I was just frustrated... and worried. I felt that no matter what I said, it would come out as something negative."

"Generous? Wouldn't you have asked me, had you won?"

"Well, yes."

"Then, what's the big deal?"

"I don't know."

"So, that settles it."

The conversation quickly returned to Heath and Isabelle. There weren't any unusual connections aside from the photographs. Maybe they just attended a ball or cotillion together. Maybe they participated in some community event together, any record would have been better than nothing. The bottom book didn't have any markings or identification on the cover. She reached over Alicia's arm and pulled it out from beneath another stack of loose papers. "What have we here?"

"Mel, I don't mean to be the carrier of bad news, but we haven't found anything here. I mean, circumstantial evidence, but that's it. She could've just as well had an interest in anyone. They might've even been related. We have to look at everything."

A loose piece of paper fell from the book. Alicia picked it up and looked at it, "Peddler Disappears," was in bold, large print.

"What do we have here?"

"It's dated August 7, 1915. Does that ring a bell?"

"Sorry," Melanie shook her head.

Alicia flattened out the crumpled paper on the table and read aloud:

"Felix McLain, a familiar peddling merchant in the area for years, has apparently vanished. He was last seen driving through the forest toward the Elysium estate. Edgar Blythe, the property owner, stated he never arrived. If you have any information on this disappearance, please notify the lawman in your area. Mr. McLain had a number of supplies needed for the quarantine at Elysium...."

"We know the peddler disappeared. We know Isabelle died. Both events happened around the same time, but what happened to Heath? "

Melanie picked up the paper, "I hate this. It feels like there's a connection, but what, and why would any connection be important?"

"I don't see anything." Alicia slumped over on her elbow. "The peddler might've run off with a married woman, or his horses could've become spooked and thrown him. Who knows?"

One of the unread books fell to the floor with a hollow thud. "What's this?" Alicia skimmed through the ancient pages. Her mouth hung open, "Oh, my God. These are death certificates."

"What?" Melanie looked over her shoulder. Alicia flipped the book to the front. There had to be some sort of introduction or opening statement. Edgar Blythe's words told the story of the records:

"This is a record of the Great White Death Epidemic that has stricken the Goodson area of Bristol, Virginia, starting in 1913. The plague has taken many loved ones and respected members of our community. I do not think of friends and family I have lost. The pain is far too great, but I will document those losses in these pages for future generations. We have administered to, and tried to heal, numerous travelers and most of our own beloved neighbors.

"Few medicines affect this vicious disease, and more and more are infected daily. Our beloved Elysium has become a quarantine hospital for the duration of the plague. We have requested the services of Pocahontas Hale, the notorious medicine woman of Bristol. Her cures have helped many, but even they aren't strong enough to eradicate this horrid pestilence. God help us all."

Alicia flipped through page after page as they read. So many people died on the grounds. Each page listed ten victims with their vital information stretching out across the second page. How many was there in all? The entries began in 1913 and ended in 1916. The hard-cover book only had two blank pages left in the back.

"Who knows who haunts my home?" She was overwhelmed. "Look at how many died here, just during the epidemic. That doesn't count the Civil War attack, any disappearances, or anything else."

"I know," Alicia didn't dismiss her negativity. "I know. I'm sorry."

She hated to burden her friend, hated to burden anyone. Why did she have to be in a situation where she was so damned dependent? She'd been self-sufficient at the apartment, and life allowed her to be independent. Now, she had more than she could imagine and felt utterly vulnerable.

Alicia quickly sat the book down, "Wait."

"What?"

Hidden amid tens of names was a simple entry for Isabelle Blythe. The cause of death given was tuberculosis. "What? We already know what happened to Isabelle. I saw her hanging in the trees." She sighed. "Doesn't sound much like what we're seeing, does it?"

"Maybe, if we manipulate circumstances just a little?"

"Just a tad." Alicia looked through the pages and tried to find something on the little girl. "Maybe the little girl is the key?" After a few minutes, her expression showed defeat. "I haven't found a 'Dahlia' anywhere."

"So, if she wasn't in the epidemic, then she must be the child that disappeared in the 1940s. She looked similar to the photograph that Matt had despite the gap in age."

"She said she was looking for her mama, but the missing child was a baby. Where was she for three or four years? Wouldn't she have thought of Isabelle as her mother?"

"She knew she wasn't." Alicia returned the papers to the stack.

She flipped through the book after Alicia finished. "We've lost all sense of direction. Maybe we should concentrate on the attack that destroyed the first house. I mean look at the evidence. It may look like Isabelle, but what's that ring of fire? We know that the attacking bandits, marauders—or whoever they were—burned everything in a circle. Hence, the ring of fire."

"Hence?"

"It's a real word."

"Yea... two hundred years ago." She grinned.

"Maybe you're right. I was so certain it was connected to Isabelle."

"Maybe it liked her form or her life?" Alicia poured two glasses of iced tea. "Maybe something evil came from the Civil War attack liked her pneuma? I don't know."

"Eesh, 'pneuma.' I don't even know what the hell that is. Isn't that a big cat? We sound like television psychics." She laughed.

"It's a fancy word for 'inner-most self,' or 'soul.' You're thinking of puma. Yes, the entity residing here is a metaphysical manifestation of eras of oppression and heinous torture at the hands of brutal men."

"Metaphysical? I felt it to be more of an existential issue. The excruciating presence of such traumatic memories should reflect the era from which they were enacted."

"Do you have any idea where this conversation is going?"

"I don't even know what I'm saying. Shall we converse in more simplistic terms?"

"Here, here. I concur."

"And why is it always the men who are bad in history?"

"Because women say so?"

"I don't."

"Me, neither."

"Has no one ever heard of Madam LaLaurie?" She remembered that much from Alicia's shows.

"Yes, the Butcher of New Orleans. No, she was a man, masquerading as a woman. Or, better yet, she was forced into her heinous deeds by a domineering husband."

"Of course."

"Similarly, Annie Hall, the White Witch of Rose Hall, in Jamaica, seduced and slaughtered her male slaves. Darya Saltykova, of Russia, tortured and mutilated her female subjects."

"Uh-huh. You know all this because...?"

"I read. A lot. So, just face it, Mel. We're far too weak and stupid to be devious. Just watch a modern historical documentary. Pointing out women's evil deeds is misogynistic."

"Well, that's convenient."

Their exchange faded as they ran through the known witness reports for the ring of fire. No formal investigation was ever devoted to it. The brief mentions were brushed aside as quickly as possible.

One book contained a few folded magazine pages. *Ghost*, an unheard-of paranormal magazine, tried to cover the estate in the 1960s. The article discussed a vague history of the home but didn't offer anything aside from ambiguities and supposition. One portion of the article was headlined, "Realities of the Red Room."

It was one theory that not even Alicia had knowledge of. Melanie read the brief introduction aloud:

"... There is a rumor amid those with an interest in Elysium's activities of a place called the Red Room. This mysterious room is little known, and the claims have never been validated. The Red Room was said to be a healing place that did not heal. Whispers have perpetuated from the time of Elysium's epidemic that the owner, Edgar Blythe, employed his own physicians briefly, but all eventually succumbed to the illness. We have never substantiated what, precisely, was done to victims, but those who survived the attempted cures were sent to a place called the Red Room to heal. It is also reported that none were ever seen again."

Maybe the presence just liked Isabelle's form. They had discussed a possible indiscretion as reason for her death, but she could've been a suicide. She could've gone insane from watching so many suffer and die. It was clear she hadn't died due to physical sickness, and a hanging death was usually self-inflicted. A suicide would've been hidden back then.

A soft noise in the hall broke her concentration from the antiquated documents. Alicia hadn't noticed anything. Her eyes never left her paperwork. The familiar sigh came accompanied by a chorus of equally soft whispers. "I need to check something." She slipped out of the kitchen as Alicia continued writing. She hoped it was Dahlia, and she might offer some answers.

The noise continued from the hall closet as she inched closer. The volume didn't rise nor did the words clarify themselves even though she drew near. She turned the long brass latch handle and pulled the door open. There wasn't anything, at first. It was just as she had left it, three boxes stacked on the right and a cluster of old coats hanging to the left, but there was something shiny behind the hanging garments.

She blinked a few times until her eyes adjusted to the darkness. Something glimmered in the back, two shiny orbs remained stationary together. As her eyes adjusted, she realized they were a pair of cold, black eyes.

She screamed and slammed the door shut, "Alli! There's someone here!" Alicia bounded around the corner with the butcher's knife from the counter set. The new chopping blade was razor sharp. "Open it..." Alicia stood beside her.

She yanked open the door as her friend lifted the weapon. Alicia crept inside with the knife drawn. There was silence for a moment and the sound of frantic turning. "Um... Mel?"

"What?"

"I just knifed your coat... there isn't anything here."

"But... the eyes. They stood where you are." She came in the house. Isabelle was in the house, and she wasn't ready. They walked back to the kitchen, she asked, "You've seen a woman here with a dirty dress, haven't you?"

Alicia responded. "Have you?"

"Yes. Who do you think it is?

"Isabelle." Alicia returned the utensil to its proper place.

"Right, she's the biggest portion of the activity. Isabelle. Isn't it strange that so much activity seems to revolve around her?" She knew the truth in her heart. It revolved around Isabelle. It was so difficult to accept such a beautiful girl could end that way.

Everything about her had seemed perfect. She had a perfect smile, perfect skin, perfect hair, and a perfect life. But the girl who seemed so perfect was the center of the activities. Perfection couldn't have been true.

A phrase whispered through her brain as they sat down at the table. The delicate delivery of the words nearly camouflaged their meaning. *She is spreading...* That was even more illogical. Hauntings didn't *spread*. They weren't communicable. *Spirits weren't infectious.* It wasn't her area of expertise, but even she knew it wasn't possible.

"I saw her at the apartment before I came here."

She couldn't resist the questions, "Where? What did she look like? Did she say or do anything?"

"She was in the corner of my bedroom, looking down. She didn't do or say anything. She wore a grimy white dress and long dark hair. She just appeared for a moment. I saw her when I was little, too, when I walked by here to school. I remembered that vividly when she appeared in my room."

"I was so sure it all revolved around the Civil War attack... but I mean we can't sidestep the ring, and the only known ring came from that attack. It's just that everything else revolves around Isabelle."

"Are they coming to dig today?"

"Yes, this afternoon, around four. They'll unearth more around the building, or whatever it is."

"You didn't show me what they found. I completely forgot."

They slid into their shoes and walked out into the yard. The warm sun was inviting, even though the backyard was in dire need of work. "You know, Mel... it is beautiful here." Alicia stretched out her arms to relish the sunlight.

"That's why I bought it. It's not all bad... just feels it right now." Melanie walked onward. "It's over here, through these trees."

"Wait, Mel." She called and grabbed her arm. "Don't go in there." Her eyes were wild and terrified as she looked into the forest.

"Why? We've been through here time after time."

Her breathing came in rapid, fitful gasps. Her hands trembled. She didn't speak for a moment. "I don't like it... something's wrong with it."

"Alicia? Are you talking about the circle? It's just salt, really, it's not poisonous... we even tasted it. Just plain ol' table salt."

They stopped frequently as she urged Alicia onward towards the circle. Her reaction didn't improve any when they arrived. Her voice whispered, "Get away from that. Don't stand there!"

Melanie's aggravation had changed to fear. Maybe such close proximity to the circle threatened to resurrect memories. What if Alicia wasn't supposed to remember the other night? It might do something to her. "Alicia, honey? What is wrong?" She reached back to touch her friend's shoulder. "Please tell me."

"It's there," she whispered and pointed to the partially uncovered structure. She took a step back. "It started there."

"What started there?"

"Bodies... where they put the bodies." Her monotone voice was flat and lifeless. Her glazed eyes were entranced by the circle. "They kept them there."

"Bodies? Tuberculosis victims? Victims of the attack?"

"All of them. The Red Room. The Disease. Victims of an attack... Yes, a horrible attack."

"So that's what this all comes from?"

"It was a horrible attack... so brutal."

"Where are you getting this from?"

"I don't know." Alicia remained pensive. Her eyes locked on the white circle. Melanie held her hand and lifted her chin to look squarely at her. Her unblinking eyes finally batted when they locked gazes. "Alicia? What are you doing?" She spoke firmly in an attempt to break her friend's concentration.

Alicia blinked a few times. "Where did that come from?"

"Were you conscious?"

"Kind of. It's like something else took over. I don't know what happened."

"Do you need to see a doctor?"

"God, no." She smiled. "They'll put me in a straitjacket."

"Why, you know it's just acute psychosis."

"Of course it is. Or just hormone-stimulated, psychosomatic hallucinations."

"If it's that time of the month, they'll have a joyous time theorizing the many chemicals of woman."

"Or the many insanities."

"Well, a little nut makes the fruitcake sweeter."

Alicia burst out laughing, "Come again?"

"I have no idea and, likewise, I'm unsure of its meaning."

"Probably for the best." She looked down in the pit once she got rid of the daze. "Wow. What's that?"

"That's what they're excavating."

"It's a building?"

"We think."

"Doesn't make sense to bury a building, does it?"

"Matt said it might've been a smokehouse. Maybe they tried to cure a large amount of meat, and it went foul? Or they buried it to avoid contamination? Or maybe it was a termite infestation? He mentioned the lethal pesticides they used back when. It might've contaminated the building."

"I guess."

"Matt seemed to think it was termites."

"Say, you're getting close to Matt, huh?"

"Well, I guess. We're friends."

"Uh-huh. Okay. I'll buy that."

Chapter 23

Ash kept an eye on the rearview mirror as he drove. It still followed, even after all this time. He couldn't tell anyone just yet. There was a good chance it might spread to the others, if they weren't already infected. He couldn't think of that. Worry distracted him and he already knew time was limited.

The activity began as soon as he arrived home from Elysium. He left his house on foot as soon as he realized he was followed. He hoped it would tire and return to the estate. He walked all evening, even ate supper in town. It didn't help that presence waited on him when he returned.

He had no idea just how strong the entity was. *So much for poltergeist activity.* He felt ridiculous for even thinking it was a mere impish spirit. It was a demon, and it was pissed... and it was also insatiable.

He couldn't involve anyone because it might attach to them, too. He had no way of knowing how it infected. He had to find a way to communicate with Matt. He'd considered emailing or texting, but that was no guarantee. If it followed him, it couldn't be at the estate. He hoped.

Spiritual activity was just energy in one form or another. It wouldn't be a problem for energy to migrate via electronics, and he did not want that entity to be viral, no more than what it was. If it got online, there's no telling where it could spread. That would be one hell of an internet virus.

He wanted to talk to Alicia just as badly. She was the best thing to come from the experience. Something happened when they met. Something clicked between them. Nothing like that had ever happened before. He never wanted to begin an investigation with a personal attachment because it might create a breach of professional conduct. He couldn't stop his feelings.

L. Chambers Wright

His first instinct was to seek refuge at his mom's house. The entity was at his place and, so long as no one was there, it should've remained there. It should have, but it didn't. That only put his mother might at risk.

The whole situation was unheard of in the paranormal world. He watched that girl outside the window in his mother's living room. The entity stood with her head down at the window. His mother remained oblivious to its presence.

She was in the rearview mirror as he drove away from her house. It was a woman, or that's how it chose to appear. She stood motionless beside the road with her head down. The hem of her filthy dress barely moved in the breeze. The form appeared in front of the car, on the side of the road, and just as soon as the latter form disappeared in the distance, it reappeared ahead of him, like a twisted jump in a film strip. It didn't matter how fast he went or which direction he turned.

He'd never even read of such an intelligent and powerful entity. The figure could appear miles and miles from Elysium's grounds. He heard those whispers no matter where he went. The facts he'd gleaned from the experience were few. It was obvious that it didn't want to kill him, not just yet. That was nearly the only advantage. It would've killed Melanie and Alicia days earlier if that was the sole purpose.

The force grew in intensity, but that alone wasn't dangerous. The danger stemmed from the entity's aggression. It had manifested a time or two for the girls when he last spoke with them, but they lived there. It had the power to follow him, which meant it could do just about anything on the grounds.

A sudden thought nearly made him slam on the brakes. *Distraction.* He was an investigator with certain psychic abilities. There was a chance the force didn't want him on the grounds. Something with that degree of power would easily identify that. It wanted him away from the property.

Elysium was evil. If they couldn't solve the problems with within a few days, Melanie would need to move. If they survived. Something needed to be done. The home needed an exorcism. An exorcism wasn't for the destruction of the entity, so much as forcing it to go elsewhere. The only reassurance was that the force couldn't be omnipotent. There had to be a weakness somewhere, there always was.

The more deeply he concentrated on Elysium, the more the activity seemed like a puzzle, and every puzzle had a solution. It might be difficult, challenging, or seemingly impossible, but one did exist. His burn itched beneath his left sleeve. Something grabbed his arm during one of the visions and he'd received a nasty burn. The cotton shirt irritated the tender tissue.

He checked the internet at the library hoping to find something he missed. He found a little more information on the mysterious Black Riders of the White Death. Matt mentioned the group years earlier, but it didn't catch his attention. It was an interesting bit of history, yet he initially believed it had nothing to do with Elysium. He was inclined to think differently now.

No matter how he aligned the atrocities at Elysium, nothing explained why it still affected the present or how it was connected. Perhaps the separate incidents interwove energies to form what was there, but that was unlikely.

Urgency was all that surpassed his frustration. He needed answers now. Every second that ticked by was irreplaceable, and the next passed more rapidly. It wouldn't be long before it manifested. He had to be ready. He suspected that if they missed the opportunity, they would all die.

He noticed a man studying Elysium, from the opposite side of the street, when he left the house. He hadn't seen the man in Bristol before, but he was familiar. It took a few hours, but he remembered a presentation given at Mountain Empire Community College several years ago. A guest professor gave a public lecture on local lore and regional myths, with a special focus on Bristol's

Elysium property. The man staring at the house was none other than Dr. Herbert Malcolm.

He'd arranged to speak with the professor in his home. It was a last and desperate attempt brought about through mild duress. The professor would barely speak with him on the telephone. Fortunately, he only needed to mention his habit of gawking at the house, and what potential ramifications voyeurism could have if the public knew. In all likelihood, there weren't criminal ramifications any more than there was criminal voyeurism, but he was desperate for leverage. If the professor didn't offer answers, they were all doomed.

Chapter 24

The group arrived around four o'clock and everyone was formally introduced. Alicia's vivacious nature had returned and made the atmosphere even more welcoming. She spoke with everyone as if she'd known them for years.

Melanie always envied her charisma when it came to social situations. She would've made a great attorney. She needed to return to college to finish that pursuit. She had been so close to law school when her parents stopped helping her, just a few semesters away. She didn't need to be a drone at Hayden. Maybe she would offer something like that to all the girls stuck in the pit.

Janelle entertained them with stories of previous investigation mishaps as they burrowed deeper into the soil. All members who were physically larger and stronger were given shovels. Devon supplied soil screens to filter the freshly dug earth for artifacts or remains. She and Alicia had well developed labor skills from Hayden, but heavy lifting was not one of them. Lifting assignments there were based upon Fillmore's whims as opposed to productivity or routine. The four men made impressive strides in around the structure. After an hour, another two feet of the object had been excavated.

She didn't have much faith in the dilapidated structure. It was a fascinating discovery, but not likely to provide any valuable insight. At most, it was just a frame of broken boards even if it was somewhat intact. Devon tapped the still solid sides of the structure with his shovel once they cleared another foot of earth. It didn't break or crumble, it didn't sound rotted or hollow.

The scroll work still posed a mystery. That amount of ornamentation shouldn't be on a disposable building. It was an elaborate fixture that couldn't have been cheap. If they buried the building, why didn't they save it? Normally, they would've stripped for use elsewhere. Maybe that was a Blythe trait, just as the house. Beautiful furniture, antiquities, priceless pieces left just like trash.

Questions only mounted as they uncovered more of the structure. Instead of decreasing, her sense of familiarity grew as they exposed more of the ancient structure. The wooden box had no visible doors or windows, but everyone seemed to think there was something inside. The men marveled at the building's condition when Devon yanked up what appeared to be a long string of dirt.

"Hey, it's a chain." He yanked the full length out of the ground and shook the packed soil from the links. "It's still in pretty good shape, too." Several coins from the 1900s were scattered through the earth surrounding the building. Melanie hopped into the pit and knocked on the sides. "Does anyone know why a building wouldn't have any way to get in or out?"

"Well, I have an idea," Scott began. "But it isn't pleasant." He threw another shovel of dirt across his shoulder.

"What?"

"The epidemic was here, right?"

"Yes, a tuberculosis epidemic, it started around 1913."

"And Elysium was a makeshift hospital wasn't it?"

"Yes."

"Maybe this was for things like dirty sheets or contaminated medical supplies, or it could be coffin for a mass grave."

"Maybe, but I haven't heard of mass graves using a containment structure. Aren't the bodies just dumped in the ground?"

"In times like that, locals often bent many laws. Maybe they viewed the corpses as contaminated, and feared they would contaminate the ground. It's just a theory, but I wouldn't be surprised if it was some sort of coffin. It would explain the ornate top, too."

"Like a pauper's cemetery for the sick?"

"Exactly. Locals could've entombed the dead, but these would've been dangerously communicable. During that era, you didn't have concrete vaults, and most didn't see elaborate headstones. The families around here mostly cared for the bodies of their own. Did you know people frequently had their coffins made in advance and stored them in attics and barns?"

"Wow. You know your death." She joked.

Matt giggled, but Scott's gray eyes didn't flinch, "I'm an apprentice. My dad owns the Eckerd Funeral Home on State Street. Dad always gives a history lesson."

"So he's a death professional." Matt said. "Dr. Death, to the rest of us."

"You know it," he echoed with another push of the blade into the ground. "I put the 'fun' in funeral."

"The 'serve' in service."

"The 'memory' in memorial." He continued Matt's joke.

"The 'form' in formaldehyde."

"The 'rave' in grave."

Levity let them briefly forget their fatigue and boosted their energy. She fingered the newly brushed scrollwork. They were already far down on the structure.

She knew how it would feel before her fingers touched it. The cold of the iron and the ridges of the detail. She also felt there was something wonderful inside. She didn't know what it could be, but she knew it wasn't death. Despite the horrors of Elysium, some things were genuinely virtuous, and a sense of sanctuary emanated from within.

She climbed out of the pit and stood at the edge for a moment. She felt like a third wheel. Every member had a distinct purpose, and they worked together like a machine. Some functioned as wheels, some worked as cogs, but everyone had a purpose, and every purpose was accounted for. She felt eyes on her and turned to see Janelle and Alicia as they sat together. She smiled at them and eventually they smiled back.

She felt like kicking herself so often. If only she hadn't been so pigheaded. She should've known there was something wrong with the place. The previous owners didn't care for it because it was cursed, haunted, because something was wrong with it. If only she had chosen a nice, normal house. She could've purchased a sweet bungalow or a nice, generic ranch, but no. She *had* to get the estate.

Obviously, they were all more patient than she was. She hated herself for the current situation. Hopefully, they knew she didn't have remedial knowledge of the property's history. She just thought it was pretty.

She approached the girls and sat with them. She resumed brushing the debris through the screen. "Show Janelle your arm, Mel." Alicia stopped for a moment.

"Okay," she pushed the spandex bandage down and held her arm out.

Janelle went through several expressions and stopped at shock. "That came from a dream?"

"Yes, why?"

"Is it a burn or a bruise?"

"I can't tell. What do you think?"

"I hope this doesn't offend you, but it looks horrible. Does it hurt?" Janelle's eyes didn't change. "I've never seen anything make this kind of mark, especially on flesh."

"Flesh?" Matt looked up from the pit. "I like flesh—" His humor faded when he noticed her face.

Melanie realized everyone was watching her, for some reason, her pulse raced. Suddenly, shovels were cast aside, and a circle formed around her. It reminded her of something terrible. Just like the iron scrollwork on the box below, something about the way they stood was so familiar—horribly familiar. "Please don't get so close," she fanned herself as if she were hot. "I need air."

The group glanced at one another and back at her. Matt knelt to examine her arm, "When did this happen?"

"Last night. I dreamed that Isabelle grabbed my arm. When I woke this morning, I had this." She pulled the bandage farther away so everyone could see the extent of the injury.

She tried to hold it still, but her arm trembled. Matt looked closely at her, "You have my wealth of medical knowledge and didn't say anything?"

It was Scott's turn to scoff, but Matt grimaced. "This looks awful... but, despite how it looks, I think it's superficial."

"Are you sure?" Janelle cocked her eyebrow at him. "With that amount of blistering?"

"I am positive, as strange as it is. What degree of pain do you feel from it, Melanie?"

"Well, it's a little tender and it throbs at times, but it's not agony. It looks incredibly painful, but it isn't."

"If this were an injury that penetrated, particularly a burn, this would be agony. Literally. A patient with a deep burn like this would require physician-administered painkillers. It wouldn't just be an annoyance."

"But it looks so horrible."

"I know.... It's amazing. I don't know how you could get this amount of swelling or discoloration without an injury requiring medical attention. Aside from this, does your arm function normally? Do you have any problems with movement?"

"No, nothing at all. Just skin sensitivity in the area. What should I do?"

"Well, if there's no pain, I don't see why you would need a doctor's visit just for this." He shrugged and stood back up. "There aren't any signs of infection, and the top layer of skin is still intact, albeit damaged. If it doesn't improve in a day or two, you should schedule an appointment."

She smiled, "Thank you."

The men returned inside the pit without further discourse. Everyone grew so quiet. Outside of nature, the only sounds were the scraping of the brushes to push the stubborn dirt clods through the sieves and the shovels cutting soil.

She never had claustrophobia, and groups of people never bothered her. There was something about the way everyone gathered. She pushed her mind to recall that evasive memory. She'd seen a crowd somewhere before... just like that, but where? She turned to Janelle, "Did you hear from Ash?"

Janelle's amicable expression darkened. Her clear eyes were in a distant, hateful place. "Sort of, we heard from his mom. She said he was fine."

"Has he contacted the group?"

"No, and that worries me."

Melanie studied her for a moment. She tried to decipher her expression. "Are you interested in Ash?" She curiously pried.

Alicia quickly looked down to the ground. Maybe she shouldn't have said anything, but she needed to ask. It would be better if Alicia heard it now, as opposed to later. She had a deep affinity for him and needed to know if he wasn't able to return it.

Janelle seemed to sense the question between them and chuckled. "I love Ash like a brother... I love everyone in the group for that matter. We've been investigating for years, and you get attached to people. We're like a family." She smiled. "Ash is unique. He's gentle and determined, a wonderful listener, and I can't imagine why he won't talk to us. I worry so much about what he's going to try alone." Her eyes became misty.

"I'm sorry," Melanie patted her shoulder. "I'm just getting used to the idea of a group. I've never had a group of friends, always just one or two."

Janelle sighed. "I know Ash has a good reason. I hope we all figure this out. It's wonderful to have a group of friends. You both should consider joining the group." She paused before adding, "I take it Alicia is interested in him?"

"How did you know?" Alicia had almost gone pale at the mention.

Janelle laughed. "I sense things... and I noticed how you acted when we talked about him."

Melanie took a deep breath and stood. She needed answers from everyone. Alicia and Janelle watched. "What is it?" Janelle smiled.

"I have a few questions for everyone." She announced. The entire group again stopped to listen. A group questioning would settle many questions at once. She began, "A simple show of hands will be the fastest way to get everyone on the same page. How many here have experienced... unusual events since coming to Elysium. I mean anything at all, dreams, visions, anything."

Matt raised his hand and seemed in the minority, even as she and Alicia raised their hands in unison. Devon shrugged when he raised his hand, "I think I have, but I'm not sure."

She ventured, "How many of them concern a young woman?"

The same number remained in the air. "Does she wear a dress that's dirty or grimy?" The hands remained up.

"Has anyone ever heard of a 'red room' at Elysium?"

The hands went back down. Scott started to answer and stopped himself. He opened his mouth again and spoke, "Actually, that sounds familiar. Was it something from the Pennsylvania Five? I don't think I've ever heard any details about it."

"The what five?" Matt stopped.

"The Pennsylvania Five? Come on, you and Ash should already know what that is."

"We don't."

"I do," Alicia stood. "I checked them out the other day at the library."

"What was that?"

Melanie sat down and let Alicia stand. "Five kids, in the 1950s, dared one another to climb Elysium's fence and pick a flower. They did, and all five were dead within days."

"Of?" Scott eyed them from his position.

"I think it was three tuberculosis and two from unexplained smoke inhalation."

"Good God."

Matt pushed the top of the shovel blade with his foot. "So, what's the Red Room?" It was Alicia's turn to shake her head.

Scott jumped in, "Rumor had it that Edgar employed a doctor after the plague came. Since the epidemic was so vicious, and unresponsive, they decided to create their own medicine.

They attempted surgeries in the Red Room to avoid attention. Patients who survived the surgeries were placed in some secret room in the house, but none of them survived, either. Those who survived the tortures of the Red Room surgery usually died in the recovery room."

"What else do you know?" Melanie walked to him. "Please, tell us everything."

"Honestly, that is the extent of it."

"What about the girl?" Melanie said.

Matt stepped out of the pit. "We don't know if she is a girl, or just assuming an appearance. We also don't know what entity it is."

It was a group of paranormal professionals. Someone had to have some idea of something. The same ghost, spirit, presence, whatever it was, followed them all. "We know it isn't just repeating the past, and it isn't just an impish spirit. If it looks the same to us all, and has the same behaviors with us all, isn't it safe to assume the same force is following all of us? If it can be spread like that, it's contagious, isn't it?"

"Why assume the figure of a girl?"

"To throw us off?" Devon suggested. "To make us let down our guard? It's brilliant, really. You would associate a beautiful girl with gentility, especially from a century ago. Who would expect that form to be a blood-thirsty demon?"

"Why does it need people to let their guard down?" She added.

Janelle stated, "So we would be open, in some way."

"Open to communication?" Matt leaned on his shovel.

"Most likely."

"Does it want us to leave?" Melanie asked.

"Apparently not. It wants us to see or hear something. I think Dahlia was telling the truth. Whatever has her form wants to show us something."

"I know the investigation just started, but I have the feeling we're on some sort of schedule." She couldn't bring herself to say she felt their time was so limited. Either they face what was coming, embrace it, and find a solution, or suffer.

"We're being timed." Alicia already knew.

"It feels like it. Does everyone else here feel it?"

Those who'd visited multiple times nodded, but the rest appeared unsettled by the admission. She had to maintain some kind of hope. Scott just told them many things. Maybe someone might say something relevant and give someone else an idea. It was her responsibility, anyway. She started the whole damned thing. She had to figure the mystery out before whatever was coming arrived.

The line of questioning brought about a sense of defeat instead of the hope she looked for. Janelle and Alicia remained equally silent as a hawk cried in the distance. The bird gracefully soared in circles overhead. Her mind returned to the little room on the top floor. That must've been the Red Room. Why did they choose that place to build their collection? Was it merely due to its privacy or was there another reason? It had to be a terrible life, enslaved to Elysium's activity.

Janelle seemed to be the most centered of the group. She was open on a level above most of them. She turned to her, "Janelle? What do you make of the circle?"

"I think it's one of the most significant elements. Someone was trying to do something, or did something, there."

"Did Scott tell you about the third-floor room?"

"No, I didn't." He looked up from the ground. "I didn't know it would be needed, but with Ash's disappearance, and this, I haven't had time."

Janelle encouraged Melanie to start at the beginning, and let everyone know what had happened since she moved in. That would bring everyone up to speed and provide a fresh perspective as a group.

It was eventually assumed that the little room was indeed the infamous Red Room. She told them about the wall of drawings and clippings, tucked away like a personal shrine. She then told them of the cache of books, loose papers, and newspaper clippings beneath the floorboards. Janelle dumped a bucket of fresh dirt into her filter, "I guess we can assume the original owners had no dealing with this?"

"I don't know what happened to the Rotherwoods. I couldn't find anything at the courthouse."

"Jeremiah Rotherwood?" Scott's unexpected expertise surfaced again. "He just moved to Tennessee. He eventually married and had several children. His home is a bed and breakfast now, or at least it used to be."

"So nothing abnormal occurred after the move, or went with him?" She called back to him.

"No, not as far as I know. He prospered in Kingsport, as his father had prospered in Bristol. They married into the King family, and you know who they were."

"What about the Blythe family?"

"As far as I know, Edgar lived a long and respectable life elsewhere. He was private, but they all were."

"But the massacre... that's the worst kind of energy to bring on a place, isn't it?" Devon argued.

"Yes, but there are no guarantees. You know that."

"What else could there be to cause all this?"

"Honestly?" Scott stuck the shovel in the ground and rested his folded arms on the top. "I think the Blythe family did something no one knew about, probably during the epidemic, and it had to be bad. Look at what they created here. I've seen things, and it doesn't look like anything from the Civil War era. Can you imagine the possibilities just from that single decade? One warped doctor who could've had a steady supply of victims? Or even a group of men claiming to enforce the law when they abused the position?"

"We're supposed to believe what the Blythes did was worse? A warped doctor? That sounds a little far-fetched. Look at how many witnesses would've been there." Matt argued.

She had to side with Matt, although Scott made some valid points. A sinister doctor seemed a bit preposterous given the number of sick at Elysium. A single family couldn't possibly enact the same evil, without a similar attack, and there wasn't one. Maybe the Manson family, but even they couldn't enact that kind of evil without witnesses. The building was a hospital. There would've been patients everywhere, not to mention the Blythe children.

"No, no, no. The Civil War attack brought negativity. I'll wager it started this. I'll give you that, but that's not what we're dealing with. This is something even more intense. No one has seen a single bushwhacker, not like the girl. No one has seen a burning piano or a burning house. We have photographs that look like the girl we're seeing."

"Really, Devon. Could anything be more intense than a massacre?" Janelle crossed her arms.

"Maybe not physically, but we aren't dealing with the physical... it's psychological and emotional."

The group didn't agree on much, but at least there were many opinions. It wasn't really a surprise. Of course everything came from the epidemic, from the Blythes. It was a case of the blind leading the blind when time was of the essence. Even a group of seasoned paranormal professionals were lost at Elysium.

Her gut told her it was Isabelle. Something happened with her. Logic protested because she was just a girl, and even if she was miserable enough to commit suicide, could it really compare to a brutal onslaught? No, it didn't seem possible.

Scott remained in concentration. His dark eyes were far off. He said, "Think of it this way, the attack in the 1850s came quickly.

The family died in one night. A few hours and they were all dead. Even if they were burned alive, it'll only last so long, especially with accelerants. Victims of the epidemic died over a prolonged period of time. There was utter agony for weeks, months, maybe years. What if this is a product from hundreds of people suffering? Intense regrets, bitter longings, and unfulfilled lives that slowly wasted away, when there was no way out, no cure, and only more illness every day."

"Maybe." Janelle nodded.

The men unearthed the bottom-most portion of the structure. "Now what?" Matt asked from the bottom of the hole. The structure's bottom lip was now visible, but still didn't offer any hint of what was inside. It was metal, as well. The flat, featureless exterior was ashen and scarred.

"Should we open it?" The decision was unanimously affirmative, but everyone had a different idea as to how to approach the task.

"We can't go through the roof," Devon felt the sides. "It's a solid sheet of metal, probably iron. The only way in would be to weld it open and if there is anything remotely fragile in there, the heat might destroy it. Plus, if it's solid iron, it might shatter with any temperature extreme."

Malcolm suggested. "We'll go in through the sides. We'll stop for the day since the sun is setting. My dad has a shed full of woodworking tools we can use."

They discussed the arrangements for the next day as if it was just another shift at work. Melanie watched the excited exchange, still amazed at the group's cooperation. It seemed impossible that so many people would help. That they would put their own lives on hold for someone else, without expecting anything in return.

Ash was found. He wasn't with them, but they knew he was okay. They didn't have any reason to continue, but they still volunteered to do so. She wasn't certain how she could ever repay their generosity.

"We'll see you tomorrow, Melanie." Janelle called from the group as they started back towards the house.

"I can't thank you all enough," Words were inadequate to express her feelings. "I would never have gotten this far alone." They all smiled and waved as they walked on.

"Well, we can't take humanitarian credit, Melanie." Matt stood by her, "We're hoping to gain something from this, too."

Alicia walked with Janelle and the others across the yard. She remained by the pit with Matt. He said, "You don't have to feel so indebted. I mean, we're all adults—no one twisted our arms to get involved. This is something we've learned a lot from. I don't know if you've considered it, but we're incredibly indebted to you. Paranormal groups all over America have attempted to investigate Elysium, unsuccessfully, for decades, but here we are. Our little group, from our little town, and we are the first. That is huge for our credibility."

"It's so much work." Her mind drifted to her mother's little vegetable garden. She planted a small garden in her mother's backyard after she moved into the community. Since she couldn't leave the house, she had visited her mother weekly to weed and care for the small patch of earth. Even that was laborious. This wasn't a little vegetable garden. It was an excavation.

He held her hand as they strolled towards the front of the house. "Well, I've enjoyed my time here."

"What is this?" She held her hand up with his attached. "What do we have?"

"Only time will tell."

They stopped at the last corner, and they kissed. Her heart leapt at his passion. He continued to embrace her, "Call me if you need me."

"Oh? And what if I don't need you?"

"Call me anyways."

"Aren't you supposed to do all the calling?"

"Why does it always fall on me?"

"Just because." She laid her head on his chest and listened to his heart race. His chest gently rose and fell, she was mesmerized by the familiarity. How something so foreign could feel so damned natural. Everything felt neatly in place, as if a million tiny events had crept by, unnoticed, to coincide within that moment.

It was wonderful to experience anything like love, or attraction, or whatever it was, again. She was always too busy to notice life's prior emptiness. There was never time to go out and meet people. When she had time, she was so exhausted she just wanted to rest.

She lingered at the corner of the house as he walked to the car. His Ford was the last vehicle to leave. Alicia stood ahead on the edge of the sidewalk. Melanie started towards her friend, but a noise behind her made her stop. It sounded like a campfire popped and cracked nearby.

She continued to listen, but no other noises accompanied it. Her body froze when she sensed something behind her. The campfire noise had softly morphed into a roar, the sickening, whirring noise. She knew she shouldn't look, but curiosity was too strong. She turned to see a sinister fire rage within the forest.

"Alicia!" She screamed as she darted towards the woods. She heard Alicia's quickly follow. They stopped at the glade's entrance as a ring of brilliant azure fire enveloped the uncovered circle. Alicia caught up to her and started to speak, but her words caught in her throat. She merely uttered a gasp.

"What is that?" Alicia finally whispered.

"I don't know." She returned. Her voice equally hushed. Who knew what could happen if noise disturbed the manifestation? It the most beautiful and terrifying display she had ever witnessed. It wasn't the typical blue that appears within a flame. It was an aggressive and volatile shade that didn't weaken or dissipate. This lingered, wanted to be seen.

"An electric blue ring...." Alicia sighed.

She couldn't speak. She couldn't move. She heard Alicia take a deep breath as the flame narrowed. The ring grew smaller and smaller until it vanished.

"Something happened there." She repeated, just as she did earlier. "I can't recall why I said that earlier. It was like sleepwalking, but I was aware. I know the group doesn't recommend psychics, Mel, but maybe we should at least try one. It couldn't hurt to just ask."

"Maybe."

"I know of one, but I'm not sure how legitimate she is. I don't know what else to do. We can't connect everything... We don't have time to pursue every event. We both know time is running out. How can we find substantial proof of anything that happened so long ago? You heard the group, they specialize in this shit, and even they are unsure."

"See if you can reach her, Alicia. I'll scour the books some more." She had to cling to hope even if it diminished with each second. She wrung her hands as they returned to the house. She couldn't stand the foreboding sense that time was running out. Her mind returned to that strange telephone call, when she believed Ash called. Who was that? It was someone who knew something and it was probably too late to ask.

Chapter 25

The sun's evening intensity filled the sky, but light made no difference. Countless professional investigators had reassured for years that the energy from sunlight interfered with paranormal energies. It was always the reason more activity occurred at night. The theory was rapidly losing credibility.

Ash was certain it was just her, but then another form came. The force they dealt with masqueraded as Isabelle but wasn't her. Likewise, there were no images from the pre-Civil War massacre, or any other time in Elysium's past. The child appeared randomly, every so often, a blond child in a frilly white dress.

Spirits always made their presence known. He was the most sensitive of the group and always had the strongest interactions. He was usually able to quickly determine what they dealt with.

The spirits in this situation were no exception, although they were deliberately vague. They wanted attention. They knew he could see them but refused to offer direction or reason for their activity. He wasn't as comfortable with his abilities now that Elysium was involved. It didn't matter in a standard haunted house but made a grave difference at Elysium.

He was the bookworm of the group, but commonly accepted concepts or procedures didn't apply with Elysium. Spirits seldom had the capacity to follow the living. They rarely attached to people, in any regard. People were temporary, ever evolving, the polar opposite of a structure or a patch of land. People couldn't be haunted, as houses were, but this was Elysium and had its own set of rules.

He briefly communicated with Matt the night before. They couldn't cover much. Matt was at work, and he was still searching for answers, himself. They briefly touched upon the ongoing investigation at Elysium.

Full investigations normally required weeks to arrange, sometimes months. For the first time, in all their years as a group, everyone was free at the same time. It was no more logical than Melanie's abrupt fortune, but he didn't believe anything happened by chance or coincidence.

Elysium somehow influenced those lottery numbers. He wouldn't admit it, but the force at Elysium obviously admired her as much as she did the estate. That abyss had indeed stared back, to paraphrase Nietzsche. The final question was that of motive. *Why* did it want Melanie there?

They knew of the massacre and the epidemic. None of the old information seemed to provide an adequate account, and that is what they needed. He hadn't counted on bizarre creatures, crawling things, and spirits of all shapes.

It had previously appeared as Isabelle, a man, several monsters, and the last solid manifestation was of a little girl in a white dress. He hadn't encountered any activity from the established events. The men weren't wearing the tattered, filthy clothing of highwaymen. Their clothes were clean and in good condition. The group openly attacked, so there was violence. They weren't sick. There was no coughing or indications of disease.

Regardless of the society's policy, there was no need for collective opinion here. The presence was indeed intelligent, deliberate, and malevolent. There hadn't been any major renovations of the physical property to justify the contempt it held for the living. It hadn't been disturbed. Melanie probably thought the estate was the most beautiful place in the world, and would hesitate to change anything, anyways.

Any possible enemy from life would have died long ago, so that discredited the idea of intelligent vengeance. The activities had to be an attempt at communication. If the force hated people so much, it would just kill them. There was a stark possibility that it didn't even know why it was enraged.

The earlier telephone call with the professor replayed in his mind. "I have an urgent situation pertaining to the Elysium estate."

"Please call my office. I'll be happy to see you next week."

"Dr. Malcolm, we don't have that kind of time."

"My deepest regrets, then."

"I noticed you staring at Elysium the other day. Is that a habit?"

"Excuse me?"

"I'm close friends with the owners. It's fascinating that you have such a strange interest in the home. Is it the structure... or its female occupants?"

"Well— I've never—" His haughty voice grew indignant.

"Stop it, Malcolm. I know it was you." He caught the doctor before he raised his voice further. "Look, we're in desperate trouble. I fear for our lives. We already know much, but not enough. I don't want to harass you, but this is an emergency. None of us knew what we were getting into. You may be the only person who can help us."

There was an extended pause on the other end of the line. He'd feared Malcolm had already hung up, but he answered, "Come to my house in the morning...."

It was an exceedingly small victory. After all, there was no promise that even Malcolm could do anything. He never wanted to resort to accusations of voyeurism, but there was no choice. He would clear his conscious when he spoke with the professor.

Alicia was already a day ahead of him into Elysium, and he had to clear it up before the time came. Whatever was coming would come for her as soon as it did Melanie. They didn't have a week. There was nothing else. Regardless. There wasn't a week or even a day to waste. It was coming.

Chapter 26

Alicia hoped she remembered correctly. She grinned when she found her number in the search engine. Moonsong Edwards was the only commercial psychic in town. Her occupation garnered her fame as much as notoriety. She waited as patiently as possible, but the line kept ringing. She started to press the end button when an out-of-breath woman picked up the other end. She recited her introduction with a slight Hungarian accent.

Alicia exchanged greetings, but Edwards wasn't receptive or concerned. "I do not perform home tours or inspections. If you want a consultation, please call during regular hours, Monday through Friday, between nine in the morning and four in the evening."

"We don't need a consultation... we need answers."

"Let me guess." she huffed, obviously accustomed to emergencies that weren't really emergencies. "Is it man trouble? You're getting married and want to know if he's the one? You want to know if you are having a boy or girl? What could possibly be so urgent?"

"My friend purchased Elysium—"

"The estate? You are calling me from Elysium... *the* Elysium property?" The accent softened with her excitement.

"Yes. I'm helping her move in and there's something going on."

"Damn straight. Are you free?"

"Now?"

"Yes—now. I'm in the area."

"Sure. When is the best time?"

"I'm on my way. If I have permission to use my work in the home for a reference, my visit will be free."

"Thank you. That sounds great—" The other end of the line clicked. She didn't wait for a response, but maybe Edwards could steer them in the right direction. At least she might provide specific time, or even a name. Something concrete is what they need. Maybe it was Isabelle's form, or maybe it was Isabelle herself. They needed confirmation, either way.

A low growl deep within her stomach broke her concentration. She returned to the kitchen to eat something before Edwards arrived. "Those things are going to make you cross-eyed." She tried to distract her, but Melanie barely nodded.

She didn't like her growing interest in those books. They'd already been through them. Melanie poured over the books as if her life depended on it. It wasn't healthy. No matter how deep she dove into that history, nothing w3ould come of it. What they needed to find just wasn't in those old volumes.

Her eye caught the exposed roof of the box in the back yard as she walked to the cabinets. The big, charred box with no entrance or exit. For all they knew, it was filled to the brim with corpses of countless epidemic victims.

She hadn't vouched her opinion, but the illness seemed more likely to cause a haunting. Gruesome murders were awful. There was no dismissing that cruelty or agony, but to waste away over months had to be worse. You didn't just endure brutality. You endured fear and panic because death approached, and no one could help. That didn't even take any physical pain into consideration. That was purely mental and psychological anguish.

If the box's builder had taken the time to seal the container with elaborate scrollwork, they should've added something about the contents. A brief message of what happened, even if it was just a few words to bring respect and honor to the dead? It was absolutely backwards to decorate a grave and not identify those buried.

Chapter 27

Melanie ate sparingly as she flipped through the books. Again. It felt like the most important piece of the puzzle was there, in plain sight, but she lacked the ability to see it. A single element permanently bound everything into a fragmented picture. She was doing the best she could with the misshapen pieces, but it wasn't promising.

How could Isabelle relate to a ring of fire, from before the Civil War, nearly a half century before she was born? She was a suicide, but she hung herself. Ultimately, there was no connection with the events aside from simple death. The dreams clearly indicated some kind of attack, but there wasn't any documentation anywhere supporting a similar attack after the Blythe family purchased the property.

Isabelle's death posed another dilemma. Why hang herself? What reason would a girl, who had everything, possibly find for suicide? It had to be the epidemic. Maybe she was infected and hung herself rather than suffer. Even if the motive were that simple, suicide was scorned in that era. Many places wouldn't bury suicides in a proper cemetery for fear of desecration.

Alicia laid her hand on the book. "Have you heard anything I've said?"

"Sorry, I was into this."

"You don't need to be. Guess what?"

"What?"

"I got her. She's coming over."

"Now?"

"Yes, now! She refused to hear anything until I told her where we were. Everyone wants a piece of Elysium."

"Maybe that'll provide something." She heard scraping from an empty mayonnaise jar and the crinkle of the bread bag.

247

Sandwiches were adequate but not satisfying. "We'll order pizza when she leaves."

They finished their snacks in silence. She waited for whispers from the hall, but none came. There were no sounds at all. It was too quiet. She suddenly suspected the house listened to her, as studiously as she listened to it.

It wasn't long before a knock came at the door. Alicia put her plate in the sink on her way to answer it. She followed. A woman in muted gypsy garb stood on the porch, her chin held high. Her icy blue eyes glared. *Well, someone apparently had to fit a stereotype, at some point.* She hoped, at least, her abilities were genuine. "Hello, I'm Ms. Edwards." She had a thick foreign accent.

"Hello, Ms. Edwards." She held out her hand. "I'm Melanie Smallwood, welcome to Elysium."

The stranger shook her hand and looked her squarely in the eyes, "You have an old soul."

"Um... Thank you." She awkwardly opened the door for the psychic.

"This is an amazing home with an amazing history." She inspected the premises as she entered. "How long have you been here?"

"Just about a week. Actually, we know quite a bit of the history, it's the activity that has us alarmed."

"The activity is strong. I could feel it outside."

"I don't suppose you might've gleaned any details as to what it is?"

"That would require a séance. Are you prepared to hold one?"

"I am unfamiliar with most aspects of the paranormal, Ms. Edwards." Melanie led the visitor towards the kitchen. "How, exactly, do you prepare for one?"

"I need a table and a dark room. You can just draw the curtains if you don't have a room without windows."

"Do you need anything else?"

"Yes, three lit candles in the center of a round table."

She gave Edwards a glass of iced tea to drink while they prepared the room. The psychic sat on a stool and looked over the room. She hadn't removed the heavy draperies from the parlor. She carried the candles in the room with Alicia behind her. They drew the heavy fabric panels to shut out the sun. They pulled a table to the center of the room and sat three chairs around it. They lit three white emergency candles and sat them in the center of the table.

Ms. Edwards had given into temptation by the time they returned. She scoured the pages in the books on the table. "It's all here, isn't it?"

"What?"

"The origins of it all."

"We suspect that."

"I'm telling you it is," she gave a curt smile. "Is the room ready?"

"Yes."

She followed them into the parlor. "Many things have been plotted here; you know."

Melanie looked at her for a moment. "No, we didn't know that. Maybe you can provide insight as to what it was."

They sat around the table and linked hands. Ms. Edwards began moving her beaded head in a circle. "Spirits come and say what you will. Say what you need to find peace."

She felt ridiculous, absurd, and completely flabbergasted. How could this possibly have a constructive outcome? The woman wore what bordered on a Halloween costume. She moaned and jerked her head repeatedly. She was ready to stand and order her out of the home when the air changed.

She couldn't see anything, but she felt it. The room became unbearably humid, just like in the cave with Matt. The once-fresh parlor air grew heavy and stagnant. The psychic now sounded like she was choking.

She studied her. This was no act. Edwards's eyes had rolled back in their sockets. Her face was ashen and drawn. "I am here." Her voice had become gravely and ethereal.

"Who are you?" Alicia looked suspicious. "What are you doing?"

"You must learn the secret."

"What secret?"

"It burns... burns so much."

"Who are you?" Alicia nearly yelled.

"Just a girl... I can't leave." The merciless voice subsided for a moment and the psychic whimpered.

"What do you want?"

There was silence and Ms. Edwards began violently coughing. She carried on for five minutes, unable to breathe, gasping when she could. Her face turned as purple as Taylor's when she signed the paperwork. "Smoke is everywhere." The deep and sinister tone came through far more forceful than the other. "I am here...." It began. "Everyone will see what happened."

"What happened?" She beat Alicia to it. "What are we supposed to see? Please tell us."

"A horrible crime. They killed me. They killed us... and got away with it. They were never punished. All will be punished, now."

"All?"

"For what they took from me."

"How did they take it?"

"They murdered us all."

"Who murdered you? The soldiers? From the Civil War?"

"My family."

"Please, tell us who you are."

"Isabelle knows... Felix knows... The Black Riders... Murderers. Thieves. Highwaymen...."

"Please let us fix it." Melanie stood without breaking the circle. "Please leave us alone."

"Only one way. Unite us. Unite us and let us be...." The girl's voice went silent. Ms. Edwards's head fell back. For a moment, she worried the experience had killed the psychic. Suddenly, she snapped upright. "What happened?" Her congested voice rasped.

"How would we know?" Alicia looked warily at her. "You're the one talking."

"I don't know what happened." Edwards stood and stumbled back from the table. The accent was gone, and she spoke with a Southern drawl. "What's going on?" Her chair fell over, and she continued backing up until she hit the fireplace.

Her eyes were wild and panicked. She stopped only long enough to grab her purse. She held it close to her body and nearly ran for the front door. "Leave this place. Leave this place and never return." She threw open the front door so hard it slammed against the wall. Her footfall darted down the hall and out the front door.

"Well, damn... back to square one."

"I guess that's why Ash didn't support bringing one in."

"Do you suppose something spooked her?" Alicia smirked.

"I don't know... maybe."

"Should we send her a card?"

"Definitely. We should express our deepest regrets."

"Our most sincere condolences."

"She can say she helped, sort of. What did they know? Isabelle, the Riders, they all knew about it, whatever it is." They walked into the living room. Alicia resumed her position on the opposite couch, and they flipped through the channels.

Despite a staggering number of channels, the television did a poor job of diversion, but anything was better than the house's foreboding silence. She held her breath when she heard the whispers start. Something was going to happen. Soon, a repetitive banging noise resounded from the back yard. "Shit, not again." She stood and walked towards the noise.

"Melanie? Again?" Alicia followed. "What are you talking about? I think something broke. I heard something in the yard."

"I have my suspicions." They crept to the backdoor without turning any of the lights on in the kitchen. Enough light poured in from the hall to illuminate what was needed. There was no need to search for a weapon. She couldn't think of any weapon that might help. She followed this pattern from previous night's dream. Who knew what it would be tonight? She flipped on the patio lights.

Alicia followed as they stole out the back door. It seemed like a false alarm. A subtle jingling sound was somewhere away from the house but approached. As her eyes adjusted to the darkness, she caught sight of what they'd heard. Alicia walked into her, and they were both knocked off balance. "Oh, God," she covered her mouth with her hand.

A horse approached from beneath the overhang of the trees. At least, it had once been a horse. She couldn't imagine what it was now, but she knew it wasn't alive. It couldn't be. The steed wasn't a pitiful ghostly animal with pale flesh or ashen colors. Its half-bony tail had slapped the branches of trees as it came through.

The animal's wet lesions and blisters clustered across the flanks. The gruesome wounds shone in the porch light. Raw exposed muscle glistened with the animal's movement beneath the deeper wounds. The whinny wasn't that of a horse, but a raspy, enraged growl. *Please go away, please disappear.* Alicia's hand tightened around her own as they held onto one another. Opaque lines of smoke emanated from its back.

The clinking sound grew louder as the horse approached. The jingle of reigns was barely audible once they exited the house. It grew louder as a carriage approached. The crack of a cruel whip made the animal walk faster, the strips of leather on the bridle slung gore as the driver yanked them back.

A few seconds later, the misshapen black carriage came fully into the light. It was as deformed and malevolent as the animal and carried an equally deformed rider. She couldn't breathe, let alone speak as they passed. Alicia had gone as white as cream. The solid black carriage appeared to have been burned as badly as the steed.

Its exterior was injured. The body of the carriage had gory wounds just like those on the horse. Tendrils of white smoke wafted from the carriage.

The driver's black clothes were covered in ash and his body smoked, like the horse. The macabre procession came to a stop in front of them. The driver's head turned with a wet, cracking noise. "Where is she?" The driver slowly looked in Alicia's direction. She couldn't describe it, but even his voice was slimy.

"Wh... Who?" She barely got it out.

"I'm looking for her... Issssabelle." The driver hissed. "I looked everywhere... for you." His head turned towards Melanie. Her heart sank in her chest.

"I'm not Isabelle." She whimpered. Alicia tightly hugged her. This must be it. This must be what happened when time had run out.

"Yes, you are. I know you. You have her mark." The driver sinisterly laughed. "We'll be together soon... my bride."

He yanked on the reigns and the horse returned towards the caves. The whip resounded again, and the horse roared in response. She was right there. He was right there, but he didn't take her.

"Alli," she sniffed. "What's happening?" The air was thick with the smell of smoke and decay.

"We'll figure this out. We both saw him at the same time. It wasn't a hallucination, we saw him. Look..." she pointed downward.

The hoof prints and the wagon's wheel imprints had left smoking impressions in the ground. "What was that?" She could barely force words out. The relief at escaping the wagon morphed into incapacitating fear at what awaited her, at what awaited them. She would be the first to succumb to whatever Elysium unleashed—she was the first to contract it.

"We need someone else here." Alicia tugged her arm back towards the kitchen. "Where's Matt's number?"

"...on the pad beside the books." She trembled as she followed her into the kitchen. She poured two glasses of whiskey while Alicia dialed the number. She spilled some on the counter but didn't bother to wipe it up. She couldn't do anything. She felt faint and dizzy.

She half-staggered to the table and dropped in the nearest chair. She just bought a house. She didn't bargain for a demon. She didn't think anything was wrong with it. She quickly wiped away her tears as they seeped from her eyes. *What have you done, Isabelle? Why? What did I do to you? What...?* Her mind raced so loudly she barely heard anything else.

The worst part of the ordeal was the familiarity. Despite the gore and smoke, the driver was familiar. She didn't dare let Alicia, or anyone else, know. Why did she feel such an urge to step into the carriage? It was brief, but it was there. *What is wrong with me?* A trip in that carriage would be damn-near instant death, but the feeling was akin to the one she'd gotten from the box in the pit.

Alicia continued her conversation, but she didn't listen. Why wouldn't her mind stop? She didn't want Matt to leave work early. So many needed him more. She finally sat the phone down, "He's coming over around midnight. He said he'd stay on the couch or wherever we had room. He wanted to see what was happening, as it happened."

She sat beside her at the table and downed half the glass of wine. "I told him about Madam Fake-psychic."

"What did he think?"

She bit her lip before she spoke. She always did that if she wanted to consider her words. "We might've made it mad."

"Oh, that's all we need."

"But he also said the driver might've offered a hint. It said you were Isabelle... that you had a mark."

"I'm terrified."

"He'll help, Melanie. They won't abandon us."

"I know."

"He really likes you, Melanie." She was the second person to voice it, but she didn't need to hear it. She wasn't in a good place and had no hope of being in a good place. Besides, he wasn't exactly falling over himself for her. They were good friends, and she enjoyed him, but she couldn't believe he liked her that much. No one liked her that much. She doubted if Aiden really liked her that much.

"I know he likes me, and I like him, too. I would be happier, Alicia, but right now I'm bound to... to this thing. I can't do anything until I see what is going on here."

"I don't think you realize how much he likes you. You should've heard him. I'm so happy. I didn't think you'd find anyone after Aiden."

"It's sweet... it is. I would love to return that affection. I just don't see it."

"Humph... you just aren't accustomed to male attention, not that any of us are. Trust me. You had nothing but work for so long I think your social skills have suffered."

"Probably." She swallowed the last of her drink.

She poured another drink of whiskey in her glass. She was probably oblivious to the subtleties of the opposite sex. She was hardly experienced when it came to men. She hadn't dated in years.

She loved men. She loved being in a relationship, but it had been impossible for so long. She was wiped out after sixty hours a week with Fillmore. Fillmore had been her man. Matt was certainly a welcome distraction from Elysium. And memories of Fillmore.

A relationship just wasn't possible right now. She couldn't think of it. None of them may live long enough to enjoy anything. Dreams of the beach may never come to fruition. They might die with her.

They walked into the living room and resumed their positions from the night of drinking and merriment. The spirit of mirth had long since fled Elysium's cathedral ceilings. Alicia flipped through the channels as she dwelt on the evening. What was hidden in the driver's words? She didn't look like Isabelle. She'd never even known anyone named Blythe. Where, or how, was she marked? It had to be the mark on her arm. She couldn't begin to imagine any other connection.

She secretly longed for those days of logic at the Happiness. Life was simple and concrete, with no need for abstracts or theories. She didn't have to dig through someone else's past in a desperate search for today's truth. There was only one concrete, tangible truth at that moment, and time was closing in.

She had a terrible feeling the next time the death coach came, wouldn't be a false alarm. She fluffed the oversized pillow behind her and rested her crown against the softness. Maybe the final event was an innate, irresistible compulsion to climb in that carriage.

The television droned on, but she just heard silence. Waiting in constant and malignant dread was the worst part. Every time Elysium showed her something, it was horrific. A knock came at the front door around twelve-thirty. "That's probably Matt." Alicia stood to answer it.

"Look out the window first. I answered it the other day and there wasn't anyone outside. After what happened earlier, I... I don't want you or anyone else taking chances."

A wave of heated resentment crept through her. She had enough of Elysium's games. She was sick of the puzzle. Yes, it was beautiful, but it wasn't worth it. She could sell it and have a nice house elsewhere. There were entire counties full of houses for sale, just in the region, but she just didn't have the heart... or the guts.

Elysium was contagious. The thing that haunted the grounds was contagious. She could pass the house on, but she would also pass on the symptoms to innocent people. That is exactly what it wanted, and she would not allow that. She would not pass the virus along and help the entity spread. Besides, there was no guarantee the weird shit wouldn't just follow her, and no promise the new residents would survive.

Matt walked into the living room, "Melanie? Are you okay?" He sat on the end of the couch with her. She sat up to face him.

"I'm as well as can be."

"Tell me everything. What happened?"

"Alicia already told you..."

"I want to hear it in your words, about Ms. Edwards, about everything...."

She told him of the brilliant ring in the circle when the group left. She gave the full story of Edwards's unsuccessful visit what happened when the psychic spoke in those two terrible voices. She slowed when she arrived at the horseman's visit, it was still so vivid. She almost told him about the urge to jump inside.

He didn't speak for a few moments, and she didn't ask him to. He could be angry with her because she'd consulted a psychic against their recommendations. He might be angry that she moved into the house in the first place, with no regard to research or history.

She sighed, "I wanted to apologize." She moved both her feet to the floor. The fine-grained wood was cold beneath her feet.

"Apologize for what?"

"You're missing work... and... just everything. If I hadn't been so stubborn to get this place, none of this would've happened. It's my fault."

"You have it completely backwards." Matt laughed and shook his head. "Don't you see how perfect it is? I mean there are no coincidences... everything has a purpose."

"Perfect? Come again?" He was trying to help, but there was no purpose, no divine intervention. Nothing was going to save them.

"It couldn't have happened at a better time. Say you hadn't bought this place, eventually someone would have, right?" He scooted closer and took her hand.

"Yes, the previous owners were eager to get rid of it."

"What if it hadn't been you? What if it had been someone in more complicated circumstances?"

"What do you mean?"

"What if an elderly person bought this place? What if a large family had? Just viewing what Elysium has showed you could injure or kill someone of advanced age, not to mention any caregivers or family. And imagine what it could do to a growing child? Think about it. What if a family had purchased Elysium and the children witnessed what you have? Wouldn't that have scarred them?"

"But you're all involved, and you have families. Isn't Scott married? What about his family?"

"His family is perfectly healthy, as is Ash's mother. I talked to her myself. She'd be ready to admit if something abnormal were harassing her, but nothing had happened. Don't forget, it only targets people who visit the house."

"But Ash—"

"Ash is doing something. I know him. He's resourceful and working on something. He doesn't want to risk the involvement of others. I didn't get to tell him it was too late... I mean, we're already involved."

"Isn't that my fault?"

"Enough of this negativity. I trust him. If there's a solution to be found elsewhere, he'll find it."

"The psychic said, when she was in that weird trance, Isabelle, the Riders, and all of them knew about it, whatever it was."

"I've thought about that all day. I think Scott and Devon have a point. Why is the activity so localized? Dahlia is most likely the little girl who disappeared in the '40s. She's here and accounted for. What about the Rotherwood family? The slaves? The animals? Considering all that, it would corroborate what the psychic said. They all knew the home's history. Any owner would have known what happened during the marauders' attack. That only happened a few decades earlier then. If the spectral carriage driver said he was looking for Isabelle, I think we need to focus on her."

"I have some notes." She stood. "What do we need?"

"Aside from the books and your notes? A hot cup of coffee."

They all entered the kitchen and Alicia started the coffee. They gathered around the table to again trudge through familiar stacks of books and papers. The house might've been new, but she'd already forgotten what it was like to have a clear table.

"The one element that links everything is Isabelle. I believe it is her, despite the differences in the photographs. You have both seen Dahlia, but neither of us have. If she were involved, we would all see her, too. We'll rule her out as having a connection to the darkness here. Janelle was probably right, and Dahlia was just another victim. We need names. Who surrounded Isabelle in life?"

"There was a picture at the courthouse of Isabelle with a group of young men. I thought they might be suitors or relatives, it didn't say. I have a copy here, somewhere."

"What else?"

"They have a full album on the Blythe family. One of the pictures was of a man named, "Heath Buckner.""

"Buckner? Doesn't ring a bell."

"I thought the same thing." Alicia flipped through another book quietly, from the other side of the table.

Melanie started on her second book. "So, we've narrowed a time period down. What else can we try?"

"Do you have internet access?"

"Yea, but it isn't connected. My laptop's still in the box over there." She pointed to the topmost box on the stack at the end of the dining room. She'd wanted a computer for years, and now that she had one, she hadn't even set it up.

"I can get it running. We'll look up Edgar. I've never known any article to mention details of his whereabouts or what happened after Elysium."

"I have an article here that says he was attacked in the caves." She began flipping through books and papers.

"Do they know who it was?"

"No, the article didn't confirm anything."

"Okay. We know he left right after he gave Andrew the place as a wedding gift. No one discussed what happened to him, as far as I know. Andrew told everyone he moved to a warmer climate due to his health."

"I wonder if anything happened while Andrew was in charge."

"I guess so. They apparently moved to another home in the fifties, I believe. Elysium was just a spare home in the Blythe family since then."

"Where'd you hear all this?"

"I've done some homework, myself. I hope you don't mind."

"As long as it isn't me doing the work, it's cool." She smiled. "Please do what you can." Matt quickly sat everything up at the table. They gathered around the monitor.

"Pull up a search engine and we'll see if we can find anything on Edgar." Alicia spoke over his shoulder.

"Didn't you research him before?" Melanie glanced at him in question.

"Well, no.... I mean he left the property after around two decades, and the property is precisely what interested us. I never considered we might learn anything from him."

She slid a stack of books over as he opened the system on the table. She and Alicia pulled up chairs on either side of him to watch. His long fingers quickly moved about the small keyboard with rapid dexterity. He typed in Edgar's name and location. At first, there wasn't anything relevant to Elysium. The location was included, but they received page after page of results from around the country.

A message board, hidden deep within the results, had seemingly obscure paranormal information. The website titled "Seeking Ghosts" discussed paranormal interests in Louisville, Kentucky. They featured an article titled, "Edgar's Blight." She studied the text:

"Our group seeks information on a recent discovery. We located numerous records for the now derelict Waverly Asylum, in Louisville, Kentucky. In 1918, a patient named Edgar Blythe, had some astounding experiences. Rumors link Blythe to the Elysium plantation in Bristol, Virginia, but we can't confirm this. We know Blythe was wealthy and once owned an estate in Virginia. Information is limited. If possible, we hope to visit Bristol to locate records on this individual and confirm the connection between Blythe and the infamous estate.

"Blythe had one hell of a case of dementia, a new term at that time, in addition to a terminal case of tuberculosis. It's the only case we have located where the patient's 'ailments' forced his physician to resign. Apparently, Edgar's real "contagion" was rumored to be a ghost. Blythe was admitted for insanity and paranoia, attributed to late-stage dementia, but the illness passed on to the psychologist. The few records of sightings describe a girl, labeled a "hallucination," who followed Blythe constantly.

"After a year, Dr. Nichols began to see her, too. A personal letter from his effects surfaced after we launched our investigation. He admitted he watched her follow Blythe on several occasions at the asylum and she followed him soon after. She appeared from nowhere and wore a disgusting dress.

"Nichols returned to his native New York, after his resignation, but it wasn't enough. The remaining years of his life was spent in seclusion. If you have any information on the people mentioned here, please contact us...."

Her heart leapt within her chest. They may not know everything at that point, but it was comforting to know it happened before. There was a history. Some kind of documentation supported the events, even if it was vague. The activity didn't start until Edgar. The Rotherwood family never experienced problems because there weren't any. There might've been minor presences from the attack, but none was akin to whatever Blythe unleashed.

"So what does it do?" Matt wondered aloud. "It just follows people for the rest of their lives?"

"I don't think so," she replied. "I don't see that as the ultimate goal. Maybe Edgar refused to see it. I think it wants to tell us about something that happened."

"What did the psychic say again?"

"When she was in her trance, she said someone killed them. She also said it was their family. She mentioned the Black Riders."

"So, it comes from another murder. Who was murdered at Elysium? The Black Riders were law enforcers."

"Judging from the past, I'd say you can flip a coin. The thing accused someone of murder, of being a highwayman, but the evening wasn't in vain. At least, we have a specific time period to explore."

"No, it's been productive. I think we can eliminate the Rotherwood history. That eliminates any residual energy from the attack. We know many died from illness, but illness isn't *murder*. A person has disappeared on these premises, but even that isn't necessarily murder."

"So, it is Isabelle." Alicia sat her mug on the table. "She wants to say something to us. Didn't you say, Melanie, you felt a weird connection with her photograph?"

"Yes, but that doesn't mean anything."

"Have you ever tried communicating with it?"

"Are you nuts? What was that thing in the carriage?"

"You're probably right. Never mind. We don't want to communicate."

Matt crossed his arms. He leaned back and his blue eyes drifted to the ceiling. "Let's run down what we know. How did Isabelle die?"

"A broken neck."

"Natural or inflicted?"

"It was self-inflicted. I saw her hanging in the trees outside before she grabbed my arm."

"Doesn't it seem odd that an influential man, like Edgar, wouldn't do more for his daughter's death? I still have issues with that."

"Meaning?"

"There should've been a memorial, statuary, something special to commemorate her memory, or at least something on her grave."

"Well, take your pick. Someone amassed a load of stuff." She waved her hand across the stacks of materials.

"No, no. If there were records like that, they would be in what we've found, don't you believe?"

"Yes."

"Where is she buried?"

"There's no record."

"What are her funeral details?"

"Who knows?"

"Daughters of wealthy men don't just disappear. They aren't hidden. There are elaborate tombstones, grand memorials, something. Even if it were suicide, a loving father would have lied. She fell down steps, she fell from a swing, or she was sleepwalking and fell; anything to make it look respectable."

"Maybe it's at her grave?"

"So, where is she buried?"

"I.... I don't know." The concept of a physical grave hadn't crossed her mind. Edgar hid his daughter's death. "None of the articles mention a burial."

"Same here." Alicia glanced up from her papers.

"But she had to be buried somewhere."

"Isn't it odd?" Matt said. "What happens when any young girl dies? People leave flowers, balloons, gifts, you name it. You didn't get richer than Edgar Blythe at that time. They should have statues, fountains, massive headstones, marble benches, anything. Epidemic or not, you don't have to be near a body to set up memorials."

"Maybe it's coincidence."

"Maybe. Or maybe foul play was involved."

"But, why?" Melanie swirled the last sip of coffee around the bottom of the cup. Fathers didn't murder their children back then. The very idea seemed preposterous. Parents did today, but the world was self-centered today. Family was the greatest threat to Narcissists.

They ran through theories as hours passed. Isabelle must've betrayed her father. Edgar might have frequented brothels, as many businessmen did during the era. He could've gambled too much or been addicted to something. He might've been abusive, and she retaliated.

She wondered if the ordeal involved Heath, in some way. Edgar could've hated Buckner, hated his family. Perhaps it was something as simple as consummating the relationship before marriage. By the time 3:00 came, even the coffee wasn't keeping them awake. They called it a night, in hopes that ideas would be stirred by sleep.

Matt volunteered to sleep on the couch in case there was activity outside. She left Alicia in the bedroom beside her own. She curled up under the comforter in the soft bed. If only she could see what happened to Isabelle. Why wouldn't the force or presence give some sort of detail as to what it wanted to say or what it wanted them to do? If she had a connection, as Matt and Ash described, she should be able to divine with clarity.

The earlier conversation churned in her brain. Why was it so hard to find information on her death? She drifted over an ocean of softness as her tumultuous mind calmed. *Where are you, Isabelle?* She wanted to talk to the girl, the tortured spirit that had whimpered through the psychic, before the beast took over.

She opened her eyes in a washed-out world. Everything from the grass to the distant mountains was pale and faded, even the sunshine was stale. Masculine voices drifted from nearby trees. She crept towards people, but instinctively knew she needed to stay out of sight.

"What do we do with them?"

"Burn them, in the pit, with the other maggots." An authoritative voice ordered.

"Sir? Shouldn't we give her a proper burial?"

"I'll not bury that worthless whore. Look at how she died... shameful. I'll not disgrace a reputable cemetery with such a pathetic deviant."

"Sir? I would never question your decision, but I am curious as to how you will do this. She's your daughter... won't the community talk?"

A low and brutal laugh dismissed the worrier. "Community? What community? The community's dead. They all died beneath my roof. What's one or two more? No, she'll get a headstone, but no rest. She can spend eternity in the pit... with her peddler."

Something stepped behind her. She whirled to see something coming towards her. It looked human, but walked backwards on all fours, like a crab, with its belly up. Its skin was white. Its head had been viciously pulled under its body; its scalp sat against its spine. The windpipe was blackened and rotted out in spots. The arms and legs, bent like a human's, were inhumanly emaciated.

It gargled and choked as it neared. Black gunk gushed out of the wounds on its throat with each guttural sound. She backed up until the tree branches caught in her hair and poked her shoulder. It wouldn't stop; the thing crawled towards her.

She stepped through the branches to run, but two creatures stood there with shovels. She'd almost collided with them before she caught herself. The humanoid figures had normal arms and legs, even stood at normal height for men. From the neck up, they were horribly deformed.

The two male beings had massive hands with no fingernails. The taller creature wore an ashen top hat, bushy white sideburns on his otherwise blank face. She knew he was Edgar, somehow. He didn't have eyes or a nose. Black sores lined his throat, and his mouth was an open wound. That mouth... that rotted mouth, her stomach heaved.

The other being had a correctly placed mouth, but it was abnormally wide. It literally stretched from one misshapen ear to the other, in a lunatic's grin. His cloudy skin resembled a sheet of dingy plastic, stretched across purple and black veins. Its eyes were solid black gashes, barely visible under the filthy derby pulled down to its ears. His gray, rotted teeth were jagged. The mouth didn't move to talk, but she clearly heard them. The two closed in on her as slowly as the crawling monster on the other side of the trees.

She tried to figure out what they were as she retreated the other way. Why was the taller creature Edgar? She got the same sense that the thing in the derby was Heath, but the creatures didn't resemble their human counterparts. She couldn't scream. She couldn't find the air to breathe. Everything was fuzzy and instable. She felt faint.

The Crawler made it to her before she could move any further before she'd even realized it followed her. It grabbed her calf. Its touch burned like fire, and scorching heat shot up her leg into her hip. The bones in her left leg felt like molten iron pokers. She was on fire. She finally found the breath to scream, she screamed as loudly as possible. She woke to Alicia shaking her shoulders, "Melanie! Wake up! It's not real!"

She gasped as she sat up, she swallowed hard. She could still feel the Crawler's hand. She furiously rubbed her calf. "Oh, God, it touched me."

"What touched you?"

"That... thing... It touched me. It was disgusting."

"It was just a dream."

Bare feet thudded up the stairwell and bounded down the hardwood flooring in the hall. Matt appeared at the threshold. "What's going on?"

"Nightmares." Alicia shrugged.

"Melanie?" He entered the room and sat down next to her on the edge of the bed. "Tell me what happened."

"I was standing in this pale, faded area. Everything was washed out...." She described the dreamscape and the two talking monsters. She described the creatures as best she could and the agonizing sensation from their touch.

"She really was murdered...." he trailed off into oblivion.

"He buried her? Himself? Where?" Alicia thought aloud. "Where would he bury her?"

"The salt circle?" Melanie snapped her fingers. "The pit! That's it. That is where it's all coming from."

"What should we do?"

"Give her a proper burial? Maybe she can't rest until we do."

"Are you sure?" Alicia looked uneasy. "That's a lot of work, and a lot of time lost, if it isn't the answer."

"We can only try."

She fell back onto the pillows. "I don't think I've ever been so exhausted."

"I'm staying in here with you." Alicia tugged the covers back on the opposite side of the bed.

"All is clear down below." Matt stood. "I'll go back to the couch and keep watch."

"Thank you, Matt." She smiled as she drifted off to welcome sleep. She didn't think she would ever want to close her eyes again, not after that dream. She nearly asked him to sleep in the bed with her. She knew nothing frightening would happen if he were there, but then again, Alicia wouldn't appreciate it.

Chapter 28

He turned onto Interstate 81 and dodged two barreling rigs that drove as if the speed limit didn't apply to them. It was time to visit Malcolm. He followed the exit and drifted down to the intersection. He prayed the right words would come.

If Malcolm didn't provide answers, there was nowhere left to go. It was too late. None of the Blythe descendants had public numbers, and it would take weeks to locate where they lived. As far as he knew, most of them were in gated communities, so it wasn't as if you could drop by.

He turned into the nondescript Cedar View subdivision. He searched Ames Street for the correct house number. Now that time was closing in, he noticed many things he'd overlooked before. Most of the subdivisions in the region were the same. Just like this one. The only real difference between the houses were the numbers. All of them had similarly paved drives and nearly identical mailboxes.

Every house was brick with a brief hint of white siding, be it the eaves, the windows, or around the porch. Cape Cod houses, ranch houses, even a few Federal designs all conformed to the same exterior. Every home featured a manicured lawn and several carefully placed trees.

He found 6450 and pulled in the drive. His heart raced as he got out of the car and walked up the sidewalk. The air smelled of freshly mowed grass and a faint floral hint of something. He rang the doorbell at the massive metal front door.

"Just a minute," came from inside the home. It was Malcolm. Thank God he'd gotten this far. He took a deep breath when the door opened. He was definitely the same man who stood outside Elysium.

"I'm Ashton Lane." He held out his hand.

"Hello, Ashton." The doctor accepted the gesture. "Please come in." He seemed in good spirits, considering the circumstances.

He was civil enough to shake hands and invite him in, instead of launching into a wave of obscenities.

The prim interior was exactly as he expected. The tactfully decorated furniture was arranged in neat, precise clusters. Everything was too meticulous, too deliberate, not even a chair was turned slightly aside. All the cushions were fluffed, and all the visible glassware and fixtures shone as though they were new.

"Please have a seat," he gestured to the armchair. "You might as well tell me what you know."

"Herbert!" A shrill female voice yelled from the next room. "Who is that?"

"Come in, mother. It's the young man I told you about." He called back at equal volume.

"The one from Elysium?"

"That's him."

An older woman with rigid posture entered the room. She sat in the oak rocker with the cobalt cushions, across from him. She almost looked down her nose at him while she studied him. "What about it?"

He looked to Malcolm for some indication of what he needed to do or say. The older man just nodded for him to go on. "Well... ma'am... we're having trouble, and I fear for us all."

"Elysium *is* nothing, but trouble."

"You know about it?"

"You haven't filled him in, have you Herbert?" Her scrutiny turned to her son. Her hard expression didn't waiver with him.

Malcolm sat on the couch across from him. "We have close ties with Elysium, Ash. I guess you've noticed. I've watched the house for some time."

"Why? What does it matter to you?"

Malcolm sat back on the couch. "Andrew, Edgar's beloved son, inherited the house. Edgar's youngest daughter, Dora, fled the home in 1920. She married her first suitor at 16. Sadly, Dora did not have a happy life. By World War II, she was twice divorced and worked as a paid dancing girl."

"She tried her best... bless her heart." His mother spoke aloud. Her expression was in a far-off place of memory.

Malcolm didn't miss a beat. He was apparently well-rehearsed in weaving through his mother's remarks, "She married a third time, later, and the union lasted until his death. They had a girl, as well, Esther. That's my mother."

"Ma'am? You're Dora's daughter."

"In the flesh."

"You know about it, don't you? The bad stuff?" He didn't really know how to word his questions with her.

The old woman issued a dry chuckle. "Oh, yes. It was bad stuff."

"Why didn't you just tell me that?" He turned to Malcolm.

"Frankly, we don't want to be linked with it. I have struggled on a long, hard road to gain any respect. You'd be amazed how even elementary sciences, which involve parapsychology, are scorned on an academic level. If I admitted such a personal connection, it would jeopardize my future work. I need to be perceived as a distant, unrelated third-party to be credited as an expert, not a victim."

"Have you ever visited?"

"No, no, not at all. Not the grounds. I know about the curse."

"Curse?"

"Oh, yes. That house is cursed and the only way to avoid it is to avoid the house." They made small strides in the discussion. It seemed everyone waited for the right moment to say what was on his or her mind. Esther watched them, amused with something only she knew.

What a week. He would've chalked it up as a terrifying and wonderful adventure, if it was over, but it wasn't over. There was no way to know when it might end, or if they would even survive the end.

Whatever lived at Elysium was driven to involve new people and to leave the premises it was supposed to occupy. It reached out more aggressively than any entity he'd read of in history. It was defiant. How could a spirit be defiant? Sure, it made great fodder for movies, but in reality, the spirit world was different. *Was different.*

Hopefully, Esther would offer answers. It wasn't likely, but he had to try. Things were getting worse. It was growing, and he had no idea what it fed on. One wrong word could mean the difference between answers and rejection. There was no room for error.

Chapter 29

She opened her eyes and felt genuinely rested for the first time in as long as she could recall. The nightmares didn't disturb her after she returned to sleep. She waited a moment and sat up. She still carried the irritating sensation that something was missing. She tried to clear her mind as she got out of bed. It was early morning and, evidently, she was the only one awake.

The exhilaration she felt when she opened her eyes vanished as she began the climb out of bed. She would go to bed much earlier tonight. There wouldn't be any solutions or discoveries without rest. She showered and dressed in navy cotton shorts and a white tee shirt. She checked on both Alicia and Matt, both were still in deep slumber. Elysium hadn't stolen anyone during the night. With everyone present and accounted for, she went to start coffee. She still didn't trust the house. Elysium was sneaky.

The home remained quiet while the coffee perked. She relished the silence. No sounds of bouncing balls or jumping rope came from the nursery overhead. No whispers drifted through the hallway. She opened the kitchen windows to let fresh air in. It was sweetest during summer mornings. The birds sang in the glades outside. There were no traces left of the hellish carriage from the night before.

How could such a beautiful place hide such horror? Her vision drifted to the glade where the circle was. The two creatures had been digging there, in her dream. The crawling monster had started towards her from the center of the yard.

How could such hideous phantoms exist anywhere within that splendor? She poured a cup of coffee and carried it to the double doors. She slowly sipped the steaming java while she drank in the morning outside.

If there were nothing more, there was peace at that moment, and she would enjoy it. The table was a mess from the previous night. Books had been left open; papers were scattered across the surface. Several had fallen to the floor. She tried to straighten it without losing their notes written in the chaos.

Her eyes caught a sheet of paper she'd written on. *"Thus with a kiss I die."* It still bothered her. She knew it was significant to whatever happened back then.

The first order of business was locating Isabelle's grave. The thing from the dream admitted she had a headstone. Now, the struggle lay in locating it. It would help to discover what kind of set-up Edgar gave his daughter's final resting place. She still couldn't accept the idea that a father would kill his daughter back then. It seemed too modernistic, although she knew it happened.

Crimes that vicious were nearly expected in our world, but not in that world. Things like that weren't supposed to happen when men were gentlemen, and women were ladies. It also introduced the question that, if he killed his own daughter, who else did he kill?

Sounds of life came overhead. Alicia was awake. Matt came into the kitchen and surprised her. "Did I miss anything?" He groggily walked towards the coffee pot. "Wow, my sleep schedule is screwed up. I should just be going to bed now."

"I'm so sorry, Matt," she sat her mug down.

"None of that." He sat down beside her at the bar. She toyed with the counter's tile mosaic top. The intricate pieces formed the image of the Grecian Diana.

"What's on the agenda today?" His coffee finally cooled enough to drink.

"I want to see Isabelle's grave."

"Ah, curious are you?"

"Yes."

"Then see her grave, we shall."

She laughed, "Are you Yoda?"

"Find answers, you must."

"Clearly speak, you must." She sat out several boxes of cold cereal for them to eat. She pulled out bowls and milk while Matt searched through local cemetery information online.

"In clauses, we talk." He eventually hit something. "Ah-hah, found it! Actually, it's just down the road. Elysium's original property boundaries exceeded what they are now... by about three hundred acres. The family cemetery was on the property as well as the main road for traveling out of Bristol. It forked at the cemetery, one way of the road lead here and the other way went into Scott County. The Blythe cemetery grew during the epidemics. They continued to expand it and gave it a formal name. In 1932, it became a formal cemetery for all residents of the area."

"Magnolia Grove..." She whispered. She should have known. Magnolia was one of the oldest cemeteries in the region. She never associated the massive cemetery with the property, although it was within walking distance, and hidden by thick line of trees.

Alicia looked fabulous when she walked in the kitchen, but she always looked best without make-up. It was something she both admired and hated. The pronounced dark circles beneath her blue eyes were gone and, while she was still pale, most of her color had returned.

Sleep deprivation tainted the room. Discussions were quieter and more reflective. Even though they had slept, everyone was still psychologically exhausted. They ate breakfast in silence and, after they finished their coffee, they left to visit the Grove.

"I never dreamed Magnolia was affiliated with Elysium." She trudged over the weeds alongside the road.

"Perhaps it's one of the blessings of the epidemic." Alicia took a high step across a patch of briars. "Otherwise, there probably wouldn't be such a public cemetery here. Matt? How did you find her records?"

"If there's a wide interest in the cemetery's history, genealogists often document them. We occasionally use genealogy records for verification. If someone suspects this person lived during this time, we like to get exact dates. Doesn't always work, but it can be faster than courthouses or libraries."

They traveled on the road when possible. The sides of the street were overgrown with weeds and brush. They stepped off into the bramble to allow cars to pass and then returned to the asphalt. It was a beautiful day, but humidity already blanketed everything. She missed the cooler shade of the backyard as they entered the cemetery gates. Sparse trees grew in clusters of two and three.

"Do you know where she is?" There was row upon row of graves that stretched across at least five acres.

"Um... Oh! Look at that...." Matt sheepishly grinned and darted off towards a statue of an angel.

"We should take that as a 'no'." Alicia laughed and walked to her side. "We'll find it. There are lots of stones here, but you just need to watch for her last name."

Matt surveyed row after row of stones, but none attracted their attention. She tried to move at a similar pace, but the astounding statuary prevented it. She could see many obvious parallels with the details at Elysium. A moss-covered fountain trickled from a bucket held by a smiling cherub. Angels and biblical statues had been liberally sprinkled across the grounds. A black tarmac walkway wove in and out of the small knolls.

She pushed all thoughts away, now was the time to focus on Isabelle. She needed to find her. She could admire the grounds, the cemetery, and all else at any other time. She had a job to do now. A strange influence drew her towards a generic corner, to the right. This couldn't be the location of any *Blythe* headstone. It was clearly the paupers' section. Some of the stones were crudely carved in fading sandstone, while others had already faded and broken, completely lost to time.

Many paupers' headstones were cracked beyond recognition. Several were broken in half with the topmost piece on the ground behind. The names of those buried would eventually be lost unless they were documented. She couldn't understand why people would neglect any part of such beautiful cemetery. It was a great dishonor to everyone buried there.

She shifted the closest broken stone upright as best she could. "Claude P. Hays," had regained his name, but his vital information had eroded into oblivion. Maybe she would take charge of it. She could save those with traces of information and give them new stones. Even a marker was better than nothing.

A relative might seek them one day and would never find them. She repaired the three remaining fallen stones in the row. She was now at the end. She glanced down at the pitiable rock in front of her and held her breath.

Matt was right.

Those things in the dream were right.

Something was terribly wrong. Isabelle's grave lay directly below, but it wasn't any different from those surrounding it. The microscopic slab of plain marble lay without adornment or ostentation. It had no design or biblical scripture. It was forgettable and had been forgotten.

Her tombstone lay flat on the ground. It was a spiteful, bitter commemoration to the eldest child of one of the richest men in the county. The only identification was "Isabelle Blythe," and "1897-1915." She flagged the other two over. The other two remained quiet.

"That is so sad." Matt knelt by the grave. "What happened?"

"She must've really pissed him off." Alicia said, but her worried voice held no humor. "Her own father buried her like this, here, so far from the family."

Matt wiped the dead grass from the stone, "You know, the rest of the Blythe family is buried over there." He pointed to the opposite corner where massive flowering trees and concrete benches sat. The highly manicured area didn't have a single leaf askew.

They paused a moment in respect for Isabelle before they ventured to the Blythe section. The Blythe family area was marked with a delicate wrought iron border. The divide was only around a foot in height, but time had given the décor a gorgeous emerald patina. Grecian urns and concrete vases sat atop tall pedestals. Each granite monument was a six-foot-tall replica of the Washington Monument. The base detailed both vital information and a picture of the individual buried.

Why didn't anyone return Isabelle to the family spot? Edgar left Elysium to Andrew. Her brother could've brought her back. Her nieces and nephews could have returned her to her family. What could a teenage girl do to justify such ostracism? She was hidden for decades after her death by all possible descendants.

Drusilla Blythe, Edgar's wife, wore a restrictive black taffeta dress in her oval portrait. The collar came up to the base of her jaw and a white broach sat in the center. She died in 1916 due to the epidemic. She appeared to be a stern woman but had smile lines from years of laughter. "Why didn't they care for Isabelle?"

"Apparently, the whole family hated her." Matt walked by the other stones. "Families were huge then. Tons of siblings, aunts, uncles, cousins, and grandparents. Someone should've said something."

"You would think so."

"She must've done something really horrible."

"She disgraced the family." She felt that shame, herself, after all this time. Women weren't allowed to do anything back then, but even with that in mind, she was a child. There isn't anything she could've done to warrant such loathing.

"Maybe she was pregnant outside marriage?" She wondered aloud.

"That's a little harsh, don't you agree? 'Shotgun marriages,' got their start during those days. All they had to do was marry."

"What if her father didn't like Heath?"

"It would have been easier for him to disown her and let her marry Heath. I mean that would have been his child and grandchild, his own flesh-and-blood."

"But she *was* his flesh-and-blood, and look she ended up."

He couldn't offer any answers. The trip would've been wasted, but at least they knew where Isabelle had stood in her family.

"Let's have another look at her grave before we go." She wiped her brow with the back of her hand. The temperature was on the rise. It was another Appalachian summer day with a beautiful morning, which led to a smothering midday. They wandered through stones and around rows as they traipsed back to her final resting place.

Poor Isabelle.

She was all alone. She was estranged from family and loved ones in death, as she most likely had been in life. In her mind, she saw a brief flash of a hand against the window on the third floor. Someone had been locked inside. They tried to get out. Someone wanted out of that hateful room. It was a feminine hand, delicate fingers. It attempted to push against a pane that would not move.

So much for the pampered rich girl.

Maybe that inhumane exile was the reason she committed suicide. A wave of sorrow pulled at her stomach. It was good that she wore sunglasses because her eyes welled up behind them. She'd never heard of Isabelle before Elysium, but that didn't hinder the sharp pain in her heart.

They gave her stone a final exam. Matt prodded the grass below the surface, but nothing on the stone had been hidden by growth.

"If only we could exhume her grave." Alicia spoke aloud.

Matt smiled, "I wonder if we'd find evidence of foul play?"

"Probably." Melanie sighed. "Most likely... I think we can all feel it. Let's go home." She moved towards the gate. "We can discuss this out of this damned heat. We've found all we can here."

She had grown unusually tired. Maybe it was stress, or the heat, but she just wanted to go home. There weren't any answers there. If they exhumed her grave, it wouldn't help. The body was never even buried there. *"In the pit with her peddler...."* She heard a hateful voice hiss but couldn't remember where she heard it.

The journey home was difficult as the sun bore down on them. Heat radiated from the asphalt below. Shimmering mirages of water pooled over every knoll down the highway. Insects buzzed beneath the canopies of the trees.

They all gasped by the time they reached the yard. The intense heat had evaporated what little energy she had left. They paused with the cool glade to catch their breath. Her sides felt like they were pulling apart. She leaned against a nearby ash as she studied the structure that now protruded from the earth in the pit.

"Maybe the building will reveal something." She knew the structure had significance but couldn't say why.

"I hope so." Alicia tried to smile. Eventually, their exhaustion subsided. They returned through the kitchen door. "I just want all of this to be over." Melanie poured three tall glasses of iced tea and splashed a generous amount of lemon juice in each.

They gathered around the table. Again, they flipped through the aged books that seemed to've been previously milked. Alicia flipped through the pile of books sitting nearest her. A letter flew out of the second. It reached the other side of the kitchen before it hit the wall and fell to the floor.

"Wow, who needs rockets? Now that was a helluva page turning. What velocity did you launch that with?" Matt grinned.

Alicia retrieved the wayward envelope and read it as she walked back to the table. Melanie started to follow up on Matt's wit but paused. Something was wrong. "Alli? What is it?" The envelope had marks from being opened and folded countless times.

"It's an envelope, you know, you mail things with it...." She returned the sarcasm with a wink. "It's a note." She studied the faded envelope, and an even further yellowed letter slipped outside of it. She handed the envelope to Melanie, who read it aloud:

"'I know you've seen the ring. I know you've found the room. Solve the puzzle before it's too late. She's waiting. She'll get you. She has no conscience. She is everywhere. She's coming and he's following.' It's signed 'Edgar Blythe, 1970'."

"Not another one." Alicia whined.

"Whoa, whoa. Edgar Blythe died long before 1970. He was a father of twelve in 1912." Matt said. "Is it a fake?"

"I don't think so."

"Wait, wait." Matt refereed. "Maybe it's a descendent. Let me see it." She handed the package to him. The note discussed Isabelle, but not the Isabelle from the photographs. She couldn't have been like that. Something changed. Someone warped her.

Matt opened the envelope and gently pulled the folded letter out. It was a message written with elegant penmanship. The brown letter was much older than the envelope. It read:

> "Meet me in the glade, my dearest. Meet me where eyes can't reveal our love to those who won't understand. Meet me where no one can see us, with our lunar chaperone. I'll go away with you this time. I accept. We should flee before you are forced to go away, and I am forced to die."

"What were they forcing Isabelle to do?" Melanie asked.

"Is that *her* handwriting?" She felt the same marvel as Alicia did. How could it be the same Isabelle at all?

"I do."

"Why would she meet anyone in private? She was rich. Even if she was a black sheep, they couldn't let the community know of their disdain. It wouldn't have been socially acceptable."

The rest of the group arrived a few hours later to continue the excavation. Everyone appeared haggard and withdrawn. The laughter had subsided. They clustered together in the kitchen before going outside.

Everyone now manifested symptoms of Isabelle's blight. The unmistakable physical traits that linked them all. Dark circles were under everyone's eyes, in varying degrees, and their expressions now held panic and sadness. Even Alicia, who'd made a remarkable improvement from the previous day, still had a trace of those dark rings.

"What is going on?" She asked everyone.

"We're all going through it," Janelle replied. "All of us."

She caught glimpse of herself in the mirror across the room before she spoke further. She looked just like Alicia. She hadn't paid attention to her appearance since the ordeal started. She had the same dark circles, and no matter how she smiled, her eyes remained afraid.

They were all faded and washed out, just like Elysium in that other world. Everything was faded and everyone was faded. You contracted the demonic infection when you visited, and no one escaped its clutches.

She couldn't look at them any longer. She couldn't bear to see the product of her own greed. She'd done it... done it to them all. She's the reason they were fading. They were all so young. She had to get away. She had to have a moment to think.

"I need to check the mail," she suddenly stopped. She feigned casual self-annoyance. "God, I haven't been out there in two days. Feel free to start without me. I'll be right out." She walked back through the house and out the front. How would she live with herself if she did survive?

She strolled beneath the shade of ash and elm as she headed towards the mail and paper boxes at the end of the drive. She heard the group start out in the backyard. They were dying, and it was her fault. She grabbed the mail and papers without looking through them. She pushed hard on the old mailbox door closed.

She walked back towards the house. She halted as she arrived at the sidewalk to the front porch. Isabelle stood less than three feet away from her. It was her, standing right there. She never noticed, but they were the same height.

The specter wore a faded white dress and hung her head. Her long dark hair hung in matted tendrils. She wasn't faded or ghostly.

She was as solid as any other person. She had so many questions for the apparition she had no idea what to ask first.

"Hello... Isabelle...." Her breath came out in a ragged whisper as she inched closer. She couldn't walk away. There was no choice but to ask the very one who made it all happen. The spirit appeared to her in broad daylight. She just stood there like any person. Matt or Alicia could round the house at any time, or someone could drive down the street.

She realized that, in the situation, none of that mattered. The figure didn't move or diminish as she crept closer. "Isabelle?" She whispered again and slightly lowered her own head. She wanted to see her face, only a portion was ever exposed. She needed to see if she really was the girl from the photographs. Perhaps this was the event she'd felt approach. The beginning of the end.

Proximity was no longer a concern. Maybe her death would stop the carnage. It wasn't as bad as a life of enduring everything at Elysium, constant nightmares, perpetual torment, and terror for those she loved. If she could give herself in their stead, she would.

She almost touched the figure, "I'm so sorry for what you went through. Please take me instead ... Just show me... and leave everyone else alone." Now was the time to stop it. She wouldn't run any longer, and she wouldn't look to anyone else for help.

She took a deep breath and gave one last look to the mansion she'd longed to own all her life. She had achieved what she wanted. She'd shown the world that she could achieve the impossible. That was more than most people did in their lifetime, and the achievement was the reward.

She gingerly opened her arms to embrace the figure. It might be the last thing she ever embraced, but it just didn't matter. The wraith's head snapped up and its arms latched onto her. She didn't fight.

The air completely left her body. The world went pitch black before light came. Time sped up as she watched the new world around her. She laid on the grass in the back yard. She couldn't see anyone, at first. She heard creaking wheels approach. A familiar wagon came towards her from the distance, but it wasn't burned. *Burned....* That was the box they dug up.

The carriage driver wore a black bandanna and wide-brimmed black hat. It was the evil man she'd watched in her dream the first night at Elysium. His eyes glimmered even in daylight. The light in this scene was the same as it always appeared in the dreams. Everything was dingy and gray, like a faded black-and-white movie.

Another flash of light seared her vision and eventually, she regained sight to find a group of men stood over her. The wagon stopped beside her.

"How'd you like that?" *Heath...* It was Heath, he stood closest to her. He spoke and her skin crawled. The other men kept their faces hidden with the black hats and bandanas. Her wrists ached from where they held her down.

Heath refastened the waist of his pants in a way that made her cringe. She had a moment of shock. *What the hell happened?* She looked at that once familiar face. A childhood friend who was gone forever. Heath Buckner was the enemy. She never dreamed he was capable of such brutality. Never in a million years. Not Heath.

"But, who...." she whispered to herself.

Heath snapped, "Who?" He grew offended by her words. "Told you I'd have you and no one else... your father even helped. See? It's for the best. What could he provide you?" He nodded his chin towards the carriage, "He was little more than a drifter. A peddler is a drifter with some pocket change. A peddler and a Blythe... married?" The men laughed at his mockery.

She tried to move, but everything was painful. Her body hurt from her head to her feet. Her back was bruised, her legs, her arms trembled, and her throat was so dry and sore. "Daddy... Let you...." She couldn't speak. Her throat hurt too much from screaming.

"That's right, sweetheart. Daddy gave me permission to deflower you and make you mine. It's against tradition, but eloping isn't tradition, either." He glared at her as the crowd thinned, "You should've watched your letter. You weren't isolated in the little room for protection against the plague. They knew what you planned."

The letter.

The letter she thought she'd lost in the forest. She wondered why they imprisoned her in that little room with the bloody walls. None of the other children were locked up.

Her eyes moved through the familiar faces that stood around her. She knew them all from childhood, all from good families. *Eli...* she remembered. Harris stood to the right. Fredrick, Able, Geoff, they all were there, and no one had defended her honor. Instead, they held her while Heath dishonored her and congratulated him for a "job well done."

"Daddy?" She whispered.

"Have you gone stupid?" Heath crouched back down in front of her. "Your peddler is dead." He stormed off to join the other riders as they ransacked the wagon. "Nail some dry boards to it," Heath grinned. "That'll make it burn faster." He walked away to help them bring lumber.

Felix. Where was Felix? They had his body, somewhere. She crawled away, but her arm hit something behind the bushes. She found a leg, and a shoe. It was Felix's shoes. His body was still, the ground bloody beneath him.

She knew he was dead. She gasped when his eyes moved to her, he whispered, "Thus with a kiss I die." She leaned down and kissed his lips, but he was gone. She felt his cooling blood against her lips. "Thus with a kiss I die," she answered. They were Romeo and Juliet, just like in the play.

"Yes, Isabelle...." A voice whispered in Isabelle's mind. *"You should be clean. You need to be clean. You need to get rid of the infection before it starts...."*

The men dragged his body away and slung it inside the wagon. They nailed boards over the wagon, but none of them knew anything about carpentry. They half-nailed the wagon shut. They pushed it beneath the tall overhanging trees.

The pit. They were sending the wagon to the pit. She heard a crash. The men cheered with the sound of breaking glass and the roar of a massive fire. They set it on fire. *Her* Felix. *Her* peddler. Heath returned to her, grabbed her arm, and yanked her up to stand. Her hips hurt from trying to prevent his violation. He half-dragged her to the pit. "Now, we'll watch him burn, like he's burning in hell."

Everything changed inside Isabelle. Melanie felt it deep within her own body. It wasn't the shocking, lashing out variety of anger that was quickly spent. It was a cold and insatiable rage.

Isabelle knew it consumed her, and she relished it. The evil had overtaken the girl's body, and it was too strong. Melanie couldn't control her thoughts, no matter how hard she fought, and she couldn't fight as hard as she wished. Isabelle deserved justice.

Her own father did this. What could she expect from the rest of the world? She would make them pay... somehow. They would pay so much more for their hatred than she ever did for love. She turned her rage towards Heath. She sprung from where she stood and lunged at his throat. She would show them all. She would show them what a monster was, and what kind of monster they created.

She managed to knock him over and he landed on his back. She frantically looked around and grabbed a rock before he caught his bearings, or the others came to his rescue. She hit him over the head, and he yelled. She pummeled him as hard as her trembling arms could. The rock's edge had turned red from his blood, but he was still so powerful.

She raised the rock to hit him again, but something grabbed her as she reared back. Her shoulder twisted behind her; further pain shot through her back. Edgar towered overhead, his eyes hard and sharp. He yanked the rock from her hand.

"How could you? He's going to be your husband." He hissed.

Edgar threw the rock with one hand and jerked her back as hard as he could with the other. She landed on her back. The wind left her body, and her head hit another rock. She saw spots and the world spun for a moment.

Her father's physical strength was unreal. "Give it up, girl." He warned as he reached out a hand to help Heath up. He apologized for his daughter's crass and uncivilized behavior.

What a laugh, Isabelle thought. She rubbed the bleeding wound on the back of her head. Heath and Edgar stood together, as... as the two men had been in the parlor when she peered through the keyhole. They were drinking and shook hands. It was just business.

She was a business deal her father hoped to successfully close. Heath's family owned the flour mill as well as many other businesses. Heath would take over several, as a wedding present.

"Congratulations, son." Edgar shook his hand. "She'll make a fine wife. She just needs to have that damnable will broke. She's like a filly, or a jackass, both need to be shown who their owner is."

Her brain still labored to wrap around the fact that Heath raped her. He hurt her like that, they all helped him, and her father patted him on the back. She pulled the blood-stained parts of her dress beneath her legs. It seemed less trashy, but now she was trash. She was as low as a prostitute and her father applauded it.

She looked back at the house and even her mother watched. Drusilla's eyes were rimmed with red, but she wasn't sympathetic. Her mother was in on it. *So what else had they done?*

She suspected them of horrific things since the plague came. Edgar was always around when someone died from the disease. The neighbors were vermin once they contracted it. The bodies were burned in the pit before anyone got a good look at them, not that there were any lawmen left.

Except the riders.

The dirty, filthy bastards.

Oh, yes, they'll save us all.

There was no stopping the white death. There was no cure. There was no way out. The only way out of the realm of the white death had been with Felix. She'd planned and prepared. She'd successfully escaped the room by picking the lock with a rusted nail. All for naught. Now, he was gone... and there was no escape.

How long until they were all diseased, if they weren't already? It was too late for hope because everything was infected. Life was an infection, just like that goddamned disease. It killed the world while she slept.

There was only more bodies and more decay every day. The stench from the dead in the pit had already overtaken the courtyard. No matter how many times you burned, that smell didn't leave. It only grew stronger.

It was too much. There was nothing left to do. They would force her to wed Heath, and even if she got away, what did she have to offer anyone now? Her precious virtue was gone. She'd wanted Felix to have that.

Now, she only had memories of him, of their hopes and dreams. The caves and the glade were the only places she could remember being with him. *Stones go in the graveyard, bury the bodies in the pit, so they can't contaminate.*

They were all damned. Maybe it was the end of the world... or maybe they were already in hell. Those who didn't die became monsters, anyway.

Time drew near for the entire world to be infected. They would all have those horrible sores that bled muck and only grew more infected. Their chests would rattle and wheeze. Their voices would change, like it did in those bad cases. They could already be infected. *Yes, that was it.* They were already infected with sin and its corruption.

Not me.

No. She would be cured. She would be cured, and she would be free. Everyone scattered once the commotion quieted down. Heath returned to the house with her parents. The boys had fled since the wagon was now ablaze. She stood and attempted to regain her balance. Blood trickled down her forehead from when Heath first pushed her down on her stomach. Her body bled from his violation, but the world bled black pus. It was gangrenous.

She stumbled to where they attacked Felix. Her legs were tender and wobbly. She stared at the ground where his blood had poured from his throat. How could the human body hold that much blood? He made circle after circle around where the wagon had been, the circles, a perpetual circle of hate.

She half-dropped down on her knees. Her body wouldn't work properly. She had to steady herself with her hand on the ground. She forced her body to stop trembling so she could gather a handful of dirt drenched with his blood. Just hours earlier, it had been life within Felix's veins. Her Felix.

She would show them a perpetual circle of hate.

She staggered, half-crawled, and fell to her knees at the edge of the pit. The outline of his wagon popped and cracked in the fire. She saw gray bone and bits of clothing protrude from the bottom of the burning box. They were the last batch of bodies to succumb, and now the house was virtually empty of victims. *For now.* Now, her Felix was in there and he was gone. It was a disgusting pit where the White Death reigned victorious.

Oh, but I'll be cured. Everyone will be cured. I won't wait on the world to heal or watch more people die. The time is ticking, father. Can you hear the ticking? It ticks on and on and on. Pretty soon, your time will be over. Heath's time will be over.

She stood up and felt something in the other hand. It was a locket. She remembered kissing Felix in the glade when he gave her the locket. She asked him to hold it for when they were married because her family would be suspicious.

Heath threw it earlier and she didn't know where it went. He threw it at her after they ripped it from Felix's throat, after they slit him open. She couldn't recall when she found it, but it had to've been during the violation. That was it. She grabbed dirt when he was ravaging her, and she felt the chain. She focused on the feel of it to get through it.

288

It was as sacred as a wedding ring to her, and Heath violated that, too. He touched what never belonged to him. It was her locket.

She would show them because there was nothing left to fear.

Her father was probably having a drink with Heath while her mother nursed his wounds. They were nothing more than corrupted corpses themselves. The other riders had disappeared, not even the sounds of their horses were within earshot. They should have left. That kind of shame would be a hideous badge that they would wear for the rest of their miserable lives.

Felix was like her. He wasn't infected... the farthest thing from the infection. They were both just in the way of a lucrative deal that would line her father's pockets. Perhaps she hated him most of all. God help her, she hated him even more than Heath. *He will never live to enjoy it.*

She crept to the smokehouse, then to the barn to retrieve the extra spool of rope. She returned to the pit without drawing attention from the house. She wound the rope in a loop and secured it into a noose. She threw the rope up and over the high branch above the pit and tightened the end around the trunk.

She would show them. She wouldn't be infected. There was no reason to wait now. He was gone. She might turn into her mother, infected with fear and vanity. Her father was infected with greed, or the bastard Heath, who was infected by lust. She was still clean, despite what he did, and she would remain that way.

She lugged the ladder from the barn towards the pit and nearly tripped. She dropped the ladder. It almost fell into the hole below. Her body leaned the ladder against the tree. She forced her shaking hands to calm as she climbed higher. She only had a minute before someone would notice. She slipped the noose around her head.

She would not be infected. She wouldn't cough up blood, or make others bleed. It wouldn't infect her organs or bones and deform them. She gave a final look to the carriage below. It had been drenched with kerosene and set on fire.

289

She paused just a moment. She wiped her bloody lips with her hand, but they were dry. There was no evidence of his blood. Maybe it was a dream. Maybe she was mad. Nothing mattered, aside from the fact that she would meet him, wherever he was.

She jumped and air was taken from her. Her pulse pounded in her eardrums for just a moment. Then, all went silent and dark.

She opened her eyes. Her arms had dropped from the embrace, but the wraith held fast. Isabelle barely allowed her to gasp for air.

"Why?" She managed to get out between ragged breaths. She thought of a girl in elementary school who suffered an asthma attack. It must've been similar. Her lungs were on fire. Her back hurt. She needed air.

"You will feel," Isabelle spoke. "All will feel."

"What did I do?"

"You asked to see. I showed you."

"No...." she couldn't talk. She had to get more air.

"Everyone will feel." Her voice was low and cold. "I will not be stopped."

"But you wanted to be united. You said to unite you."

The figure paused. It seemed to be caught off guard. A girlish voice cried, "Please, please reunite us." It was the same feminine voice that first spoke through Edwards.

"No," the forceful voice commanded. "No reunion... it's too late."

Alicia emerged from around the side of the house. Her face went white, and her eyes grew wide when she saw Isabelle. She sprinted towards them, "No!" She screamed, "Let her go, Isabelle!"

When she reached the sidewalk, Isabelle released her grip and faded into nothing. Melanie coughed, but she could breathe. She had precious air inside her tender lungs. She couldn't believe it. Dahlia told them everything. She told them all they needed to know when she jumped rope in the nursery. She hadn't paid attention.

Infectious

"Isabelle, Isabelle, where did you go?
Are you hanging in the trees like you were before?
Who did you tell your daddy you would marry?
It better be the one who is big and scary!"

"What the hell is going on?" Alicia cried with her. She knew what was going on and she was going to die. Alicia supported her as they stumbled inside. She dropped at the table as soon as they reached the kitchen.

Alicia poured a tall glass of water for her and shouted to the group outside. She drank as quickly as she could between coughs. Her parched throat felt like it would never be normal again.

Matt ran inside, "Where's smoke coming from?"

Alicia ran to the sink for a wet washcloth, "I smell smoke, too. I think its Melanie."

She leaned down and smelled her hair, "Melanie? You smell like smoke." She nodded in agreement. The reek from the burning wagon hadn't been that far away.

"The wagon..." She got out before her throat prickled again. She coughed and tried taking slow deep breaths.

"What happened?" Janelle came in with Scott. "What's going on?"

"That's what we're waiting on, Janelle." Matt said. They pulled up chairs around the table. Janelle and Alicia poured drinks for everyone as they silently waited for her. After five minutes of deep breathing, and two glasses of water, Melanie spoke. Alicia handed her a paper towel to wipe her eyes. "Isabelle grabbed me out front."

"That's impossible," Scott scoffed. "Can you prove it?"

"Excuse me, Scott." Matt raised his voice. "Alicia saw her, too."

Scott's smirk faded. She continued. "I saw things... They happened in the past."

"What kind of things?" Janelle scooted next to her. "We need you to tell us exactly what you saw. Don't leave anything out."

"Isabelle didn't love Heath. It was an arranged marriage for Edgar's business." Janelle shook her head.

"They killed the peddler, Felix. Isabelle loved him... they were going to elope. *Romeo and Juliet*, they believed they were like them. Isabelle wrote Felix a letter accepting his proposal to elope, but lost it in the forest, or so she thought. Her parents found it. They knew she was going to elope. Heath raped her, and all the young men she knew helped."

Alicia sighed, "God, how sad. What did her family say?"

"Her father congratulated Heath because that meant she 'belonged' to him. He deflowered her. Their marriage was to unite two wealthy families."

She gingerly tried to clear her throat. The pain subsided, but it still felt like she inhaled an ashtray. "Her mother and father were there when he raped her. She tried to kill Heath with a rock, but her father pulled her off and threw her aside. It was all planned. She saw them together after it all happened. The Black Riders were her friends and previous suitors."

"What happened?" Janelle held her hand.

"Isabelle knew there was no way out. Something snapped when she realized what had happened." She took another generous drink, "She then believed everyone was infected. Everyone had something horrible growing inside, like tuberculosis. She didn't want to wait until she was infected.

"She made a noose and suspended it from the tree over where the salt circle is now—the pit. They burned the contaminated waste there. I woke just as she hung herself... Alicia came around the house and saw us."

"It's true." Alicia asserted. "I didn't know who it was until I got closer and saw that dress. That's what the black stains are in the middle of her skirt on either side. Blood. She was as solid as any of us. She disappeared."

Melanie finally let go of her mail and the newspaper. She still clutched them against her body. "What does she want?"

"She wants everyone to pay. She wants everyone to feel what she did."

"Isn't there something that will appease her?"

"No. Nothing. A small voice said something about a reunion, but I don't know if that matters. The stronger voice said it didn't."

"This is insane. How could she be like that? It's brutal and merciless, just like the riders were. She wasn't angry in life so why would she be like this in death?"

"Wait... Melanie? You said something changed in her. Describe it clearly." Janelle squarely eyed her.

"She was in shock, I think. She couldn't believe Heath and the boys did that. She'd known them all for years. Then, her father came into the picture, and she was overwhelmed, she'd always loved her father, she thought he loved her. She watched as they congratulated one another. Her mother was there.

"She was stripped of everything. Her parents, her life, she kept thinking everything was rotten. She became enraged, and after a little while, she wanted to use it against them, but she didn't know how."

"Maybe it really isn't Isabelle, Melanie." Matt held her hand. "This might have been an entity back then."

"What's the difference?"

"What does an entity have? Its purpose is to destroy. It is often summoned at the scene of something horrible. It remains there. That's all it knows."

"Sounds like any other ghost to me." Alicia shrugged.

"But an entity has no morals, no sense of right and wrong." Matt continued. "No real thought aside from destruction."

"Can someone perform an exorcism?"

"No," Matt nodded emphatically. "No, none of us are that experienced. We investigate, document, 'prove,' if you will, but it takes a great amount of spiritual strength and knowledge.

Considering how we've all been plagued by her for days, I'm not so sure any of us are at the right point to attempt something like that. You must be both physically and psychologically strong."

Melanie noticed the newspaper had unfolded on the table. She whimpered when she noticed the headline, "Celebrated Realtor Dies Mysteriously." Beneath the large letters was a picture of John Taylor.

Alicia snapped herself and ran outside. "What do you want?" She screamed into the courtyard. The group seemed unaffected, but tension hung in the air. Taylor had died of asphyxiation. Somehow, he died from smoke inhalation in a hospital room.

They were all going to die.

"Would I have died like that if Alicia hadn't come around?" Isabelle was some unquenchable hate and rage that had lived for so long. "Oh, my God. The telephone number we couldn't trace, 276-555-2591. That's Taylor's! That's why it was familiar."

Matt continued, "Did Taylor say how long the home had been open?"

"He said a week or two, but I don't know for certain. He might've just said that to cover for the lack of interest."

"She could've killed you, Melanie. She didn't. Why didn't she?"

"Because of me?" Alicia toyed with her hemp bracelet.

"She got Taylor in the middle of a friggin' hospital." Matt disagreed. "What did you do that Taylor didn't? If she had wanted to kill you, she would have. I think she was making a point. You evaded her full grasp, but you still suffered some of what she did."

"Well, she can't *like* me.... That voice didn't like anyone."

"I didn't say you were liked. You just did something that earned you some mercy... because you are alive. It didn't stop her... didn't come close to stopping her, but you weren't killed. Did she say anything to you?"

"That she wanted everyone to suffer. She said I was looking for her."

"Were you?"

"Of course not!"

"But you felt a connection with her from her photograph at the courthouse, didn't you?"

"Yes, but to think I called this... this thing?"

"No, not the thing. Tell me, did anything strike you as familiar when you went through their album at the courthouse?"

"Not really. I recognized my home, but it is Elysium. Many would do that. I had a slight impression that Heath Buckner was not very nice, but nothing like what I saw."

Matt seem to search for the right words. "Something drew you here, Melanie. Sure, it's beautiful, it's historic. Yes, it has a fascinating history. No one else is breaking their backs to own it. Even people with money didn't want it. I can't imagine one person would buy this place as soon as they came into enough money for a home. But you did. It came naturally, didn't it?"

"Yes. I've always liked it, though." She defended. "You can't possibly think I wanted any of this—"

"No. I'm not saying that. Just let me finish."

"Okay."

"That isn't a negative. It's kind of romantic. This discussion has little to do with you, personally, because few people choose what they're drawn to. With that said, what else was it? Think. Isn't there anything else that influenced your decision to buy this place?"

"It just felt like home." That was the simplest way she knew how to explain it. You had to live a lifetime of tiny, cramped apartments, crowded in between drug pushers and prostitutes to understand. You had to experience walls so thin you heard conversations next door to understand.

How could she not want a massive, rambling home? Why not a place where she could invite guests that didn't offer neighbors' beds banging against the walls? She would never be kept awake all night by the singing drunks next door, or scary men coming and going at all hours again.

Matt smiled, "Look at your fortune, too. Isn't it strange you won the lottery? What are the odds? Do people from this region ever actually win anything from it? But you did. What if that was influenced?"

She couldn't respond. She hadn't considered anything like that. She had a sudden realization. "We're digging it up, aren't we? The wagon?"

"No, Melanie. It can't be." She nearly ran out of the house with the others trailing behind. She had to see the structure they were uncovering. She felt a twinge of unease as they crossed the yard. She remembered so much that had happened, even though it never happened to her. The mark on her arm was nearly gone. What had she done? How could she replicate it? How could she save everyone?

Chapter 30

Ash sighed with relief as Herbert and Esther grew a little more open. The small talk seemed to be gaining momentum. Esther even joined as time passed. The exchange shifted, and Herbert was a mere listener.

Isabelle, or whatever it was, would not listen. She grabbed his arm at one point, and he was breathless. He watched through her eyes as Buckner did the unthinkable. Isabelle's friends helped him.

Esther revealed the endless stream of White Plague victims virtually depleted the once vast Blythe wealth. The family had no choice but to care for them, or watch the world become contaminated by something that would not die.

Their affluence became their downfall. They couldn't turn anyone away. As the pillars of the community, people came to them for help and expected to be helped. What would their peers have thought if they allowed people to die in their gardens? It had been everywhere. Death and sickness had walked, not only in Elysium, but in the surrounding states. Everyday more and more came with fevers and perpetual coughing.

Edgar changed the most after the plague started. He became cold and distant, primarily concerned with the family name and wealth. Isabelle recalled him as a kind, generous father, so she was the most impacted by the change.

Her once-loving father became abusive, withdrawn as the plague's reach grew. Apparently, not even Edgar was safe from the negativity that lived there. It didn't take a great deal of thought to see the entity influenced his actions.

Four cats ambled into the living room and gathered around the old woman's feet. "You seem like a nice young man. I think I'll answer your questions but only discussing because it is an emergency." She warned.

He held up his hand. "It is an emergency. The owner is experiencing things, and I don't know how to help. She doesn't deserve what's happening."

"*Deserve*?" Esther whispered with a sarcastic chuckle. "That has little to do with anything in life, doesn't it? Children don't *deserve* cancer. Mothers don't *deserve* to suffer for their children's addictions. Fathers don't *deserve* to be punished for their wives' deceit. Patients don't deserve to suffer at the hands of careless doctors." She shook her head, "No, doesn't work like that. Isabelle didn't deserve what happened to her."

"How can we stop it?"

"Stop it?" She gave a cold laugh. "You think you can stop it? What's done is done, boy. Some wrongs can't be made right. Believe me, everything imaginable has been done. Why do you think my mama ran? She saw Isabelle's agonies and couldn't do anything. When she came of age, she fled as quickly as she could be married. She got away from it because she knew it was poisoned."

"Poisoned?"

"Yes. Isabelle has never left Elysium... in any way. Even when they sold much of the property and offered the cemetery to the city, she never left, and the evil didn't leave the forest." Her statement introduced new questions. The *spirit*? What spirit was beyond Isabelle?

"She's buried in the cemetery, isn't she?"

"She has a marker there, far off in the pauper's corner. Her body isn't there, though."

"Why not with the family?"

"Because she killed herself."

"Why?"

"I remember mama talking. Isabelle was the best big sister... she was outgoing and vivacious. She was empowering. But, that last month or so when she was engaged to Heath, it all stopped. The warmth and energy was gone. It all came down to the last night Felix visited. It was so sad. Mama always broke down when she talked about it."

"What happened?"

"Edgar discovered Isabelle loved the peddler. He knew how she loved him and how much she looked forward to his visits. He even saw them kiss in the glade behind the house. Mama said she glowed when she talked about him. They communicated through letters when he was gone. She wrote to him accepting his elopement proposal, but thought she lost it in the woods. It fell from her pocket in the yard. Her mother opened it, read it, and told Edgar."

"Edgar did something, didn't he?"

"Damned straight. Edgar Blythe wasn't to be outdone by anyone. Isabelle was sequestered in the third-floor room so she wouldn't run. They told her it was to prevent infection. She found a way out by the time Felix visited. Edgar had a mob waiting. The Black Riders of the White Death. Some were good, but the ones here were bastards. I don't care if that was the only time they did something wrong, look at what they did. That absolutely overshadowed any good they did. They attacked his carriage and then pushed it into the pit to burn. They slit his throat from ear-to-ear."

She gestured to the pattern the riders' cut. "He ran around his wagon after. I don't know why, maybe shock from blood loss, or maybe he wanted something to cover his wound with. He ran until he fell dead. That circle of blood surrounded the wagon. Isabelle couldn't get near him, the mob stood between her and Felix. She never even got to tell him good-bye."

He'd seen much of it already but couldn't tell her. Esther moved her mauve rocker back and forth. "When he died, they threw his body in the wagon. They set fire to everything in the pit."

"Isabelle watched?"

"Oh, that wasn't the end for her. It was only the start. Heath attacked her. Mama never went into details, but she described a horrific gang rape if ever there was one. Heath 'violated' Isabelle, as

299

she put it, while the riders held her down, and Edgar stood by. He thought it would 'seal the deal' if Isabelle believed she had no choice but to marry Heath."

She sighed. Her expression despondent. "I don't know what the poor girl thought after that. She tried to defend herself with a rock, but her parents attacked her for it. They left her in the yard. They probably thought she would just sit there and pout, but she showed them. She made a noose and hung herself right there in the glade, suspended from a limb over the burning pit."

"They didn't bury her in the cemetery?"

"Edgar wouldn't hear of it. His daughter committed suicide and wasn't fit for holy ground. That damned her to hell. It was more like she was damned to hell because she went against his wishes."

"Why did he put a stone there?"

"To offer some sort of proof that she received a burial. Her body isn't there, just a stone. No one cared to investigate anything because TB was rampant and so many had it. Graves were in constant demand."

"Where is she buried?"

"She hung herself over the pit. They just cut the rope and let her fall into the fire."

"There's no way to stop her?"

"None. If you bring someone to the house and expose them, you'll be free, but there is no end."

"Expose them?"

"Like an infection. Vaccinations often contain traces of the disease they fight off. The flu shot has a slight amount of the flu in it. Once someone is exposed at Elysium, they must spread it to another, if they want to live. You never actually get rid of it. It lingers with them for the rest of their life, just like tuberculosis. Well... You see this?" She threw down a copy of the Bristol Herald newspaper. "This is what I mean."

Popular realtor Robert Taylor was splashed over the front page, along with an article about his sudden death. "How'd you know he was there?"

She spoke, "We still talk to a few people from the old neighborhood. Mamma didn't stop all contact with cousins and neighbors. Taylor didn't invite anyone, you see. They had to call him to schedule an appointment. We saw him in the doctor's office the other day. Mama had one of her migraines and she knew what was wrong with him just by looking at him."

Esther got a knowing look in her eye and said, "Ashton? Let me see your left arm."

"Why?" He pulled up his sleeve and exposed the fading burn.

"That's her hand." She nodded. "It's fading, so I think you'll survive."

"But, what about the others?"

"What about 'em? They must invite someone Isabelle can infect."

"How long will it go on?"

"Always." She appeared oddly amused. "She'll never die. Edgar made a monster that drove him to an asylum in Kentucky."

"What happened to Buckner?"

"He inherited his family's fortune and lost it all in the Depression. He was institutionalized in Williamsburg. Every single one of the Riders died horrible deaths before 1930. She got 'em, got 'em all. Those who didn't succumb to TB died in other ways, typhoid, pneumonia... a couple were murdered."

"Did your mother remember Isabelle's death?"

"Yes. Mama said all the children were together that night, in the opposite side of the house. Grandmother wouldn't let them leave the room. When she left, she demanded the cook stay with them. They heard screaming, but she wouldn't even let them look."

She reached up to toy with her left earlobe. Her eyes were sad and distant. "Mama never wanted anything to do with the Blythe family after that. She was 13 when it happened. She said they'd do

301

it to her just as fast as Isabelle. She believed they, and their money, were cursed."

"Does Isabelle go away?"

"Sometimes, if you survive the initial wrath."

"If I might ask...." He turned to face her. "What happened to her? Is she still a person's spirit, or is she something else?"

"That would be Herbert's forte, Herbert?"

"I think it's something that used Isabelle. I think it used Edgar, until the night of the attack, and it saw potential in Isabelle. Perhaps she retains some of her human self, somewhere, but I can't imagine what might provoke that."

"What was the spirit of the forest?"

"After the Civil War attack, the forest behind Elysium was never quiet. Of course, it was avoided even before that. It was difficult because the main road went through it. Several carriage drivers refused to enter the area if the day was so much as dim."

"Were there unexplained things before the Blythes?"

"Yes. The forest became notorious after a series of strange deaths in the 1880s. In 1883, Robert Clark was well-loved until he joked with the wrong woman. He was a black man but greatly respected for his carpentry and general handiwork. She claimed he was going to rape her and got her husband involved. A lynch mob formed who wrapped him in chains and hung him. His family retrieved his body, but he was buried in those chains, somewhere in that forest. Later on, no one really remembered precisely why they hung him."

"You said a 'series' of them. What else?"

"In 1884, a man fell over dead, and his face was frozen in a scream. No cause of death was ever found. In 1885, a chain gang was cutting the growth away from the road when the deputy went berserk. He shot every man in the gang and went home for supper. He couldn't recall any of it. In 1888, two men hunting in the area disappeared. Their tracks just ended near a tree, their weapons lay on the ground and hadn't been used. Even dogs couldn't find their scent. It was quiet after that, until the Blythes came, and Edgar was the first to change."

Esther leaned forward. "Edgar never believed in ghosts. I guess that bastard learned a thing or two." She sat a feline on her lap and stroked it. "You know, if it hadn't been for him, none of this would be happening. Do you know how many people in my family have died since, just over his greed?"

"No, ma'am."

"Far too many. My cousin Harriet died at the last cotillion; her baby vanished. I remember that still. I was just a kid, but mama knew."

"Did your mother attend?"

"Oh, no. She wasn't invited to anything after she fled."

He thought aloud. "I just don't understand why she would do this to innocent people."

"Are you serious?" She stopped rocking and looked at him. "She went crazy. The girl is gone. She died decades ago. What lurks there is not that girl. That thing grew inside her."

"How did we get where we are?" He asked more rhetorically than anything.

"You visited the house. That's why it was closed for years, why it was sold. That's why Mr. Realtor choked to death on smoke when there wasn't any around. It was the circle of flames."

"The ring kills?"

"Yes. The circle of flames closes in on you but doesn't touch you. The smoke eventually chokes you to death, like a hanging, like Isabelle died."

"The fire is his blood, isn't it? The peddler."

"Yes."

Was that what the cotillions and social activities were all about? "That was the reason for the social events?"

"Yes."

"How many died over that?"

"No one knows. Mama wouldn't let us near the house or even discuss visiting. My cousin and her baby weren't so fortunate to be told what they needed to do."

"Were they sacrifices?"

"I've always wondered that," she looked away. She took a deep breath. "I can't give you what you're looking for, any more than I could Cousin Edgar. That house drove him insane. They locked him in a nuthouse until he died. He thought he could solve it or stop it... thought he could save us. Even dug up the old wagon, pulled some stuff out, and poured a ton of salt over top thinking it might stop a spirit. Old timers said it might. It didn't. It couldn't. He stayed in that little room on the third floor for thirty years just watching...."

She sat the cat back on the floor. When she looked back at him, her hardened expression had become sympathetic. "I can't tell you it's going to be peachy and sweet when it isn't. You have two choices at this point, period. You can invite others to save your friends or let it stop. Just remember, even if you die, it won't stop for others. No cure for that curse has ever been found. The burn fades when you invite someone. After all, an infection is an infection. I don't know why it connected with that damned disease. You will always be infected, I'm afraid. You'll not be killed, if you've appeased it, but you will suffer. The family always did...."

He had to get back. He had to tell everyone what he'd learned. It had to have spread to more in the group, and the remedy was as dark and horrific as the disease. He didn't know how he would tell them what they needed to do. He delivered the worst message possible, and time was up.

Chapter 31

The group feverishly dug to unearth the entire bottom portion of the structure. Since there wasn't enough room in the pit to dismantle the boards, they fashioned a hoist from thick rope. Every person in attendance grabbed the ropes and, eventually, maneuvered it out of the pit.

Her stomach grew queasy. All of those plague victims were incinerated in that pit, like trash. Isabelle and Felix were in the pit. The pit where people were disposed of like contaminated waste.

It wasn't symbolic or dream fodder any longer. Countless human remains would still be down there. Tears streamed down her cheeks as they continued. She couldn't save the group, couldn't even save herself. The soil below was ashen black, residual ashes from fires a century ago.

Janelle dropped her shovel and coughed hard. Scott ran to her side and put his hands on her shoulders. They strolled away from the pit. She took a deep breath, but her breathing wasn't normal. She heard the sickly rasp deep within her friend's chest. "Sorry, everyone." The episode quieted. "I must be allergic to something."

Alicia's shoe snapped a twig as she approached the edge of the dig. Everyone looked up to see why she was quiet. "Alicia? Alicia, what is it?"

Alicia held the newspaper open. The headline read, "Local Psychic Diagnosed with Ancient Tuberculosis."

She grabbed the article and skimmed:

"Authorities were shocked to find a resilient case of Tuberculosis in the Tri-Cities area. Ms. Francis Edwards has been placed in a quarantine unit at the Ft. Shelby Hospital, in Bristol, Virginia. Ms. Edwards exhibited classic signs and symptoms of third-stage tuberculosis....

"Cases, such as Ms. Edwards's, have not been reported in our region since the 1950s. She was unconscious upon arrival and there is no known origin of where she contracted this illness. This incident has alarmed many residents. Medical personnel are confident this is nothing more than an incredibly horrible misfortune.

"The public is encouraged to undergo quick and painless tuberculosis testing if they are concerned. Tuberculosis testing is an effective tool for early detection and can be performed by all area physicians and health departments...."

"God, that's horrible." Wasn't everyone vaccinated against the illness? Even cows were inoculated against something as old as tuberculosis. Or were they? Alicia escorted Janelle back inside the kitchen when it became clear her cough wouldn't stop. She stepped away from the box to make sure Janelle arrived inside without fainting.

"Melanie? She's got it hasn't she?" Matt gravely whispered behind her.

"I think so."

"It's time, isn't it?"

"Yes." Time had run out. It was all due to her. To Isabelle. Everything stemmed from her. "Our clock has run out," she sighed.

They returned to the gigantic box. It appeared to be a plain wooden container, at first glance. There was a thick, wooden foundation and the rest was boarded up. There were blackened streaks and scorching across the sides.

"Why is the top iron, but not the bottom?" She already knew. It was Felix's wagon. She just couldn't bring herself to speak it.

Scott grabbed a pick and thrust it in the corner of the building, between two boards. He angled the tool, and the board popped off. "There's a substructure."

Malcolm and Matt loosened the rusted nails while Scott and Devon yanked the boards away. The black structure was eventually uncovered. "Look," Matt wiped the metal protrusions with his already grimy hands. There were handles beneath the black soot. Scott quickly took his tee shirt off and wiped the side. The surface beneath started to shine as he rubbed more of the ash and residual smoke away.

The metal fixtures on the uppermost doors had melted against the wood during that original fire. The lower doors were in relatively good condition. She quietly cried as the shock left from Isabelle's embrace. It was Felix's wagon. Where was Isabelle's body?

"Wait," Scott scooted his shovel around the bottom. "There's something underneath here... You were right. This is a wagon, not a building."

A sensation exploded through her body in an electric pulse. Isabelle hanged herself but didn't leave. She watched Heath and her father cut her body down and let it drop into the pit. They stood above them and laughed as the flames burned the top of the wagon.

"That's how we take care of a problem, boy." Edgar had slapped Heath on the back so hard he almost fell into the pit himself. They told neighbors she slipped on the steps and broke her neck. They set a stone at her pauper's grave because they claimed they feared contamination from a gathering.

It was as clear as Elysium's original glass. Other people held the key to survival. She brought Alicia, and that saved her. Alicia brought Ash, and Ash inadvertently involved Matt. Matt had unknowingly brought the entire group.

As long as others were brought to Elysium, they would live. Heath and Edgar were the two monsters from her dream. The two creatures that closed in on her, just before the Crawler grabbed her. Who was that beast on all fours? Suddenly, she saw Isabelle's mother

307

walking out of the house. She was completely pale, and her eyes were stark. She looked sick. She had the plague. *Everyone has a plague.* The voice that spoke in Isabelle's mind came through.

Scott and Malcolm pried the largest board on the wagon, wood groaned before it popped off. The structure beneath had many small doors, and a large one towards the front. They pried the tall, narrow door open. The hinges grated together with nearly a century of rust. They waited for the compartment to ventilate as dust flowed out through the gaping door.

Everyone sat to rest for a moment. "So, this is it." Matt sat beside her.

"Yea, I guess it is."

"Do you think it will stop her?"

"No."

"What did you do, that Taylor and Edwards didn't do?" He faced her.

"I invited someone... Alicia."

"So, that spreads it. Alicia did, too. She invited Ash. That's why she's not coughing or anything."

"I've noticed."

"I'm not, either. But I invited the rest. It's like we passed some kind of test or passed an infection. We did something that lifted the severity of it."

"I'm scared. Ms. Edwards was just here. She seemed perfectly healthy. Will Janelle suffer like that?"

"I hope not."

"What do we do now?"

"Wait and see what happens."

Janelle coughed in the kitchen and each wave sounded worse. It was a dry, hacking sound that permeated the air. She wanted to cover her ears from the familiar sound. She'd heard that cough before.

"Did you start without me?" Ash's voice broke the silence like a welcomed messenger. The group turned and all gawked at him. He was unbelievably healthy, without a hint of disease. He was now confident in opposition to his previous stature.

"Ash?" Matt overcame his shock. "We thought something awful had happened."

"No. I did something, and the rest of you have to do something, too." He paused a looked around for a moment. "Where's Janelle?"

"In the kitchen," Matt walked to Ash and explained the circumstances around Janelle, as well as what happened to Taylor and Edwards. Scott and Malcolm motioned for Melanie to come to the unearthed wagon, "It's on your property. Do you want to be the first to go inside?" Scott held the door open for her.

"Yes, thank you." Who knew what she would find? There could be terrible rewards for the first visitor. What if the things she never wanted to see again waited in there? The driver of the hellish wagon could be in there, but it was her property, and her responsibility. She'd endangered enough innocent people as it was.

She took a deep breath. She gathered her strength as she approached the structure. She knelt and peered inside the opening. It was an efficient, albeit primitive, wagon. Every space had a clear use, and nothing was wasted or frivolous. The exterior was scorched in places, but the inside hadn't been affected by the burning. There were even some papers that survived the fiery onslaught. She maneuvered into the space.

She pulled a handful of papers from the floor. One folded paper opened, "The Door-to-Door Company, supplier to merchants nationwide." The supplier had addressed the peddler from the books, "Felix McLain of Williamsburg, Virginia."

She reached for another handful from the floor in front of her, her hand hit something hollow. She brushed the dust from the object and jerked her hand away. It was a shoe with what appeared to be petrified leather. It was the driver of the carriage in that dream. It was Felix. She could tell by the fabric of the trousers. She turned to yell, but Matt and Ash were already leaning in the door. "Look!" She proclaimed, "See? He's still here!"

Ash handed her a flashlight and she crawled further into the cab. If anyone protested, she didn't hear it. At first, she clung to the wall opposite the body. She shone a light on the figure and found the corpse as she expected. The only indication it was male, or female, was the clothing. McLain had been there for almost a century with his head against the wall in the wagon.

She neared the body as curiosity overpowered caution. Even in his decomposed state, he was familiar. It was something beyond the purchase of Elysium... or winning the lottery. It was instinctive. She remembered a man in those clothes, with mahogany brown hair and clear skin. Everyone else had been pale because they were all infected.

The door to the wagon slammed behind her. She tried to push it back open, but it wouldn't budge. She heard them yell and answered, "I'm fine. I'm just stuck." Their frantic voices calmed, but they struggled to reopen the door.

Her flashlight darkened, but the interior brightened with a strange, unearthly illumination. The white light seemed to come from everywhere. She saw a reverse of the body's decomposition within seconds. Suddenly, he smiled at her, and his eyes were so clear and bright. They didn't carry a trace of grief or illness. She reached to embrace him. "I told you I would come back." He smiled as he whispered.

Her terror was softened only by her fascination. "You can't be," was all that would come out of her parched mouth. "I don't know you." She finished. She didn't want to see him. She wanted to defy him, to defy what she felt. It was the same man she repeatedly saw upstairs while she showered. He was in the flesh and in front of her. He was the most gorgeous man she'd ever saw in her life.

"I know you, Isabelle." He reached up and placed his hand on her cheek. It was abnormally warm and dry. He was so familiar. It couldn't be real. The situation playing out in front of her couldn't possibly be real.

"I'm... I'm not Isabelle.... Felix." She couldn't get away, couldn't move. Her eyes locked with his. She spoke in a daze. She was finally with him, and he was amazing.

"I know a Blythe anywhere." He smiled. His grin was warm and inviting.

"Wha—I'm not a Blythe." She regained her sense of speech.

"Yes, you are. I see it in you. Edgar will never die as long as there are descendants."

"Is that why we're suffering?"

"No, not because of ancestry, and not because of me." He shrugged. "It's her."

"Isabelle."

"My Isabelle is gone."

"But...."

"That *thing* is not my Isabelle."

"But I'm not, either. Why do you—" he pulled her into him. He kissed her and held her. She was taken aback. Her body seized up. There was a party. Attendees wore 1940s clothing. Women wore their hair in shoulder-length styles with victory rolls and form-fitting dresses. Big band music drifted through the double doors in the ballroom and into the courtyard.

A woman strolled outside with her baby in her arms. "Look at this sweetie! Your Uncle Andrew owns all this. Isn't it beautiful? Your daddy will own this one day and you will play here always."

A dark figure lurked in the background, behind the ivy and carpeting of hydrangeas and rose vines. Her dark eyes glittered in the light from the veranda as they did in the hall closet. Isabelle waited on the mother and her baby. They walked onward through the tangle of foliage and into the glades. The salt circle wasn't yet there.

She screamed for them to stop, but they couldn't hear her. Isabelle waited for them in the forest. The mother continued with the baby in her arms. Suddenly, the picture went dim. A horrible choking sound filled the darkness. She darted into the forest after them.

She reached the center of the glade. The mother hung from the tree overhead and the baby lay on the ground. Isabelle reached for it and picked up the cooing infant. Melanie ran to catch up with them, but everything went through her as if she were vapor.

Branches passed through her. She ran to Isabelle and tried to grab her arms. Since they were both spirits, maybe she could grab her. Her hands passed through the wraith with no affect. Isabelle turned back and gave a monstrous grin as she walked away with the baby. The mother's feet were swinging beside her face.

She followed Isabelle through the cemetery. She walked for a long time before entering an abandoned house in a place she'd never visited before. The baby cried, but Isabelle didn't attempt to comfort it. Suddenly, they were both gone. The crying stopped, and all was silent. She ran back to the glade and the mother was still hanging.

There were people on the veranda yelling, "Harriet." She tried to yell back to them, "*Harriet's here, hanging in the tree, and a monster has the baby!*"

No one heard her. She waved her hands. She hoped they would see her as a ghost, but they would see Harriet when they got there. Maybe there was hope, maybe she could change history.

All hope was dashed when she was found. There were no ambulances or screaming sirens. There was only crying. They summoned a doctor, but there was no rush. Harriet was dead.

Where did Isabelle take the baby? She darted back towards the cemetery and stopped by the caves. There was a doorway in the largest, center cave. A bright light shone from inside. She crept into the cave. She couldn't see anything aside for the blinding white light.

The air inside wasn't hot or cold, she felt nothing against her skin. She stepped through the mysterious entrance, but it appeared she was going back to the house. How could the cave both start and end at the same place, without any curvature or turns?

There was bright day on the other side of the exit. Everything seemed so white, and traces of black were a sharp contrast. She emerged in a sick world. The trees were barren and black. The sparse grass grew in thin patches. She thought of the pet cat she had when she was little. It contracted the mange and its fur fell out. The ground was diseased.

Isabelle had disappeared. A girl in a long filthy dress walked in the distance, but she wasn't Isabelle. She walked sluggishly and appeared to be in pain as she moved.

A white-tailed deer stood beside her. Its swollen neck was covered with sores and its fur was matted. It shook as if it convulsed from a seizure. The animal's stomach had shrunk, and its ribs protruded from its flesh.

The birds didn't sing here. They screeched and emitted sounds that resembled a cat's purr. The fields were filled with dead animals. She didn't have to feel pity for long. Many of them stood back up and grazed as she watched, as if they were healthy.

A large sow stumbled as it paced in the sty beside the field. Its throat was equally rotted, and it sounded like it was choking. She neared the house and heard horrible noises, like in her dream. She held her breath when she saw the creatures from her previous visit. She'd been here before. The baby was in the house. It was the only normal sound in this world.

The Crawler crept across the porch. The other two creatures sat beneath a tree in the front yard. No one spoke but the sounds of wheezing and choking filled the air. Isabelle walked out of the house with the baby in her arms, oblivious to the horror around her.

Another strange woman emerged from the house and limped towards the Crawler. Who was she? Her neck was swollen past her chest. Her breathing rattled so hard she heard it from the bushes at the end of the yard. The woman had white hair and gray skin.

Someone coughed behind her, and she quickly turned. A man limped towards her. He looked like Heath, in that nightmare. His sickly yellow skin was stretched across bones that cracked and popped with each step. His filthy brown derby was pulled down over his face, covering his eyes. All that was visible was an abnormally massive mouth with sharp, white pointed teeth. The thing didn't choke or wheeze, he growled. He wore an antique black suit that was covered with dirt and debris.

She backed up as he neared. "Who... who are you?" She whispered. He closed in on her even as she moved.

"She wants to see you now." He spoke with a deep and eloquent voice.

"Who?"

"Isabelle."

"I don't want to go to the house. Please, I'm ready to go home."

"You are home."

"No, I'm not."

"But it's a welcome party." He grinned widely. Black gunk dripped from the corners of his mouth. "She has a baby now."

"She has a baby?"

"Isabelle has a child. We need to celebrate."

"What does she want with a child? She killed it."

"The child is very much alive. She will continue to live... as long as she doesn't contract the disease."

"Remain alive? She can be here and remain alive?" *Dahlia.* She really lived beyond that night. What a horrible existence, cared for by a demon, and raised in hell. *The poor baby.* She never knew life beyond Elysium.

"If Isabelle wishes it."

"Why does she need a baby?"

"Sadly, Isabelle is still part human. The power over her decided to allow her some companionship to appease her melancholy. She simply wishes to raise the child."

314

"What does she wish for me?"

The thing paused. It finally answered, "You'll find that out when you speak to her."

She bolted past him and went back towards the caves. She didn't want to be there. She needed to get out quickly, before her time ran out. She should never have followed Isabelle. Why did she? Why did she think she could change anything? What was done was done.

She ran faster through the glades, towards the caves, past the diseased wildlife, out of the contaminated world. She followed her steps through the cave and emerged on the other side. She returned to the night when the mother went missing. Everything went black when Felix withdrew his kiss.

She opened her eyes as he held her, but he didn't back away. Their noses almost touched. She faintly heard a woman's laugh as she returned to the present.

"How do we stop her?" She whimpered.

"You can't," his voice started fading. He laid his head back against the wall, as it had been for a hundred years. His healthy skin became pale, veins started to appear. He was returning.

"Don't go," she whimpered. "Why do I have these feelings for you?" It was wrong, all wrong. She wasn't supposed to feel the way she felt. He was dead. He'd been dead nearly a century.

The decay stopped. "There's a part of her alive in you. You feel for me what she felt for me. You don't want me to go, do you?"

"Never."

"Even though you don't know me at all."

"I don't need to." She leaned towards him. She never felt that way for anyone. Here he was in front of her. She could barely breathe. Why couldn't she go? She wasn't prepared to see him, but it didn't matter. None of it mattered. She just wanted him. She ached for him. If it were insanity, she didn't want to be sane. They could institutionalize her, and she would remain in bliss.

He gently nudged her back. "It isn't me." He grabbed her hand and held it to his cheek. It was soft and warm. "You feel a kinship with Isabelle. Your father was a Blythe. His mother was an illegitimate child of Andrew. You know I can't stay."

"Take me with you." It meant death. It didn't matter. She was already damned. They were all damned to Isabelle's wrath.

"You don't love me." He smiled. "You aren't mine to take."

He leaned back in and kissed her again. She felt a shock that went from the top of her head down into her feet. She couldn't breathe and, for once, she didn't want to. The world went black as she clung to him.

"Melanie?" Matt called. "What's going on?" They'd opened the door, and she hadn't even noticed.

"Matt?" She was alone in the wagon. She was stretched out beside a skeleton. Her left hand still held Felix's skeletal hand, and the right held a bunch of dry rotted fabric from his dusty lapel.

"He said I was a Blythe. I saw him... Felix. He was right here."

"Are you? What happened?"

"I don't know. I passed out." She couldn't very well admit what happened. In reality, she just kissed a skeleton. She kissed a dead man, and wished he would return and do it again. God help her.

"That would explain your attraction to Elysium," he poked his head in and looked around. "Cozy quarters, huh? Room for one more?"

"Well, considering there's company here already, I'm not sure." *Christ, what's wrong with me?* She didn't want anyone else in the wagon. She didn't even want to talk to Alicia. She wanted Felix back. She'd been driven mad. That was it. Elysium had claimed her mind, just as it claimed John Taylor's life.

He looked over and found the body, "Yikes. I see we found our peddler. Now, where is she?"

"She's supposed to be here."

Where was Isabelle's body? She should've been somewhere around the wagon. But—wait. What happened that morning? They set the wagon on fire first. Isabelle wasn't inside.

"I'm calling 9-1-1!" Alicia screamed out the back door. The group fled the area of the wagon and leapt across piles of earth. She quickly wiped her eyes as she followed.

Why did she have to come back? Why did she have to go through this bullshit again? Felix's image still burned in her brain as did the wonderful sensations of safety and sanctuary. She just wanted to stay in his arms. There was little reason to return. They were all going to die horribly, and it was her fault.

Janelle collapsed on the kitchen floor and was unconscious. Her breathing was hauntingly familiar, in wheezes and gasps. Her chest rattled. Her face had grown pale and sallow. She had to see Janelle's eyes. She knew the look and would know if there was reason to panic.

She kneeled beside her and looked deeply into her eyes. It was there. She saw the sharp glint of someone who was infected. She held her hand as she tried to comfort her. Janelle motioned for her to come closer. "Melanie, she's here." Janelle whispered so she wouldn't alarm the others.

"I know." She felt Isabelle near-by. A hollow and sickly feeling of familiarity. Her presence was cold and damp.

"I see her standing behind Matt."

"What is she doing?"

"Smiling."

"What does she want?"

"To spread her infection."

"Do you know how to cure it?"

"You can't. I need to ask my cousin Gerald to visit." Janelle had made the decision. She chose a person to come in her stead. What decisions they had ahead of them. It was a monstrous task that made them monsters, just as Isabelle now was.

"Are you sure?"

317

"If you dial... I will ask." She ran and grabbed the receiver. She quickly dialed the number Janelle gave her. "Gerald?" Janelle tried to smile as Melanie held the telephone. Her voice became hoarse. "You'll never guess where I am..." She spoke about Elysium. Eventually, they came to the subject of why he needed to visit. "The current owner is getting rid of some antiques... you might make some quick cash."

She hung up the telephone. Everyone was resigned to what transpired, and what would happen to Gerald. "He's a heartless leech. He bankrupted my grandmother." She wheezed, but the rattling already sounded like it was fading. "Just let me rest a minute."

She made a remarkable improvement by the time the paramedics arrived. Her coughing came in random fits, but the EMTs attributed it to a minor asthma attack brought on by allergies.

Matt spoke with them while they examined Janelle, but there was no longer any evidence of a serious illness. Her chest had cleared, and her vitals were normal. As the EMTs left, their eyes darted about the room. She didn't have the heart to tell them about what they'd been exposed to. Maybe they would all be dead by the time the demon reached her arms out to infect the region.

They all knew what had to be done in order to survive. There were mixed looks through the group. Several were prepared to offer someone. Others were stricken with panic and fear. "What if we have no one we wish this on?" Malcolm asked, although it was obvious he already knew the answer to it.

"Malcolm, what do you need us to do?" Melanie walked to him. "We're in this together. We have to be. Either it ends with us, or this is just starting. I can't tell you what to do. You'll have to live with what you decide, either way."

"I know. I just can't do it." He shrugged.

"You do what you think is best," Matt patted him on the shoulder. "We'll respect your decision."

Those who were ready to spread the disease made the call. Those who felt compelled to end it were supported. They were all together despite the great divide in solutions.

Isabelle had won. She had won and they would suffer for complying with her rules. Melanie couldn't stand it. What choice was there? You could murder or endure a protracted and excruciating death. Scott dialed his phone. She sensed Isabelle in the room, carefully studying those who passed the test.

Malcolm began to cough, and it was only minutes before he appeared as sickly as Janelle had. Between gasps, he seethed, "I will not let it go on. She will not get another victim from me."

Those who were supposed to visit were on their way. She scrounged around the place for odds and ends to offer. After all, people simply needed to visit, not go away happy. As more visitors promised to come, more of the group returned to normal. Malcolm worsened and Scott drove him on to the hospital. They wouldn't risk exposing even more first responders.

"I wish he would've found someone," Matt finally spoke. Everyone who expected company drifted to the hall where they'd moved tables and objects to appear like the remnants of an indoor garage sale.

"Me, too."

"Where is she now?" Melanie asked Matt.

"She's spreading."

"What should we do?" He looked to her. "We're murderers."

"No, Matt." She corrected. "Isabelle is the murderer." She wanted to comfort him, but he was right. They were complicit. They were murderers, just like Edgar and Heath. Why would Isabelle want others to be like them? She hated them. Regardless of what that woman told Ash, there was still something missing.

She heard clinking and rattling outside and held her breath. It was the wagon she'd watched with Alicia. "Quiet!" She shouted. The noise drew closer. She ran outside with everyone calling after her. She had to see this through because her time just might be up.

The courtyard was in chaos outside the kitchen. The exhumed wagon now stood on four wheels. All the charring had vanished. The entire carriage was in perfect condition. She gawked as a second smoldering carriage approached from across the yard in the opposite direction, the one she'd witnessed with Alicia. The demonic driver shrieked, and the horse growled when they noticed the peddler's carrier.

Isabelle emerged from somewhere behind the group. She fully solidified by the time she passed Melanie. She walked hesitantly, as if she were afraid, until she saw the wagon. A piercing, unearthly shriek came out of her mouth. Melanie covered her ears and fell to her knees. The group either hadn't come out or remained silent. She couldn't look away.

Isabelle put both hands to her head and the spectral figure bent over. There was a growl from the ground, and the figure split. A beautiful girl emerged from the filthy rags of the malevolent presence. There were two Isabelle's.

The apparition ran as quickly towards Felix's wagon as her long dress would allow. The small door opened, and Felix leapt out to meet her. She could barely watch them embrace within that ethereal and blinding light.

The demonic Isabelle attempted to run from the smoking wagon, but it was too late. The wagon door exploded open and a tendril of something inside, as black, and smooth as smoke, shot out and latched onto her leg. It dragged her into the smoldering wagon. The figure grabbed at weeds and ground until she was inside.

The beautiful, spectral couple was again visible, but hadn't let go of one another. "She never got to say good-bye," Ash whispered behind her. She was terrified of interrupting. Isabelle was with him now. She was with her Felix. Within seconds, both wagons had disappeared. She wept as she watched.

"What's going on?" Janelle walked outside. "What happened?"

Melanie fell to her knees and cried. It was over. She knew in her heart they found the cure. Everyone sat on the ground or in the antiquated iron garden chairs.

She should be thanking God, and rejoicing for such a miracle, but she couldn't. How could she go on without seeing him again? It wasn't fair.

After a few moments of silence, she felt she had just woken up. Felix became faceless in her memories, just like her father. Maybe that was a blessing. Elysium had removed that longing from her mind. She knew where she came from.

For the first time in decades, she remembered her father's face.

Good God, her father had looked like Isabelle. She watched everyone embrace and cheer. "No one ever exhumed the wagon and left it!" Ash rejoiced. "No one brought them together. Isabelle couldn't resist."

"What was the hideous wagon?" Alicia grabbed his hand.

"The smoking wagon was for the entity. Ironic, isn't it?"

Someone embraced her and she felt happy enough to burst. It was wonderful. It was so familiar. Felix? He had returned to take her with him. She whirled with a smile. She would go with him. She would go anywhere with him.

But... Matt held her. His embrace felt exactly as it had with Felix. He kissed her and she knew what Felix meant. She belonged to someone who was already with her. She returned the kiss, oblivious to those around her.

"We survived." He broke long enough to smile. Words were inadequate as they watched everyone. All traces of illness were gone. The sickly skin and sallow eyes were again healthy. She kissed him again. She was home. She made it after all. She knew who she was, and she knew it was over.

Chapter 32

The primly dressed anchor on the evening news announced, "Medical authorities are puzzled by a miracle at the hospital today. Local psychic, Francis Edwards, was placed under quarantine several days ago due to an active strain of tuberculosis. Her condition had reached the point that she wasn't expected to live another 24 hours. Hospital staff remains baffled as all traces of the disease have disappeared. Doctors now question their abilities to effectively diagnosis. More news as it develops...."

Everything that revolved around Elysium's virus resolved itself without further intervention. She mused over the previous events as she pulled a blue cotton blouse on. Life returned to normal without the slightest consideration as to what happened or what could've happened.

The society found traces of activity after that day, but nothing akin to what had been. It even appeared that Dahlia had found some semblance of peace. She slipped into her jeans and flipped the television off.

Recollections of her father's face were as shocking as the sudden resolution. It had only been days, and already she'd forgotten so much about Isabelle and Felix. She looked forward to a vacation. They hadn't decided on a beach just yet, but she and Alicia were going to a cabin in the Smokey Mountains with the guys the coming weekend.

All traces of disease had vanished with the diabolic wagon. Everyone immediately returned to normal. The group went for tuberculosis testing the following day, but everyone's test site faded with no sign of reaction. The relatives who'd been candidates to spread the infection arrived to see the first grand Elysium yard sale. They were escorted in and ushered out by those who'd invited them. She sold a few miscellaneous items from the apartment.

She slipped on suede boots and gathered her equipment. The next investigation would begin in two hours. They were now official members of the same group that helped them. She gave it much thought before they accepted, but it was only natural that they shared their expertise with others.

Her friends even helped her clean some of the house before they left. Their generosity continued to astound her. The situation had quickly escalated, and ebbed just as rapidly, with virtually no proof of the fatal haunting at Elysium.

They spent hours searching the pit for human remains, or any materials left from the epidemic. It didn't seem right to simply hide it and forget everyone. Any remains needed to be found and properly buried. Ash collected samples of soil to be tested. Tuberculosis could live in soil for a long time under the right conditions.

She ran a brush through her hair. She looked much better. The dark circles under her eyes were gone. Her hair's dull shine had vanished. Alicia would probably be ready. She was always ready first. It was a new life for all of them. The brush with death had put so much into proper perspective.

Her arm remained tender where Isabelle grabbed her, but that would probably last a while. The burn vanished, and all bruising faded, but the pain didn't go. She needed to have it checked, but she hadn't figured out a reason to justify her arm injury. She couldn't very well say it came from Isabelle. There was no indication of physical injury any longer. She'd go in a day or so if it still hurt.

They were going to investigate the Rotherwood estate. The structure had long been reported to have activity, and the owners wanted more information, but they also wanted privacy. Who better for the job than the group that infiltrated Elysium? Elysium's current owner remained anonymous, as so many articles stated.

The once-vivid memories of Felix were nearly gone. She remembered he was a peddler, and she felt something towards him, but she couldn't remember why. She couldn't really remember what happened in the wagon outside of a kiss. She'd omitted that when discussing the events with the group. Of all the things to recall from a time like that, it had been a kiss.

She ascended the steps to the foyer as she double-checked her bag. Alicia waited in the living room. "All set?"

"Sure."

"You really think we can do this?"

"Ha!" She stood up off the couch. "After what we've seen, we can do anything."

They both did their last-minute checking before the knock came at the door. Ash and Matt stood together.

"You ready?" Matt leaned into her and kissed her cheek.

"I think so."

"You'll probably be bored out of your mind." Ash started as they walked to the SUV. "After what you're accustomed to, I'd say a routine investigation will bore you to tears."

"Good." That was a relief. She never wanted to encounter another entity like that. She closed the door behind her and listened. Sometimes, when the house was silent, she thought she could still hear Dahlia upstairs.

She finally learned who Creepy was, of all individuals, a professor. She'd invited Dr. Malcolm and Esther to Elysium. For the first time in decades, Dora's legacy was welcome. It took a little persuasion to urge Esther, but she eventually consented to come by and visit the coming Saturday. She admitted she'd always been curious, but they didn't want her, and she didn't want the curse.

"There are some things I still question." She spoke from the passenger's seat as they pulled out of the drive. Alicia and Ash sat together in the next row back.

"What?"

"How did the entity enter Isabelle's body? Why, when so many horrible things had already happened to her? Why did it push her to commit suicide?"

"There are no certain answers." Ash responded as if he'd already considered it all. "It might've been deliberate. I think it was when she kissed his body, just before she hung herself."

"But wouldn't it have wanted her to live? Didn't death limit her abilities?"

"Not necessarily. It probably wanted complete control and figured it would be easier if she had no will. Life would've been a limitation."

"Why two wagons?"

"I think that was a way of getting at the entity. It lived so long as Isabelle, and its time was up. Evidently, something was looking for it. It might have assumed Isabelle's form to avoid being caught, itself."

"If Edgar unearthed the wagon and poured salt, why didn't all that happen, then?"

"It had been years since the last victim visited Elysium, by then. It was probably dormant. Apparently, it was only uncovered long enough for him to look in the wagon and then recover it with salt. Look at all the new visitors Elysium had, just in the past week. Taylor probably woke her, and by the time you purchased the house, she was ready to infect."

She was terrified by thoughts of encountering another entity but knew that feeling of loneliness. No one should have to go through that. If she could help anyone in a comparable situation, even slightly, she would.

They drove down 11-W, towards their destination. Traffic grew denser as they neared. Now, it was time to see what happened to Jeremiah Rotherwood after Elysium. He reportedly enjoyed a good life, but his descendants weren't so fortunate. Several tragedies in the home came about over the century.

She felt a hand on her leg. She put her own on top of Matt's. Everything worked out for all of them. In the grand scheme of life, maybe she owed Isabelle some gratitude.

If it hadn't been for the curse, she would likely still be at the apartment. If it hadn't been for her, she might never have patched things with Alicia, met Matt, or found the new group of friends she had. Goodbye Happy Hell, and the life that went with it.

Author's Note: This book is dedicated to the nameless peddler who was killed in Bristol, Virginia, by a band of murdering thieves. The "Ring of Fire" haunting, which followed, is the inspiration for this story.

About the Author:

L. Chambers-Wright, also known as Laura Wright, has spent a lifetime crafting stories that bridge the gap between the real and the uncanny. With publishing credits spanning nearly every genre—from poetry to nonfiction—her work is as diverse as it is captivating. Raised on the eerie whispers of Appalachian folklore and ghost stories, she weaves the chilling, the mysterious, and the forgotten into her writing, ensuring that legends never truly fade. You can find more of her work at Laurawrites.net.